Dear Fellow Chocoholic

Hope you're going to enjoy the further adventures of the Chocolate Lovers' Club ladies. Every time I finish a chocolate lovers' story, I think it will be my last, but these characters just keep on giving.

I love spending time with Lucy, Autumn, Nadia and Chantal. As a writer, when I come to the end of some stories, I know that I've finished with those characters – not so with these ladies. They seem so real to me now, that I worry what's happening to them when I'm not writing about them. I always keep thinking what if this happens or what if that happens to them. I feel as if I'm part of their gang and I hope that you will too.

They also enable me to do lots of fun things in the name of research! Mainly eating chocolate, it has to be said. But what's not to love?

So please enjoy *The Chocolate Lovers' Wedding*. Make sure that you have plenty of chocolate to hand – I don't want you to have to do any of those late night runs to the petrol station in your PJs for chocolatey goodies. Happy reading! Happy chocolate eating!

Carole ☺ xx

Also by Carole Matthews

Let's Meet on Platform 8
A Whiff of Scandal
More to Life than This
For Better, For Worse
A Minor Indiscretion
A Compromising Position
The Sweetest Taboo
With or Without You
You Drive Me Crazy
Welcome to the Real World
The Chocolate Lovers' Club
The Chocolate Lovers' Diet
It's a Kind of Magic
All You Need is Love
The Difference a Day Makes
That Loving Feeling
It's Now or Never
The Only Way is Up
Wrapped up in You
Summer Daydreams
With Love at Christmas
A Cottage by the Sea
Calling Mrs Christmas
A Place to Call Home
The Christmas Party
The Cake Shop in the Garden
The Chocolate Lovers' Christmas

Carole Matthews

The Chocolate Lovers' Wedding

sphere

SPHERE

First published in Great Britain in 2016 by Sphere

1 3 5 7 9 10 8 6 4 2

A CIP catalogue record for this book
is available from the British Library.

ISBN 978-0-7515-6021-3

Typeset by Palimpsest Book Production Ltd, Falkirk, Stirlingshire
Printed and bound in Great Britain by Clays Ltd, St Ives plc

Papers used by Sphere are natural, renewable and recyclable
products sourced from well-managed forests and certified
in accordance with the rules of the Forest Stewardship Council.

MIX
Paper from
responsible sources
FSC
www.fsc.org FSC® C104740

Sphere
An imprint of
Little, Brown Book Group
Carmelite House
50 Victoria Embankment
London EC4Y 0DY

An Hachette UK Company
www.hachette.co.uk

www.littlebrown.co.uk

The Chocolate Lovers' Wedding

Chapter One

In London you are never more than ten feet away from a Twix. True fact. There is one, right now, in my desk with my name on it. Third drawer down. Back left-hand corner. It's now twelve thirty and its siren song has been calling me for the last hour.

I'm holding strong. And there's a very good reason for it. I, Lucy Lombard, aficionado of all things chocolate-based, am a recently engaged person and, as such, am of course on a diet. No one wants to sashay down the aisle at their wedding with the congregation sniggering 'lard arse' into their hands, do they?

I sigh with happiness. Not about the diet. I'm not a weirdo. I'm happy because I'm actually to be married to the love of my life, Mr Aiden 'Crush' Holby. After years of unsuitable boyfriends – Marcus Canning in particular springs to mind – and one previous abandonment at the altar – due to Marcus Canning – I am betrothed to someone who is not only undeniably handsome, but is kind, loving, can cook, likes small animals and, most importantly, is willing to overlook my various foibles and flaws to make me his wife. To the point that he wouldn't *actually* mind if I was packing a little more punch in my wedding frock. Hmm.

Right. That's it. The Twix gets it.

'Lucy.'

Guiltily, my fingers snap back from the drawer. My boss. Wearing his usual expression of harried disdain. How did he know I was about to eat The Forbidden Twix?

'Did you get those figures for me from the finance department?' he growls.

Oh, right. That. 'Ah, no.'

'I'm sorry to interrupt your daydreaming. Again. But they are quite important.'

In the short time I have worked here at Green Information Technology, or GIT as the employees call it, I have found that Mr Robert Simmonds gives great sarcasm. Sometimes – quite often – he does have a point.

'Sorry. Sorry.' In fairness, he asked me ages ago to get his figures or whatever and I've completely forgotten. I got a bit sidetracked Googling wedding favours and such on the internet. I'm thinking of heart-shaped chocolates or personalised chocolate lollies. It's tough. What would you do?

My boss drums his fingers on the filing cabinet. Mr Simmonds likes to make out that he's a laid-back hippy. He brings a quinoa salad in for his lunch, for heaven's sake. But he's *so* not a hippy. He's old, grumpy and a total stress bunny. He wears a suit and tie when everyone else in this office favours faded jeans and open-necked shirts. My easy-going approach to my job is totally at odds with his uptight, starchy nature. We are terminally unsuited and I should discuss this with my temp agency.

My eyes slide back towards the chocolate bridal favours.

More drumming. 'And you're waiting for?'

'Right. Right.' Must. Stop. Thinking. About. My. Wedding. And. Chocolate. 'I'm on my way.'

With a theatrical tut that's not even necessary, Mr Simmonds – never Rob – slams back into his office. This is a company

2

that is supposed to care about the environment and the planet and all that but, frankly, doesn't give a toss about its employees.

Wearily, I push myself from my desk and head towards the finance department. I could probably just call them, but this will help to fill my endlessly dull day and also burn off some calories to balance out the imminent Twix consumption.

Before I depart, I ease open the desk drawer and take a sneaky peek at it. 'Wait for me, baby,' I coo. 'Mummy won't be long.'

Then I head off to . . . where was it again? Finance. Finance. That's where I'm going.

I've been working here at Green IT for three months. Three months since Marcus Canning – dastardly ex-fiancé and serial cheat whom I may have already mentioned – only went out and bought the best café and chocolate emporium in the whole of London: Chocolate Heaven. This was my sanctuary, my home from home, my life. Beyond my wildest dreams, I had become the manager. And I was good at it. Bloody good. Then, beyond my worst nightmare, the owners sold it to said ex-fiancé, the lowdown dirty dog, and I had no choice but to leave. I thought I'd be serving behind the counter of Chocolate Heaven until I was old and grey. But Marcus spoiled it all.

I vowed then and there, as long as Marcus was calling the shots, that I'd never darken the door of that blessed place again. True to my word, I haven't entered its hallowed halls ever since. Three months. It makes me feel quite dizzy to say it. In all that time, the good ladies of the Chocolate Lovers' Club – Chantal, Nadia, Autumn and my good self – have been wandering the hinterlands of north London like nomads. Having our favourite haunt cruelly snatched from us, we've been meeting at a variety of inferior, less chocolatey cafés across the capital city to indulge our cravings and finding that nothing really floats our boat in quite the same way. No wonder I'm depressed.

These same long months I have also been back in the dreary, dead-end world of office temping. And, to tell you the truth, I feel as if I'm hanging onto even this poxy job by the skin of my teeth. This could, potentially, be a great company to work for. Saving the planet and everything is very fashionable, right? But the other problem is that, as a temp, I'm given No Responsibility. Therefore, I turn off my brain the minute I arrive at my desk. Then, when I am actually given something to do, I usually make a total cock of it. Vicious circle.

I think I'm skating on thin ice after putting together an important PowerPoint presentation for my boss on the Anthropogenic Effects on the Natural Environment, which he was giving to some bigwigs in the industry and which, somehow, mainly featured wedding dresses. Gah! I have no idea how that happened. Still, a lot of people found it amusing. Well, some people found it amusing. One in particular didn't, though. Ahem. The proper presentation was *really* boring, anyway.

There are some upsides to being at GIT. This is a great building to work in. It's an enormous, contemporary office block right on the river by Blackfriars bridge – prime location. It's stuffed full of bright artworks and multi-coloured chairs. It has floor-to-ceiling windows and, because that makes it like an oven, we have the air conditioning pumping out all day. If you ask me – and no one does – that doesn't seem all that green. Clearly, we prefer to tell other people how to cut back on their energy use rather than have the inconvenience of doing it ourselves. I have, however, connived to surreptitiously manoeuvre my desk further towards one of said windows so that I can admire the splendid view of the Thames at my convenience.

Before Mr Simmonds can come and chase me again, I scuttle out of the office. Normally, even in the face of adversity I'm a cheerful soul but I'm out of sorts today, restless and unsettled.

Out in the main corridor, where I'm alone, I hold up my hands and lean against one of the windows, resting my cheek against the cold glass. It's March and it's chilly outside. However, it's one of those days that make you hopeful that spring is just around the corner. The Thames is a shimmering silver ribbon and trees along the Embankment are shyly coming into bud. The sky is a quite promising shade of blue.

I look down over the river and, on a bench, three floors below me, a figure looks up and waves.

'Marcus?' I jump back from the window and press myself against the wall. I'm sure it was him. Could I be hallucinating due to lack of chocolate?

My phone pings with a text and I glance at it, warily.

Hi, Lucy! Surprise, surprise. M xx

I summon up the courage to look again. Sure enough, it's Marcus who's down there and he's waving at me again.

Go away, I text back.

No, he answers. *Come and talk to me.*

As I watch, he pulls his coat round him and lies down on the bench. He'll freeze out there. When he sets his mind on something, he doesn't falter until he gets the result he wants. He could be out there for days waiting for me to crack. I know Marcus only too well; I will not win this staring contest. I am always the one who blinks first.

With an exasperated sigh, I head downstairs and, after getting my security pass all in a tangle at the gate, flounce outside and into the cold. Marcus sits up, smiling triumphantly as I approach. His blond hair is tousled by the breeze coming from the river. He's wearing a sharp grey suit and a black cashmere coat. As always, he looks devastatingly suave. This is the man who has broken my heart into a thousand pieces time and time again. I should never forget that.

'I have nothing to say to you,' I tell him firmly.

'Shall we do it over a coffee?' he asks. 'Or I could buy you lunch?'

Lunch. My stomach growls. I check my watch. It is, technically, my lunch time. Sort of.

'Just hear what I've got to say,' Marcus pleads.

He turns those devastating china-blue eyes on me. The ones that I have loved so much. The ones he thinks always reduce me to a quivering wreck of compliance. Ha. Not today, Marcus Canning. Today, I am braced against your wily ways.

'There's nothing you can say that I want to hear.' I hold up a hand. Talk to that.

'I love you,' Marcus offers.

'Don't be silly. You haven't sat out here in the freezing cold just to tell me that.' I shiver and Marcus, as quick as a flash, whips off his coat and wraps it gently round my shoulders.

'I can't manage without you,' he tells me.

I purse my lips. 'Emotionally or physically?'

'Both,' he admits, boyish smile giving it all it's got.

'Stop it, Marcus. I'm immune to your charms these days.' But still my stupid heart remembers how much it once loved him. It's like a favourite white blouse with a chocolate stain that always remains no matter how much Vanish you scrub it with; yet you still can't bear to part with it.

'Half an hour,' he cajoles. 'You owe me that.'

'I don't *owe* you anything.'

Despite my protestations, Marcus takes my hand in his and starts to walk in a determined manner towards the bridge. 'This could change your life.'

'It won't.'

'Just hear me out.'

I make some show of resistance, pulling against him. But it's futile. I so desperately want to know how things are going at Chocolate Heaven without me. I want to hear him beg me to go back.

I won't. Obviously.

But I want to hear it all the same.

'Oh, Marcus.' I fall into step beside him.

I'll hate myself for this. I know I will.

Chapter Two

'I thought we'd eat at the OXO Tower,' Marcus says.

'No.' I stop stock-still. 'No OXO Tower.'

'It's fabulous there,' he insists.

'And that's exactly why.' Plus it was the scene of my first proper date with Crush and I don't want to sully that memory. Well, no more than falling down the stairs and breaking my leg afterwards did. 'You think you can ply me with fine food and wine and I'll be putty in your hands. Well, it's not going to happen.'

Marcus's face falls. 'I've already booked us a table.'

I tut. 'Then ring them and cancel.' Does he really think that I'm so malleable?

'OK. Whatever you say, Lucy.'

He looks so miserable, but I hold my ground. 'We'll grab a sandwich. A quick one, mind you. I have things to do.' Which reminds me that I should be on my way to the finance department right now.

Reluctantly, Marcus calls and cancels the table. He thinks I'm a pushover, I know. Well, I'll show you, Marcus Canning.

We walk further down the South Bank until we come to a

small chain café. Perfect. Scruffy enough and grubby enough not to impress me. Inside, every table is strewn with the detritus of the previous customers' meals.

'You really want to eat here?'

'Yes.'

Marcus sighs in resignation. 'Grab a table, then. I'll queue up. Coffee?'

I nod. 'Get me something low calorie to eat. I'm on a diet.'

He laughs out loud at that.

'I am!'

I shrug off Marcus's coat so that I can load up a tray swimming in tea with empty sandwich wrappers and crisp packets and move them onto the next table. Then I wait, twiddling my thumbs, until he returns.

He puts a latte and a plate with a giant slice of chocolate cake in front of me.

'I said low calorie.'

'Just inhale it then.'

'I'm *seriously* on a diet.'

'You look sensational exactly as you are. I like a woman with curves.'

'You like a woman who *breathes*,' I counter. As many and as varied as possible all the time we were in a relationship together, if I remember rightly. 'Anything else is a bonus.'

He laughs. 'Oh, Lucy. You can be so very cruel.'

Not cruel enough, I think.

While Marcus faffs with our coffee and sets the cake in front of me, I catch sight of my reflection in the window. I thought I'd melt away to a size eight after leaving the temptations of Chocolate Heaven behind. Truly, I did. But no. I'm curvier than ever. I think I've been comfort eating since I was cast adrift at Christmas. And who wouldn't in my circumstances?

When Marcus bought Chocolate Heaven, I lost the best job

in the world and nothing, not even a Wispa and a Bounty combo can make up for that. So I'm not just curvy, I'm heading towards the positively rotund. And no one wants to be a fat bride, right? No one wants to waddle down the aisle next to the man of her dreams. I want to be a sliver of my former self at my wedding and must keep this, at all times, at the forefront of my mind.

'I'm losing weight for my *wedding*,' I remind him.

'Ah.' He stirs his coffee thoughtfully. 'To whatshisname? Still going ahead then?'

'Yes, Marcus. Of course it is.'

'No sudden change of heart?'

'No. I *love* Aiden and he *loves* me. The date is booked. The venue decided. The invitations have gone out.' Not strictly true, I admit.

'I didn't get mine.'

'As if.'

He does his cutest lost-little-boy look. 'Not for old times' sake?'

'No. You're the last person I'd want there.'

'You didn't say that last time we were at a wedding together.'

'That's because you were the groom, Marcus. And I was the bride. This is probably a good time to remind you that you didn't actually stay around for the ceremony.'

He frowns. 'You're never going to forget that, are you?'

I laugh, because what else is there to do? 'No. I'm never going to forget that. Or forgive you.' I get an unwanted flash-back to the day Marcus jilted me and feel sick to my stomach all over again. It was the worst moment of my life and, frankly, there are a lot of worst moments to choose from. This time it will be different. I know it. Crush is not Marcus. And thank the heavens for that.

Picking up my fork, I toy with the chocolate cake Marcus has bought me. If I eat this and forgo the Twix then I'm really no worse off than I would have been. I could just eat half. That's all. I'm thinking that I should order my wedding dress a size too small so that I can slim into it. All brides lose weight, right? I have about three months to shed a stone or so. Doable? Tomorrow, I'll really get a grip on it.

Hmm. This chocolate cake is delicious. A moist, light sponge filled with rich ganache – even though we are in a place where I might have expected inferior quality chocolate treats. Marcus grins at me as I eat it.

'What?'

'Come back, Lucy,' he says, earnestly. 'Chocolate Heaven needs you. I need you. It's not the same without you. It's where you're meant to be.'

That, if I'm brutally honest, is music to my ears.

'I bought it for you. So that you could run it. That was the whole point of me owning it.'

He did. I have to give him that. But he bought it so that he could own me, too. I'm not a fool. 'Who's running it now?'

'I've got a manager in.'

'A woman?' As if I need to ask.

'Er . . . yes.'

'Is she pretty?'

'No, she's French. A double bagger. Awful woman.'

A likely story.

His eyes go all gooey and he reaches out to curl a lock of my blonde hair round his finger. 'Come back,' he pleads. 'Come back to me.'

'Don't do that.' I slap his hand away.

Marcus is unperturbed. 'She doesn't have your way with the customers, Lucy. She doesn't have the vision or the passion for Chocolate Heaven. Without you, it's nothing. You know the business like no one else. You were born for it.'

All of these things are true. There is chocolate flowing in

my veins. I wasn't cut out to be a temporary secretary to a bad-tempered, not very green IT director.

That pulls me up short. Yikes! The finance department! All this banter with Marcus may have slightly sidetracked me.

As the realisation dawns, my phone rings. It's my Mr Simmonds.

'Hello.' I try to sound as if I am in the quiet of the finance department and not in a noisy café on the Embankment.

'Where exactly are you, Lucy?' my boss asks somewhat tightly. 'I have been down to the finance department to get the figures for myself and they say that they haven't seen hide nor hair of you.'

'I had to pop out. Urgently. I'll be back in five minutes,' I promise. Then I remember that I'm on the wrong side of the river and will have to run. 'Make that ten.'

'Make it that you don't bother to come back at all,' he hisses. 'I'll call the agency and get someone else who's actually interested in doing this job. You're fired.'

He hangs up. I'm left staring open-mouthed at the phone. When I look up, I see that Marcus is grinning.

Chapter Three

We, the members of the Chocolate Lovers' Club, are sitting in a boring little café just off the Strand. I have a plastic-looking ham sandwich, Nadia is staring forlornly at a limp chicken wrap, Autumn is gingerly dipping a biscotti in a not-quite-hot cappuccino and, horror upon horror, Chantal is eating a salad. I feel faint looking at it.

'Look at us,' I say. 'We are the good ladies of the Chocolate Lovers' Club and there's not a morsel of chocolate in sight. What's happening to us? We are failing in our mission to embrace all things chocolatey in our lives.'

'It's just not the same without Chocolate Heaven,' Autumn muses sadly.

'But it's our *raison d'être.*'

Nadia shrugs. 'Lucy has a point.'

I'm on a roll now. 'What, I ask, is the reason for lettuce?'

Chantal prods at her bowl of shrubbery and grimaces.

'It is the most pointless foodstuff on the planet,' I pontificate. 'Even rabbits don't really like it.'

'It isn't the lettuce that's the issue, Lucy, is it?' Chantal points out. 'You're just disenchanted with yet another substandard café.'

'You're right,' I admit, sagging. 'It's not Chocolate Heaven.'

'This is OK,' Nadia says. We all look around. It is a McCafé. We could be anywhere. Magnolia walls, wooden chairs, grubby vinyl floor. Not a comfy brown velvet sofa in sight. And, more importantly, very little in the way of chocolate goodies on offer. None, in fact. Not even a measly brownie for succour.

They have *plain* flapjack. What's the thinking behind that?

To console myself, I look round at my lovely companions. These are my dearest friends. Friendships that were born out of our mutual love of chocolate. We used to meet at Chocolate Heaven, the finest of fine chocolate emporiums, every single day. We laughed, cried, gossiped, ate chocolate. Now we are homeless.

In spite of everything that has happened between us, Marcus, somehow, thought that I could carry on working there as if nothing had happened. Worse, he thought I'd be *pleased*! But I couldn't, not in a million years, work for Marcus. He would have had me in his thrall again and there's no way that I'd ever want that. It has taken me a long time – longer than I'd care to admit – to be Not in Love with Marcus anymore. And I don't want prolonged close contact with him to threaten that.

Thus, it has left us ladies all wandering aimlessly through inferior cafés and, in my particular case, inferior jobs too. But, in times of darkness, I don't know what I'd do without these girls in my life. They have gone from being mere friends to the sisters I never had.

Chantal Hamilton is the oldest among us and, more often than not, the wisest too. She's currently in the throes of divorcing her husband, Ted – which, despite being reasonably amicable, is still taking its toll. She also has a delicious baby, Lana, who we all adore. She was previously a journalist on a magazine featuring stunning homes throughout the UK, though she's not working at the moment as she can't bear to leave Lana every day. I guess, after the divorce is finalised, that might have to change. Lana must be coming up to a year old soon and I have no idea where that time has gone.

Autumn Fielding is the youngest member, the earth mother among us. She is optimistic, idealistic and would have been far better working at Green IT than I ever was. She would have made them turn off the air conditioning. She would have made Mr Simmonds smile. Probably. Usually she's the calm and laid-back one but, at the moment, she's got a lot on her plate too. She fluffs her unruly mop of auburn curls and my heart goes out to her.

What can I tell you about, Nadia Stone? She's curvaceous, a real beauty with gorgeous caramel skin and a skein of dark hair. Her son, Lewis, is four now and she's had a struggle bringing him up alone after the death of her husband, but I think she's finally met someone to put a glimmer back into those stunning hazel eyes of hers.

Last, and maybe least, there's me. I'm Lucy Lombard. I'm the wrong side of thirty, still a spinster – but not for much longer. I'm overweight, overwrought and if I can mess something up, then I invariably will. But I'm loyal and steadfast and I'm loved by the loveliest man on earth. And I may get a lot wrong – an awful lot – but I was good at running Chocolate Heaven. I really was.

Staring down at my sandwich, I'm disconsolate. 'Look at what we're eating.' I cast another particularly withering glare at Chantal's salad. 'This is not the stuff of life.'

'I've lost *pounds* since we stopped going to Chocolate Heaven,' she remarks. 'This is the first time I've been pre-baby weight.' She strokes her admirably flat stomach lovingly.

It's true that Chantal is slowly regaining her pre-pregnancy glossiness. Now that Lana is a little bit older, she's no longer cutting her own fringe with the kitchen scissors or nibbling her nails off instead of getting expensive manicures. Her hair is groomed and shiny once more, her nails slicked with pink pearl varnish. I think this has more than a little to do with the fact that she now has the lovely Jacob Lawson in her life on a more permanent basis. 'I don't like to remind you, but you're supposed to be losing a little bit of bootilicious too, Lucy.'

'Yes, but this is all wrong,' I protest. 'I'm having to comfort eat. This is not our spiritual home.' I gesture inadequately at the equally inadequate café. 'We are *meant* to be at Chocolate Heaven.'

'But we are boycotting it because of Marcus,' Nadia says.

'It *was* your idea,' Autumn chips in. 'And we fully back you,' she adds hastily.

'We are wandering from unsuitable café to unsuitable café trying to find somewhere that you *do* like because you never want to clap eyes on him again,' Chantal adds. 'Remember?'

'Ah.' All heads swivel to look at me. I hesitate to tell them. I really do. Because I know what they'll say.

They wait, mouths pursed, for the revelation.

'I sort of saw him at lunchtime,' I confess.

'Oh, Lucy.' Collective voice.

'What? I didn't mean to. He turned up outside my office and begged me, *really begged me*, to go back and run it for him.'

'You didn't agree?'

'Weeeeeell.'

'Lucy!' More group gasping.

'I got sacked today. Again.' I sigh as the overwhelming knowledge that I'm once more unemployed hits me low in the stomach. I bite into my unlovely ham sandwich and it tastes like sawdust in my mouth. What comfort does that provide, for heaven's sake? I could lie on the floor and weep.

'What for this time?'

'It was Marcus's fault. I should have been doing important

16

things in the finance department and he persuaded me to go out to lunch with him instead.'

They all look at me, aghast.

'He offered me my job back.'

Shaking of heads.

'I didn't say I'd go back to Chocolate Heaven.'

They don't look convinced.

'I did say I'd think about it, though.' And, if I'm honest, every fibre of my being is yearning to say yes.

'Could you handle seeing Marcus every day?' Chantal asks. 'He'd be all over you like a rash. It wouldn't stop at Chocolate Heaven, Lucy. You know what he's like.'

'I need the money.' I gnaw my fingernails a bit. 'This wedding is rushing up and Crush and I are trying to do it on a budget, but the bills are mounting already and we've hardly started. How will I manage without a salary coming in?'

They all exchange anxious looks, as well they might. They know I am a snowflake in a fan heater when it comes to Marcus.

'There would be a plus side of me going back to Chocolate Heaven. We won't have to try out any more rubbish cafés. We could re-stake our claim there, go back to the old faithful sofas.'

'I can see the attraction,' Nadia says. 'I know you're desperate to get back, but there will be a price to pay.'

I sigh. 'I'll have to chat to Crush about it. See what he thinks.'

'Let's hope he can talk some sense into you,' says Chantal.

'Go back to the agency,' Nadia says. 'Tell them to find you another job. Or I could ask if there are any vacancies at the call centre where I work. There's a high turnover of staff.'

'That's because it's hideous,' I remind her. Nadia has only been there a short while and already she hates it.

'Yes,' Nadia agrees. 'It is.'

'Let's not be too hasty,' Autumn says. 'Lucy loves Chocolate

Heaven. We all do. Is there not a way that she could manage to make this work?'

'That way danger lies,' says Chantal. 'You need to keep your distance, Lucy. Part of you will always be in love with Marcus.'

'I'm not,' I protest. 'I'm over him. Truly.'

No one looks as if they believe me.

'That might be so.' The look she gives me is sceptical. 'But Marcus can't be trusted. We all know that. No one more than you, Lucy.'

And she's right. He still knows exactly how to wind me round his little finger. There's no way that I could ever consider working for him. Could I?

Chapter Four

When I leave Unsuitable Café number nineteen, I jump onto the Tube and head off to meet Crush at the wedding venue I've got in my sights. We've made a preliminary appointment with the wedding organiser there to discuss our requirements. Even though I'm squashed and bashed on the Underground and people stand on my feet and poke their copy of *Metro* in my eye, I get a thrill of excitement as I think that, very soon, Crush and I will become husband and wife. I love him so much, I just hope I don't do anything to mess it up.

Oh. Momentarily forgot that I have yet to tell Crush that I've lost my job. Again. I just hope I don't do anything *else* to mess it up.

I skip off the Tube and, with wings on my feet, fly to the park entrance where I'm to meet Crush. Golders Hill Park is one of my favourite places in London. Its leafy green spaces offer a calm oasis away from the hurly burly of the metropolis. When we come here, it's like being transported to another world. Our poky flat in Camden doesn't have any outside space at all, so we try to come here as often as we can to enjoy watching it change with the seasons, having brisk, wrapped-up walks in the winter with a hot chocolate to finish, and long leisurely hours reading and listening to music with an ice-cream in the summer. It would be lovely if we could get married here.

Crush is leaning against the wall by the entrance gate, arms folded, eyes closed, making the most of a glimpse of cool afternoon sunshine. My heart lifts whenever I see him. As he's come straight from the office at Targa, he's still wearing his sharp work suit and looks so smart. He's classically tall, dark and handsome and every time I look at him I feel as if I'm punching above my weight. Not only is he good looking, but I know that I can lay my heart at his feet and be certain that he'll never trample on it. Not even by mistake. Not like some I could mention.

I tiptoe up to him and kiss his cheek. He opens his eyes and smiles as he sees me. 'Hi, Gorgeous. Good day?'

'In parts.' I try not to sound too cagey. I want to break the news of my newlyunemployed state gently. My heart melts further and I slip my hand into his warm, strong fingers. 'Ready to do this?'

'Of course,' he says with a twinkle in his eye. 'You?'

'I've truly never been happier.' I take the opportunity to kiss him again and we go together into the park.

We meet Yvette, the wedding organiser, and she's a lovely lady who efficiently takes us to the areas where we could hold our marriage service. I grip Crush's hand tighter. We pass through the walled garden where the spring flowers are waving their cheerful heads in the breeze. We could be married by the pond in the Hill Garden Shelter, a more formal area, or in the Rotunda – an elevated pavilion. Both are gorgeous in their own way.

Yvette is clearly used to dealing with gushing, giggling brides-to-be as she lets me dart about, cooing over each feature while

Crush stands patiently, smiling indulgently. She points out the pluses and minuses of each area; where we would stand to take our vows, where our guests would sit. All the while she takes details on an iPad. We're keeping the wedding small – close family and friends. That's all. I went for the big church wedding and meringue dress with Marcus and don't want to go down that route again. At least if Crush abandons me, there won't be over a hundred guests to witness my pain.

Not that he will. Crush is cut from better cloth. Cashmere to Marcus's polyester.

Then, finally, Yvette takes us to the last area, the Belvedere – a temple in a slightly overgrown area of gothic columns and gardens which takes my breath away. It looks like something out of a fairy tale and is surrounded by wisteria, jasmine and roses that are just in bud. Lush greenery winds itself round slender stone pillars and embraces wrought-iron gates. The vista over the rest of the park is breathtaking.

'Oh, Aiden,' I breathe. 'What do you think?'

'It's great. I love it,' he says.

'Really?'

'Better than I could have imagined. But it's what you want that matters, Gorgeous.'

It's so much better than I could have dreamed, too. 'I feel that this is The Place.'

It looks like a film set. It's classical, elegant and wild all at the same time. There's a stone balcony where tendrils of clematis and ivy hang down. The stone is worn, mellow and looks like it holds stories. Each area is beautiful in its own way and I'd be happy with any of them, but this one has stolen my heart. I think Autumn would be proud of me – it's quite bohemian.

'Is it horribly expensive?' I ask.

The wedding organiser tells us and it seems quite reasonable too, compared to other places I've considered. But it's still worryingly high for our meagre budget.

'I've had a cancellation for June in the Belvedere,' Yvette says. 'You need to make your minds up quickly though, as I'm seeing another couple who are interested tomorrow morning.'

Oh, I couldn't bear it if this went to someone else. I know that it's not all about the venue. It's what comes afterwards that's important – and I don't even mean the cake. But this is perfect and I want our special day to be wonderful. I'm doing this once and I want to get it right.

Then Yvette gives us her card, wishes us well and leaves us to think on it.

When she's gone, Crush and I stand looking at the area for a few minutes longer.

'You like it?' he says.

'I do.'

'That comes later,' he teases.

I slip into the comfort of his arms.

'It's beautiful. I could just imagine us getting married here. Can we really afford it, though?'

'Just about.'

'If we have a picnic afterwards, that will really keep the costs down.'

'Are you sure you don't want a sit-down meal in a hotel?'

I shake my head. 'This will be different. Fun. We can make up some hampers, sit on picnic blankets. Get someone to play a guitar or something.'

'It sounds lovely,' he agrees. 'But what if it rains?'

'There's some shelter here,' I point out. 'Besides, it won't rain on our wedding day. Even the clouds will be happy for us.'

'I would opt for telling our guests to bring umbrellas.' He grins and then kisses me deeply. 'You are the eternal optimist. That's why I love you.'

'There's just one little thing I need to talk to you about.'

Crush frowns at me. 'Should I be worried?'

'A bit,' I concede.

'I thought everything was going too well.' He stifles a sigh. 'You haven't accidentally photographed yourself naked with any strangers recently?'

He's never going to let me forget that. In my defence, I was wearing some underwear and I was only trying to help Nadia get rid of her sleazy brother-in-law by posing for incriminating photographs with him. Perfect plan. Slightly backfired. Never meant for Crush to see them on the computer. Obvs. But he did.

'You haven't swallowed any diamond rings, either?'

That too was a low point in our relationship and not entirely unrelated to the first one. It's fair to say that Crush's first proposal to me didn't go all that smoothly. I ate the ring that was hidden in a chocolate. What was he thinking? Of course I was going to eat the chocolate! Still, they were very nice in Accident and Emergency. Maybe I should invite the nurse to the wedding?

'You haven't broken the company you're working for? Yet.'

'Ah,' I say, in as enigmatic a way as I can muster. 'Maybe we need coffee and cake.'

'Oh, Lucy,' he says with resignation and I lead him down towards the café, while I think exactly how I'm going to word this.

We sit opposite each other on the terrace even though the sun has more or less given up the ghost. When I've plied him with a frothy cappuccino and a slice of paradise cake and he's looking reasonably content, I pull my coat tightly around me and begin. 'It wasn't really my fault . . .'

He laughs, but it sounds a bit forced. 'It never is, Gorgeous.'

I met Crush when he was my boss at Targa, so he is well aware of my deficiencies in the workforce department.

'I'm not cut out to be in an office.'

'Many businesses across London have discovered that to their detriment.'

I flick froth at him, but I can't actually argue my case. I am not a born employee.

He reaches out and takes my hands. 'I know you're missing Chocolate Heaven.'

My mouth goes dry with anxiety. 'I wanted to talk to you about that, too.'

Crush's face darkens and he shakes his head. 'Please don't tell me Marcus is behind this.'

'Er . . . only slightly.' Let's face facts, it was only a matter of time before I got the bullet. One misdemeanour or another would have had me out of the door before long. Marcus just expedited it.

'I hoped we'd seen the back of him. It's been months now, Lucy, and you can't say that our life hasn't been a lot quieter without him in it.'

'I know.' Can't argue with that. But here he is again. The bad penny. 'He came to see me at lunchtime today,' I confess. 'He asked me to go back to Chocolate Heaven.'

'And you, of course, told him no.'

'I did . . . '

'Now you're having second thoughts.'

'I was good at running Chocolate Heaven. It's the only thing I've ever done well in my life. His current manager is rubbish.'

Crush looks unconvinced.

'Completely unsuitable,' I reiterate. 'He offered me the chance to work there again.'

'It would cost you dearly, Lucy,' Crush points out. 'Marcus would be right there in the middle of our relationship again. Exactly where he wants to be.'

'I think he's changed.'

Crush guffaws at that. As well he might. Marcus will never change. Even I know that and I am blind when it comes to Marcus.

'Shouldn't I consider it? We're getting married. Weddings are expensive – even on a budget. How can we go ahead with our plans if I'm not working?'

'We'll manage,' Crush says tightly.

'We could postpone it,' I offer. Even though it's the last thing I want. 'Get married later in the year.'

'No,' he insists. 'We should book it now. We'll find the money. Call your temp agency tomorrow. I'm sure you'll find something.' He looks at me earnestly. 'I know that you once loved Marcus . . . '

'But not anymore.'

'I know that you love Chocolate Heaven, too. I also know that you feel cut loose without it, but there are other jobs. Jobs that don't involve you being under Marcus's thumb again. You *can't* do it, Lucy.'

'I know.' I know that in my head. I do. But my heart is telling a very different story.

Chapter Five

Chantal opened the post. Before she slit the large brown manila envelope she knew what was in it, but she still had to steady herself against the kitchen counter. So that was it. The first batch of divorce papers had come through from Ted. Suddenly, it felt more real.

The speed of it all was quite shocking. They'd paid some fancy lawyer a lot of money to fast-track the process and they were carving up their assets with alarming alacrity. Yet why not do this as quickly as possible? The only thing that bound them together now was their daughter, Lana. For her sake, they would have to maintain a civilised relationship and, if she was honest, she might have fallen out of love with Ted but had never really reached the point of disliking him. There was still affection there between them and they should, if at all possible, hang on to that. If they tried hard, it should be feasible to keep things amicable. It didn't seem to happen often once lawyers and custody issues became involved, but they were trying to pick their way through it carefully. She wasn't yet sure if it helped or hindered their relationship that he was now several thousand miles away in New York.

He'd moved there to start a new job and a new life with his lover and her former friend, Stacey, and their daughter, Elsie. Theirs had been a very complicated setup. Ted had fathered Elsie when he and Chantal had been briefly separated and she'd done her best to assimilate the little girl into their family. Perhaps she'd done too much. She'd befriended Stacey, too, and it seemed that while they were friends, the woman had continued her affair with Ted behind her back when they'd both insisted it was over.

In some ways she still missed Stacey, as they were so similar in many ways. Elsie was adorable too. The girls were half-sisters and she'd wanted them to grow up together, have fun together, enjoy a stable family together. She realised now that was probably pie in the sky. Occasionally she spoke to Stacey when she called Ted for something to do with Lana or, more usually, the divorce proceedings. When Stacey picked up the phone instead of her ex-husband they were always pleasant with each other, but the warmth and closeness they'd once shared had all but gone. She wondered how Stacey was really settling in New York. On the phone she told Chantal that she enjoyed it, but the truth of the matter was that she probably hardly ever saw Ted and was on her own in a strange and busy city with a small baby. That was never going to be a bed of roses.

Still, that was Stacey's problem now. She'd chosen that situation and there was too much distance between them – emotionally and physically – for Chantal to be able to help her as she'd once tried. She couldn't quite forgive her – not so much for taking Ted, but for not being straight with her about her feelings for him. It was clear that Stacey also felt guilty about the situation and kept her at arm's length. Because of it, Stacey would be very much alone.

Turning to Lana in her high chair, Chantal said, 'Hey, baby girl. What have you done there? Have you given yourself a new hairdo?'

Lana had been left to her own devices with a small pot of yoghurt for a few minutes, but it was amazing to see just how much it had contained. She'd barely taken her eyes off her child to read the decree nisi, but now most of the yoghurt was in Lana's hair, which stood up in clumps. It was also in her ears, up her nose and all over the highchair. She gently took the spoon from her daughter's chubby fingers before she could do any more damage. Her daughter grinned at her proudly, clearly pleased with her efforts.

'What are we going to do about that, missy?' Thankfully, it wasn't very long until her bathtime.

It was tough bringing up a baby alone. Luckily, she and Ted had been well-placed financially, so that was one less thing to worry about. They were in the process of selling the properties they owned and Ted had been very fair in their settlement. It wasn't often that she heard that from friends. Usually there was a terrible embittered battle over money, but Ted hadn't indulged in that. Perhaps it was guilt that was motivating him. He had, after all, not just left Chantal but had essentially put his career ahead of seeing his daughter.

Looking at her baby contentedly gurgling and talking nonsense to herself, Chantal wondered whether there'd come a day when Lana would be unhappy about the situation her parents had left her in, due to their inability to get along. All she wanted was for her child to be happy.

Soon, she'd look for a job, but the settlement and a general downsizing in lifestyle meant that she had enough money for it not to be a pressing issue. She'd take her time, enjoy Lana and find something she'd like to do that could work round her daughter. The world of magazines might be too demanding. She'd had to travel a lot with her last job and there was no way she wanted to do that now. Maybe something online would be the answer. Perhaps Autumn's partner, Miles, who was a website wizard, could give her some ideas.

Plus, at the moment, she seemed to be so tired all the time, and though she'd been trying to lose a few pounds, the weight seemed to be dropping off her. Not that she was complaining about that, but perhaps she needed some vitamins or a herbal tonic to give her a boost. It had been niggling her for a few weeks now.

Jacob came into the room. His hair was still damp from the shower and her stomach flipped. He was a beautiful man from head to toe, inside and out.

'Feel better?'

He nodded. 'It's nice to wash the day away.' She handed him a glass of wine and he sipped it gratefully. 'Just what the doctor ordered.' Then he twined his arm round her waist and nuzzled her neck. It always felt so good to be held by him. Lana and Jacob gave the best cuddles. 'Speaking of which. How are you feeling today?'

'Still a bit tired,' she admitted. 'I managed to have a nap this afternoon when Lana did.' It wasn't often she managed synchronised sleeping with her daughter, but recently she'd become so fatigued that she'd tried to catnap when Lana did, rather than trying to race round to achieve something useful in her day. Achieving something useful, she hoped, would come later. 'I feel a bit better now.'

'Did you call the doctor?'

'I don't think it's anything to bother the GP with. I expect all mums with young babies are permanently exhausted.'

'I'd be happier if you made an appointment. You don't seem yourself at the moment.' Jacob frowned with concern. 'Maybe the stresses and strains of life have piled up a bit. Don't they say that divorce is one of the most stressful life events?'

'Moving house is up there too and we'll be doing that soon,' she said.

When the family home was sold, she and Jacob were going to move in together. She'd bought a small terraced house in a nice, quiet mews street not far from where she currently lived. This part of north London was nice and trendy with lots going on – not that she availed herself of it now that she had Lana, but it was still good to know that it was close to hand. She sometimes wondered whether Jacob minded being thrust into the full flow of parenthood, but he didn't seem to. He'd made a fantastic surrogate father to Lana, who was too young to have noticed the transition from Ted to another man; that in itself was so sad.

They'd got together at Christmas when she'd rented a huge farmhouse in the Lake District for everyone to stay in. It had taken some organising, but all the members of the Chocolate Lovers' Club had come along. The cottage had been fabulous and they'd all enjoyed the snow, the roaring fires and spending a relaxing time together. After she and Ted had broken up, Nadia had invited Jacob to come along too as a surprise. The truth was that she'd loved Jacob for a long time, which had never helped her marriage. Now it was their chance to be together.

Despite the pain of the looming divorce, Christmas had been a great success. If anything, it had helped her to fall in love more deeply with Jacob. All their previous time together had been snatched moments. In the seclusion of the cottage, they'd been able to spend time together as a couple.

'I'll start dinner,' Chantal said.

'I'm famished. Lunch was a quick espresso.' Jacob's event-planning business was keeping him very busy. He was quite often out a couple of evenings in the week and at the weekends, though he did his best to delegate those.

'I have no idea what's lurking in the depths of the fridge, but I'm hoping there's something edible.' As she turned away, she felt a sharp pain, high on her chest, that took her breath away.

'Are you sure you're OK?'

'Just a twinge,' she said, rubbing the area. 'Lana's getting very heavy to lift now. Perhaps I've pulled a muscle. I'm sure it's something and nothing.'

'Promise me that you'll phone the doctor tomorrow.'

'It's impossible to get an appointment. You have to be on the phone from eight o'clock in the morning and sit in a holding queue of a dozen people. I'll either be cured or dead by the time I get through.'

'Try. Promise me.'

'I will.' She had no intention of doing so, but when the pain seared through her again, she thought that Jacob might have a point.

Chapter Six

Autumn held Flo's tiny hand as they all came out of the cinema, both of them blinking as they hit bright daylight. Miles's young daughter was happily singing the typically annoying theme tune to the movie. In the months that she'd been with Miles she'd become used to seeing more films featuring princesses than the usual rom-coms or soulful art-house films that she loved. But it was a small price to pay to be with a man who was as kind and loving as Miles Stratford.

She felt as if she'd been looking for someone like Miles all her life. He loved her in the way she had always hoped existed. Their relationship was quiet, caring. There was no walking on eggshells, no histrionics, no rollercoaster of highs and lows. They simply got along well, shared the same values, had similar interests. And if that all sounded a bit boring, there was passion – rather a lot of it – in all the right places. Autumn smiled to herself.

'What are you grinning at?' Miles asked.

She threaded her arm through his. 'I'm just thinking that I'm very lucky.'

'And here's me thinking that you were happy that the fairy

princess found her true love – even though it was an ogre.'

'That too,' she conceded.

They headed to the nearest restaurant for an early meal. It was a cheerful, fast-food type of place, but they gave Flo a rainbow range of crayons and a sheet of cartoons to colour in which kept her happy. Plus she'd get a balloon to go home with – no greater treat when you're nearly four.

When they were seated in their booth by the window, Autumn watched how Miles helped his daughter with her colourful creation.

'The dog needs to be *pink*, Daddy,' Flo insisted.

'Pink is an excellent colour for dogs,' Miles agreed, amiably. 'You don't see nearly enough of them.'

He winked at Autumn while Flo scribbled furiously, tongue out in concentration. She was a lovely little girl and looked just like her dad. She had his hazel eyes, his wiry chestnut-brown hair, his full mouth, the same smattering of freckles over the bridge of his nose. Two peas in a pod. Autumn had fallen as much in love with the child as she had with her dad.

It was lovely to see how much Miles adored Flo – she was his life. Autumn knew that it was difficult for him to be a part-time dad, but he did a really great job. Miles was the first man she'd had a relationship with who she thought was excellent father material. He was a natural parent and, one day, she'd love to have children with him. As always, it made her think of her own daughter and how much she'd missed out on.

Autumn had been forced by her parents to put her baby girl, Willow, up for adoption when she found she was pregnant at fourteen. It had been the worst moment of her life and there wasn't a day that went by that she didn't regret her compliance. Recently, she'd started to come to terms with it and had begun to reach out to her daughter through sites that aimed to reunite separated families.

She never imagined that Willow would be looking for her and yet, at Christmas time, she'd had a call out of the blue from the Find Families agency to say that her daughter would like to make contact. At that moment, she felt that her heart would burst with joy. In her mind, she'd imagined a tearful reunion, a tentative period of getting to know each other and then they'd all live happily ever after. Perhaps she had been watching too many princess-based films. Instead, they were still to get out of the starting blocks.

Months had passed and she'd yet to make contact with her daughter. Autumn was reliant on the Find Families agency, and spoke to Eleanor there regularly. She was the go-between between Autumn and Mary Randall, Willow's adoptive mother. They'd organised phone calls and a few times had tentatively set up a date with a view to meeting. Then it seemed that Willow shied away from making contact again. It was like a slow-motion game of cat and mouse. Mary wasn't very forthcoming, Eleanor told her, and was clearly worried that Willow was too young to handle the situation. And although Eleanor was supposedly facilitating the meeting between Autumn and her daughter, she didn't seem to be in much of a rush either. Her advice was to take it at Willow's pace. Which meant that Autumn was calling on all her reserves of patience. But, having got this far, she didn't want to frighten her daughter away by being pushy. That was the last thing Willow needed. She would just sit tight, continue to be there and wait for her daughter to choose her time.

Reaching into her handbag, she turned on her phone again after silencing it for the film. There were a few missed calls: one from Lucy, one from Nadia and, more surprisingly, one from Eleanor.

'I need to make a call. Eleanor's been trying to get hold of me.' Autumn couldn't help the hopeful note in her voice. 'I'll just pop outside before our food arrives.'

'Fingers crossed,' Miles said as she slipped out of the booth.

Standing outside on the pavement, she pressed to return Eleanor's call. Her heart was in her mouth, as it was every time she spoke to the Find Families agency. There was always the fear that her daughter might sever even this most tenuous link.

'Hi, Eleanor,' she said. 'Sorry I missed your call.'

'Hello, Autumn. I think we might be on again,' Eleanor said. 'Mary called to suggest a meeting.'

'She did?'

'Don't hold your breath,' Eleanor advised and Autumn realised that was exactly what she was doing. 'But she sounded more positive this time.'

'I can see them anytime, anywhere. I'll be led entirely by what they want to do.'

'They're coming into London,' Eleanor said. 'They'll meet you at a venue of your choice. I'd suggest a nice café, maybe in a museum.'

'I know just the place.' It had to be Chocolate Heaven. She'd have to sweet-talk Lucy so that she could go into what was now enemy territory, but it would be the best place to meet Willow and Mary. If Willow's DNA was anything like her birth mother's, she would love it.

'I'll keep my fingers crossed for you this time,' Eleanor said.

'Thank you. Me too.'

Autumn went back into the restaurant with a spring in her step. Maybe, just maybe, this time it would really happen.

Miles glanced up. 'Good news?'

'She's trying to arrange another meeting. This time she thinks that I really might get to meet Willow.'

'I hope so.'

'I'll just keep praying and making myself available.' Autumn knew that it would be a huge step for a young girl to take. She wondered how she'd feel herself in that situation. All she wanted

35

was a chance to explain to Willow why she'd been compelled to do what she'd done. 'That's all I can do until she's ready to see me.'

She was so very desperate to see her daughter, to hold her, to care for her, to love her as a mother should.

Chapter Seven

Nadia knelt on the floor and helped her son, Lewis, to put the last piece of his Lego castle in place.

They sat back on their heels together and admired their efforts. 'Nice work.' She held up a hand for a high-five and Lewis obliged. 'Now it's time for bed.'

'Ten more minutes, Mummy,' Lewis pleaded.

'Not even one,' she said, firmly. 'You're going to school in the morning and Mummy's got to go to work. We both have to be up bright and early.'

At least she'd managed to get a job with reasonable hours. She was on a permanent day shift with only one late night each week, so wasn't having to juggle childcare quite as much as she used to. For the time being, Lewis was only at school in the mornings but would be starting full time in September. Luckily, Autumn was still available to pick him up for her and look after him for a couple of hours in the afternoon until she got home. On the late shifts, Autumn gave Lewis his tea, bathed him and put him to bed, which was a bit more time-consuming for her friend, but Autumn never seemed to mind. And it wouldn't be for long. Thank goodness.

She'd received a cheque from the insurance company at Christmas and it was a not-insubstantial sum of money. It wasn't enough to retire on or to buy a mansion, but it was enough to see them right and would be a welcome cushion for times when she might be out of work. It seemed as if the company had really dragged their heels over paying out after her husband's death, but they'd finally done so and it had taken a huge weight from her shoulders. Now she could start to plan the rest of their lives.

She'd taken the call-centre job when it came up because she didn't want to start eating into their capital. That money would have to last them a long time, provide a future for them both, and she didn't want to squander it. The work was mind-numbingly tedious and she was in a soulless office without windows all day long. Fielding account queries for a big online firm meant that most of the people on the end of the telephone were very angry. Not the ideal way to spend your working day, but it would do for now. The money from the life insurance would enable her and Lewis to move to a nicer house in a more salubrious area and she'd look for a better, permanent job – hopefully more of a career move – when she knew where they'd be settled. She might even have enough money left to start up her own little business or something. There was a lot to think about.

Lewis had already been in the bath and was in his pyjamas, so she took him upstairs and tucked him in bed. It was rare that he spent an entire night in there. Nadia was sure by the time she came up later he'd be sprawled across her double bed and she'd be sleeping on a sliver at the edge as usual. But at least she made a show of putting him in his own room to start with. He was growing up fast and soon he'd want his own space. Despite the fact that he spent most of the night wriggling, she cherished the time they had together. She stroked his dark hair. He was doing well, her beloved son. They'd been through some tough times together and yet he still managed to be happy and sunny every day. Well, almost. She didn't think her heart could hold any more love for a person. Everything she did, she did for him and she wanted to give him a better life than they had now.

'Story?' Lewis said, hopefully.

'Not tonight, sweetheart. You bargained that one away for Lego instead.'

He snuggled down beneath his duvet and slipped his thumb into his mouth. 'Love you, Mummy.'

'Love you more. Sleep tight.'

She turned out the light and left his door ajar as she headed downstairs.

There was a time after Toby's death when she dreaded the evenings, and spending them alone. The hours seemed to stretch interminably. But now she looked forward to a little quality time by herself – surely that had to be progress? Added to that, she now had someone else in her life and that had definitely brought the sparkle back.

Nadia made herself a cup of coffee and delved in the cupboard for the special grown-up stash of chocolate that she hid at the very back of the kitchen cupboard, well out of Lewis's reach. Tonight a bar of deliciously dark Green & Black's would be receiving her care and attention.

Settling herself in the living room, Nadia turned down the television and picked up her phone to call James – the highlight of her day. She'd met James when she and the girls had spent Christmas in the Lake District. It was James's cottage that Chantal had rented for them all over the holiday period, and he just happened to be the rather handsome farmer who lived in the farmhouse further down the track.

Nadia punched in his number. James had two children – Seth, who was six, and his sister Lily, who was eight – and this was usually the best time to catch him, when his day was finished and the children were likely to be in bed. As always, she felt her heart quicken as she waited for him to answer.

'Hey,' he said, and instantly her heart lifted.

'Hello, love. How has your day been?' Since she'd returned home after Christmas, she'd called him every single day. Their conversations were always soothing, relaxed and increasingly lengthy. They talked about nothing much other than the minutiae of their days, catching up with what their kids were doing, but it was nice to know that there was someone at the other end of the phone who looked forward to her calls each evening. She wondered how she'd manage without this little highlight to look forward to.

'Good,' he said. 'The weather was perfect today. Crisp, cold. There was a frost on the mountains first thing, but when the mist cleared we even had a bit of sun to burn it off.'

Nadia thought about the miserable, damp and interminably grey day in London.

'We'll be bringing the ewes down from the fells to the meadows for lambing soon,' he added. 'That's a busy time for us. All hands to the pump.'

It was a world away from her own life and she loved to hear about it. If he could get a signal, he'd sometimes send her a photo of where he was on the fells and it helped her to feel closer to him, as she could imagine exactly where he was.

'You should come up with Lewis. The kids always like to muck in. He'd love it. There's always a few sickly ones that need to be coaxed with a bottle feed.'

'He'd like that.' She thought of the day they'd all gone down from the cottage to spend part of Christmas at James's farm. It was a sprawling place and had probably once been quite a grand house. Now it was very scuffed around the edges, but it was cosy and homely. There were animals everywhere you turned. Four cats curled up on armchairs, bookcases and hogging the fireside intermingled with a couple of dogs – an elderly Labrador and a lively Jack Russell.

Trips to the city farm in Spitalfields were the closest Lewis ever got to animals. It was a great place, for sure, but it couldn't really compete with the wild and rugged landscape of the Lake District. Lewis always badgered her for a pet, but with them both out of the house so much during the day, it wasn't fair on an animal. His new school had a pet hamster in class and that was the closest he'd got. No doubt they'd be on the rota to look after it at weekends and in school holidays. That would have to be enough for now.

'I haven't seen you since Christmas,' James murmured down the phone. 'I'm missing you.'

'I know. I feel the same.'

James had made them all very welcome that first day. The kids had all got on great together and had spent hours outside playing in the snow. The adults, by contrast, had taken up residence round the roaring fire with a fair few bottles of good red. With a thrill, Nadia remembered them casting increasingly long glances at each other all day. She'd spent time alone in the kitchen with James, helping him to put together a spread of homemade bread and a dozen different cheeses for their lunch. They'd talked as if they'd known each other for years and he'd made her laugh more than she'd done in months. By the end of the week, they'd spent every day together and she'd relaxed with him in a way that she hadn't with anyone else.

He'd told her about his life in the Lakes and that his wife, Helen, had died of cancer three years earlier, leaving him to cope with the farm and the children. In turn, she opened up about Toby and her struggles to bring up Lewis alone. Because they'd both experienced tragedies there was an instant affinity, but it was more than that. She was comfortable with James as well as being attracted to him. He had an easy manner, a gentle charm.

'You should come up to see us all,' he said. 'What's stopping you?'

It had been so hard to leave at the end of the holiday and head back to London. She was thirty-odd and getting swept away by a holiday romance. What a cliché. She'd laugh at anyone else doing the same thing and yet she'd really fallen head over heels for James.

She'd fully intended to go back to see them all in Cumbria during Lewis's half-term holiday, but they'd been snowed in up there and the trains were all up the spout. It was too far and too expensive to go for a weekend – Lewis would be exhausted – and she hadn't accrued enough holiday to take time off until now. Yet it had begun to feel as if the gap was too long. There was a lot of distance between them. They talked every day, but three months had passed since she'd seen him. Was he as kind and as handsome as she remembered or had time played tricks on her? Was it better to have this safe, unthreatening relationship at a distance rather than take the next step?

'I'm working,' she said, and it sounded a lame excuse even to her own ears.

'It will be Easter soon,' he countered. 'They must give you some time off from that dreadful call centre. They don't chain you there twenty-four seven.'

She laughed at that. 'They do!'

'And Lewis will be off school. So will Seth and Lily,' he added smoothly, ignoring her protests. 'I'll take some time away from the farm to show you around. Come and stay with us for a week. More if you want to. There's really no reason not to. Unless you don't want to.'

'It's not that. Of course it isn't.'

'Then why the hesitation?'

'I'm frightened,' she admitted. 'It was all so lovely at Christmas. We got on brilliantly. What if we can't recreate that?'

'Come,' he said, suddenly serious. 'We need to see if we can make this work. You can jump on the train. I'll send you the money.'

'It's not the money.'

'Then come. Are we really going to spend the rest of our lives doing nothing more than calling each other every night?'

'It sounds like a good proposition to me,' she teased. Yet she knew in her heart that there was some truth in her words.

'Not to me,' James said. 'I want to see you again. I want to hold you, Nadia.'

Her mouth went dry.

'I want to show you my world, because I think you'll like it very much.'

'That's partly what I'm scared of.'

James laughed softly. 'What's the worst that could happen?'

They could fall in love and that would turn her world upside down. Or she could stay here, call it a day and never know what she might have missed.

When she didn't answer, he said, 'We could see if we have a future together. After all that we've been through, don't you think we owe ourselves that?'

She imagined him striding over the open fells, sheepdog at his heels, and glanced out at her rather scruffy garden that was the size of a postage stamp. What would it mean if she went up there and still liked what she saw?

'I'll think about it,' she said. 'I promise.' Her stomach gripped with anxiety even saying it.

'Don't think too hard,' he said. 'Or you'll talk yourself out of it. Just do it. Book your ticket.'

If she dithered for too long, James would move on. She knew that. Perhaps the odds were stacked against this relationship working, but wasn't it worth giving it a try?

Chapter Eight

I put on a long dark wig with a blunt-cut fringe and, despite the grey day, add mirrored aviator shades. I've also bought a dark trench coat from one of the vintage second-hand shops on Camden High Street to complete my disguise. Perfect. No one will ever know me now.

I'm going undercover, visiting Chocolate Heaven to get a handle on exactly what's happening. I jump on the Tube, sweltering in my big coat after the walk up there. The wig is nylon and my head itches. Perhaps I could have done with a more lightweight, yet equally cunning disguise.

When I arrive at Chocolate Heaven, hot and bothered, I stand across the street from my spiritual home and gaze longingly at its window. The display is rubbish. Totally rubbish. It makes me grind my teeth in frustration. What is this new manager thinking of? I always made sure that there were gorgeous cakes and chocolates on show to tempt in the customers. Now there's nothing remotely enticing there at all. It looks very neglected, but it would take me five minutes to sort it out.

My heart squeezes with longing. Oh, I do miss it. I haven't

even walked past here since Marcus took over running the business. I couldn't bring myself to. Now he wants me back and I need to know why.

I turn the door handle and the bell tings my arrival. There are hardly any tables occupied – a couple sit at the one in the window; two guys are stretched out on the sofas that were the favourite and daily haunts of the Chocolate Lovers' Club. Only a short while ago, particularly in the run up to Christmas, you could hardly move in here and the till never stopped ringing all day. I was run off my feet and was happy to be so.

Even the cakes in the glass counter don't look as appealing. Our usual cake maker was a lovely lady called Alexandra who lived just around the corner. These don't look up to the standard of her work. I'd have another attractive display of products I'd bought in too, but now the shelves stand empty. It's coming up to Easter – the chocolate feast to end all chocolate feasts! Chocolate Heaven should be groaning with beautiful chocolates and Easter eggs, cute gingerbread bunnies, iced biscuits. Marcus will be missing out on a great opportunity if he and his manager don't get their act together pretty soon. No wonder he wants to replace her.

Listen to me. Like I should care. None of this is my problem anymore. If Marcus can't motivate or deal with his manager then he shouldn't be in business.

I'm standing staring at the counter, still dismayed by what I'm seeing, when someone comes out of the back into the shop. Ah. Now I can see the attraction of this particular manager. Her skills may not lie in window display or stock ordering, but she has other assets in spades.

The woman is tall, as slender as a reed and supermodel beautiful. Sigh. Marcus is nothing if not predictable. Her long black tresses fall in heavy waves over her shoulders and she flicks them back as I watch, grudgingly admiring. Her skin is the colour of creamy latte, her nose tiny, her mouth full and luscious. Sigh, sigh, sigh. She's wearing one of those timeless wrap dresses in a light navy blue that suit everyone on the planet but me. Of course, I don't need to tell you that it clings to her body in all the right places, flattering every curve. Her legs are like those of a gazelle.

She comes to stand in front of me and looks me up and down. Uncomfortable, I adjust my aviator shades.

'Hello,' I manage.

Her chin juts in response and I assume this is my cue to place my order.

'I'd like a flat Americano and one of those brownies, please.' The shelves are covered in crumbs and, clearly, no one has rubbed around with a J-cloth this morning. I stuff my hands in my trench coat pockets to stop me from leaping over the counter and grabbing one to whisk around.

She turns away from me to the coffee machine. Interesting customer relations. When I was here, I knew all our regulars by name and, needless to say, none of them are in here now. The supermodel crashes and bangs away with the coffee machine while I stand and wait. A minute or so later, she plonks it down on the counter in front of me, followed by the brownie. It seems that table service has been dispensed with.

'Thank you.'

'No problem.' An accent. French, I think Marcus said. And, actually, it did look like it was quite a bit of a problem for her. She looks as if she'd rather be on a yacht in the South of France or shopping in the Champs-Élysées. Before I move away from the counter, she's already heading into the back of the shop.

Taking my coffee and cake, I sit at a table. There's no music playing as there used to be, which makes the atmosphere a little stilted. You can hear every coffee cup rattle and the few people who are here are speaking in hushed tones. What is Marcus thinking? Does he not come in here and see how dire it is compared to how it used to be? It would take so little to get it on track again. And, of course, I'm exactly the right person to do it. No wonder he wants me back here. Thank goodness he's not around. I should drink my coffee and leave as quickly as I can.

No sooner has that thought passed through my brain than I hear the roar of a super car and a familiar red Ferrari pulls up outside Chocolate Heaven. My heart sinks. Right on cue, Marcus appears. I just hope that he doesn't recognise me in my cunning disguise. Pulling up my collar, I sink down into my seat.

'Hey, Lucy,' he says, marching straight over to me. 'Good to see you.'

Gah.

'What's with the sunglasses?'

I whip them off.

'And the wig?'

I whip that off too. Quite relieved really, as the itching was becoming unbearable.

'Take off your coat,' he suggests. 'If you're staying. You look all pink in the face.'

I hesitate. Why should I do what Marcus tells me?

'You have got something on underneath?' His eyes twinkle mischievously.

I whip off my coat. Get an eyeful of my woolly jumper, Marcus Canning!

'Don't scowl at me, Lucy,' he says. 'Chill out. Eat your brownie. More coffee?'

'No thanks.' I wouldn't like to interrupt Ms France's relaxation.

He drops into the seat opposite me. 'So? What are you doing here? Couldn't stay away?'

'I just came to see what's going on and why you're so keen to get me back.'

'Look at the place,' he leans forward and whispers. 'It is a shadow of the former Chocolate Heaven. I know that. You know that.'

I don't disagree with him.

'Question is . . . ' Marcus settles back again and crosses his arms. 'What are we going to do about it?'

'*We* are going to do nothing,' I point out. 'This is all down to you and the lady you have in charge.'

'Ah,' he says. 'So you've met Marie-France?'

'Of course I have. She served me. In a manner of speaking.'

Marcus could be a customer and yet she hasn't reappeared. Her boss is here and she hasn't even acknowledged that, let alone offered to get him a drink. I know I'm hardly the world's best employee, but even I have my standards.

'She's a great girl,' he says with a wistful glance towards the counter where she should be but isn't.

'Great in what sense of the word?' I ask and I sound bitter even to my own ears. 'She might look as if she should be on the catwalk, but she's ruining your business.'

'I know.' Now it's Marcus's turn to sigh.

'Then do something about it.'

'I'm trying to,' he points out. 'I'm attempting, rather unsuccessfully, to lure you back.'

I don't like to point out that, as we both can see, my efforts to stay away have been futile. Biting into my brownie, I find it wanting. First thing I'd do is get Alexandra on the phone.

'Come back, Lucy. Please. This place is in your DNA. I know you're miserable not working here. And you've lost your job.'

'Yes. Thanks to you.'

'I'm doing you a favour. Trust me.'

'Oh, Marcus. Time has taught me that I can't trust you as far as I can throw you.'

'I offered this to you on a plate. It could have been yours. It still can be.' He makes his baby-blue eyes go all wide and innocent. 'I'll do anything – *anything* – to have you back.'

'We're just talking about work.'

'Of course.' Marcus looks wounded. 'I know that I've lost you, Lucy.' He fixes me with a loving gaze. 'You're still planning to get married to whatshisname?'

'Aiden. Yes. Soon. We've booked a venue.'

'Then you'll need the money.'

One nail hit on the head.

'I can help,' Marcus rushes on. 'Name your price. What will it cost me to get you to come back and work for me? This place is haemorrhaging money and it was a great business when I bought it. I *need* you.'

'I don't know, Marcus.' I'm wavering. It would be so good to be back behind the counter in my rightful place, get Alexandra to bake the cakes again, stock up with fabulous chocolatey goodies in time for Easter.

'I'll pay you whatever it takes.'

I pluck a ridiculous sum from my head and blurt it out of my mouth.

Marcus doesn't even flinch. 'Done.'

The speed of his acceptance takes even me by surprise.

'When can you start? Now?'

'I'm not sure about it, Marcus.'

'You'd be mad to turn me down.'

'Or maybe I'd be mad to agree to come and work for you.' Would I be foolish to trust him yet again?

'We'd make a great team,' he assures me. 'We did once. We could do it again.'

'We were a great team in the bedroom,' I remind him. 'Not behind the counter of a small café and chocolate emporium.'

'Oh yeah.' He winks at me. 'I remember that too, now you come to mention it.'

I abandon my brownie – that's how bad it is – then I pick up my wig and my sunglasses. 'I need to think about it. I need to discuss it with my *fiancé*.'

Marcus does flinch at that. He reaches out and touches my arm as I go to leave. 'I'm begging for your help. Only you can dig me out of this hole. Please don't let me down.'

'I'll call you,' I say.

I walk out of Chocolate Heaven. I either return here as the manager or I never come back again. The choice is as stark as that. And you might think I'd be happy that the boot is on the other foot for once – that Marcus needs me more than I need him. Yet all I can think of is the number of times he's let me down in the past. I so want to believe that we could work together and get my old job back on a wonderful salary. It's very tempting. But is Marcus Canning nothing more than a power-crazed, cheating bastard who still has his sights set on my heart? Can he really have changed this time?

Chapter Nine

Another day, another inferior café that isn't Chocolate Heaven. We are all sitting staring miserably at the measly offerings on our plates. Sadly, Chocolate Lovers' Club meetings aren't quite what they used to be. I'm not even going to describe this place to you as, frankly, it's too flipping depressing.

'We have to up our game,' Chantal says. 'We are failing to maintain basic standards here.' She scowls at the soggy, chocolate-free shortbread in front of her. 'The only plus side is that I'm losing loads of weight. I'm finally back in my pre-baby clothes and then some.'

I glance up nervously. 'I could go back to Chocolate Heaven.'

'No.' Chantal is vehement in her objection. 'Absolutely not. We *will* find somewhere else. Don't do it.'

'Marcus is desperate,' I venture a little more boldly. 'I went there yesterday and it's looking so neglected. It breaks my heart.'

'Oh, Lucy,' Nadia says. 'I know you really want to do this, but Marcus would wrap you round his little finger again in no time. You can't say that your life hasn't been a lot easier without him in it.'

Never a truer word has been spoken.

'What does Crush say?' Autumn asks.

'He's never going to be mad keen on anything that involves Marcus,' I confess. Which should tell me something.

We look around at our miserable surroundings. Worn wooden chairs, scuffed flooring, no wonderful chocolates. There's only the whiff of cleaning products in the air rather than the heady scent of vanilla and cocoa.

'There are *thousands* of cafés in London,' Chantal protests.

'Yes, but they're all ghastly, impersonal chains and we need somewhere intimate and quirky.' One exactly like Chocolate Heaven.

'We just have to find the right one,' Chantal insists.

'We did find the right one. The *perfect* one,' I point out. 'And it was cruelly taken from us.'

'Bloody Marcus and his meddling,' Chantal says. 'He's the cause of all the misery in your life. Never forget that.'

'He's offered me a massive salary.' I pull a discontented face. 'Ridiculously massive. It would go a long way towards paying for our wedding.'

'If you let Marcus back into the mix, you might never get to the altar,' Autumn says. And Autumn never sees the bad in anyone.

'If you could only go there and see what's happened to it in our absence, you might think differently. There's a horrible, surly French woman behind the counter. She didn't even say hello. She just threw my coffee and brownie at me.'

'This woman doesn't happen to be extraordinarily beautiful, does she?'

'Er . . . yes,' I admit.

'There you go. If Marcus appointed his management with his brain rather than his cock, he wouldn't be in this mess.'

'I think he's realised that,' I say, coming to his defence. 'And I know that I could help him out of this hole. I don't want to see Chocolate Heaven go to the wall for the lack of a little TLC.'

'Don't do anything hasty,' Nadia warns.

They all laugh at that. As well they might. My entire life is spent doing hasty things.

'Talk it over with Crush again,' she continues when the laughter subsides. 'See what he thinks.'

He'll say no. Of course he will. If it was up to Crush there would be a restraining order on Marcus that prevented him from coming within five hundred miles of me. He has, indeed, been the cause of much trouble in our relationship. But I can't help thinking . . .

Chantal stands up to check on Lana, who is snoozing peacefully in her buggy next to us, unaware of the drama in our lives and the fact that we are having to deal with it in unsuitable premises with substandard beverages and a life-threatening dearth of chocolate. Chantal tucks the blanket round Lana's neck, adjusting her pillow.

'What else has been going on?' she asks when she sits down again. 'I feel as if I'm out of the loop now that we don't meet as often.'

'I've got another meeting fixed up with Willow,' Autumn tells us. 'I just hope she turns up this time.'

'We'll keep everything crossed for you,' I chip in. 'Do you need any moral support?'

'I think I'll be OK. I'm a bit nervous, but I think I should do this alone. I'm sure it will be quite emotional and I want to make it as easy for her as possible. She's coming into town with Mary and I was planning to take her to Chocolate Heaven. I thought she'd love it there, but after what Lucy has said, maybe I'll try somewhere else.'

Damn this. It's ruining all our plans and socialising. How can Autumn meet her long-lost daughter in an inadequate establishment? Marcus has to do something urgently! It's all I can do to stop myself picking up my mobile and telling him yes.

'I've got a dilemma too,' Nadia says thoughtfully. 'I need your advice.' She pushes aside her slightly stale croissant. 'I was talking to James last night and he wants me to go up to Keswick to spend Easter with him.'

'I'm not seeing a problem,' I tell her.

'Neither should I,' she confesses. 'But I'm scared to take it to the next level.' She lets out a sigh. 'I sort of like it as it is. We have cosy chats every night and we get on really well.'

'What are you frightened of?' Chantal says. 'That if you go up there you might not like him as much as you think, or that you might like him too much?'

Nadia puts her face in her hands. 'Both!'

'Then you do have a problem,' I agree, with a gentle smile.

'If I don't like him, then that ends our cosy chats and I go back to lonely evenings.' She shrugs. 'If I do like him, then where does that leave us? I don't know exactly how far it is from London to the Lake District, but I know it's a bloody long way. It must be at least three hundred miles. James can't leave his farm, so it would be down to me to go up there for holidays and weekends. What kind of a relationship could we have long term?'

'Love will find a way,' I say.

'Oh, Lucy. You're such an optimistic romantic,' Nadia says. 'I have to be practical for Lewis's sake. I can't drag my son up and down the country just because I fancy a hottie gentleman farmer.'

'But you *do* fancy him?' I wiggle my eyebrows suggestively.

'Yes,' Nadia laughs. 'Like mad! But is that enough? Why couldn't I have met someone who lives in the same postcode as me?'

'You said you were thinking of moving,' I remind her.

'Yes, but not to the Lake District. I'm a townie. I always have been. Plus my family are here.'

I don't point out to Nadia that she's still currently estranged from her parents. They cut her out of their lives when she married Toby against their wishes and haven't relented since he died. Seems harsh, but that's families for you. She's grown close to her sister, Anita, again but I know Nadia's worried it will all end over another disagreement. It's a big thing for her, I realise, but are families all that they're cracked up to be? If you don't get a good one, they can cause you more grief than joy.

In my own case, I hardly ever see my folks, who are too busy chasing their own salacious relationships. My dad is still with the much younger Pilates instructor. My mother is now in the New Forest with a retired grocer called Greg whom she met online. It won't last. It never does. My mother will be off and he'll be left by himself with his cabbages and carrots. I hope that when Crush and I say 'I do' that we both mean it with all our hearts. Marcus might drop in and out of my life, he might profess love for me and he certainly likes to make mischief, but there is only one man for me: Mr Aiden Holby, love of my life, soon to be my husband.

'Back in the room, Lucy,' Chantal says.

I snap back to the present.

'Your face had gone all dreamy.'

'Just thinking about my wedding. I've booked the venue now.' I think I'm in danger of going all goo-goo ga-ga again. 'It's a beautiful temple in Golders Hill Park. We can have the ceremony there and then a picnic afterwards.'

'What if it rains?'

'It won't rain,' I assure them. 'It will be great.'

'This is England in the summer, Lucy,' Chantal points out. 'Not Southern California. It *might* rain.'

'No,' I say. 'It won't.'

'Umbrellas,' the girls agree in unison.

'Nothing will spoil my wedding day,' I assure them. And no one. If Crush doesn't want me to go back to Chocolate Heaven and work for Marcus, then I simply won't. Even though every fibre of my being is telling me that I should, that it would be different this time.

'You'll still be my bridesmaids?'

'Of course!' they all say.

'What happened to the dresses from last time?' Chantal asks.

'Sold them on eBay.' For a lot less than we paid for them, I can tell you. Perhaps I shouldn't have been so hasty – that word again. But then I want to do everything differently with Crush. I want no shadow of my wedding with Marcus. This will be small, informal, al fresco. No big frock or big church or big venue.

'What do you want us to wear this time?' Nadia asks.

'I was thinking tea dresses. Floral. Nothing too fancy.' Or expensive. Particularly if I'm not working. 'Would that suit?'

'Sounds great,' Autumn says and the others nod in agreement.

'Could James come down for the wedding?' I ask Nadia.

'I don't know. We'll have to see how we get on at Easter.'

I grin. 'So you are going to see him?'

She wrings her hands and looks anxiously at us. 'You think I should?'

'Yes!' We are unanimous in our decision.

'He's a great guy,' Autumn says. 'You should at least give it a chance to see how things go.'

'Now I'm really terrified,' Nadia says.

Lana grizzles from her buggy. 'Looks like Madam is ready for her lunch.' Chantal picks her up and cuddles her. The grizzling stops.

'Let me have a snuggle while you get her lunch ready,' I say. 'She hasn't seen her Auntie Lucy for days.'

Chantal reaches to hand her over, but gasps in pain as she does. I grab Lana from her and her hand goes to the top of her breast.

I frown at my friend. 'What was that?'

'Nothing,' Chantal says. But the colour has drained from her face. 'I keep getting these twinges at the top of my ribs.'

'I hope you're going to the doctor,' Autumn says.

'I did. I finally managed to get an appointment this morning. Jacob bullied me into it. The doctor didn't seem too concerned. She gave me a good check over and said that she couldn't feel a lump or anything. She said it was probably muscular or maybe a blocked duct. I'm sure there's nothing to worry about.'

'Better to get it checked, though,' I say.

'I'm just getting to that age, unfortunately. She's sending me for a breast scan anyway, as it's gone on for a while.'

Nadia, Autumn and I all exchange a concerned glance. That doesn't sound good. It's not like Chantal to be unwell and she really does look drawn.

'Want me to come with you?' I offer. 'I can look after Lana while you go in. Don't go by yourself.'

'That would be great, Lucy. Let me text you the date.' She does so while she stands there and it pings into my phone.

I give her a hug. 'We'll get you sorted out. We all want our Chantal fighting fit and as feisty as usual.'

'Me too,' she admits. 'I'm fed up with feeling under the weather.'

We pay our bill. 'Where shall we meet next time?'

'I'll look for something,' Nadia says. 'There must be somewhere nice and welcoming where we'd look forward to going.'

There is, I think. And we all know exactly where.

Chapter Ten

'No, Lucy!' Crush says, emphatically. 'I won't have it.'

'But—'

'It's not often I put my foot down, but I won't have you working for Marcus. It's a ridiculous idea.'

'But—'

'No buts.' He holds up a hand. 'There are dozens of jobs out there that you could do. You'll find something else. Something that doesn't involve Marcus bloody Canning.'

'The salary's enormous.'

'I'd rather live off baked beans than be beholden to Marcus for our money.'

I tell him the exact sum. Crush has the good grace to gasp. It is a very gasp-worthy amount.

'I won't be able to earn that anywhere else, you know that. I just plucked a number out of my head and he agreed.' Makes me wish that I'd plucked a bigger number now.

'It makes me worry even more that there will be a catch.'

'What if I do it – just give it a try – until the wedding? If it's not working out then, after that, I'll leave.'

'It won't be that simple, Gorgeous. It never is with Marcus.'

'I don't know what it is with Marcus – why everyone thinks he has some Machiavellian hold over me. He's just a bloody annoying ex-boyfriend, nothing more.'

'Remember the canal incident in Bruges?' Crush reminds me.

How could I forget? Marcus tricked me into going to a chocolate conference in Bruges, which he just happened to pop up at. Also due to him, I ended up going for an impromptu midnight swim in one of the many canals there. If it hadn't been for Crush coming to my rescue I could have drowned at the bottom of that murky and, frankly, rather smelly stretch of water. It was *so* humiliating. I had a fish in my bra, a cold in my nose and a deep loathing of Marcus in my heart.

But, here's the rub. I'm not the sort of person to hold a grudge. He's made mistakes. I've made mistakes. Rather too many of them, it might be said. Who hasn't? Let he who is without stain and living in a glass house cast the first stone. Or whatever.

'You could get to know Marcus,' I suggest. 'Then you might not see him as so much of a threat.'

'Why on earth would I want to do that?'

'For me,' I say and, as all the fight goes out of Crush, the doorbell rings. I really hope that isn't Marcus or I'm a goner. 'I'll get it.'

I bolt downstairs to the door, praying, praying, praying that Marcus Canning isn't standing there. But he isn't. It's my dad. With a suitcase.

'Dad? What are you doing here?'

'I find myself temporarily homeless.' He is red-eyed and looks miserable. 'Patty has thrown me out.'

Patty the pencil-thin Pilates instructor.

'Oh.'

'Your mother said that I could stay in the flat for a while.'

'That's very nice of her.'

'I didn't know where else to turn,' he confesses. 'It was kind of her to be so accommodating.'

'Yeah, I'll say. Has she forgotten that Crush and I live here?' Technically, my mother owns this place, but she hasn't been near it in years. I rent it from her at a knock-down price which gives me a great address and the ability to take in random lodgers of her choosing, it seems.

'It won't be for long and I won't take up much room.'

That looks like a very big suitcase to me.

'Don't keep your dear old dad standing at the door.'

'Sorry, sorry. Come on in.' It's just that my brain is trying to process where my father is actually going to sleep, being as there's the slight inconvenience of the flat only having one bedroom and that being already occupied by me and my loved one.

'I haven't been here in a long, long time,' Dad puffs as he hauls his case upstairs.

Long enough to forget that he's going to be on the sofa tonight, it would appear.

When he comes into the living room, he recoils slightly. Now he's remembered just how small it is.

Crush is still a little bit purple in the face after our Marcus-related spat and he looks even more shaken when he claps eyes on my dad.

'Hello, there. Nice to see you.' Crush recovers well. 'What are you doing in this neck of the woods?'

'He's come to stay.' I roll my eyes behind Dad's back. 'My mother said he could. It's just for a few days.'

'Or weeks,' Dad chips in. 'A couple of months at the most. Until I can get on my feet.'

'Well.' Crush grasps his hand and shakes it. 'That's great.'

We all know that it isn't.

'This is it, Dad,' I say, gesturing at the not-very-extensive

60

extent of the lounge. 'Our humble abode. We haven't knocked through into next door or gone up into the attic, because there isn't one. We haven't gone iceberg with a two-storey basement with staff quarters because the hairdressers might object. There's one bedroom and you're on the sofa. I love you to bits, but this has to be a *very* temporary measure.'

'Right,' Dad says, looking a bit paler than he did before. 'Right.'

Crush gives me a sideways glance. 'I'll put the kettle on.'

'Have you got any organic soya milk?' Dad asks. 'Patty weaned me off dairy. She thought I was lactose intolerant.'

'No,' I say. 'It's the usual stuff that comes out of a cow's bum or you can lump it.'

'That'll be fine then,' Dad says, looking a bit put out.

Organic soya milk, my arse. How do you even milk a soya?

He glances round him in dismay. 'Where shall I put my case?'

'Anywhere as long as it's not in front of the telly,' I suggest. 'I'd better find you some spare sheets.'

'I hope I haven't interrupted your evening.'

'No, no, no,' Crush says as he returns with the tea.

Yes, I think. Yes, you flipping have. I was hoping to conclude our evening's little misunderstanding with some fabulous, mind-blowing make-up sex on the rug in front of the fire. That's certainly not going to happen now. In fact, these walls are so paper thin that it's not going to happen in the bedroom either. It's not that I'm an over-enthusiastic moaner or a screamer, but no one wants sex in the room right next to their parent, right? I shudder just thinking about it. I wonder if we could get away with doing it in the bath with the shower running. Maybe not.

While Dad is faffing about with his stuff, I pull Crush into the bedroom. 'I'm really sorry about this,' I whisper. 'I had no idea.'

'It's fine,' he says, ever affable. 'We'll manage.'

But will we? I know my father. He's very annoying. And has the hide of a rhino. I don't like to see him turfed out on his ear, but we must not make him *too* comfortable. My dad's idea of temporary might not be quite the same as mine.

Chapter Eleven

Autumn adjusted her jumper and looked at herself in the mirror. Tidy. Ish. Not too bohemian. Today, she wanted nothing more than to look like she was capable of being a respectable mother. She'd even tried to tame her mad hair, with somewhat mixed results. Bits kept escaping from the knot she'd twisted it into. In the end, she gave up and let it do its own thing as usual. Perhaps Willow would like her just as she was. Her stomach churned with anxiety simply thinking about it. She didn't think she'd ever been quite so nervous about anything.

Miles came behind her and slipped his arms round her waist. 'You look great,' he said. 'Stop worrying.'

'I'm terrified,' Autumn admitted. She'd arranged to meet Willow and her adoptive mother, Mary, this morning and her stomach was churning at the very thought.

'She'll love you.'

'Will she, though?' Autumn chewed her lip. 'What if she hates me and simply wants to tell me that to my face?' Another wave of nausea rushed up. 'I've never been to a meeting that's more important to me. It *has* to go well.' She felt as if the rest of her life depended on this moment. If it didn't, she could lose Willow all over again.

'Are you sure that you don't want me to come with you? I hate to see you so worried. We could ask Lucy to look after Flo for a couple of hours.'

'She's going with Chantal for her breast screening today, so I know she's not around.' Autumn had already called Chantal first thing this morning to wish her luck with her mammogram. 'Besides, much as I'd love to have you there, I think I should go by myself. This is going to be difficult for all of us.'

'You might be surprised. Keep an open mind.'

Autumn felt a tear roll down her face, making a track in the make-up that she'd so carefully put on for the occasion. 'I just want her to like me.' She wiped the tear away with a tissue. 'That's all. I want the chance to explain that I loved her and always have.'

'Surely she wouldn't have looked for you if she didn't want to hear that.'

'You're right,' Autumn said and she turned and hugged Miles tightly. He was such a caring man and she felt so lucky that he'd come into her life. She couldn't imagine it now without him.

'I'd better get a move on. I'll sort the kitchen out and take Flo to the park. She's missing Lewis now that he's at school every morning.'

'It won't be long before she goes herself,' Autumn said. 'Enjoy this time with her.'

'It will be better for us financially when she starts school, and it will mean that I don't have to work so many evenings, but I don't want to wish the time away either.'

Autumn didn't like to point out to him that the last thing they needed to worry about was money. Her parents might be cold and detached, but it meant that they were always keen to dole out cash. Even if what was really needed was emotional support. She shouldn't complain, though. They'd been generous to her recently and she had a large sum of money just sitting in her account waiting for her to do something with it. She could start a business, give it to a charity, use it to help a friend – there were endless possibilities.

'I'll get your coat,' Miles said and Autumn snapped back to the present.

'Thank you.' She went into the kitchen where Flo was finishing her breakfast. 'Give me a kiss, sweetheart.'

The little girl jumped down from her chair and Autumn cuddled her. Miles had washed Flo's hair last night and she still smelled of strawberry shampoo. Autumn breathed it in. She really wanted this relationship to work out, as she would love to have another child – one that would be with her, that she'd see grow up. She wanted to teach him or her to walk, talk, make their way in life and only hoped that she'd have a second chance to get it right. 'Have a lovely day with Daddy. I'll see you later.'

'Love you for ever.' Flo squeezed her with her chubby little arms and Autumn's heart melted.

'Love you too, pumpkin.'

Autumn headed to the front door and Miles was standing there waiting, her coat in his hand. Most of her stuff was now spread between their two places. She loved seeing Miles's toothbrush, his sweaters at her flat, his book on the bedside table even though he could only stay over when it was his ex's night with Florence. They were already thinking of moving in together but, understandably, Miles wanted to take it slowly and let Flo get used to the idea. Not to mention letting his ex-wife get used to the idea, too. She suddenly seemed to be feeling a little strange about Miles having someone permanent in his life. Autumn just hoped that she didn't cause any trouble.

Miles kissed her deeply. 'Call me as soon as you can. Let me know how it went.'

Putting her hands in her pockets, Autumn was surprised to find something already there. She pulled out a bar of chocolate.

Grinning, Miles said, 'Emergency supplies.'

'That's very thoughtful.' She pecked him on the cheek. 'Wish me luck.'

'You won't need it,' he said.

They were meeting at a café near Blackfriars Tube – somewhere that Miles had previously used for business meetings and had recommended. How she missed Chocolate Heaven. She would have been more at ease there, in familiar surroundings and with Lucy's smiling face behind the counter. Meetings as critical as this needed the perfect backdrop. Damn Marcus and his manipulation, although part of her wished that Lucy could go back there. It had been Lucy's ideal job and Autumn hated to see her friend rudderless without it. It was a shame that she hadn't been able to buy it instead of Marcus. Perhaps if it wasn't going well he would consider selling, but it was a huge financial commitment for anyone. Property prices around here weren't conducive to setting up a small business.

The Literary Café was small and decorated to look like a bookshop. The walls were lined with shelves of battered paperback books; each coffee table had a library desk lamp and was flanked by blood-red Chesterfield sofas. There was a table of the latest bestsellers for sale in the middle. It was as nice and cosy as Miles had said. A good choice. If it wasn't quite so out of their way, it might have made a good replacement for Chocolate Heaven. Perhaps she would bring the ladies of the Chocolate Lovers' Club back here for a trial run. Though, no doubt, Lucy would find some reason to dislike it.

There was no sign of Willow and Mary yet and Autumn

checked her watch. Ten minutes to go. She ordered a coffee and perused the counter display. Ah. Weakness spotted. Lucy would certainly pour scorn on their poor choice of chocolatey cakes. Autumn chose a breakfast muffin covered in seeds and sat by the window. She sipped at her coffee and nibbled the muffin, even though she wasn't in the slightest bit hungry, and leafed through the couple of paperbacks she'd picked from the stack on the table without really seeing them.

Her stomach was steadily tightening with anxiety when, at last, a woman came in and looked around nervously. She was obviously searching for someone and Autumn wondered if it was her. This lady was alone, though, and Autumn's heart sank. If this was Mary then, for some reason, Willow hadn't come with her.

The woman scanned the tables, her face creased with concern. She looked kind, a little harried and was in her late forties or possibly a little older. She was well-groomed, her clothes expensive, classic. Autumn was glad that she'd made a little more effort with her appearance this morning, but she still felt very young in comparison. This woman was probably much the same age as Autumn's own mother and that was something she hadn't really considered before.

It was now or never. Autumn stood up and spoke out. 'Mary?'

Her head swivelled in Autumn's direction. 'Yes.'

'I'm Autumn.' She held out her hand.

'Oh,' the woman said, taken aback. 'I was looking for someone older.'

Autumn smiled. 'I was very young when I had Willow.'

'Oh. Yes, yes. I did know that.' Mary took her hand and covered it with her own. 'It's just that, well. Well . . . ' She seemed lost for words.

'This is all terribly difficult, isn't it?'

'Yes. Dreadful.'

'Thank you for coming. I do appreciate that it's not easy. For either of us.' Autumn double-checked that the woman was alone. 'I hoped that Willow would be with you.'

'So did I.' Mary frowned, worried. 'I'm afraid that I have rather a lot to tell you.'

Autumn felt her mouth go dry and her heart was racing. She hoped that nothing too awful was wrong. Let it not be a terrible setback before they'd even started. She tried to sound more calm than she felt. 'Then you sit down and let me get you a coffee.'

Mary looked relieved and grateful. Autumn took her order and headed to the counter. When she went to pay for the cappuccino, her hands were trembling. Putting the coffee on the table between them, Autumn sat down again. She forced herself to sit back and not perch on the edge of the sofa.

'I'm shaking inside,' Mary said.

Autumn managed a thin laugh. 'Me too.'

'I never thought this day would come,' Mary confessed. 'I always knew that it might be on the horizon, but you think if you do a good enough job, if you're the best mother that you possibly can be to your child, that they'll never want to find their birth mother. You always hope in your heart that you'll be enough.'

Autumn didn't know what to say.

'But it's not, is it?' she continued, letting out a weary breath. 'Blood, as they say, is very much thicker than water.' There was an edge of bitterness in her tone that she couldn't hide. Mary sipped her coffee and composed herself. 'I've done my best for her, for Willow.'

'I'm sure you have.'

'She was a lovely baby,' Mary said. 'So happy, contented.'

Autumn was both relieved and saddened to hear it. She'd missed it all, but Willow had clearly had a mother who'd loved her dearly. She couldn't have hoped for more.

'She was always so easy and she was the apple of her father's eye. I've brought some photographs.' Mary fumbled in her handbag and handed them over.

Autumn looked at the family shots. It was like looking at a mirror image of herself. They had the same-shaped face, the same mouth and, of course, the same wild auburn hair – she couldn't have escaped that.

'She was three then,' Mary said, smiling fondly. 'Six in that one by the seaside.'

'She looks lovely.'

Mary raised a disapproving eyebrow. 'Willow doesn't look like that now. Goth phase.' She shook her head, bewildered. 'I think that's what you call it. All black eyeliner and ripped tights.'

Autumn had toyed with that look herself, more to annoy her parents than for any other reason.

Mary handed her phone to Autumn. A sulky teenage girl, caked in make-up, glowered back from the screen, but there was still no mistaking the family resemblance. It was like looking at herself at the same age. A lump came to her throat and, tenderly, Autumn ran a finger over the image. This was her child. After all these years, she finally knew what she looked like. She fought down the sob that threatened to escape. Her baby.

'She's quite headstrong,' Mary said, regretfully. 'All the sunny side of her has gone. I told her she's too young to be looking for you, but she wouldn't listen. I wanted her to wait until she was eighteen, at least. It used to be more difficult for adopted children to trace their birth mothers, but now with the internet . . . ' Mary shrugged. 'It really wasn't that hard. We've never hidden anything from her. You think that's for the best.'

She couldn't stop looking at the picture of her child. The ache of the lost years was almost unbearable. 'Did you ask her not to come?'

'No.' Mary grimaced. 'If I'd done that, then she *definitely* would have been here. Whatever I ask Willow to do, she'll invariably do the opposite.'

'If it's a consolation, I'm sure most teenagers are the same. I know I was.'

'I suppose you're right,' she agreed grudgingly. 'Doesn't make it any easier to deal with.'

'No,' she sympathised. 'I'm sure not.' Oh, God, how she wished that Willow had just come along today. Now her insides were even more twisted with anxiety than they had been. It was easy to sympathise with Mary but much harder to know how to address the situation.

'My husband died two years ago. Quite unexpectedly,' Mary continued. 'That's him there with Willow.' She pointed to one of the photographs. He was a tall, handsome man with an easy smile. 'We'd been a happy family until then. She was a very affable little girl. Everyone adored her. We'd all jogged along contentedly. We were lucky, there were very few lows. We gave her an idyllic childhood, you know.'

Autumn choked back the tears. 'I'm very grateful for that.'

'Willow has struggled since Charles has been gone. She's not the same child. There's a hole in her world and she doesn't know how to fill it.'

Oh, my poor child, Autumn thought. She knew what it was like to be grieving. 'My brother, Rich, died too young. And I still have the feeling that something's missing in my life. It doesn't ever end.' She hated to think that Willow was going through the same pain. How much worse to lose the only father you've known.

Rich had been the only person who knew about Willow. He'd always supported her, always assured her that one day her daughter would come to find her. She only hoped he could see her now. She'd like to think that he could.

'She thinks that finding you will be the answer,' Mary added, reluctantly.

She was terrified to ask, but she had to know. 'And you don't want her to?'

'Willow talks about nothing else, but I'm frightened for her, Autumn.' Mary reached out to touch her arm and then thought better of it. She let her hand fall back. 'Despite her fierce make-up, she's very vulnerable. I don't think she's mature enough to cope with this. She thinks she is. Of course she does. But she's still a child and Willow is pinning a lot of her hopes on you. I don't want her to be let down again.'

Autumn felt her throat tighten. Her heart went out to her daughter, that bonny, beaming baby from the photographs in front of her who'd grown into a troubled teenager. 'I loved her, Mary. I never wanted to give her up.'

'I understand some of your background. The adoption agency told me a little about it.'

'I was forced to give up Willow by my parents. It was the worst decision of my life.' Autumn fought back another sob. 'I've regretted it ever since. But I was dependent on them for everything and I felt that I had no option. I had nowhere else to go, no one to turn to. I'm only glad that you were able to give her a loving, stable home.'

'I'm afraid that isn't always enough.' Tears filled Mary's eyes. 'She wants you, too. But as much as she wants it, she's scared. Just before we left she engineered an argument and stormed off. She's done it each time we were due to meet. I was on the verge of cancelling again, then I decided that I would come alone to talk to you. I hope you don't mind.'

'I'm very glad that you did.' If she could build a relationship with Mary, then perhaps Willow would feel more able to trust her.

'I confess that I wanted to see what you looked like, too,'

she admitted. 'If you'd been covered in tattoos and high on drugs then I would have done everything I could to dissuade her from seeing you. She needs a positive role model in her life, not someone to lead her astray.'

'I understand that. You're only trying to protect her.' In Mary's position she would have done exactly the same.

'I think she's afraid of being rejected.' Mary shook her head. 'It would break her heart to see you if you then didn't want to have anything to do with her.'

'I have no intention of doing that. I would love the chance to have even a small part of her back in my life.'

'I feel happier now that I've met you.' Mary dabbed at her eyes with a tissue from her pocket. 'I'd built this up in my mind to be a terrible hurdle. I dreaded seeing you.' She gave a watery laugh. 'It sounds silly now. I didn't really know what to expect. I pictured the worst. You seem like a very sensible and stable young woman.'

'I'm in a good place, Mary.' She thought of Miles and Flo at home and knew that she could offer Willow something good and wholesome. 'And I'm grateful that you felt able to make contact with the agency for Willow.'

'I didn't want to,' she admitted. 'I'm worried that everything I've done for her will count for nothing in the end.'

Autumn slipped across and sat on the sofa next to her. She put her arm round Mary and hugged her tight. 'I'm not a threat to you. I want to do all I can to make this easier. I'm sure that, together, we can steer Willow through this and help each other.'

'I'd like that,' Mary said. Then they held onto each other and cried.

Chapter Twelve

Nadia finished her shift at the call centre and hurried out of the overheated office into the chilly evening air, eager to get home. She pulled her coat around her and dashed off towards the Tube. The office was down by The Gherkin and there were very few people around at this time of night. It was one of her weekly late shifts and the rush of commuters had long gone. She hated this part of her journey when it was dark. Her footsteps echoed on the pavement and the wind whipped cruelly, funnelling between the skyscraper buildings. Putting her head down, she hurried on. All she wanted to do was get home now, relieve Autumn of her babysitting duties and get into a hot bath.

She was getting cold feet about her impending trip to the Lake District; it was weighing on her mind. A few times during calls this afternoon, she'd found herself drifting off, letting one irate customer or another shout down the phone at her pointlessly. The sooner she could leave this job the better. The pay was reasonable, but the work was soulless. She needed to get out before she lost her sanity.

Nadia had checked the train times from London to Cumbria

and the journey, though long, would be easy enough. They could go direct to Penrith station, where James could come to collect her and Lewis. No need to struggle with luggage as they changed trains or anything, so that wasn't the issue to hide behind.

She went over it for the hundredth time in her mind as she walked. What she was really scared of was seeing James again. She liked him – a lot. But that wasn't the issue either. In fact, she wasn't even sure which way she wanted this to go. What if they didn't get on when they were together rather than having lovely, long remote telephone conversations? She couldn't bear it if that ended. It was her late evening lifeline, something she looked forward to every day. What if the relationship they'd developed was nothing more than a delicate illusion?

On the other hand, what if they got on like a house on fire as they had at Christmas? What then? James was rarely able to leave the farm, that much she'd already established. And why would he want to? That was his life. So where did they go from there? How easy would it be to conduct a long distance relationship with three school-age children between them? Nadia sighed to herself. Why couldn't she have met someone who lived two Tube stations away? That would have made life so much easier.

On the Underground, she dropped into an empty seat. This line was relatively quiet now and she picked up a discarded copy of *Metro*, flicking through it to distract herself from the jumble of thoughts going round her head as the train rumbled and grumbled through the stations.

At the other end of her journey, she walked up the escalator, swiped her Oyster card and swung out into the street. Her heart lifted. Not far now. She strode out as she turned the corner, home almost in sight. The lights would be on; it would be lovely and warm inside. She desperately wanted to know if Autumn had heard any more about a possible meeting with Willow. Maybe she and Autumn could share a cuppa and some chocolate digestives before her friend left. That would be a nice way to end the day.

Then, out of nowhere, she felt someone grab at her handbag from behind. She was wearing the strap across her body and the force caught her off balance and wheeled her round. There was a man, early twenties, in a black hoodie, towering over her. He was wide-eyed and wired. Where had he come from? She hadn't heard a thing. He snatched viciously at her bag again, agitated, and she stumbled forward to her knees. Before she could do or say anything else, his fist slammed into her face and she felt the taste of blood in her mouth. He aimed a kick which connected with her ribs and doubled her over.

'Give me the bag,' he snarled. 'Give me the fucking bag and you won't get hurt.'

In her disorientated state, she tried to gather her wits. Her brain struggled to make the connection between what had been happening a moment before and this. Nadia thought about fighting, but what could she do? He already had her at a disadvantage.

'Give it to me!' he shouted again.

Hands shaking, she peeled off the bag and handed it up to him.

He spat in her face and shouted 'Fucking bitch!' at her before running off down the road.

Nadia tried to get up but the kick had winded her and she stayed on the pavement on all fours, breathing heavily. Her whole body was trembling. Her tights were torn, her knees bloodied and scraped where she'd fallen. Gingerly, she felt her lip and thought that it was split. There was an excruciating pain in the left side of her ribs and she wondered if they were broken. Shaking, she wiped the spittle from her cheek with the back of her hand. It felt as if it was burning like acid and bile rose to her throat. She steadied herself, worried that she'd be sick out here on the pavement.

A young couple walked towards her, but crossed the road when they looked up from their conversation and saw her. Hot tears rolled down her cheeks. What sort of place was she living in? She was angry with herself that she'd let her guard down, as she prided herself on being streetwise. Well, not today and it had cost her dearly. She stayed where she was until she'd got her breathing under control and then pushed herself to her feet. She staggered as if drunk. It was a vicious punch and a kick, but nothing more. It could have been so much worse. Yet she felt as if she'd done a dozen rounds in the ring with Ricky Hatton.

Clutching her ribs, she made her way home holding the wall outside the terraced houses for support. This hurt like hell now and was going to be so much worse in the morning. As she got to the door, she went to get her keys from her handbag before she remembered they were gone – like going to switch on the light in a power cut so that you could find a candle. Instead, she rang the bell. She'd have to call the bank, cancel her credit cards and, more importantly, get the locks on the house changed as soon as she could. Somewhere out there was a violent man with a set of her house keys. Nervously, she checked that he hadn't followed her but, thankfully, there was no one else in the street.

A moment later, Autumn opened the door. 'Nadia?'

She fell inside, holding onto her friend. Thank goodness she was here. How would she have dealt with this alone?

Autumn was clearly shocked by her appearance. 'What on earth's happened?'

'Some drugged up shithead mugged me,' Nadia lisped. Her lip was swelling painfully. 'Just a few houses down. I was nearly home.'

Then she burst into a flood of fresh tears. Autumn held her tightly. 'Are you hurt?'

'My ribs,' she said. 'And he punched me in the face.'

'Your lip's split,' Autumn said, her own voice shaky. 'And there's blood all over your coat.'

Was there? She hadn't noticed that.

'Come on,' Autumn said. 'Let me help you to take it off. I'll call the police and then I'll make you a cup of tea.'

Autumn gently eased the coat from Nadia's shoulders as she winced in pain. It felt as if all of her body had been assaulted.

'Do you think you need to go to A and E? I can get Miles to come in the car.'

'I don't think so. But I could do with a hot bath.'

'Are you sure? What did he do?'

'He just punched and kicked me.' Nadia cried again. 'Then he spat at me.' She wiped her cheek again, longing now to scrub her whole face.

'Bastard,' Autumn fumed. 'I'll phone this in now. They might have a chance of catching him. Then I'll run you a bath and you can have a good, long soak.'

'Is Lewis all right?'

'He's fine. Fast asleep for more than an hour.'

'Good.' She was glad that her son hadn't seen her like this; he would only worry. Though how she'd disguise her lip in the morning, goodness only knows. It was starting to sting like hell.

Autumn called the police and Nadia gave them the details of what had happened. They said that someone would come round to see her, though Nadia had little hope that they'd catch her mugger. This went on day in and day out round here and there were very few prosecutions. It had become a part of life. How awful was it to say that?

She thought of James's farm, the wide open spaces, the

glorious hills and thought that there were probably very few muggings there. You were more likely to get trampled by a cow or a sheep. Trying to smile at the image, she felt her lip split wider.

Autumn got a flannel from the bathroom and gently wiped the blood from Nadia's mouth and chin, then made her tea. While she ran a bath for her, Nadia went in to see Lewis. He was in his own bed, arm thrown back over his head, deep in sleep. Oh, to be so contented, so unaware. Her heart was full of love for her sleeping child. She wanted a better life for him. What about when he was of an age to be out on his own? She'd be sick with worry every time he moved. Stroking his hair, she kissed his warm cheek. He was her life and she had to do all that she could to protect him.

In the bathroom, she sat on the loo seat and sipped her tea through the straw Autumn had found for her as it was too painful to touch the cup to her lip. Autumn swished the bath water, adding some vanilla-scented foam.

'I'll sit here,' Autumn said, her face still etched with concern. 'I don't want to leave you alone. I can stay the night too.'

'I'd like that,' Nadia said. Physically, she'd probably got off lightly. Emotionally, she felt like a total wreck. It would be good to have Autumn here.

'I'll phone Miles in a minute and tell him what's happened. We can put Lewis in your bed and I'll climb into his.'

Nadia let out a wavering sigh and tears sprang to her eyes once more. 'What am I going to do? I need to move away from this place.'

'It's no wonder you're feeling jittery, but don't do anything hasty.' Autumn helped her off with her T-shirt, wincing along with her as she lifted it over her head. 'It will all look better in the morning.'

But would it? Nadia thought. Autumn always looked on the

bright side, but the reality of the situation made her feel sick to her stomach. Both the front and the back doors were double locked and bolted, yet she still felt vulnerable. She'd been thinking about selling up for a while; maybe now was the right time.

Chapter Thirteen

Chantal flicked through the battered glossy magazine in her hand. There were a couple of dozen other ladies in the hospital waiting room. It was clearly a busy clinic.

If she was honest, she was feeling a bit of a fraud. She'd only had a few twinges, a bit of an ache; she hoped that she wasn't wasting everyone's time. Some of these women could be genuinely ill and she was taking up valuable space. Until they separated, she'd always been on Ted's private health insurance and never had to consider these things. Now she didn't want to waste valuable NHS resources.

'Nervous?' Lucy asked.

Chantal nodded. 'Terrified. No one likes hospitals. I hate being poked and prodded about.'

'Look.' Lucy nudged her. 'I've got a handbag full of choco-late-chip cookies in case of emergencies. Want one?'

Chantal shook her head. 'I'm not hungry.' Despite having had a flippant attitude about the dull ache that had been troubling her over the past few months, she was now feeling anxious about this appointment. She'd never had a breast scan before and was quite surprised when her GP had suggested it. She'd fully expected the doctor to give her a prescription for painkillers and send her on her way.

Lucy put her arm around her. 'You'll be all right. I can feel it in my bones.'

'It's probably nothing,' Chantal agreed. 'I'm convinced there's a pulled muscle in my ribs somewhere. Lifting Lana up and down all day is like a boot camp workout in itself.'

'Absolutely,' Lucy said readily. 'But still best to get it checked out.'

'You sound like Jacob.'

Lucy laughed. 'That's because he adores you.'

At least that made Chantal smile. 'I think maybe you're right.'

'I'm *so* glad that you two finally got together. You're made for each other and he's a total star with Lana. If ever there was a man who should be a father, it's Jacob.'

'He's taken her to Borough market to entertain her, bless him. He *is* good with her. I'm so lucky.' Jacob had wanted to come with her for this appointment, but she felt happier with one of the girls accompanying her. He was better caring for Lana, so she didn't have to stress about her. 'I said I'd text him when I come out.'

'Hopefully, you'll be done soon,' Lucy said. 'They seem to be moving quite quickly. Though I'd be quite happy to sit and work my way through these biscuits for a bit longer. Sure you don't want one?'

Chantal shook her head as Lucy helped herself to another one. She'd had no appetite at all recently. 'Maybe when I'm done.'

'Has Ted been in touch?'

'Yes. But I didn't bother to tell him about this. You know what Ted's like. He doesn't do illness. He'd rather not know if there was anything wrong. Other than that, he's fine. I'm glad that it's worked out for all of us.' Chantal sighed. 'I don't know how Ted and Stacey are faring behind closed doors, but they seem happy enough.' Even if they were struggling, she didn't think Stacey would confide in her now.

'How's Elsie?'

'Thriving, by all accounts. I think Ted and Stacey will be over to visit soon. Ted has work back in London and there are dozens of papers still to sign. Perhaps we can all get together then.'

'You're being very civilised about this,' Lucy noted.

'We're trying. We're all stuck with each other now. I think it would have been a lot harder for me if I hadn't been able to lean on Jacob.'

'He makes a very good shoulder to cry on.'

'I don't know what I'd do without him.' They weren't living in the same house yet, but when they sorted out the property from the divorce, they would move in together. Jacob was planning to keep his own place and rent it out. It was very much a bachelor pad and not suitable as a family home. She couldn't imagine Lana's sticky fingers all over his beautifully lacquered kitchen cabinets or her toys over his white oak floor. She smiled to herself. Poor Jacob. He'd have to get used to a few years of standing on unexpected Lego bricks.

'Not thinking of following me and Crush down the aisle?'

Chantal shook her head. 'I don't think there's any need for us to rush. It's still early days and we're just happy as we are. Moving in together is a big enough step for now.'

Lucy sighed. 'I can't wait to be Mrs Aiden Holby.'

'I can't wait either,' Chantal said. 'I sincerely hope nothing goes wrong this time. I'm having sleepless nights for you. And I have *everything* crossed!'

'*Nothing*,' Lucy stated emphatically, 'will stop my wedding this time.'

'You're with the right man,' Chantal said, resting her head

on her friend's shoulder. 'How lucky are we that we've both found such love.'

'And Autumn's doing all right, too. Miles is great. They make a lovely couple. We just have to get Nadia fixed up.'

'I have a good feeling about James the gentleman farmer,' Chantal said. 'Let's keep our fingers crossed.'

'I don't know if she'll go back to the Lakes by herself. I think she's getting cold feet.'

'We could all have another road trip.'

Lucy giggled. 'I don't know what James would think if we all descended on him. It might put him off her for ever. He takes on Nadia and he gets all four of us into the bargain.'

'God help any man who takes on the Chocolate Lovers.'

They both laughed at that. It had been a good idea to bring Lucy. You could always count on her to take your mind off your troubles.

While they were still giggling, a nurse came out of a side door and called out, 'Mrs Chantal Hamilton.'

'Yes,' she said. But not for very much longer. Soon she'd be Ms Hamilton, or she might even change back to her maiden name. She turned to Lucy. 'Wish me luck.'

Her friend squeezed her arm. 'You'll be fine.'

Chantal felt a trickle of cold dread in her stomach as she followed the nurse to the door, but fought it down.

'Good luck,' Lucy said. 'I'll be right here.'

She let out a long, uneasy breath. 'Don't eat all the biscuits while I'm gone, Lucy.'

Chapter Fourteen

The mammogram wasn't nearly as uncomfortable as Chantal had feared. It was never going to be the best time of your life, but the nurse was brisk and efficient and the scan had literally taken a few minutes to complete.

Now she was back in the waiting room and nibbling her nails anxiously. 'They said they'd give me the results right away.'

'Wow,' Lucy said. 'What service.'

'Are there any of those biscuits left?'

'No,' Lucy admitted. 'Do you want one? I can pop out for more. There was a shop by the entrance.'

Chantal shook her head. 'I just noticed all the empty packets.'

'What can I say? I eat when I'm nervous.'

'It's *me* who should be nervous,' Chantal pointed out.

'I'm coming out in sympathy with you.'

'Thanks,' Chantal laughed.

'You've nothing to worry about,' Lucy said. 'The consultant will give you the all-clear. I have no doubt.'

Lucy was probably right. If there was something untoward there, then surely they would have felt it during the scan. Yet the radiographer had given absolutely no indication that there was anything amiss.

'Can I get you some coffee?' Lucy said.

'I'm jittery enough,' Chantal admitted. 'Better not add to it with a caffeine hit.'

A few minutes later a petite, pretty doctor strode into the reception and shouted out Chantal's name.

Nervously, Chantal stood up.

'Hello, I'm Livia Davis.' She held out a hand to her. 'Come on through.'

'Can my friend come with me?' she said.

'Yes, of course.' She shook Lucy's hand, too. 'Always good to have some moral support.'

They went into her office and she closed the door behind them. It was a functional room with a tired desk and equally tired chairs. The NHS certainly wasn't squandering any money on furnishings for consultants. Chantal wondered idly about the patients who'd passed through here before her. For some of them, it wouldn't be good news. The consultant sat behind the desk and opened Chantal's folder while she and Lucy took the other chairs. Lucy gripped her hand.

'Well,' Livia Davis said. 'I won't beat about the bush, Chantal. There is a lump in your left breast.'

Chantal felt her mouth go dry. Lucy's hand tightened on hers.

'It's flat, disc-shaped and is sitting quite high.' She indicated where on her own chest. 'You haven't felt it?'

'No.' Chantal shook her head. 'Nothing.'

Livia stood and put her scan pictures in a light box on the wall to point it out. 'Can you see it here?'

She nodded, unable to find words. Lucy was saying something, soothing words, but she couldn't tell what. It sounded as if she was speaking underwater. All she could hear was the word

85

'lump' on repeat in her head. She touched the place on her chest that corresponded with the shadow on the screen. Even now she couldn't feel it. How long had it been there, lurking unseen?

'Are you OK, Chantal?' That was Lucy. Her friend stroked her cheek.

She nodded.

'I'd like to do some more tests right away,' the consultant said. 'I've requested an ultrasound scan, some blood tests and a biopsy. Then we'll know exactly what we're dealing with. Does that sound OK?'

'Yes. Of course.'

'Can you stay now?'

'So soon?' Chantal had expected to wait days, at least, maybe even weeks. Was it an indicator that something was seriously wrong that she was being sent for more tests straight away?

'I'd like to organise it today, if possible.'

'We can stay,' Lucy said to her. 'I'll sort everything out.'

'I'll stay,' Chantal agreed, dazed.

'There's nothing to worry about,' Livia reassured her as if reading her thoughts. 'But I'd like to strike while the iron's hot. The quicker we move, the better the outcome.'

Chapter Fifteen

We're sitting in a restaurant down the road from the hospital. There's too much noise in here, too much cheerful chatter. But we're committed now. I've ordered some food, which is on the table between us. Neither of us is hungry.

'You have to eat something,' I say. 'We could be at the hospital for a while this afternoon.'

'I feel sick.'

'Maybe this will settle your stomach.' I just got a sharing platter of cheese and bread. To be honest, I'm in such a state of shock too that I didn't know what I was choosing. I just pointed to the first thing I saw.

At the table next to us there's a children's birthday party. The little girl is in a pink dress in a highchair, which she's currently banging with her spoon. There are balloons all around. I should have asked them to seat us somewhere else. Chantal takes in the scene disconsolately. Fuckfuckfuck.

'She thinks I've got cancer, doesn't she?'

How do I answer this one? 'Not all lumps are cancer,' I try. It doesn't ring true, even to my own ears. 'It could be . . . ' I run out of words as my medical knowledge of lumps is scant. 'As the doctor said, she can tell us more this afternoon.'

'I can't have cancer, Lucy. I haven't got time. Who will look after Lana?'

Tears fill her eyes, then they spill over onto her empty plate. I take her hand and squeeze it. 'It will be all right,' I say, soothingly. 'I promise you. Let's wait and see what the doctor says before jumping to any conclusions.'

'It must be bad if they're doing more tests this afternoon.'

'We don't know that,' I counter. 'They might just be really efficient.'

'I should ring Jacob.' Chantal reaches for her phone.

'Have a drink first,' I urge. 'Settle yourself. He'll only be more upset if you are.' I push the cup of chamomile tea towards her.

Much as I feel we could both do with a big glass of wine, I don't think it's right if we're going back to the hospital. Though I'm not sure chamomile tea and a cheese platter is quite the right combo.

'Have some bread.' I butter a tiny slice and put it on the edge of Chantal's plate. 'Go on. You should have something inside you.'

She picks it up and chews. I do likewise to show solidarity. It tastes like cardboard. 'Bread was a bad idea.'

We both laugh.

Chantal wipes away her tears, but more come in their place.

'Do you want me to get you some soup or something instead?'

'No. Nothing, Lucy.'

'I'll get them to wrap this up in case we want it later.'

A waiter brings a cake to the next table and they start to sing 'Happy Birthday'.

'I need to speak to Lana,' Chantal says. 'That will give me the courage I need to face the tests this afternoon.'

'This isn't the place,' I say. 'Go out into the sunshine. There was a bench just across the road. Sit there and I'll be out in a minute.'

Chantal dabs her eyes again and then leaves. I pay the bill, get them to box up the cheese and bread. I have no idea why, really. At the moment, I feel like I'll never eat again, so I can't imagine how this must be affecting my dear friend. I call Crush and leave a message to tell him what's happened and that I might be back late. I think about calling Autumn and Nadia but don't want to worry them just yet.

By the time I get outside it isn't sunny, it's cold and cloudy. I try not to shiver. Chantal is already speaking to Lana. I drop onto the bench next to her.

'Hello, baby girl,' she coos. 'Have you been good for Jacob?'

I can hear Lana's scribble talk in the background and it brings a smile to Chantal's lips.

'Mummy loves you very, very much,' she says and a sob catches in her throat.

I slip my arm round her shoulders.

'I'll be home soon.' Jacob takes over the phone. 'See you later,' Chantal says. 'I'll call you as soon as I'm done.'

I hear him say, 'I love you.'

'I love you, too,' Chantal responds. Then she hangs up.

I hand her a tissue and she blows her nose. 'Better?'

'Yeah. Much.'

Glancing at my watch, I say, 'Ready to do this?'

'Do I have any choice?'

'No, but you're made of strong stuff. You can cope.' I've never seen my friend look quite so afraid.

'I'm glad you're here, Lucy. I don't think I could face it without you.'

I wish I was having the tests instead of her. I hook my arm through hers and together we stand. Then we exchange a glance and head off back towards the hospital.

Chapter Sixteen

First Chantal had some blood taken and an ultrasound scan and now, less than two hours later, she found herself lying on the bed in a tiny room waiting for a biopsy. She'd told Jacob not to worry. If she was honest, she was doing enough worrying for both of them. The speed at which everything was moving was quite alarming.

'This is terrifying,' Chantal whispered to Lucy, who sat at the other end of the bed.

'You'll be fine,' Lucy said, sticking determinedly to her view that all this would produce a positive outcome. Now Chantal wasn't quite so sure. 'The doctor said it won't take long.'

When the doctor came he produced some sort of implement that looked like a gun and took tissue samples of the breast tissue. But it wasn't fine. It hurt like hell. Lucy gently stroked her feet to distract her as she winced in pain while he punched enough holes to turn her into a colander.

When it was over, she and Lucy sat in the waiting room for another half an hour. Lucy got them both tea from the machine and they sat in silence. At this point, even Lucy had run out of comforting things to say. They both felt and looked drained.

Chantal's fingers trembled as she drank the scalding, weak tea.

Shortly they were called back into Livia Davis's office and she sat behind her desk. Her face was grim. 'I believe in straight talking, Chantal, and I'm sure you do. This is never easy to say, but I'm afraid that you do have cancer.'

Chantal felt her head swim and Lucy gripped her arm tightly. 'I can't believe it,' she managed.

'I know everyone hates that word and it's a big shock to hear it. Cancer isn't the death sentence it once was. We have excellent success with treatment now.'

The brutality of it hit her all over again. Livia certainly wasn't dressing this up. 'What does that mean?'

'It means that even with the more aggressive cancers we can often give people five to ten years of good-quality life. Many survive much longer.'

Chantal felt her world cave in.

'I can't die,' Chantal said. 'Not even in five or ten years. Never. I have a baby. She's not yet a year old.' She thought of the little girl in the restaurant having her birthday party, the balloons, the cake and candles. She wanted to do that for Lana. Not once, but for years and years to come. 'I have to be here to look after her.'

'And I'll do absolutely everything in my power to make sure that happens,' Livia said.

There was no way that she'd seen this coming. Despite all the tests, in the back of her mind, she'd still somehow expected that the scan would find nothing and that the consultant would be cross with her for wasting her time. Inside she was going hot and cold. Her brain had completely imploded and there was no space for rational thought. Turning to Lucy, she saw that her friend's face was as white as a sheet and she suspected her own mirrored that. Chantal tried to stop herself from shaking, but couldn't.

'Fuck,' she said, clutching at Lucy. 'What do I do now?'

Chapter Seventeen

We're all in a state of shock when we meet up for coffee the next morning at yet another crappy café. This one is too busy, too bustling, the tables too close together. And, no matter where Chantal positions it, every time someone walks past they knock Lana's buggy. Another place to be ticked off the list as unsuitable.

It's also totally the wrong place to discuss the fact that our friend is too young and too beautiful to have anything as awful as breast cancer. It's too bright and cheery to talk about the bruises on Nadia's face, her split lip. The man whistling away behind the counter is too happy as a backdrop to Autumn's news that Willow didn't turn up to their arranged meeting. Everything about it is wrong. The whole situation is wrong.

While we're reeling from Chantal's news, a text pings into my phone. Marcus.

My pining for Chocolate Heaven has reached epic proportions and, of course, Marcus is texting me ten times a day asking me to go back.

Ping. Yet another one arrives.

All the girls look up. 'Marcus,' I confirm.

This is inappropriate in the midst of our misery, but then Marcus's timing was always questionable. Ping. Ping. Ping. I ignore them all.

'Are you weakening, Lucy?' Autumn asks.

'I am,' I admit, 'but Crush isn't. He doesn't want me anywhere near Marcus.'

'You can't really blame him,' Chantal adds.

'No.' Can't argue with that. 'But who cares about Marcus and Chocolate Heaven? We have more important things to discuss.'

Chantal has breast cancer and it's beyond awful.

'What's the next step with your treatment?' Nadia asks her.

'I've got another appointment soon. Jacob will want to come with me to that one, I'm sure. Livia, the consultant, told me that she'll give me a plan of action then.'

We're all shaken to the core, not least of all Chantal.

'It will be fine,' I tell her. 'Livia was very positive.'

'She was,' she agrees, but I can see the fear in her eyes. And who wouldn't be scared?

I don't mention that all that's sticking in my head is that Livia also said that most people can survive another five to ten years. That's nothing in the scheme of things. Nothing. Chantal can't go so soon. She has too much living still to do.

'How did Jacob take the news?' Autumn asks.

'We cried a lot,' she says and then her face crumples and she cries a bit more. 'No one expects to be hit with this. It happens to other people.'

We all huddle round and I hug her.

'It's Lana I'm worried about,' she adds tearfully. 'If anything happens to me, who'll look after my baby?'

'You're going nowhere.' I'm absolutely certain in my conviction. Five to ten years, pah! 'You'll fight this and come out the other side. If anyone's got the strength to face this down, then you do.'

'Look at the state of us,' Chantal says. 'What a sorry bunch. It's a good job they've got decent chocolate-chip muffins here or we'd have fallen to pieces. Anyway, enough of my woes.' She turns to Nadia. 'How are you feeling, sweetheart? What a bloody awful thing to happen.'

Nadia touches her lip, gingerly. There's shadowy bruising round her mouth and even though she's drinking her coffee through a straw, it's clearly painful. She looks up self-consciously. 'I know. And so close to my own home. My front door was literally in sight. I think that's what's so scary.'

'It must have been terrifying,' Autumn agrees. 'I remember when one of my brother's dodgy friends threatened me outside my flat. I was a wreck for weeks.'

'Thankfully, the locksmith came and changed the locks this morning. It was an expense I could have done without but I hated the thought of someone out there with a set of my keys. He didn't seem to follow me, but I was in so much of a hurry to get indoors that I'm not sure if I checked properly. You begin to doubt yourself.'

'You did the right thing,' Autumn says. 'You can't be too careful. There's no price on peace of mind.'

'I've had to cancel all my credit cards,' Nadia continues. 'I was just about to book a ticket to go up to see James, too.'

'I'll pay for it,' I volunteer. My credit card might protest, but I don't want Nadia to miss out on this chance.

'I was wavering,' Nadia admits, wincing as she takes another sip of her drink. 'But after this, I just want to get away for a few days. I think it will do us good.'

'We'll book it on my phone before you go.'

'Thanks, Lucy. I feel a bit shaky but I'm going to go into work later. I think it will take my mind off things. If I stay at home, I'm sure I'll just dwell on it.'

'It's probably a good idea, but be kind to yourself, too.' I pick at the cake in front of me. 'You've had a shock. Don't underestimate how that can make you feel. If you take a turn for the worse, come home. Ring me and I'll be right round.'

'Thanks, Lucy.' Nadia manages a smile and then winces as it splits the cut on her lip again.

'I went to the agency this morning,' I tell them. 'I think they were quite annoyed that I'd been sacked from the last job.' Bit of an understatement, really. The woman rolled her eyes and tutted a lot. She told me it was a wonderful job and that they'd struggle to place me elsewhere. I fought the urge to roll my eyes and tut back. It wasn't a 'wonderful job', it was really boring and, if I hadn't been sacked, I'd have left anyway. Probably. 'They gave me the details of three jobs to think about, but none of them really float my boat.'

'You need the money for the wedding,' Nadia reminds me. 'Just think of that.'

'I know. I'll ring them and get some interviews fixed up. I can't stay at home with my dad under my feet. He's driving me potty.'

'No sign of him moving out yet?' Autumn asks.

'He's looking far too comfortable on my sofa,' I say. 'It's worrying. He keeps assuring me he's heartbroken, but he's looking *way* too perky for my liking. He's on the phone to my mother every ten minutes. I could kill her for telling him he could stay with me. What was she thinking? The place is barely big enough for two.'

'Fingers crossed that it won't be for long,' Autumn says. 'How's Aiden coping with having him there?'

'They're sharing a couple of beers every night, watching football on telly. It doesn't seem to be wearing thin for Crush, despite the fact that we can't have any . . . erm . . . *conjugal relations* due to the fact that my old man is in the next room and the walls of the flat are like tissue paper. You can't have

95

sex when one of your parents is in the next room, can you? It's wrong on every level. He'll have to go soon.'

Chantal laughs. 'Oh, Lucy. You are a tonic.'

'My problems are minuscule compared to everyone else's,' I say, feeling ashamed that I'm concerned about such trivialities when my mates are really suffering. 'I shouldn't be so selfish.'

'That's the last thing you are,' Nadia says.

'So what if I never grace Chocolate Heaven again? It's not the end of the world, is it?' Though inside it feels as if it is. 'Nations won't fall. Marcus will find someone else.' Don't even think about weeping.

'He will, Lucy,' Chantal tells me, softly. 'You shouldn't feel guilty about not doing exactly what he wants. I know what you're like.'

'We're all in a sorry state,' Nadia agrees. 'We need something to cheer us up. Autumn, tell us some good news. Any progress with Willow?'

'I hope so. Mary's going to try to set up another meeting soon. I'm so glad I saw her. It cleared the air a lot between us. She's a lovely lady and I was so relieved to hear that they'd given Willow a good life. She's very loved.'

'Did you get a photograph of her?'

'No. The only current one Mary had was on her phone. But she looks identical to me. Same hair.' Autumn picks up a strand of her own locks. 'She'll really be delighted I gave her this. Poor girl.' She rolls her eyes. 'We look like two peas in a pod, even down to the way she dresses. I was a Goth too at her age. She's all black eyes and moody face. She still looks adorable to me, though.'

'We can't wait to meet her.'

'Me neither. I think Mary was worried that I wanted to steal Willow from her or that I was unsuitable in some way to be in her life. I can't blame her. I suppose all sorts of things go through your head. But she's happier now she knows that isn't my intention at all. I can only wait and hope now that I can meet my daughter soon.'

'Keep us posted,' Chantal says. 'We're all rooting for you.'

Autumn glances at her watch. 'I'd better be going. Miles isn't working this morning, so we're taking Flo to the park.' She stands up and kisses us all. 'Are we going to meet up tomorrow?'

'Hopefully,' I say. 'Should we come back here?'

They all shrug.

'It's not the best, is it?' Chantal says.

'No.' I shake my head. We know where the perfect place is and it's unavailable to us. Until we find a new home, we are the Wandering Chocolate Lovers' Club.

'Promise me that you won't go near the place,' Nadia says.

'I won't.' I hold up my hands in submission. 'I'm not completely stupid.'

My friends exchange a knowing look.

Then another text comes in. I hold up the screen to them. Marcus.

Chantal shakes her head. 'Don't do it. You'll only regret it.' And, sadly, the others seem to agree.

Chapter Eighteen

My dad, Crush and I are all sitting on the sofa staring at the telly. It's ten o'clock at night and we've been watching football for hours. Hours and hours. How long is a football match, anyway? I'm getting to the point where I want to claw my own eyeballs out when the match, thank heavens, ends.

'Right.' Dad does a big, theatrical yawn.

Clearly it's time for bed, which means that we have to vacate the sofa and the living room.

'Mind if I use the bathroom first?' he says.

'No. Fill your boots.'

He plods off to the tiny bathroom. That'll be no hot water left for us. I sigh in his wake.

'I'm sensing that the thrill of having your dad here is wearing off,' Crush says.

'This flat really isn't big enough for the three of us. And we can't do what *we* want to do.'

Dad isn't the easiest of house guests. Everything has to revolve round him. We have to go to bed when he wants us to and, because he's not sleeping all that well scrunched up on our sofa, he's up with the lark and crashing about in the kitchen. He hogs the bathroom and his dirty laundry is *everywhere*. As he's not working, he's mooching about the flat all day, yet when I come home his dishes are still sitting in the sink. And he hasn't bought so much as a pint of milk yet. Organic soya or not. I could go on. And on and on.

Worryingly, he doesn't seem to be missing the Pilates instructor all that much, either. I thought this one was supposed to be the Love of His Life. Yet I haven't overheard any calls in which he's been pleading earnestly to go back home. In fact, he seems to be spending more time on the phone to my mother than anyone else. 'We can't watch what we want to on the telly. We can't have sex on the rug.'

'We can't actually have sex anywhere,' Crush points out. He comes to wrap his arms round my waist and pulls me close, nuzzling my neck. 'Unless we pull the covers over our heads and be really, *really* quiet.'

'Our bed sounds like a creaky old ship at sea at the best of times,' I remind him. 'Every time we turn over it squeaks and groans. It's bad enough when there's *not* someone closely related to me in the next room.'

'Good point, well made. So what do we do?'

If Dad looked as if he was about to depart next week then it wouldn't be a problem, but my dear father is not showing *any* inclination to move in the foreseeable future. It's not that I'm sex mad or anything, but quite how long are we supposed to stay celibate? A woman – as well as a man – has needs. I chew my lip and dredge my brain. 'What if we go and spend the night at a cheap hotel?'

'How cheap?' Crush says. 'We don't want to make love among bed bugs – that would be just as off-putting – and, with the wedding coming up, I'd rather save our money. What about we give him the money for a curry and ask him to go out for a bit.'

'While *we* have a bit?' I joke.

We snarf together.

Then I sag. 'He'd know. That would just be embarrassing all round.'

'True.'

Suddenly, I'm desperate for this man's body. I have to have him. I *will* have him. I feel one of my cunning plans coming on. My eyes light up.

'What?' Crush says warily. 'I recognise that twinkle in your eye and it's scaring me.'

'I know where we can go.'

Now he looks very worried.

'Trust me,' I whisper, casting a glance at the bathroom door.

'Where?'

'I'll surprise you.'

'Now I'm not just scared, I'm terrified.'

'Let's do it,' I urge. 'It will be like an adventure.'

'What will we tell your dad? We can't say that we're sneaking off to have sex. He'll want to know where we're off to at this time of night.'

'We'll tell him that you've got to go back to work for a couple of hours and I'm coming with you to keep you company. Sorted.' In fact, if we hurry up, we can just leave him a note and not face the trauma of having to lie to him.

'Do we need to pack a bag?'

'No,' I say. 'Let's be spontaneous. If we're quick, we can be gone before Dad comes out of the bathroom.'

'We can't,' Crush says. 'That would be terrible.'

'I'm feeling *very* naughty,' I say, in my best seductive voice. 'You wouldn't deny me?'

'Oh no,' Crush says, grinning.

'I'll write Dad a note.' So I scribble on a yellow Post-it and stick it to the telly.

BACK LATER, it says. AIDEN HAD TO POP BACK TO WORK AND I'VE GONE WITH HIM. DON'T WAIT UP. LOVE LUCY XX

Then we grab our coats and tiptoe out of the flat, giggling like teenagers. This is fun. And such a great idea. One of my very best.

Chapter Nineteen

'You can't be serious?' Crush turns in the passenger seat and stares at me, aghast.

'I've still got the door keys,' I tell him. 'And the code for the alarm. There'll be no one here at this time of night.'

Sure enough, Chocolate Heaven is in total darkness.

'I do *not* want to make love in Chocolate Heaven.' He sounds quite emphatic.

'It'll be fun. No one will ever know.'

Crush glowers at me darkly, which makes my heart beat even faster.

'Let's do it,' I say. 'I'm feeling really mischievous.' I titter nervously. 'Think of that squashy brown velvet sofa. That doesn't squeak.'

'No,' he says. 'Couldn't we just go somewhere very dark and do it in the back of the car?'

'Noooo. That's really sleazy,' I insist. 'Besides, someone might come along and see us. Everywhere that's dark and secluded is a dogging site now. It would be horrible. We'd be right in the middle and some perv would turn up in a flasher mac with a torch. Chocolate Heaven is warm and comfy and safe.'

I can tell that he's weakening, so to seal the deal I run my fingers up his thigh.

He shakes his head as if perplexed. 'Against all my better judgement, Gorgeous, I'll go along with this.'

'You won't regret it. I'll be fun, fun, fun.'

So, before he can change his mind, we jump out of the car and, hand in hand, rush across the road to Chocolate Heaven.

Standing at the door, I fumble with the keys.

'Want me to do it?' Crush asks.

'No. I've got it. It just feels a little weird being back here.'

'Especially in the dead of the night with the sole intention of having some nookie.'

'Yes,' I agree.

'Supposing Marcus has changed the lock or the alarm code?'

My heart quickens. Didn't think of that. What if he has? I hold my breath and cross my fingers when I say, 'He won't have. I know Marcus.'

There's a momentary flash of panic as the lock clicks but the door gives and swings open. He hasn't changed the lock and I rush to punch the code into the security box. Then I breathe a sigh of relief when there's no clanging alarm. So far, so good.

I take Crush's hand and we step inside. Oh, how I've missed this place. Even at night I love it. The scent of vanilla and cocoa hang enticingly in the air. I could be tempted to pinch a few chocolates to add a frisson to our illicit lovemaking session, but maybe Marcus's new manager has tighter stock controls than me and would miss a few truffles in the morning. From what I've seen of Marie-flipping-France it's unlikely, but we have to be careful. Better not risk it. Not even for one little chocolate, even though I'm feeling slightly drooly now. We must make absolutely sure that no one knows we're here.

In the darkness, we move towards the sofa. Stealthily, stealthily.

Crush kisses me deeply. All I've had since my dad arrived is a few pecks on the cheek and I'm ravenous for more. Hurriedly, I unbutton his shirt and he strips me of my blouse.

Together we hop out of our jeans while trying to keep our lips moving in harmony together. I think it's a sign of the strength of our relationship that we very nearly manage to do it. We fall on the sofa; I divest Crush of his undies and he's quick to get me out of mine. We're on the sofa, lying full-length, kissing gloriously. Crush moves above me.

'This is madness,' he whispers hoarsely. 'But *so* much fun. I love you, Lucy Lombard.'

'I love you, too,' I murmur back. I pull him down towards me.

And that's exactly when the burglar alarm starts to shriek.

Chapter Twenty

Within seconds, the police arrive. I'll swear that there must have been a squad car parked right around the corner, just waiting. Crush and I have managed to put our undies back on at the speed of light, but the rest of our clothes are still in disarray when they're banging at the door shouting, 'Open up! Police!'

Crush looks at me ruefully. 'Shit.'

'I don't want them to break the door down.' Then Marcus *will* be cross.

Hurriedly, he dashes to the door and opens up. The two policemen stride in. 'What's all this, then?'

They look at me shivering in my bra and pants. All idea of romance has gone and now I just feel a little bit stupid. Why on earth did I think that this would be a good idea?

'I'm sorry,' I say. 'I used to be the manager here. We didn't think we'd be doing any harm.'

The officers look round and can clearly see that nothing – other than my clothing – has been disturbed.

At that moment, Marie-France appears from the back of the shop. She stares at us with absolute disdain.

'Thank you for coming, officers,' she says in her French accent which some people – if you like that kind of thing – would find sexy and appealing. She is tousle-haired and in a slinky, kimono-style dressing gown. Some people – if you like that kind of thing – would say that even in a half-dressed, sleepy state she's still incredibly beautiful. 'I was very frightened. I live upstairs and thought that I heard intruders.'

'Looks as if you were right, Miss.'

'But I can explain—' I begin.

'Quiet, you two,' he says.

'I can only offer my sincere apologies—'

'Shut up,' the officer says.

I leave my mouth hanging open for a moment, then I do shut up.

'Can we at least put our clothes back on?' Crush pleads. Not unreasonably, if you ask me. Which no one has.

Completely ignoring Crush, the officer says to Marie-France, 'You were lucky we were in the area.'

Us, less so.

This is awful, I think. How can I have let myself be so compromised? If Marcus learns about this – and, of course, he will – I'll never hear the last of it.

The policeman flicks a thumb towards me. 'This young woman says she used to be the manager here.'

Marie-France regards me coolly. 'I have never seen her before.'

'I'm Marcus's ex-fiancée,' I start. Then I can tell from the slight narrowing of her eyes and her tell-tale smirk that she knows exactly who I am.

'I'd like to take down some particulars,' the policeman says and I'm sure I can see them both sniggering.

My voice sounds tremulous when I ask, 'You're not going to take this further, are you?'

'That will, largely, be down to the owner and whether he wants to press charges.'

I turn pleading eyes to Marie-France. 'Please don't tell Marcus,' I beg. 'We can sort this out.'

Then, when I think that nothing can make this evening any worse, the roar of a throaty sports car cuts through the air and the oh-so-familiar red Ferrari belonging to one Mr Marcus Canning pulls up outside the door.

My heart would plummet to my boots, if I was wearing any.

He bounds in grim faced and yet the minute he sees Crush and me standing there like lemons – particularly guilty lemons – he breaks into a wide grin.

'Good evening, officers. What's going on here?' Marcus looks Crush and me up and down. Especially me.

'Marcus,' I say, trying to cover as much of myself as possible. 'Tell them that you know us. That you don't mind us being here.'

'Don't I?' he counters.

'Do you know them, sir?' the officer asks.

'Hmm.' Marcus strokes his chin as he considers.

'Marcus!' There's a warning note in my voice, though I hardly have the high ground here.

'Yes,' he says eventually. 'I think I do.'

Crush looks as if he wants to kill someone and I'm not really sure if it's me or Marcus who'd be first in the firing line.

'Do they have your permission to be here?'

'Hmm.' More chin stroking from Marcus. 'Not exactly.'

I'm shaking inside and I don't know if it's with fury or terror. I don't want to go to jail for having a bit of rumpy-pumpy in a chocolate shop. Is that a punishable offence? We might not exactly have Marcus's permission, but we haven't broken in, either. I used my key. It's Marcus's stupid fault that he didn't take it off me. How was I supposed to know that Ms Flipping France was living upstairs?

'Are we needed here?' the officer says. 'Can you resolve this yourself or do you want to take it further?'

'Oh, I'm sure that we can come to some amicable arrangement,' Marcus says smoothly. Then he turns to me and raises a questioning eyebrow. 'Can we, Lucy?'

It's fair to say that Crush doesn't look happy.

'What exactly did you have in mind?' I feel my negotiating stance is somewhat undermined by still being in nothing but my bra and knickers.

Marcus takes my elbow and steers me to one side, away from Crush, away from the police officers.

'Come back,' he murmurs. 'Come back and run this place and I'll say nothing more about it.'

I fold my arms across my chest. 'That's blackmail, Marcus.'

'Yes,' he says, unperturbed. 'Do we have a deal?'

I feel backed into a corner and excited at the same time. 'Aiden will be furious.'

'Quite probably.' Marcus has the smile of a man who knows he has won.

'The salary I proposed?'

'Yes,' Marcus says. 'I don't want you on the cheap but, make no mistake, I *do* want you.'

'And, if I agree, you won't press charges?'

Marcus nods.

'And we'll never speak of this again?'

'Never.' Then his smile widens. 'Well, not *very* often.'

'I hate you, you know,' I tell him.

'There is a very thin line between love and hate, Lucy Lombard.'

'I'll come back,' I say. Inside me is the perfect storm of trepidation and exhilaration. I'm coming home. Chocolate Heaven is to be our domain once again. The girls will be thrilled. Though quite how I'm going to break this to Crush, I have no idea.

'Excellent.' Marcus pretends to spit on his hand and holds it out to me. 'Done.'

And, do you know, a significant part of me feels that I have been.

Chapter Twenty-One

Autumn thanked her lucky stars. Only a few short days after the last abortive meeting and she'd been able to arrange to meet Mary again. And, hopefully, Willow too. This time she was biting the bullet and going to their home turf as Mary felt that it would be easier for her daughter. Autumn could only hope that Willow would be happy to go along with that. She was so desperate to meet her and now that she knew the girl was struggling, Autumn wanted to help as much as she could.

Miles and Florence stood on the pavement and waved her goodbye. Flo had given her a bag of Minstrels for the journey and she blew her a kiss. They were both heading straight to the park while Autumn was borrowing Miles's car to drive up the motorway – hopefully – to her reunion with Willow. Although Miles and Flo hadn't been long in her life, she already hated to be away from them for any length of time. But this was an important day for her.

Mary had already explained that she and Willow lived in the heart of the Cotswolds and that their home was a farmhouse that they'd converted into a bed and breakfast. It was hard to imagine her daughter living somewhere like that – she'd always imagined that she'd been in London somewhere or the suburbs rather than the country – but she was glad of the chance to see where she'd been brought up.

Traffic was heavy, yet just over an hour later she was turning off the M40 and leaving the built-up towns behind, heading out into the gently rolling hills of the Cotswolds. Ugly brick houses gave way to gorgeous mellow stone cottages; the tangle of busy roads dissolved to meandering lanes and acres of untrammelled farmland. It was a beautiful area and a glorious day. Autumn felt some of the tension leave her shoulders.

A short while later, instructed efficiently by the sat nav, Autumn pulled up at the edge of a small village, outside Manor House Farm. Finally, she was here. She breathed a sigh of relief. In the last few miles her palms had gone clammy on the steering wheel and she was as nervous as she could possibly be. Nothing had ever meant this much to her and she was desperately anxious for it to go right.

She took a moment to compose herself and absorb her surroundings. The farmhouse was double-fronted, Georgian, both grand and homely at the same time. The yellow stone building was surrounded by a low wall covered with sprawling purple aubrieta and white rock which was in bloom. A riot of spring flowers in a multitude of colours filled the mature garden – daffodils, tulips, irises, grape hyacinths and a dozen other plants that Autumn didn't know the names of. A delicate pink rose draped itself around the front door. It looked idyllic and she was glad to think that Willow had grown up somewhere so lovely.

Getting out of the car, Autumn went to the door, feeling shivery inside. This was the moment she had never dared to dream would happen. She rang the bell and moments later, heard the snappy bark of a little dog and the sound of footsteps in the hall. A moment later, Mary opened the door, wiping her hands on a tea towel.

'Do come in, Autumn,' she said. 'Nice to see you again. Have you had a good journey?'

'Yes. Thank you. This is a lovely place.'

'And you found us all right?'

'I managed not to get lost once,' she said.

It was a big hall with stone tiles and stripped pine doors. A large and quite imposing wooden staircase with a tartan carpet runner dominated one side. On the other was a table full of family photos, a phone, a rack of pamphlets about the attractions of the area for the guests and a book for comments. There was a lamp, too, switched on even though the day was bright, with a shade in a tartan pattern that differed from the carpet.

It was cosy and welcoming. If you arrived here for a few nights' break, Autumn imagined that you'd be quite pleased.

The little dog – a Jack Russell – jumped up to be fussed, his claws scrabbling on the stone floor.

'Don't mind him,' Mary said. 'He's normally restricted to the kitchen when guests are here. Get down, boy. Leave our visitor alone.'

'It's all right, really. I like dogs. I'd love to have one but I live in a flat with no garden.'

Mary lowered her voice. 'Willow *is* actually here – which is a bonus.' She shook her head as if perplexed by the ways of her daughter. 'But I have to warn you that she's very scratchy today.'

'It's understandable.'

'She's a teenager and is going through the usual hormonal angst. She's been through a lot. I think she's trying to find her place in the world and part of that is knowing her history.' Mary seemed just as anxious as Autumn was. 'I can't blame her for that, but it makes me nervous, too. I'm sure you'll take things slowly with her.'

'Of course. I'll go entirely at her pace. However, I have to say that I can't wait to see her.' Autumn put her hand on Mary's arm. 'I can't thank you enough for agreeing to this. It must be hard.'

There were tears in the woman's eyes again. 'You have no idea.' She managed a weak smile and put down her tea towel. 'I'll go up to get her. You go through and make yourself comfortable in the conservatory. We haven't got any guests in until later this afternoon. When you're settled, I'll make myself scarce and put the kettle on while you two get to know each other.'

Butterflies whirled in Autumn's stomach at the thought. Mary turned away from her and climbed the stairs, a little weariness evident in her step. The dog bounded after her.

Autumn walked through to the kitchen, which was large with an ancient-looking range cooker. Pots and pans filled every possible shelf. A blue jug filled with daffodils stood on the huge, scrubbed pine table. Beyond it, the conservatory ran along the length of the house. The end nearest to the kitchen was taken up with four small tables, already set for breakfast. The far end had two sofas facing each other, both of which looked well-loved. They were covered with hand-crocheted throws and an excess of mismatched cushions. Autumn went to sit in one of them.

A few minutes later, Mary came back looking agitated. 'Here she is!' Her voice was too cheery and forced. Behind her trailed Willow, exuding reluctance.

Autumn stood, mouth dry, eyes brimming with tears. After all this time, the child that she thought she might never see again was standing right in front of her. She wanted to run to her, gather Willow in her arms and hold her for the rest of her life, but that clearly wasn't going to be an option. Instead, she simply stood up and made do with saying, 'Hi.'

Willow nudged closer to Mary and mumbled back, 'Hi.'

The girl was a small, angry mirror image of Autumn. If Willow was in any doubt about her parentage then this must surely confirm that Autumn was her birth mother. They were like twins, only separated by years. Willow was slender and dressed head to toe in black – Doc Marten boots, lacy tights, black denim shorts and a hoodie with a pentagram on the front. You certainly couldn't mistake her leanings. Her face, naturally pale, looked more so due to the thick black eyeliner around her eyes and the slash of red lipstick on her mouth. The sprinkling of freckles probably matched Autumn's dot-for-dot. Her hair – as bright in colour and clearly inclined to be as exuberantly corkscrew as Autumn's – had been straightened and gelled within an inch of its life. Obviously, Goths didn't do crazy curls.

'Why don't you sit down with Autumn?' Mary said, shepherding the girl forward. 'I'll leave you alone for a bit while I make some tea. I'm sure you have a lot to talk about.'

Willow shuffled forward and plonked herself on the sofa opposite Autumn, the scowl never leaving her face. The little dog came and sat next to her and Willow pulled him to her side and fussed his ears. Autumn took her seat again and wondered how to fill the awkward silence.

'He's a lovely dog,' Autumn said, voice cracking. 'What's he called?'

'Jack.'

'Did you have him as a puppy?'

Willow nodded.

'Why did you call him Jack?'

She looked at Autumn as if she was an idiot. 'He's a Jack Russell.'

'Oh. Of course.'

114

Willow softened slightly. 'He came from a rescue centre. That's what he was called when we got him.'

'It's a nice name.' Willow stared at her. This was going to be like pulling teeth, so she might as well just get to the crux of the matter. 'I expect you have a lot of questions that you want to ask me.'

The girl shrugged.

'Then I'd like to hear all about you, if you wouldn't mind.'

Willow stuck the toggle of her hoodie in her mouth and sat back on the sofa.

'Or I could tell you a bit about myself first?'

'OK,' Willow mumbled.

So Autumn took that as her cue to begin. 'It's hard to know where to start.' Her voice sounded shaky. After a deep and steadying breath, she continued, 'I'm twenty-nine years old and I live in a flat in north London. I'm not working at the moment, but I've been teaching at a drugs rehabilitation centre. I run classes on how to make stained glass.' Autumn tried a laugh. 'That must all sound very dull.'

The expression on Willow's face didn't contradict her.

'I live by myself, but I have a really nice boyfriend called Miles and he has a little girl of his own. She's called Florence and she's three. Will that do for now?'

'Dunno,' Willow muttered.

'I was so thrilled when Mary contacted me. I didn't think you'd be able to look for me until you were eighteen and I always hoped that you would.'

'I just wanted to know who I looked like. That's all,' Willow ventured with as much condescension as she could manage. 'I'm not like Mum or Dad.'

Autumn held out her curls. 'Same hair.'

Willow's resulting smile was reluctant and barely noticeable, but Autumn was sure it was in there somewhere.

'You've done a better job of straightening it than I've ever managed. I gave up years ago and decided to let it do its own thing. Thank goodness for GHDs.'

Willow examined her split ends as if they were the most interesting thing that had ever existed.

'This is a lovely place to live,' Autumn tried.

'It's boring,' Willow said, emphatically.

'Have you got a nice group of friends?'

'No.' She shook her head. 'They're all farmers' kids,' she said as if they had a terrible, incurable disease. 'Straw-chewers. I've got nothing in common with them.'

'That must be hard. I remember when I was at boarding school with a lot of posh, high-maintenance girls. I was a bit Goth too – so I thought – before I veered towards bohemian. I'd just had enough of the eyeliner on my pillow, really. I was the only vegetarian in my class and I supported the Green Party. Everyone thought I was weird. The rest of the girls just wanted to talk about boys.' She tried a laugh at the memory, but it had been painful at the time and it was more than ironic that she was the one out of all of them who had ended up pregnant. 'It was terrible. I didn't have lots of friends. None, really. I know what it feels like to be on the outside.'

Picking at her black nail varnish, Willow said, 'I don't care.' When, patently, she cared very much.

Mary came back and fussed and fiddled with the cups while she poured. Then Autumn and Mary sat drinking tea and making excruciating small talk while Willow glowered at them both.

'Why don't you and Autumn go for a walk?' Mary said brightly when conversation was clearly drying up. 'Take Jack across the field.'

Willow shook her head.

'Maybe I should go now,' Autumn said. 'It's been a lot to take in.'

'Half an hour wouldn't hurt, would it, Willow? Autumn has come a long way.'

The girl shrugged as if she didn't care one way or the other. Her face said that Autumn could have come from the moon as far as she was concerned; it still wouldn't impress her. 'OK.' She stood up, hands jammed in her pockets.

'Show Autumn the wood. It's lovely up there. A bit early for the bluebells, but it will still be pleasant.'

Willow rolled her eyes.

Autumn hadn't expected it to be easy. She'd just have to do this on Willow's terms. She owed her that much.

'That sounds nice,' Autumn said, trying to look hopeful.

'It'll be boring,' Willow countered. 'Like everything around here is.'

Chapter Twenty-Two

Autumn and Willow fell into step next to each other. The little dog ran ahead. They strode away from the farmhouse, crossing the meticulously maintained back garden. Willow had her head down, shoulders hunched, hands buried in the depths of her hoodie. Autumn noticed that Mary was watching them through the window with a worried expression.

At the far corner of the garden was a half-hidden gate. Willow pushed aside some rampant climbing plant and opened it. Then they headed along the track beside the field. Green shoots of a future crop were pushing hopefully through the earth. Autumn dipped into her pocket and pulled out a bar of Galaxy.

'Sustenance.' She broke off a few squares and handed them to Willow. 'I'm a total chocoholic,' Autumn admitted. 'I forgot to mention that.'

Willow's first proper smile. 'Me too.'

'My boyfriend gave me this bar for courage. This isn't easy for either of us.'

Willow said nothing.

'What's your favourite?'

'I like Fairtrade chocolate. Dark is my fave.'

'Me too,' Autumn said. 'Though I do like a good white chocolate, too.'

They walked a few more paces in silence.

'There's a great place in London that I'd like to take you one day, if you'd let me. It's my favourite café. Chocolate Heaven.'

'Sounds cool.'

She was sure that, despite their misgivings, Lucy would be back in control there soon. Her daughter would love it.

'If you're up for it, I'll ask Mary if we can organise it.'

'She just wants me to be happy,' Willow said, flatly.

'Me too.' At the risk of sounding like she was interrogating her daughter, she asked, 'What kind of music do you like?'

'Retro Goth, some old-style punk,' she said, a reluctant air of enthusiasm finally coming out. 'The Cure, Evanescence, the Damned, Siouxsie and the Banshees. That sort of stuff.'

'At least I've heard of those,' Autumn said.

'I play the guitar,' Willow offered.

'Any good?'

'No,' she said. 'Totally rubbish.'

Then they both laughed. At that moment, she knew that it was going to be all right and tears prickled behind her eyes once more.

'I'm glad that you looked for me,' Autumn said.

'I sort of wanted to know where I came from,' Willow mumbled.

'Doesn't everyone?'

'I guess so.'

'I'll tell you whatever you want to know,' Autumn said. 'You only have to ask.'

'Usual stuff,' Willow said, sullenly. 'What happened. Why you decided to get rid of me.'

'OK.' Now the tricky bit. They walked in silence for a few moments while Autumn tried to find the right words. She'd rehearsed this in her head so many times, imagined this situation, but now she finally had a chance to tell her side of the story, she didn't want to make a mess of it.

Autumn took a deep breath before she said, 'I fell pregnant with you when I was fourteen years old. About the same age as you are now. I didn't know the boy very well, but I thought I loved him madly.' Her throat was closing with emotion, but she forced herself to plough on. 'My parents sent me away to have you – to Switzerland – and, very soon after you were born, they made me put you up for adoption. I was too young, too naive to understand what was really being asked of me. I was in a state of panic and had no idea what to do. I just did what my parents said without question. I couldn't see another way. I know that it broke my heart, though. You were my baby and I adored you the moment I set eyes on you. There hasn't been a day in all these years that I haven't thought about you.'

Willow walked beside her, stony-faced, digesting the information. 'So you wanted to keep me?'

'Desperately.' Autumn brushed away a tear. 'But I had no way of looking after you. I felt, at the time, that I had to accept what my parents had planned. They thought it was for the best.'

Willow's chin jutted defiantly. 'Was it?'

'No. Not for a minute. It was a terrible thing to do.'

Her daughter looked deep in thought for a moment, then said, 'What happened to your mum and dad?'

'They live in London. They're both lawyers.'

'Do they know that you've come to see me?'

'No,' Autumn admitted. 'I'm not very close to my parents. They have busy lives.'

Willow processed this. 'Where's my dad now?'

That question was much harder to answer. 'I don't know. Sadly, he doesn't even know about you. He was a gardener at my boarding school. He was a few years older than me, but only seventeen or eighteen – I'm not sure now. When the school found out about our relationship, he was sacked immediately. I was sent abroad and never saw him again.' She wondered if he'd ever come back to the school looking for her, but thought probably not. He'd been just a kid, too.

They kept to the track alongside the hedgerow as they climbed up away from the house.

'We go in here,' Willow said. 'This is what Mum thought would be "pleasant".'

It sounded strange to hear her call someone else 'Mum'. She wondered if Willow would ever come to know her well enough to be able to call her that, too. Currently, it seemed a long way off. Perhaps she'd given up that privilege for ever.

'It looks lovely.'

'It's just stupid trees,' she said with disdain.

It was a small copse with a narrow winding path – just enough room for them still to walk alongside each other. The sun shone through the trees casting dappled shadows at their feet. It was, as Mary had said, too early for the bluebells, but it wouldn't be long before they were out. The dog snuffled happily through all the mounds of leaves, still abundant on the ground from last year's fall.

Willow finished her chocolate and Autumn broke off some more to hand to her.

'What was his name?'

'His first name was Finn. I can't even remember his surname.'

Willow's face showed her disappointment. 'Not much chance of me finding him then.'

'I wouldn't know where to start,' Autumn acknowledged. 'I knew so little about him. But he was kind, funny.' And he had shown her some love and attention. That was the main reason she used to sneak out of the dormitory to meet him. Like

Willow now, she felt so alone, so isolated. It was no wonder that she clung to the first crumb of affection she was offered. 'Perhaps my old school would have some information on him. He was a casual worker and only there for a short time, so it's a long shot.'

The girl brightened. 'Worth trying, though.'

Autumn wondered how she'd feel to be reunited with Willow's father after all this time, and how he'd feel to learn that he had a daughter. She hadn't even had a chance to tell him that she was pregnant. It had been easy to turn a blind eye to missing a few periods, to put the fact that her tummy was becoming rounded down to the stodgy school meals. It was only when it became impossible to ignore that she'd sneaked into the local town and had bought a pregnancy test. She'd crept out of the dormitory before everyone else was up to use it in secret and had never known fear quite like it when the test showed positive. She didn't have a friend she could share her terror with, no one to confide in. Autumn ended up having to tell the school matron, who immediately summoned her parents. They didn't take her anywhere quiet where she could break it to them gently. They sat upright on hardback chairs in the headmaster's study with the matron and the headmaster watching on while she blurted it out. She'd known exactly how they'd react and the thought of that conversation made her feel sick even now.

She was bundled out of school that day, an embarrassment to all, and never went back.

'I thought you'd be old,' Willow said, pulling Autumn back to the present. 'Like Mum.'

Autumn smiled to herself. Mary was probably late forties at the most. 'I was just your age when I had you.'

'If I had a baby now, I'd keep it,' Willow said, defiantly. 'No way I'd give it away. No matter what anyone said. I'd run away with it.'

'There isn't a day that goes by that I don't regret what I did,' she replied sadly. 'I think, if you had a baby, that Mary would support you. She seems like a lovely mother.'

A pink flush came to Willow's cheeks.

'I wasn't so lucky. My parents were very harsh and I hadn't learned that I could stand up to them.' She still wasn't sure that she had, even now. 'I didn't know what else to do, so I did what they wanted. It was the biggest mistake of my life. I should have kept you, whatever it took.' She wasn't sure, but it looked as if Willow brushed a tear away from her eye with the sleeve of her hoodie. All Autumn wanted to do was hug her. 'But I'd like to try to make up for the time we've lost. If you'll let me.'

Willow stopped and stared at her. It seemed as if she was trying to look into her soul, to work out if she could allow this woman into her life. She was hurting and didn't want to risk getting hurt even more. She looked so tiny, so vulnerable.

Autumn opened her arms and, with only a brief hesitation, Willow stepped into them. Then her daughter cried – her body tight with tension, pressed against Autumn.

'It will be all right,' Autumn soothed. 'Everything will be all right now.'

And she hoped with all of her heart that she could keep her promise.

Chapter Twenty-Three

Chantal linked her arm with Jacob's, strolling alongside him as he pushed the buggy. The spring bulbs were waving their cheery heads in the warm breeze. Swathes of daffodils and crocuses covered the grass by the pathways. St James's Park was one of her favourite spots in London and the bright sunshine made it even more special. Lana was sleeping blissfully, unaware of the beautiful day. Chantal had even taken her jacket off, the first time in the year. Summer would soon be on its way. Her heart felt both happy and sad at the same time. She wondered if you experienced everything more keenly when you realised that it might be taken away from you. Was the brilliance of the day more poignant when you were made keenly aware that you may not have many more of them?

'You're quiet,' Jacob said.

'Just thinking.'

'I don't want you to worry.'

'I'm not,' she assured him. Well, not *too* much. That was partly because she still felt it was unreal, that it was happening to someone else and not to her. 'The weird thing is that I don't even feel unwell. I'm a bit tired and still having a few twinges, but I'm prepared to believe that's just my age. And what mum with a baby isn't tired?' Surely with a cancer in her body, she'd *know*; she'd feel worse than this. Perhaps when it came down to it, the doctor might be wrong. It happened.

Now all she could do was wait to hear from the clinic for an appointment to remove the offending lump. Livia said it would be a very straightforward operation. Thankfully, she'd been told that she'd likely only have to wait a few days rather than weeks. Until then, it would gnaw away at her, no matter how much bravado she tried.

'I'll take time off work,' Jacob said. 'I've already started delegating. I can be at home to look after Lana while you're in hospital, and when you're recuperating I want to be there to care for you.'

Chantal rested her head on his shoulder. 'What would I do without you?'

'No regrets?' Jacob asked.

'None,' she said, emphatically. 'Absolutely.'

'We should get married,' he said suddenly, stopping in his tracks.

Chantal laughed. 'I'm not actually divorced yet.'

'But it won't be long,' he countered. 'It would be good to make plans for our future.'

Future? She wondered, bleakly, if she'd have one at all.

'Let's see if I come through this,' Chantal said, her voice catching with unexpected emotion.

It had all seemed so set, so easy. She and Jacob would take things slowly, deepening their love before they moved forward onto the next step. Now she felt as if someone had started an alarm clock ticking. Like one of those red LED displays on a bomb in action films. Except this time the clock was ticking on her life.

'There is no question that you'll survive it,' Jacob said with conviction. 'I'm not waiting all this time to be with you only to have our days together cut short. That's just not in the plan. It won't happen.'

'I'm happy to believe that.' But inside she was scared. Her cancer was a non-aggressive type. The consultant had been very keen to point that out. And it had been detected early. That wasn't to say that it was going to be a bed of roses. Despite what Livia said, Chantal was well aware that not everyone got their happy ending. 'You shouldn't be tied to me until you know that I'm going to be around for a long time to enjoy it.'

'Shouldn't I be involved in that decision?'

'You know what I mean, Jacob.'

'Promise me as soon as you're well again that we'll get married?'

'Yes.'

'I think I need more than that. It seemed like a very feeble assurance to me.' Jacob left the buggy abruptly and went to pick a daffodil.

'What are you doing?'

'I'm sure that the park can spare one. This is an important occasion.' When he came back, clutching the cheery yellow bloom, he dropped to one knee in front of her and proffered the daffodil. 'Chantal Hamilton, would you do me the very great honour of being my wife?'

Tears spilled over her lashes as she took it from him. 'Yes,' she said. 'I'd like that very much.'

'When this is done, when you've been given the all-clear, I'll go down on one knee again with the biggest diamond I can lay my hands on.'

'This is all I need,' she said, looking at the daffodil. 'It's beautiful.'

Jacob stood and took her in his arms. He held her as if he never wanted to let her go. The few people passing by that had paused to witness his proposal burst into spontaneous applause. Chantal felt herself blush, and her heart wanted to burst with love.

'Now you have to get better,' he said. 'You have a promise to keep.'

Chapter Twenty-Four

As much as Nadia tried to pretend not to be, she was still quite shaken by her mugging. The bank card and credit card had been cancelled, the locks changed, her mobile phone replaced, but, despite all those measures, it had still left her feeling more vulnerable than before.

More than ever she was left wondering what she was doing living in a run-down area and working at a rubbish job. She'd had no contact from the man who'd pushed her to the ground and stolen her handbag, thankfully. He'd just disappeared into the night with her belongings, but that didn't stop her being scared now every evening on her way home from work. Even when it was still light. From the minute she left the office she was anxiously looking over her shoulder until she was safely behind her double-locked front door. She'd bought a panic alarm, which she kept tightly gripped in her fist. She kept her phone, credit cards and money on a pouch around her waist inside her coat. It was a ridiculous way to live.

She'd started to put Lewis straight into her bed too, not wanting to sleep alone. Just feeling the warmth of another human being alongside her comforted her, and she could protect him too. She tucked him in and kissed his head.

The trip to Cumbria couldn't come soon enough.

'How many sleeps until we go to see Seth and Lily?' Lewis asked.

'Not many now,' Nadia said. She was glad that he was excited about their trip and a change of scenery would do them both good. 'If you go to sleep straight away, then it will be here even quicker.'

'Love you, Mummy.' He stifled a yawn.

'Love you, too.' Everything she did, she did for her son. She turned on the nightlight and left him snuggled down with the bedroom door ajar.

Downstairs, she opened a bottle of wine and, from the cupboard, right at the back, pulled out the box of chocolates she'd bought yesterday. They were a supermarket brand and nothing wrong with that – needs must. But she was desperately missing Chocolate Heaven and its delights.

Her sister, Anita, was coming over to see her tonight. She'd been horrified when Nadia had told her about being attacked in the street and had wanted to rush round straight away, but Nadia had managed to persuade her that she was all right; all she'd wanted to do was to crawl into her bed.

Now Nadia would be glad of the company. It was proving even more difficult than usual spending her evenings alone. Anita had asked her to go over to her house for dinner with Lewis but she couldn't face it. Unless she needed to for work, she didn't have the inclination to leave the house after dark. Her confidence had taken a serious knock. When the evenings got a bit lighter, she hoped that would change but, for now, she just wanted to batten down the hatches and stay safe. She kept getting flashbacks to that night and a fresh jolt of nausea would grip her. What would become of Lewis if something dreadful happened to her? It didn't bear thinking about.

She wouldn't call James tonight, as he'd told her that he was going into Keswick for a rare night out and she didn't want to interrupt his fun. He was heading to one of the pubs to listen to a local band, which one of his friends played in. She hated how much she missed their usual chat. They might not have seen each other since Christmas but he'd become very much part of her life. He, too, had been horrified to hear of her attack and had to be dissuaded from jumping in the car and coming to collect her. She was in no doubt that it had left him feeling helpless, as they were so far apart. Now when she spoke to James she felt as if she never wanted to hang up.

Before she poured the wine, she texted him. *Have a great time tonight. Missing you. Xx*

James texted straight back. *It's loud and crowded, but fun. Wish you were here. Xx*

Soon she would be and that thought made her feel warm inside.

As she was pouring herself a glass, the front door bell rang and she went to open it, checking the security spy hole before she unhooked the chain – all the little measures that she hadn't bothered with before. Anita bowled in and hugged her tightly. 'Are you all right?'

'I'm not so bad,' Nadia said, easing herself from Anita's grip. Which wasn't strictly true. Her ribs carried a dull ache and her lip still kept splitting open if she wasn't careful. Though the bruises had faded, she was very much aware of them; they'd left a mark that was far more than cosmetic. 'Glad to see you.'

Anita didn't let go. 'You should have come to me. I would have taken care of you.'

'I'd have found it difficult to get a babysitter and Lewis has school in the morning.'

'You can't stay at home every night by yourself.'

'I know.'

'Tarak would have come to collect you.'

'I don't like to trouble him.'

'No trouble. You're family. He'd be glad to do it.'

Nadia thought that she'd be less than keen to be in a car alone with Tarak. Her brother-in-law might seem like a reformed character but in the past he'd had sleazy moments that were hard to forget.

'Are you going to pack in that awful job?' her sister continued. 'You could come back to the shop tomorrow if you want to.'

'I don't think so. I'll look for something else soon.'

'I hate to think of you travelling home at night on the Underground by yourself. You should get a taxi home.'

'It's a good idea, but it would be too expensive, Anita. My wages don't really run to such decadence.' They walked through to the kitchen. 'Besides, I don't work too many late shifts. Just one a week. I'm generally travelling home with the crowd and I have a personal alarm now, which makes me feel a bit better.' However, the undeniable fact was that now she was just a little bit more jittery. It was the first time she'd ever experienced real danger. She'd felt so helpless, so threatened, and that feeling hadn't yet left.

She finished pouring the wine and gave a glass to Anita. 'Cheers,' she said. They clinked glasses together. 'Though I'm not exactly sure what we're celebrating. Unless you count the fact that there's a good rom-com on the television for us to watch and I have a box of chocolates that I managed to keep hidden from Lewis.'

She lifted the lid off the box.

'I have some good news to tell you,' Anita said, sounding excited. 'I hope that it will cheer you up.'

Nadia waited patiently.

'Mummy and Daddy would like to see you,' Anita said. 'I talked to them on your behalf and they've agreed to meet you.'

She'd become estranged from her parents when she'd gone against their wishes in marrying Toby. It was years ago now and yet they'd never relented, not even when Lewis was born. She could take them cutting her off, but shunning their grandson, too? That she couldn't get her head around. They hadn't responded to the photographs she'd regularly sent. Not even a phone call or a birthday card for him.

Her mind stuck on one word. 'Agreed?'

'You know what I mean. They *want* to see you.'

She wondered how much persuasion Anita had to employ to get them to agree. 'What changed their minds this time?'

'I talked to them for you.'

Nadia rolled her eyes.

'Don't be like that. You can be as stubborn as they are.'

'I've sent them cards, photographs. Every year. I've had nothing in return.'

'I know. And that's dreadful. But they're not getting any younger,' Anita said. 'Dad's health is failing. Perhaps they realise that if they don't make amends soon, then they might miss the opportunity.'

A few years ago, it was all she wanted to hear. She'd missed her parents, her family, desperately. If they'd stepped in and helped her when she was struggling then maybe everything would have turned out differently. They had vehemently disapproved of her marriage and, in turn, it was their censure that had made her determined to stick with it when perhaps she would have been better to leave. Still, it was no good dwelling on that now. It was done and nothing could change it. Anita was right. Her parents were getting older and, if this was an olive branch, then she should grasp it.

'Say something,' Anita urged. 'Is that not good news?'

'Yes,' Nadia agreed. 'Great.' Yet inside her there was an emptiness. The elation she should feel at the possibility of being reunited with her parents just wasn't there. The girls of the Chocolate Lovers' Club had stepped into the gap created by her family and she wondered if she could ever really forgive her parents for abandoning her when she most needed them.

'Shall I set up a time?' Anita chattered on. 'What about a Sunday lunch at my house? It would be just like old times.'

In truth, nothing would ever get that back again. Too much had happened. Too much had been said. It could never be the same.

'Let me see.' Nadia saw Anita's face fall. 'I've got a lot on at the moment. I'm going up to the Lake District to visit James. Perhaps we could fix something up when I get back?'

'I hope you're not chasing this man, Nadia.' Anita pursed her lips in disapproval. It reminded Nadia of her mother.

'I don't think so, sister,' she said. 'But, if I am, then that's my business.'

'Lewis doesn't need a stranger in his life.'

'James isn't a stranger. We've grown fond of each other.' She'd had more heartfelt conversations over the phone with him than she ever had with her husband when he'd been in the same room. 'He's a very nice man.'

'You said that about Toby,' Anita reminded her.

'He was a kind man and a loving father. Unfortunately, he had a weakness. As many men do.' It was a barbed comment and she hoped that it struck home with Anita. *Her* spouse wasn't exactly ideal marriage material either, with his philandering ways. Who was perfect? She and Toby had enjoyed a good relationship until gambling got a grip on him. 'He needed help, which he never got.'

'He nearly dragged you under with him,' Anita said sharply. 'You can't afford for that to happen again.'

'You're right,' Nadia said. 'But what do you want me to do? Spend the rest of my life alone? Lewis needs a father figure. I do the best I can, but it's hard bringing up a child on my own.'

'You need a good husband. A solid man.'

Nadia had to bite her tongue. It was hard not to point out that Tarak was hardly a contender for Husband of the Year. She knew secrets about him that Anita didn't. Who was her sister to preach to her?

'You be careful, Nadia,' Anita warned. 'You are too quick to love.'

Perhaps there was an element of truth in that. Despite her protests, she *was* actually running up to the Lake District to be with a man she'd met only briefly.

She took a swig of her wine, which tasted bitter in her mouth. And when she bit into one of the chocolates – a dark truffle of indistinct origin – it failed to soothe her at all.

Chapter Twenty-Five

I'm back behind the counter of Chocolate Heaven, beside myself with joy. Mr Aiden Holby, less so.

Crush thinks that Marcus is blackmailing me into returning and I can see his point of view. Sort of. Marcus simply took advantage when an opportunity presented itself. Which, let's face it, is what he does best.

There have been several arguments *chez* Lombard, all in hushed tones as my dear father is still sleeping in my living room. In the end, I persuaded Crush – against his better judgement – that this is my spiritual home. It is where I am meant to be. I am never happier than when I'm in my apron behind my rows and rows of delicious chocolates and delightfully displayed cakes.

Mind you, it has all gone to pot since Ms France has been in charge. The whole place looks a bit shabby and unkempt. The cushions aren't plumped, the chairs are askew, the shelves aren't fully stocked – I could go on. Instead, on my first morning back, I'm already hard at work with a damp J-cloth and a mop.

I'm sure when Crush sees how delirious I am, he'll come round. The pay is great. Marcus has been true to his word. He's advanced me a month's salary and it's a not inconsiderable sum. This will help our wedding fund no end. Though I'm hardly going to point that out to Marcus. Plus Crush and I can now come and have sex here any time we want to! Ha! I bet Marcus never considered that, did he? One to cunning chocolate-shop manager. Nil to scheming ex-fiancé.

Though, in fairness, maybe Crush will be traumatised for life by his previous experience and may never be able to . . . ahem . . . *perform* in a chocolate shop again. I shudder at the thought.

Just as I'm considering my options, there's the familiar throaty roar of Marcus's Ferrari. If he's come to gloat about his victory, he'll get the sharp end of my tongue. From now on this is going to be a proper business-style relationship: he will treat me with the respect I deserve and not try to snog me over the summer berry tarts or anything like that. I might be back at Chocolate Heaven and on Marcus's turf now, but nothing he can do – *nothing* – will come between Crush and me. Nothing.

'Hey, Lucy.' Marcus swings in. He looks like the cat who's got the cream. 'It's great to see you back where you belong. You and this place are meant to be.'

'It feels good,' I have the grace to admit. I can now call all the girls and tell them that it's safe to return once more. They've yet to discover that I'm back in the 'hood. 'The place is a bit of a state, Marcus. No wonder business has been slow. It will be nice to get it up to speed again and I have great plans for the future. I'm so glad you got rid of that awful woman.'

'Ah,' Marcus says. He goes a little bit pale.

'What?'

'I've been meaning to talk to you . . . '

I give him my best death glare. 'Please tell me that she's gone.' I'm hoping that at this moment she is standing alone at Paddington station with her little suitcase and her sexy accent waiting for the Eurostar to whisk her back to Paris where she belongs.

'*Mais non*,' a voice comes from behind me. 'I am *still* very much here.' *Steeeeel.*

I turn, and lounging in the doorway in her silk kimono thingy again is Ms France. Gah. I look back to Marcus for an explanation.

'Ah. I haven't yet had time to convey our new working arrangements to Marie-France,' he tells me.

Frankly, how long does it take to say, 'You're out on your ear, love – Lucy's back in town'?

Ms France bristles and folds her arms across her chest. 'What new working arrangement is this?'

Eeeeez. Theeeeez.

As the new manager, I'd really like her gone *tout de* flipping *suite* and be able to get in someone who has a passion for this like me. She's really let this place down in the short time she's been here. That's never going to win her an Employee of the Month badge, is it?

'What is *she* doing here?' Ms France wants to know. As well she might.

'We can sort this out, ladies,' Marcus says smoothly. 'I've brought Lucy in to help, Marie-France.'

Help?

'Lucy ran this place before and I know that you can't manage by yourself.'

Ms France pouts.

'You'll get on brilliantly.'

We both know that we won't. Besides, I came back thinking that I'd have free rein, not be encumbered with someone whom Marcus has employed for skills other than those with chocolate. And customers.

'I want her gone.' Ms France flounces upstairs.

'And I want *her* gone,' I say when I look back at Marcus. 'Looks as if you have a tricky situation on your hands.'

Marcus sighs. 'You can win her round, Lucy. She needs you.'

'*If* she stays and *if* I stay, she does know that I'll be her manager?'

Marcus goes a little pink. 'Let me talk to her.'

'If she's your girlfriend, Marcus, why do you even want me here? I'm your ex. This was always going to be a bad idea.' It breaks my heart, but maybe this isn't workable. Perhaps Crush was right all along. Anything involving Marcus is never straightforward. 'It's probably for the best if I just leave. I was silly to think that I could work for you.'

'You can. You can.' Marcus sounds desperate. 'Marie-France and I are just, well . . . you know.'

I know only too well. There have been so many women that I'm surprised Marcus can actually remember her name.

'Just give it a chance. Please. I've sunk a lot of money into this, Lucy. And it was all for you.'

'Then don't jeopardise it by letting other parts of your body rule your head.' I give a pointed glance in the direction of the offending article.

'A week. See how it goes after a week. If you and Marie-France aren't best friends by then, I'll sort something out.'

All the fight goes out of me. I really want to be here and I can't fall at the first hurdle. I can't go home to Crush after one morning and tell him that he was right all along.

'OK,' I say. 'But you tell her that I'm in charge. You tell her that she needs to buck her ideas up.' I don't know what the French is for that. Buck *vos idées* up, chuck.

Marcus is nodding furiously.

'You tell her that and I'll stay.'

'I will,' he says. 'Of course, I will.'

'We do this on my terms, Marcus, or not at all.' I even frighten myself by how stern I sound.

This is the new me. Lucy 'Ball Breaker' Lombard. And Marcus Canning better not mess with me.

Chapter Twenty-Six

The minute that Marcus leaves, I text all the members of the Chocolate Lovers' Club. *CHOCOLATE EMERGENCY*. This is our call sign for everyone to come running. *Chocolate Heaven asap*, I add.

Just wait until they get here. They won't believe their eyes. I'm still not sure that I believe it myself.

Already there are a few customers coming in today. I turn on the charm and serve them in my usual friendly and welcoming manner. A few boxes of chocolates to go are whisked away and there's a couple sitting in to share a gorgeous cappuccino cake. It's like getting back on an old, familiar bike. A few of them tell me that it's good to see me back – I need to woo these people to return as regulars, and quick. They are all happy and smiley by the time I've finished with them. I tell you, Ms France could learn a thing or two from me. I might not be able to pout as if my life depended on it or have the legs of a supermodel, but I know a thing or two about customer service.

Of course, I had completely forgotten about the very best perk of the job. Ahem.

With my little chocolate-deprived heart beating faster, I

pick out a couple of chocolates that are new to the range and savour them. An almond cream in a white chocolate shell with a caramelised almond on top, then a dark truffle with cocoa nibs smothered in cocoa powder. And, for good measure, a gianduja coated with nibbed hazelnuts and smooth milk chocolate. Ah, bliss. They both taste divine and it's good to see that the standards here haven't slipped. My waistline is totally going to take a battering this week, despite the continuing Wedding Diet. But it's a small price to pay for being so contented.

My very next job is to phone Alexandra and get her back on board as my cake baker; there's no way that the current cake offerings are up to scratch.

Half an hour later and Ms France returns. This time she is dressed and groomed as if she's about to do a magazine photoshoot. Her long dark hair swishes glossily and her perfect mouth is enhanced with red lipstick. She's wearing black spray-on leggings, a loose white linen shirt and killer heels. I'm in a T-shirt, jeans and aged Converse. I seriously have to up my game on the style front tomorrow.

She pouts at me, which I take as my cue to say, 'Could you possibly dust those shelves and restock them? I like to see them nice and full. I haven't had time to check what's in the stock room yet, so is it all right if I leave that to you?' That was really polite, right?

With a flick of her hair, she disappears again and then comes back with a duster and a few boxes of chocolates. She might not like me being in charge – resentment radiates from every cell of her sexy French being – but at least she's doing what I ask.

While Ms France is occupied doing that, I titivate the window display. The chocolates here look a bit faded and tired, so I replace them with new offerings. And, though it goes against all that I stand for, with a slight whimper, I throw the old ones in the bin.

Marcus texts me. *All OK?*

Yes, I text back. *Chocolate Heaven is in safe hands again.*

I love you, he sends back and there's a big row of kisses, too.

I'll say one thing for Marcus: he never gives up.

While I'm arranging some fresh muffins on a plate, Autumn arrives. She does a double take as she sees me behind the counter.

'Hi!' I give her a cheeky wave.

'What are you doing here?' Her eyes widen. 'More importantly, what are you doing here on *that* side of the counter?'

'It's a long story and I'll tell you when the other girls arrive, but I'm certainly glad to be back.'

'It's great to see you.' She frowns. 'Everything smoothed over with Marcus?'

'Kind of.' I nod towards Ms France tidying the shelves.

'Oh.' Autumn grimaces at me and I shrug.

'Now then, can I get you your usual, Madam?'

'I'm so glad we're back!' Autumn claps her hands with excitement. 'This is permanent?'

'I hope so.'

'Wow. I'll have a celebratory latte and a selection of chocs, please. I'll let you choose.'

'I can heartily recommend the almond cream in white chocolate.'

'Hit me with it,' she says. 'Yay! This is just like old times.'

We have only been displaced and nomadic chocolate-eaters for a few months, but it does feel like a lifetime.

Next to arrive is Chantal. She manoeuvres Lana's buggy through the door with the skill that comes with a lot of practise. Nevertheless, I go to help her. I think she looks quite drawn today and that makes me worry about her even more.

141

'All well?'

She shakes her head. 'So, so. Once I've had a double espresso to restore my equilibrium, I'll tell all.'

'What do you think?' I point to my Chocolate Heaven apron.

'You are a Malteser above a candle flame when it comes to Marcus.' She sighs at me. 'I knew you'd be back. It was only a matter of time.'

'He's giving me a great fat salary.'

'And a load of grief to go with it, no doubt.' Chantal looks at me ruefully. 'But you look happier than you have in ages, so who am I to criticise? You go for it, girl.'

'I can manage Marcus,' I assure her.

My friend raises her eyebrows and I think better of telling them the story of Marcus finding Crush and I getting jiggy on the sofa in here and cajoling/coercing me into returning. When I think about it, it doesn't sound that great. Instead, I opt for, 'Anything to eat?'

'Cake.' A relieved breath. 'A *huge* slice of it. The biggest you've got.'

'Coming up!'

She goes to sit with Autumn while I oblige. I kick the coffee machine into life, the peculiarities of operating it all coming back to me. And to think that I could be in a temporary office position now doing filing. Hurrah for me!

I've just delivered Autumn and Chantal's order when Nadia arrives. She hugs me straight away. 'Look at you!'

I give her a twirl with my apron.

'It's as if you've never been away.'

'I swear that my soul has relaxed today.' Even the scent of cocoa is making me chill.

'And so it should.' She gives me a look. 'I'm sure Marcus pulled off some hideous scam to get you in here.'

'Yeah,' I confess. 'He did.'

'Wouldn't be Marcus otherwise.'

'Latte and a muffin?'

'Sounds good to me. I can't stay long.'

I make up the order and, because the girls are currently the only customers, I sneak a minute to sit with them. I can dash back to the counter in a second if a customer comes in. Rather that than let Ms France serve them in her customary style, eh?

I'm so happy that we're all here again, where we should be – The Chocolate Lovers' Club back at Chocolate Heaven. I could jump for joy.

'Marie-France,' I shout over to my colleague. 'These are my friends. You'll be seeing a lot of them in here.'

She turns and regards them all coolly. *'Bonjour.'*

'Hi,' they say as one.

I wave to her. 'Come over and join us for a minute.'

'I am busy.' Ms France returns to her task, flicking her duster a little more briskly.

Tricky, Chantal mouths.

Very, I echo. But even the one fly in the ointment can't rain on my parade – if you know what I mean.

'Right. News,' I say. 'I want to hear it all.'

'Well,' Chantal says, looking very coy. 'Jacob has proposed to me.'

'Fabulous!' We all smother her with hugs and kisses.

'That's really great news,' Autumn says. 'And just the tonic you need right now.'

'It will give you something to look forward to,' Nadia agrees. 'Another chance to be bridesmaids!'

'Not so fast.' Chantal holds up a hand. 'I did point out to Jacob that I'm not even divorced yet.'

'Technicalities,' I say. 'When is the wedding?'

'I've told him that we can only go ahead when I've had my treatment,' Chantal says. 'I don't want that hanging over me.

Plus I don't want to steal your thunder, Lucy. We have your wedding first.'

I clap my hands with glee. 'Now that I'm back working again we can actually go ahead and book the venue.'

'That's great,' Chantal says. 'I can't wait!'

'And you *have* to be better by then.'

She laughs. 'I'll do my very best. I've got another appointment tomorrow to see the consultant. Hopefully, she'll have more to tell me about my treatment then, and I can start making arrangements.'

'I can change my plans if need be,' Autumn says. 'Don't go alone.'

'Jacob's coming along,' Chantal replies. 'He's organised the time off work. But it would be a big help if you could look after Lana.'

'No problem. I've got Flo, too. I can take them both to the park.'

'You should just set yourself up as a permanent childminder,' Nadia says. 'You're brilliant.'

'I do love it,' Autumn agrees. 'Maybe it's something I should think about. I've been out of work for too long and I need to do something constructive.'

'How did it go with Willow?' Chantal asks.

Autumn grins happily. 'Better than I could have hoped. She's an amazing girl. You can't believe how relieved I am. It was a bit difficult at first. She didn't exactly rush into my arms, but she's young and hurting. I'm sure it's been a lot to take in.'

'Did you get a photo?'

Autumn opens her handbag. 'She took a lot of coaxing, but eventually she let me take one.' She passes round her phone and a miniature Autumn stares back. But with more make-up.

'She's confused, very cross about everything and a bit lost,' Autumn says. 'Yet she seems willing to have a relationship with me. She's agreed to come down to London so that we can go out for the day.'

I give Autumn a big squeeze. 'I'm so pleased for you.'

'If you'd told me last year that this would happen, I'd never have believed you.'

'You'll have to bring her here so that we can meet her. When is she coming?'

'I'm not sure yet, but as soon as we can arrange it. I can't wait to see her again. I just regret all the years we've been apart, but I'm so grateful that she looked for me. She's struggling a bit at the moment but, underneath the hard little exterior she's trying to create, she's lovely.'

'She's her mother's daughter,' I remind her.

'I feel as if I'm trying to tread a very fine line. I don't want to undermine all that Mary has done for her. She's the one who's been there for Willow all of her life. I want to take it slowly so that Willow doesn't feel crowded.'

'You know that we'll do anything to help you,' Nadia offers.

'Thanks.' Autumn grins. 'Miles has been brilliant, too. So understanding.'

'You deserve some happiness after all you've been through.' Chantal pats her knee.

'It's only sad that Rich will never get to meet her. He would have loved to be an uncle.'

I don't think Autumn will ever get over the death of her brother and it's times like this that must bring it all to the forefront again. Thank goodness she's got Miles now.

'What about your parents? Have you told them that you've been reunited with Willow?'

'No,' Autumn says. 'That's something I've yet to address. Part of me feels that they don't even deserve to know about her. They were so quick to give her away and I don't know if I can ever forgive them for that. I'm going to have to think on it a bit more. It also depends what Willow wants to do. If she wanted to meet me, then surely, she'll want to meet her grandparents, too.'

'It might soften their hearts,' I suggest.

'The death of their only son simply served to make them even colder,' she says, 'so I won't hold my breath.'

That's a bleak view for Autumn, the eternal optimist, but she may be right.

'I had a visit from Anita last night,' Nadia says. 'My mum and dad want to meet up with me again.'

'Oh, Nadia,' I say. 'That's great news.'

'Is it?' she says with a weary air. 'After so long, I thought I'd be thrilled, but I don't feel much at all. You've been my family through the difficult times. They weren't there for me at all. Perhaps my heart has hardened towards them.'

'You never know, you might feel differently when you see them,' I offer.

'It's not long before I go up to Cumbria, so I'll wait until I get back. It might not go well and I don't want anything to spoil the mood.'

'Are you excited?' I'm beside myself with glee for her. After all that's happened recently, it will be good for her and Lewis to get away from London for a break.

'Yes,' she admits with a shy smile. 'But I don't feel I can go with you unwell, Chantal. I should cancel until you're better.'

'I don't even feel that bad,' Chantal says. 'A bit tired, but who isn't? You must go. You can't put your life on hold just because I've got a lump that needs to be gone.'

'I could rebook the tickets for the summer holidays.'

'No,' Chantal says. 'Absolutely not. You need to get up there and grab that man before some tweed-wearing country type gets her claws into him.'

Nadia laughed. 'Now you've given me something else to worry

about! I admit that since I've finally plucked up courage to book the tickets, I can't wait to see him again.'

'This is all so lovely,' I say. 'I think it deserves another round of coffee and chocolate.'

Strangely, none of my friends disagree.

'Before you do that,' Chantal says, 'I think you need to tell us how Marcus finally lured you back.'

'I've sworn myself to secrecy. You'll only laugh.'

'Promise we won't,' Autumn says.

'You know you can't keep a secret, Lucy,' Chantal says. 'It will come out one way or another.'

I sigh. 'Promise that you won't laugh,' I say. 'Or think badly of me.'

'Promise.' All of them.

I take a deep breath and lower my voice so that Ms France can't hear. 'My dad's still living with me, so Crush and I can't . . . well . . . you know. My walls are paper thin. I hadn't given my keys back to this place, so I let myself in here, so that Crush and I could have some . . . er . . . *privacy*.'

They all stare at me.

'What? Tell me you wouldn't have done the same if you were desperate.' I plough on regardless. 'Things were just getting interesting when the police arrived. Apparently, Ms France had called them. She thought we were intruders.'

'You were,' Nadia points out.

'Yeah, I know. But not in the strictest sense of the word.'

Already there are little outbreaks of giggling. I do my best to ignore them.

'So while I was still standing there in not much more than my undies and the policemen were swinging their handcuffs, Marcus coerced me into coming back by promising not to press charges.'

Now there is a group guffaw.

147

I'm mortally wounded. 'You promised you wouldn't laugh.'

'Oh, Lucy,' Nadia says. 'Even for you, that's priceless.'

Between chuckles Chantal manages, 'Marcus will never, ever change. You'd better have your wits about you, girl.'

'Well,' I say, 'by hook or by crook, I'm back. And I'm delighted.'

Then they're all falling about with laughter again, which I assume means that they're glad too. So I stomp off and get more chocolate.

Chapter Twenty-Seven

I've been back at Chocolate Heaven for a week now and Marcus is behaving himself. More or less. He's been in every day and there's a lot of giggling in the staff room when he disappears with Ms France, but business is on the up already and he's pretty much staying out of my hair.

I'm tidying the place, ready to leave for the evening, when his car roars up.

'Hey,' he says as he swings in through the door. 'What's new?'

'We have some lovely pecan pralines on offer, if you'd like to try one.'

'You know I'm not a big chocolate fan, Lucy.'

'Strange for a man who owns a chocolate shop. I should educate you.'

Marcus grins at me. 'That, I'd look forward to.'

I tut at him. 'Don't forget I'm leaving early tonight. I did text you to remind you.'

'You did.'

I undo my apron and strip it off. 'Because you are paying

me a fabulous salary, it means I can afford to go and book my lovely wedding venue. So thank you for that, Marcus.'

'Aw.' He pulls a face. 'Don't marry him, marry me.'

'We've been there before, Marcus. Remember?'

'I was young, foolish.'

'Now you're older and even more foolish. You could be one of my bridesmaids, if you like.'

'Harsh.'

'Besides, I'm not sure how Ms France would like you proposing to me.'

'Marie-France and I are just good friends.'

'It looks like it.'

'You're determined to go through with this?'

'Of course I'm going through with it. I'm in love. I'm happy.'

Marcus does his best sulk. 'What has wotsit got—'

'Aiden,' I supply.

' . . . that I haven't?'

'Integrity. Loyalty. Fidelity.'

'You could get a puppy if you wanted that. Don't you like a challenge, Lucy?'

'No. But clearly you do.'

'You must miss us just a little bit.'

'That'll be a no again,' I tell him. 'I'm marrying Aiden and that's all there is to it. Don't waste your words, Marcus. Wish me well and let me go.'

'If only it were so easy. You're a hard woman to forget.' He takes my hand, lifts it to his lips and graces it with a lingering kiss.

That moment, of course, is the one that Crush chooses to arrive. He's all smiles, but when he sees me and Marcus, his expression darkens.

I pull away from Marcus, who stands there grinning smugly.

Crush nods tightly at my boss. 'Marcus.'

'Hello, er . . . '

'Aiden,' I supply.

'We'd better get a move on, Lucy,' Crush says. 'We've got an appointment with the *wedding organiser* soon.'

I don't think any of us missed the emphasis on that.

'Yes, yes. I'll get my coat.' So I rush into the back room and grab it off the hanger. I don't want Crush and Marcus left alone together for more than two seconds. Goodness only knows what might happen. There could be a full-on brawl. Coat in hand, I scurry back.

When I return, they are, indeed, standing as if they're squaring up to each other. Crush's hands are clenched into fists by his side. Time to leave.

'I'll be in first thing in the morning, Marcus,' I say. 'Don't meddle with anything.'

Marcus raises his hand. 'Have fun.'

We swing out onto the street.

'He's not a problem,' I say.

'Marcus is *always* a problem,' Crush counters. 'I know only too well what he's like. I can't help it, Lucy; I just don't like you spending time with him every day.'

'He's totally wrapped up in Ms France at the moment. He's not bothering me.' I stop still and turn to him. 'And it's you that I love. We're on the way to book *our wedding*.' I get a thrill just saying that. 'Let's not argue about Marcus.'

Crush breaks into a smile. 'You're right. I'm being an idiot. A possessive one at that.'

'Don't ever stop,' I say and I wind my arms round him to kiss him.

'I called Jacob,' Crush says. 'We're meeting him at the venue. He's never organised a wedding at this place before, so he's looking forward to it.'

'Me too.'

* * *

151

One crowded, stuffy Tube ride later and we rock up at Golders Hill Park. Jacob is helping us with the planning and, as agreed, is waiting for us at the gates. We go into the park. It's a beautiful evening. Every day is stretching out that little bit longer and the sun is still making a respectable effort to warm us. We walk down to the wedding pavilion that we've chosen and the area is bathed in a golden glow. It's even better than I remembered. Jacob is suitably impressed.

'This is a fabulous setting.' He looks round him. 'You've picked a great place.'

'I want it to be casual and informal,' I tell him. 'There'll only be a few family and our friends.'

'Bridesmaids?' Jacob asks.

'The girls, of course. But I don't even want them to have matching dresses. Everyone can come as they are.'

'You want flowers, though?'

'Maybe. Nothing starchy. I don't want a prissy bouquet.' What could possibly compete with the abundance of flowers cascading around us? And in June it will be fabulous.

'You could have a simple, casual arrangement.'

'Sounds just right.'

'I'll take some inspiration from here.' Jacob studies the flowers around us, the colour of the rambling roses, the lavender that will soon be in bloom. He's making copious notes on his iPad.

'Then I thought we'd have a picnic here afterwards,' I tell him.

'What if it rains?'

'Everyone says that! It *won't* rain,' I assure him. 'Not on our wedding day.'

Jacob laughs. 'I love your optimism, Lucy, but I might just make a contingency plan. Caterers?'

'I'll leave it to you, Jacob. But something fun. And, preferably, inexpensive.'

'Involving chocolate?'

'But of course.'

He taps that in, too.

'Are you sure this is the place?' Crush asks.

'Absolutely sure.'

So when Yvette, the wedding organiser here arrives, we book the date – which, miraculously, is still free. That has to be an omen, right? When I watch her enter it into her diary it feels so positive that I could turn a cartwheel. Maybe two. We're on the calendar! The date is sealed! Ain't no stopping us now.

Jacob talks to Yvette about chairs and where the celebrant will stand and the form of our service, but I'm drifting on a cloud of happiness somewhere above it all. I'm finally marrying Aiden 'Crush' Holby and my little heart couldn't hold any more love for him.

When Jacob has done his bit, we all say goodbye to Yvette. Then I kiss Jacob and Crush shakes his hand and he heads for home, leaving Crush and me alone. We sit on the worn stone steps surrounded by tendrils of luscious ivy, sweet honeysuckle and blousy clematis. The sun is sinking in the sky and Crush holds my hand.

'It's a done deal,' he says. 'Nervous?'

'No. Not at all. You?'

'Not one bit.'

'This is heaven,' I say. 'I could happily sit here for ever.' I lean against Crush's chest. 'I can't wait to be your wife.'

Wife! Me, a wife!

'I love you,' Crush says. 'For better, for worse, for richer, for poorer, in sickness and in health.'

I think about what Chantal is going through and my heart goes out to her. Jacob is proving that he's just as much here for her in sickness as in health and I know that Aiden would be exactly the same. He is a good person. One of the best. It's true that you never know what's around the corner and I want to spend as much of my life with Crush as I can. 'I like the sound of that.'

We will love and cherish each other for ever. I know that nothing will come between us. And that includes Marcus Canning.

Chapter Twenty-Eight

Autumn lay in bed next to Miles, both of them drifting in and out of sleep, neither wanting to fully wake and face the day. She was meeting Willow for the second time later and already she was nervous and excited.

A moment later, Florence jumped on the foot of the bed, crawled up and plonked herself between them. 'I'm awake, Daddy,' she bellowed.

Autumn smiled to herself. For someone so delicate looking she could be quite a bruiser. Still, fair play to Flo – it probably was time that they all got up.

'Oh, no,' Miles said. 'Does that mean it's time for your first tickle of the day?' He pulled his daughter onto his chest, while she shrieked with happiness.

'I wish you were both coming with me today,' she said as she turned to Miles.

'Me too.' He put Flo down and settled her against his pillow. 'But you need time on your own with her.'

'I know. I hope she enjoys the exhibition.' Autumn had booked for them both to see Hollywood costumes at the V&A museum. It was the hot ticket. If conversation was difficult between them, then surely that would give them a lot to chat about.

'If it goes all right, maybe we could meet up for something to eat later. Ed's Diner might go down well. Or Bill's. Text and let me know. What time is her train home?'

'Not that late,' Autumn said. 'I wish she was staying over.'

'That'll be the next step,' Miles assured her. 'A little bit at a time.'

An hour later, Autumn was up, showered, dressed and ready to head out of the door. She was meeting Willow's train at Paddington mid-morning and didn't want to be late. There'd be nothing worse than leaving her daughter waiting for her. Autumn wanted her to know that, although she may have let her down once, she could be relied now. She'd never do anything to hurt Willow again.

Kissing Miles and Flo goodbye, she headed to the station. It was a good half hour before Willow's train was due to arrive, but that was fine. She grabbed herself a coffee and a chocolate croissant while she waited.

At the allotted time, Willow's train pulled in. Autumn's heart lifted when she saw her coming along the platform. Willow was dressed head to toe in black again, wearing a short black lace dress and black denim jacket with her Doc Martens. This time her hair wasn't straightened and her mop of curls mirrored Autumn's.

'Good to see you again,' Autumn said as she hugged her tiny, tense body. 'You look great.'

Willow studied the floor. 'Thanks. It's just something old.'

'Did you have a good journey?'

Shrugging, she mumbled, 'It was OK.'

Willow had retreated again and was shy, reluctant. But that was fine. At least she was here.

'It's the first time Mum has let me travel to London on my own.'

'Hopefully not the last,' Autumn said. 'We can head straight to the museum. We've got timed tickets, but I think it's going to be really busy. We'll grab something to drink before we go in and then have a bite to eat afterwards. Does that suit you?'

The girl nodded and they fell into step together. Autumn felt emotion well in her chest. This was her daughter and, beyond her wildest dreams, they were going for a day out together.

The exhibition was all Autumn could have hoped for. The range of costumes and memorabilia from Hollywood films old and new was quite staggering. There were costumes from the Indiana Jones films through to Marilyn Monroe's dress from *Some Like it Hot*, plus sumptuous period dresses from *Dangerous Liaisons* and *Elizabeth: The Golden Age* through to Morticia's gloriously gothic gowns from *The Addams Family*. Surely Willow would like those? It was a feast for the eyes. The slow-moving queue snaking through the halls meant they could take their time and look at everything.

Soon the awkwardness fell away and they were chatting more easily about the displays.

'Look,' Autumn said. 'There's the ruby slippers from *The Wizard of Oz*.' She bent down to point them out to Willow, who broke into a rare smile.

'Cool.'

'It was one of my favourite films as a child.'

'I like the old films,' Willow ventured. 'I was never into the whole Disney thing. Audrey Hepburn in *Breakfast at Tiffany's* is an icon.'

'Her dress is here too, I think,' Autumn said.

'Wow.' The smile was nearly a grin.

This had been a very good choice and Autumn thanked her lucky stars that she'd been able to get her hands on tickets.

'I wanted to be in the drama group at school,' Willow

admitted, as they moved along in line. 'But that's where all the It girls hang out. I don't belong. They spend their lives as if they're auditioning for *Glee*. It's nauseating.'

'I know what you mean,' Autumn said. 'I was never one of the cool girls either.' She wondered if Willow was bullied at school. Anyone who didn't fit the mould tended to be. 'But you have your own style and you're an individual.'

'I stand out like a sore thumb.'

'Don't let them thwart that. And don't let them mess with your dreams. You should follow what your heart wants to do.'

'I'd like to come to drama school in London,' she said. 'Or maybe do something with fashion. I hate the countryside. I don't fit there either, but Mum won't let me go.'

'It's a tough world,' Autumn said, 'and I'm sure that Mary's only worried about you.'

'I'm not a kid,' she said defiantly and Autumn smiled to herself. 'I know my own mind.'

'I wish I'd been half as feisty as you at fourteen.'

'Maybe you wouldn't have given me away then.' Willow's chin jutted.

Autumn took the jibe. 'There's no question about it. I was too weak to stand up to my parents and I can only apologise for that. The decision was taken out of my hands and I simply went along with it. I felt that I had no choice, but I should have fought harder for you and I've lived with that regret ever since.'

'It's OK.' Willow's lip quivered. 'Mary's been a great mum.'

'I never want to step into her place. I want to assure you of that,' Autumn said. 'But you're my flesh and blood and we've spent too many years apart. I hope that we can become good friends.'

'Yeah,' Willow said. 'We'll see how it goes.'

That's all she could ask and, for now, she'd hold onto that

crumb. Then the line moved forward and they inched past a plethora of costumes until they finally stood in front of Audrey Hepburn's iconic little black dress.

'That is one *sweet* dress,' Willow said in awe. They both gazed at it in admiration.

'You can be anything you want to be, you know,' Autumn said. 'You're bright and you're beautiful. Let the world see what you've got. You know that if I can do anything to help you, then I will.' Autumn grinned at her. 'I've got your back, kid.'

Willow smiled back and tears sprang to Autumn's eyes when she felt her daughter's arm hesitantly link through hers.

The day ended too soon. After the exhibition, the two of them went for a cream tea at the café in the V&A. They sat in the old part, beautiful with its stained-glass windows and dark wood panels, enjoying the hubbub. A pianist played in the corner while they chatted easily about what they'd seen in the exhibition. Here in London, with all its different fashions and cultures, no one turned a hair at Willow's appearance and she seemed a lot more relaxed than when she'd arrived. Despite all her bravado and fierce style, did she really just want to be like everyone else?

When it was time, Autumn took her back to Paddington station to catch her train. She felt tearful, and it was clear that Willow was feeling the same.

She hugged her daughter tightly. 'It's been a fantastic day. I hope you've enjoyed it as much as I have.'

'It was great.'

'You'll come again soon?'

'I will,' she said.

'Good.' She kissed her cheek and Willow didn't pull away. 'You'll have to hurry to catch your train.' They'd lingered too long over tea. 'I'll call you.'

'OK.' Her daughter left her and ran down the platform. The guard was blowing his whistle and she swung onto the train as the doors closed. Autumn stood and watched it pull away, taking her daughter with it and the hole opened up in her heart once more.

Chapter Twenty-Nine

Chantal was in her hospital gown. Once the lump had been discovered, it seemed that everything was moving at breakneck speed. Practically, that was a great thing. Emotionally, she felt all over the place. But at least she didn't have much time to dwell on it.

Today she was having isotopes injected, to check that the cancer was contained in the offending lump and that it hadn't spread to her lymph nodes. She didn't believe in God, but she'd never prayed so much in her life. She had to be well for Lana's sake.

Jacob was here holding her hand, but she wished that the girls could have been with her too. Nadia and Autumn were sharing the childcare duties between them and she'd handed Lana over at seven o'clock this morning, a bit grisly and out of sorts. Chantal had squeezed her within an inch of her life.

Chantal had been glad to hear that Autumn's first solo day out with Willow had gone well. She didn't even want to leave Lana while she was in hospital, so how difficult must it have been for Autumn to hand over her child for adoption? She couldn't even begin to imagine. Would there come a day when

Ted would want to take Lana back to America, maybe for holidays? She didn't think she could cope with that. Hopefully, it was a long way off. Even more hopefully, she'd still be here to experience that dilemma.

The girls had given her an amazing bouquet of flowers and there was a signed card for her, which she was now displaying on her bedside table. They'd all just texted her, too. They might not be here in the room with her, but there was no doubt that they were all rooting for her.

The consultant came in to see her. 'Hi, Chantal. Big day. Lots of procedures. We're going to be removing the lump for you and also checking the lymph nodes to make sure that the cancer hasn't spread to another site. All good?'

Chantal nodded, shakily. She was trying to be strong for Jacob and Lana's sake, but her insides felt like liquid.

'We're going to turn you into one of my Smurf ladies, I'm afraid.' Livia glanced at her notes. 'We're going to inject you with radioactive tracer and also a blue dye. They attach themselves to all the bad stuff to show us what we're dealing with. But it means that you'll wee blue and you'll poo blue. You may even turn a bit blue for a while.'

'I'll look forward to that,' Chantal said wryly. That, she was sure, was the least of her worries. As long as they got this cancer out of her then they could turn her whatever colour they liked.

'If I think any of the nodes look as if they have cancer cells, I'll remove those too and send them to the lab.'

Chantal blew out a wavering breath.

'We'll have a much better picture of what we're dealing with after today. Are you doing OK?'

'I'll be a lot better when this is over.'

'You will,' Livia assured her. 'I have no doubt about that. Ready to go?'

She nodded and Jacob hugged her tightly. 'I'll be right here waiting for you. I love you.'

'I love you, too,' she said. And she'd never meant it more.

Chantal struggled to open her eyes, which felt as if they had lead weights on them. Jacob was gently rubbing her arm and he smiled when he saw that she was awake.

'Hey, sleepyhead,' he said softly.

'Have I been out for long?'

'Quite a while. How are you feeling?'

'A bit bashed and bruised.'

'You look OK.' He stroked her hair. 'Your lips are a bit blue. I was worried for a while, but they said it was only the dye.'

'My mouth's dry.'

Jacob passed her a glass of water and she sipped gratefully at it.

'The girls are coming in soon,' he said. 'I'm going home soon to put Lana to bed. I just wanted to be here until you woke up again. Livia popped in afterwards and said that it had gone well. She'll be back in to see you again soon.'

'You look exhausted.' There were dark shadows round Jacob's eyes and his face looked grey with tiredness.

'I'm fine. Worried about you, that's all. I'm happier now you're back from theatre and awake again.'

'Me too.' Chantal let her head rest back against the pillow. She felt weary down to her bones. She let her eyes close again as they were heavy and it was an effort to keep them open. She didn't drift off to sleep, but was grateful that Jacob sat quietly next to the bed, hand covering hers, until Livia came in.

'How's the patient?' she asked brightly.

'Still here.' Chantal eased herself to sit up, feeling the ache across her chest and down her arm.

'Well, you'll be pleased to know that the surgery went well. I got a good, clean margin round the lump and that's what we always look for. I've taken three lymph nodes and sent them off to the lab for analysis. It'll be a day or two before the results come back and we can decide then what you need next in terms of treatment. We'll keep you in overnight but, all being well, you can go home tomorrow.'

Chantal wanted to weep with relief.

'That's good news,' Jacob said, squeezing her hand. 'Great news.'

'It is,' Livia agreed. 'I'll leave you to it now, but I'll be back to see you in the morning.'

'Thanks, Livia,' Chantal said.

'I wish they all went as well as this,' the consultant said.

Livia left and, a moment or two later, Nadia and Lucy arrived. They tiptoed into the room and whispered, 'Hello.'

'I'm awake,' Chantal murmured. 'Drowsy though.' Her eyes kept threatening to close again.

When he'd kissed them both on the cheek, Jacob said, 'I'm going to take this as my opportunity to go home and relieve Autumn from her babysitting duties. Is that OK?'

'Of course,' Nadia said. 'Lana's fine. She's been a little poppet all day.'

He turned to Chantal and caressed her cheek. 'I'll call you later, hun, and I'll be back in the morning.'

'Kiss my baby for me.' She could have wept for the want of a cuddle with Lana.

'Will do.'

'Anything you need, just phone me,' Lucy said to him. 'Whatever the time.'

'Thanks, Lucy.' And he left.

The girls both kissed her and Nadia asked, 'Are you pleased with how it went?'

164

'I'm not quite out of the woods yet, but it all sounds positive,' Chantal said. 'Livia's really pleased with how it's gone. Thank goodness.'

'We'll have you out of here and back at Chocolate Heaven in no time.'

'That sounds wonderful.'

'The Chocolate Lovers' Club needs you. You're not going anywhere on our watch, Chantal Hamilton. You just remember that.'

Then she cried with relief, with fear and gratitude, with having come through the first step and, most of all, for having the best of friends.

Chapter Thirty

'It is totally pants having a meeting of the Chocolate Lovers' Club without Chantal,' I declare. 'We should have a minute's silence for her before we eat our cakes.'

'She's not flipping dead, Lucy,' Nadia says with a tut. 'Stop being a drama queen.'

'But what if it had been worse? She's so lucky that she went to have that lump checked out and they found it early.'

'I know. It's too awful to think about. How can I possibly trot off to the Lake District while she's in the hospital?' Nadia asks forlornly. 'I'd feel terrible. I'll have to cancel.'

'No!' Autumn and I shout together, making her jump.

'You *have* to go,' I say. 'Chantal will be furious with you if you change your plans on her account.'

'You'd lose a lot of money, too,' Autumn reminds her. 'She wouldn't want that, either.'

'You needn't have paid me back so quickly,' I tell Nadia. 'It would have waited.'

'I know you're not flush with cash at the moment,' Nadia says.

'It's better since I've been here,' I admit. 'Autumn's right, though. Chantal would definitely be upset if you cancelled because of her. Besides, you and Lewis both need the break.' The cut on Nadia's lip was healing nicely now, but you could tell that she'd lost some of her nerve and was jittery.

'I suppose you're both right, but it doesn't feel proper going off to have fun while she's poorly.'

'I insist that you have *lots* of fun. We need some juicy gossip when you get back.' It would make a change for someone other than me to be the number one topic on the gossip list.

'That'll cheer her up. Promise me that you'll go and that you'll behave *really* badly while you're there.'

Nadia laughs. 'I'm not sure that's going to be possible when we've got three kids in tow.'

'Give it your best shot,' I beg. 'For the team.'

'You'll make sure Chantal's all right until I get back, won't you?' Nadia is clearly worried.

'As soon as we've eaten this very delicious chocolate cake in her honour, Autumn will be going to look after Lana so that Jacob can go to the hospital and I'll be taking over as soon as I've finished my shift here.' We have the rota down to a fine art.

We'd all been hoping that she'd come out today, but the consultant has said that she's to stay in for another night. 'Why do you think they're keeping her in?'

'They said it was a precautionary measure.'

I don't like the sound of that, but I don't voice my opinion. I do know that I'll be relieved to see her tonight.

Ms France is having a day off today, so I'm at the helm on my own. Bliss. Had I remembered that I wouldn't have dressed up quite so much this morning. As it is, I'm getting up half an hour earlier so that I can do my hair, put make-up on, iron things. It's all bloody hard work having a glamorous assistant.

I'd like to tell you that she's stopped rolling her eyes and making some sort of disdainful French guttural noise in her throat every time I ask her to do something, but she hasn't.

'I'd better eat my cake and get going,' Nadia says. 'The train is just after lunch. I'm collecting Lewis from school and going straight to the station.'

'Aren't you excited?' Autumn asks.

'I'm terrified,' she admits. 'This could make or break our relationship.'

'You shouldn't think of it like that,' I say. 'It's simply taking it to another level. And it's a week. If you find that you can't stand each other, you'll be back before you know it. Chantal will be out of hospital by then and everything will be back to how it was before.'

Nadia downs her coffee and has the last bite of her cake. 'I hope you're right on all counts.' She plants a peck on my cheek. 'I'd better get a wiggle on. I've still got a few things to pack.'

'Jeans and wellies, that's all you'll need, woman,' says me, style adviser. 'You're going to a farm in the middle of nowhere. Leave those killer heels at home.'

'I'm looking forward to walking on some of those hills we saw at Christmas.'

I shake my head knowingly. 'It must be love.'

'On that note, I'm off.' Nadia goes round to kiss Autumn goodbye. 'Wish me luck.'

'Text us when you get there to let us know you've arrived safely,' I tell her.

'I will. And keep me posted on how Chantal is doing.'

'I'd better be going, too,' Autumn says. 'Jacob will be wanting to be with her.'

'Give them both my love,' I say and then they both disappear, leaving me to clear up.

While I'm tidying the tables, Crush comes in. 'Hello, Gorgeous.'

'This is a nice surprise.'

'I'm on my way back to the office from a meeting and took a very slight detour.'

I put the tray of crockery down and give him a big hug. 'I'm glad you did. Have you time for a coffee?'

'Just a quickie.'

'We can't do that,' I joke. 'Look where it got us last time.'

Crush shudders. 'Don't remind me of that. Marcus isn't here today, is he?'

'No. I haven't seen him all week. Thank goodness. Now that the figures are picking up again, he seems happy enough to leave me alone.'

'You do seem in your element here. Glad you came back?'

'Yes. I love it. And Marcus really isn't a problem.'

Crush doesn't look convinced.

'Let me make you a cappuccino. And I've got some mini coffee and walnut cakes that you might like.'

'Sounds great.' He follows me to the counter. 'How's Chantal doing? Have you had an update?'

'They're keeping her in for another night, which I'm a bit worried about.'

'She's in the best place.'

'Yeah,' I agree. 'I keep trying to tell myself that. Stay positive and all.'

'You're going to see her tonight?'

'I can't wait.'

'I can come with you, if you like.'

I shake my head. 'Go straight home after work. Make sure that my dad isn't up to any mischief.'

Crush laughs.

'I won't stay long at the hospital. I just want to pop in for a few minutes.'

Crush stands and waits patiently while I serve a couple

169

of other customers before him, then I make his coffee.

'We should get one of these for the flat,' he says.

'No way. It's a beast. I'm glad to see the back of it when I leave. Plus, if we start making great coffee at home, we'll never get my father to leave.'

'He does seem quite comfortable.'

'He's *got* to go. He's driving me nuts. His stuff is everywhere. We can't get near the television remote. He leaves his dirty dishes in the sink. His laundry is all over the bathroom floor. No wonder Patty the Pilates instructor got fed up with him if he was like this. Do you think I should give him an ultimatum?'

'We should give him a few more weeks yet. Let's just start making strong hints.'

'You're being so patient.'

'It's one of my biggest virtues.'

I laugh at that, but it's true. 'We should be making wedding plans. The date is rushing towards us and I haven't done anything yet.'

'We're keeping it low-key, remember. And Jacob is on the case.'

'I'd be a lot happier if I'd found my dress. Or even started looking.' I'm thinking something a bit sticky-out and fifties style. Something that doesn't scream 'wedding gown'.

'It will all be fine,' Crush assures me. 'The sun will shine. We'll have a great day. And, most important of all, the groom will be there.'

And that's why I love him. Crush is calm, collected, chilled. Reliable. The perfect partner for me.

Chapter Thirty-One

Nadia looked out of the window with Lewis. It was a three-hour journey on a direct train from London to Penrith and she'd brought plenty for her son to do to entertain him. By the time they were beyond Manchester, he'd exhausted the delights of his sticker book and a dozen different games on her iPhone, plus he'd eaten most of the stash of chocolate she'd brought to bribe him with. She'd hoped that he might be able to have a little sleep, but he was far too excited. They hadn't been on holiday together by themselves before and Lewis had been buzzing for days. But, for the moment at least, he was content to snuggle into her and look at the passing scenery. She wrapped her arms around him and hoped that she was doing the best thing for Lewis as well as herself.

They were getting closer to their destination now and the train was whizzing through open countryside that was becoming increasingly green and rugged. As the size of the hills increased so did the number of butterflies in her stomach.

'Are we nearly there yet?' Lewis asked in time-honoured fashion.

'Yes. Not long now and you've been a good boy all the way.'

'Will Seth and Lily come to meet us?'

'I think so,' Nadia said. 'If not, they'll be back at the house. You'll see them shortly.'

'Will there be lambs yet?'

'Yes. James said that they've got quite a lot now.'

She'd hated leaving the girls behind. It had been a lot of fun when they'd spent Christmas up here together. Making the solo journey was much more nerve-wracking. She knew that one of them would have readily come with her if she'd asked, but that wasn't really the point. It was time to decide whether she and James could possibly make a future together and part of that was to see how feasible the journey up here was on a regular basis. The train tickets alone had cost an arm and a leg. How often would she be able to afford that expense?

Eventually, the train slowed into Penrith station and she pushed down the feelings of terror and concentrated on hauling their case onto the platform, fussing with Lewis as she did. When she stopped and looked up, James was standing there waiting. The smile on his face told her that he was as delighted to see her as she was to have finally arrived.

What she wanted to do was drop her case and run into his arms like they did in the movies. Instead, she stood there feeling embarrassed and inhibited, waiting until he came to her. When he did, he gave her a stilted and awkward welcoming hug, though she could feel the warmth behind it. Perhaps he just felt as unsure as she did.

'Hi,' he said. 'It's good to see you.'

'I'm glad we're here.' He was taller, more handsome than she remembered. He wore a Barbour jacket and a flat tweed cap. His face was rugged, lined, but kind. At forty-three, he was ten years older than her but didn't seem it. She liked that he was solid, reliable and had lived a bit.

'We saw *massive* mountains,' Lewis said, bouncing up and down. 'Everywhere!'

'It's one of our specialities,' James said. 'Fancy walking up one or two of them?'

Lewis was wide-eyed. 'Now?'

James laughed. 'Not right now. We've got to go home and see Seth and Lily. They're waiting for us. But you're here for a whole week.' His eyes caught Nadia's and he smiled softly. 'Perhaps we can do it tomorrow? How does that sound?'

'Cool. Can we, Mummy?'

'I came prepared,' she said. 'At least I think so. I brought jackets and sturdy shoes.' As Lucy had advised, she had eschewed her pretty dresses and shoes in favour of jeans and trainers. She was sure that she didn't own nearly enough waterproof clothing. If it rained in London, you simply did something indoors – one of the museums – but she wasn't sure if that was an option up here. If they wanted to go out, it could be in all weathers.

James smiled. 'You'll certainly need them in this neck of the woods.'

'I'm looking forward to it.' She wasn't generally an outdoors kind of person, but she found to her surprise that she was keen to give it a go.

'Ready to head home?' James picked up her case. 'The Land Rover's outside.'

They fell into step beside each other and he took her hand and squeezed it. 'Glad you made it.'

She suddenly felt shy with him. 'Me too.'

In the car park, he loaded their case into the Land Rover, which looked very spic and span; she wondered whether it had been spruced up especially for her arrival. There was a sheepdog sitting on the back seat and Lewis clambered in next to him. The dog tried to lick him to death.

'Sit down, Jep,' James said.

He helped Nadia to climb into the passenger seat. 'This looks suspiciously tidy,' she noted.

James grinned at her. 'The kids earned some extra pocket money yesterday. This is usually more used to being a taxi for sheep rather than people.'

'You and your country ways,' she teased.

'Had to make a good impression. I didn't want you getting the next train home.' James got into the driver's seat and gunned the vehicle into life. 'Not long now.'

He set off from the station and they were soon out in the country once again. Dusk was gathering and Nadia wanted a hot bath. Lewis, still excited, would soon be overtired and tetchy. They both needed something to eat and then to get him straight to bed so that he'd be fresh for tomorrow. After that, a glass or two of good red might be in order. It had been a tiring day.

It wasn't long before they got back to Keswick. It would be rush-hour in London, but the traffic here was light. Though, clearly, it wasn't yet the start of the main tourist season.

The farmhouse, when it came into view, was much as she'd remembered. It was an imposing building constructed from traditional Lakeland stone and nestled into the landscape. It wasn't as big as the cottage that James had rented out to them further down the lane, but it was still a substantial family house – certainly compared to her cramped London terrace.

They swept up the gravel drive past a large pond which she hadn't been able to see at Christmas as it had been covered with snow. The whole place looked so different. The hills that loomed behind the house were now less bleak and looked inviting. James parked up.

'That's Blease Fell and Blencathra,' he said as he got out of the Land Rover. 'This place is known as Fell Farm. It's stood here for quite a while now. It was my father's home before it was mine and it belonged to my grandfather before him.' Then he laughed. 'But I'm sure I must have bored you with all this before.'

'I don't find it boring at all. It must be nice to have such a heritage.'

'Yes, but it's a responsibility too. It's a mammoth effort to keep this place going, yet I wouldn't want to be the last of the Barnsworths to be at the farm. One day, I hope that Seth or Lily will take over from me. But kids these days, they want the bright lights. I couldn't hold either of them here if they don't want to stay. Thankfully, for now . . . ' James crossed his fingers, ' . . . they both seem to love the mountains and the farming life as much as I do.'

They walked to the house and he swung open the heavy door. They entered straight into the kitchen and a blanket of warm air enveloped her. Clearly something wonderful was cooking in the oven.

'I hope you're hungry.'

Her stomach rumbled. 'I am now.'

'Penny's got supper on for us. Chicken stew with a posh name.'

'Penny?'

'A woman from the next village who helps me out,' James said. 'She was away with family in Cornwall over Christmas.'

'Oh. You haven't mentioned her before.'

'I haven't? She's a treasure.'

Wasn't it a bit strange that he'd never said anything about this lady?

'I don't want you lifting a finger while you're here. This is your holiday. So she'll still pop in every day. She collects the kids for me from school and, more often than not, gives them their tea. Then she puts something in the oven so that it's ready when I get home. I don't know what I'd do without her.'

Hmm. Truly indispensable. She wondered how long Penny had been on the scene and what else James hadn't told her.

'She'd normally be here still, but she had to rush off for something tonight. You'll see her tomorrow.' He took off his cap and hung it up. His hair stood up in untidy tufts and he ruffled it with one hand, making it worse. 'Come in. Take your coats off. Make yourselves at home. *Mi casa es tu casa.*'

There were a few steps down into the main kitchen area, which was fitted out with hand-crafted oak cupboards. A dark blue range took precedence on one wall. Centre stage there was a large kitchen table, filled with the detritus of a busy and untidy family. There was a sturdy log burner kicking out heat in the fireplace. It was so cosy and welcoming.

'Kids!' he shouted out. 'Our guests are here.' A second later they both barrelled into the kitchen cheering. 'Whoa,' James said. 'Calm down. Calm down.'

'Daddy, can we show Lewis the lambs?'

'Dinner's ready now,' he said. 'But you can go out afterwards for half an hour, if you're good. I want you in bed early though as tomorrow we have an action-packed day planned. We want to show Nadia and Lewis our lovely lakes, don't we?'

They both nodded, earnestly.

'We have our own pet lambs,' Lily said proudly. 'Daddy said that you can have one, too.'

Lewis's eyes widened. 'Can I?'

'Let's talk about that in the morning,' Nadia said.

'Aw! Mummy!'

'It teaches them about the farm,' James said. 'You have to do everything for them, right? No slacking.'

Lily and Seth nodded again.

'If you pick out a lamb, you couldn't take her back to London,' James said to Lewis. 'She'd belong here. But Seth and Lily would look after her and she'd be here whenever you came back.'

'I'd like that,' Lewis said. 'I haven't got a pet.'

'OK then.' Nadia held up her hands in surrender. 'Looks as if I'm outnumbered.'

James turned to Nadia and grinned. Her insides melted. 'We're going to have a great time,' he said. 'I can tell.'

Chapter Thirty-Two

I'm weary when I climb the stairs to the flat after a long day at Chocolate Heaven. I think we've had more customers through the café today than ever before, which means more money has gone into Marcus's coffers. Perhaps I should have negotiated a bonus along with my salary.

I popped into the hospital briefly and Chantal seems to be doing fine. She's weary and a bit teary, but who wouldn't be? Now my feet are aching like mad and all I want is a glass of wine, a nice hot bath and some chocolate-based treats. I've been so busy today that my chocolate consumption has fallen to dangerously low levels. However, I'm about to remedy that.

For once I'm hoping that there's wall-to-wall football on the television so I can leave Crush and my dad to their own devices and wallow in the bath until I'm in a vegetative state.

When I reach the top of the stairs Crush, unusually, is waiting for me. 'Hey, Gorgeous. How's Chantal?'

'She's doing OK. She still looks a bit battered and bruised, but they're letting her go home in the morning.'

'That's good news. She must be relieved. Nothing like your own bed to make you feel better.'

Never a truer word spoken.

He strokes my cheek. 'You look tired. Busy day?'

'The busiest. I'm knackered.'

Raising an eyebrow, he flicks his head back towards the living room behind him. He lowers his voice when he says, 'We have another visitor.'

'We do?'

'Your mother's here.'

I should be delighted to see her, but instead my heart sinks. My mother is never the easiest of people. 'She is?'

'Arrived about an hour ago.'

I can't help the groan that escapes my lips. 'Really?' I peel off my coat and Crush takes it from me. I wonder what she's come here for. Maybe my father has done something heinous – again – and she's come to have it out with him in person. 'I hope there's not going to be a fight. I've no energy for that.'

'Actually, they seem to be getting along *rather* well,' Crush says.

'It won't last,' I assure him. 'Give her another hour and she'll remember how annoying Dad can be. Then we'll have to put up with them trying to out-bicker each other.'

He hugs me. 'Thought I'd better come out and warn you.'

'Thanks. I love you. One day we *will* get our flat back for ourselves.'

Heavy of heart, I follow him into the living room. It's not that I don't want to see my dear mother, but I'd like to do it on my own terms sometimes. Also I'm way too tired to go through the usual knockabout routine of my parents' relationship.

My mum and dad are sitting together on the sofa watching *The One Show*. Mum has her feet curled underneath her and she's leaning against Dad's shoulder. To the untrained it could almost look as if they're sort of snuggling. But I know better.

179

'Darling.' Mum jumps up and bears down on me instantly.

'Hi, Mum.' I allow myself to be smothered with kisses.

She strokes my hair. 'You look tired, poppet. Working too hard?'

'Yes, yes. I'm back at Chocolate Heaven. Busy but I'm loving it.'

'And Aiden tells me that you've booked the wedding date.'

'We have. Only just.'

'That's lovely. I'll have to check my diary,' she says pointedly.

Ah, yes. Didn't actually consult the parents to see if they were around before we organised it. My bad.

'What brings you here?' I ask. 'You didn't mention you were planning on dropping in.' I gain a bit of ground back there, I think.

'Daddy and I have some things to talk about.' Alarmingly, she bats her eyelashes in my father's direction.

I recoil. He doesn't. Worrying.

'What shall we do for dinner?' Crush chips in. 'There's not much in the cupboards. I can nip out to the Tesco Express, if you like. What do you fancy?'

'I don't want you to go to any trouble on my behalf,' Mum says. 'Is that nice Chinese restaurant still down the road? Shall we go there? My treat.'

All I want to do is lie flat on the floor and sleep, but we'll have to entertain my mother somehow – she's not a staying-in-with-feet-up kind of person – so it might as well be with some steamed pork dumplings.

'Chinese it is then,' I say. 'When are you going home?'

'Lucy!' my dad says. 'Your mother's only just got here.'

'I know, but I'm concerned about where we're all going to sleep. There's one bed. One sofa.'

My mother giggles like a little girl. It's not attractive. 'I'm sure we'll manage.'

Not for the first time since my dad arrived, I consider booking into a hotel. Though I'm now legitimately allowed in Chocolate Heaven, I'm not even thinking about going back there. Besides, Crush would never agree. Once bitten, twice shy and all that.

'Have I got time for a shower?'

Crush nods. 'Let me make you a strong coffee to perk you up.'

'I'll be ten minutes,' I say to my parents.

'Excellent.' My mother clasps her hands together. 'Martin Sheen is on in a minute and I don't want to miss him.'

Even my television is not my own anymore.

I grab some fresh clothes, go through to the bathroom and turn the shower to hot while I strip off. A few seconds later, Crush comes in with my coffee.

'Are you sure you want to go out?'

'No,' I say. 'Let them go by themselves. We'll stay here and have sex standing up in the shower.'

'Much as that sounds like an excellent plan, I do feel we have to make an effort. I feel bad that we hadn't told them about the wedding arrangements. We should have.'

'I was getting round to it,' I say. 'I just had other things on my mind.'

'I'll keep them happy until you're ready. There's a cheap bottle of white in the fridge. Unless you want me to stay and wash your back?'

I press my naked body against him. 'I can think of nothing nicer.'

'We'll never get out of the house if you do that, you naughty lady.'

I sigh. 'Ten minutes then.'

Crush winks at me and leaves. I stand in the shower and let the water do its thing.

*　　*　　*

181

'Will you have your usual, darling?' Mum says to Dad. My father looks blank. He's not even sure what his usual is.

'I'll have whatever you're having,' he manages rather gallantly.

'I'm having steamed vegetables and a side of seaweed.'

'Oh,' Dad says. 'Make that sticky spare ribs, sweet and sour chicken and special fried rice for me then.'

Mum giggles. Does she think he's joking? Or is she simply determined to find every single thing that he says witty and amusing?

Despite my nice, hot shower, I'm still tired and increasingly irritable. We all order.

I bite the bullet. 'We've booked Golders Hill Park for our wedding venue.'

'Lovely,' Mum says. She barely takes her eyes off Dad.

'We thought we'd make it informal. Very informal. Bordering on casual.'

'Nice.'

I turn to Crush and he shrugs. It seems as if we are slightly superfluous to the proceedings. The food comes and Crush and I eat ours largely in silence while my parents – mainly my mother – go on some romantic trip down memory lane.

It's all 'remember when we did this, darling?' 'Remember when we did that?' Quite a lot of it my dad doesn't really seem to remember at all. I think sometimes my mum confuses him with other husbands she's had. But, nevertheless, he's playing along gamely.

After what feels like the longest meal in the history of long meals, we leave. My mum might remember all the fun they were having together twenty or thirty years ago, but she clearly doesn't remember her earlier promise to treat us to the Chinese. Crush pays the bill.

We walk along Camden High Street back to the flat. It's a beautiful balmy night – if you ignore the drunks sleeping off their binges in doorways – but that's doing nothing to soothe my soul. My mother is high on wine and something else. They're behind us giggling together and holding hands. I try to hurry up our leisurely stroll. They're like teenagers. Teenagers with no respect for their elders.

When we get back home, the fact that we've not addressed the sleeping arrangements cannot be ignored.

'So,' I say. 'What's the deal?' Best not to beat about the bush. 'There's one bed. One sofa. I haven't even got a spare duvet.'

Mum goes coy. 'Oh, I'm sure we'll manage somehow.' She flutters her eyelashes at Dad for the millionth time. 'Won't we, Cuddlebunny?'

Cuddlebunny? I think I'm going to be sick. And I can't even blame it on the chicken with black bean sauce.

She sidles up close to him.

My dad looks like the cat who's got the cream.

I can't cope with this. 'Right,' I say. 'We'll leave you to it.' Crush and I beat a hasty retreat.

With cursory ablutions, we're in bed within a few minutes. I can still hear the low murmur of my parents talking in hushed tones. Then I hear embarrassed giggling and the sofa springs start to creak.

'Oh, no.' I put my hands over my ears. 'Please tell me that's not my parents *shagging* on my sofa.'

Crush doesn't even try to hide his laughter. 'I think it might be.'

'That's horrible,' I say. 'No daughter should have to hear that.' I stick my fingers in my ears, but I can still hear it. 'Make them stop.'

'Perhaps they won't be long.'

'Aaaaargh. I can't listen to that. Put a pillow over my face and press it tightly.'

'I have a feeling that might end badly, Gorgeous.'

The creaking and giggling increase in volume. I feel like whimpering. I'm going to be traumatised for ever by this.

'We should encourage your mum and dad to get along,' Crush says.

'I don't think they actually need any encouragement,' I point out. Another bit of moaning and groaning. And not about there being nothing on the telly, the football results or the useless government that my dad usually moans and groans about. These are my parents' sex noises. Aaaaargh! 'Haven't we got any earplugs? I can't handle this.'

'Maybe if they get it together again, they'll go home to your mum's house.'

I gasp. 'Oh, that's a cunning plan, Mr Aiden Holby.'

'I have another one,' he says. 'Come with me.'

Chapter Thirty-Three

Crush grabs the throw from the bed and leads me to the window. He opens it and climbs out onto the ledge.

'Are we going to jump?'

'I hadn't planned on it,' he says. 'Come on, Gorgeous. Trust me.'

He takes my hand and I climb up after him. Below us is the flat roof of the hairdressing salon.

'I've been having a sneaky look out here over the last few weeks,' Crush says. 'I thought if we were going to stay living in the flat, perhaps we could put a door in where the window is and turn this into a roof terrace.'

He makes the short jump, then he holds out his arms and lifts me down too. It's not very inspiring at the moment: a bit of patchy roofing felt, some broken tiles and a moderately interesting view across the roofs of Camden, but I see what he means – with some money and effort thrown in, it could be great.

'It wouldn't be that hard,' he continues. 'It needs a good tidy, but we could put a bit of trellis up, add a few pots, some cheap and cheerful garden furniture and Bob's your uncle.'

'He's not going to move in with us too, is he?'

Crush laughs. 'A roof terrace is a nice idea, but maybe moving somewhere with more bedrooms would be more practical for when your relatives descend on us unannounced.'

Then he wraps the throw round our shoulders and we sit down with our backs to the wall, sheltered from the breeze. The moon is high in the sky, the clouds scudding across it. Huddling together for warmth, we gaze out over the rooftops and even the usual background hum of traffic fades away. I'm wishing we'd thought to bring a bottle of wine out with us – but that would have meant accessing the kitchen, which is currently a no-go zone as it means traversing the flesh-pot of my living room.

Flicking my head back towards the flat, I say, 'This has shown me that this isn't entirely my home. Mum owns it. She could sell it tomorrow or, God forbid, move in. I seem to have no say in the matter. If we can, I would rather get our own place.'

'It'll be tough if we want to stay in London. We're both on half-decent salaries yet we'd struggle to afford a cupboard.'

I cosy up to him some more. 'But it would be *our* cupboard.'

He laughs. 'Your glass is always half full.'

'There's a flat above Chocolate Heaven. Ms France is living there at the moment, but she's not going to be around for ever if I know Marcus.' Which I do only too well. 'Perhaps I could persuade him to rent it to us while we save up for a deposit.'

'You know how I feel about Marcus. I don't want our lives mixed up in his. It's bad enough that you work for him.'

'It's fine,' I say. 'He's happy that the business is back on track and he doesn't have to worry about it. He's being quite sweet.'

'That's when he's at his most dangerous.'

'You're right.' I sigh. 'As always.'

'I only have your best interests at heart.'

I rest my head on his shoulder. 'I'm really glad that I'm marrying you. You're so sensible.'

Crush chuckles softly. 'I hope I have more qualities than that.'

'I would regale you with them all,' I say, stifling a yawn. 'But it's a long list and I'm getting very sleepy and we both have to be up early in the morning. Do you think my parents might have . . . um . . . *finished* by now?'

'Want me to check whether the coast is clear?'

I nod.

Crush lifts himself back through the window. A few seconds later, he pops his head out again. 'All quiet on the Western Front.'

Thank heavens for that. Now all we'll have to contend with is the snoring.

'Give me your hands and I'll pull you up,' Crush says. 'Step on that little pile of bricks.'

With less elegance than I'd like, I also clamber through the window and back into our bedroom. Then I creep down the hall to the living room and, as all is still quiet, I risk a peep at my parents.

They're snuggled up together, a tangle of arms and legs on the sofa. There are contented smiles on their faces and – despite the noisy bit – it warms my heart to see them happy.

I wish they could be in love like this all the time. They seem to be unable to live together, yet life apart doesn't seem that great either. If only they could find contentment with each other as they grow older. My dad can be really annoying and my mum's so high-maintenance, but there's clearly something that pulls them back together. If only they could nurture that. They might drive me to distraction, but I love them so much and do worry about them. I don't want either of them to be alone. Doesn't everyone want a companion in life, even if it's one who leaves the loo seat up or spends too much in Debenhams?

Leaving them in peace, I go back to the bedroom. Crush is already under the duvet and I cuddle into his side.

'Let's be in love for ever,' I whisper.

'OK,' he murmurs back. 'I'm up for that.'

I want a strong abiding love that grows as we do. I don't want drama, distrust and broken dreams. I want slow, steady, settled. I want to build a family that sticks together through thick and thin. I want to be with Crush in the sunset of our lives when we've got bent backs and fingers that can't open jam jars, but maybe would still be passionate enough, every now and then, to have noisy sex on the sofa. But only when the kids are out.

He puts his arm round me and I feel loved and protected. I rest my head on his heart and, feeling its strong, steady beat, I fall asleep.

Chapter Thirty-Four

Autumn stood outside her parents' house. It was big, imposing and had never felt like her home. Now she could hardly remember when she'd last been to visit them here; you could certainly never just drop in. If she wanted to see her mother and father, she had to make an appointment. They both had very busy schedules.

When she rang the bell, her father opened the door. Until recently they'd had a number of staff running their home – a housekeeper who had been with them for many years, a cook and a cleaner. They were from old money and expected to be looked after. Since the housekeeper had retired, they managed with one Romanian lady who came in each day to clean and leave them a prepared dinner. She supposed it was their way of becoming more modern.

'Autumn,' her father said by way of greeting. No hug. No kiss. 'We're just finishing supper. Come through.'

They were sitting at a table in the kitchen opposite each other, a plate of cold meats and cheese between them.

'Hello, darling.' Her mother, fork in hand, looked up from the pile of legal papers that were next to her plate. 'Have you eaten?'

'Yes,' she said.

'Wine?'

'That would be nice.'

Her father poured her a glass and she took off her coat, hung it on the back of one of the spare seats and then sat down. In any other family, this would be a nice, cosy scene, Autumn thought.

'What are you doing with your days?' her father asked.

Which was the same as asking if she'd found a job yet. She hated the fact that at her stage in life she was still entirely dependent on her parents. They paid for her flat, a not ungenerous allowance went into her bank account every month and yet the one thing that she wanted from them was never on offer. Their time and their love was doled out piecemeal, as it always had been.

'I'm considering my options.' It sounded as if she was dodging the question, but she wasn't. She literally had no idea which direction her life should take. She wanted to settle down with Miles, have another baby – one who would stay in her care. But, beyond that, she just wasn't entirely sure what the future held.

'You wanted to see us about something?' her mother asked.

It showed the state of their relationship that she couldn't simply drop in without reason. They knew so little about her life. She hadn't even told them about Miles or Flo.

'Yes.' She tucked her hair behind her ear. 'I have something to tell you.'

Perhaps it was the tone of her voice, but they did both have the grace to pay attention. Autumn took a strengthening swig of her wine before she said, 'I've found Willow.'

There was no recognition on either of their faces.

'My daughter,' she added.

Even then, it took a moment to register with them both. Her mother flushed scarlet.

'She's a beautiful young woman now,' Autumn continued.

Her mother took off her glasses and laid them on the table. Autumn noticed her hand was shaking. 'Oh, my.'

'She's fourteen now.' Her mouth was drying. 'The same age as when I had her.'

'Autumn,' her mother said. 'I can understand you wanting to see her. But are you sure this is the right thing to do? This could cause an awful lot of upset. It's all in the past now.'

She turned on her mother and spoke crisply. 'Do you really think that? How can you possibly imagine that it's in the past for me? Not a day has gone by that I haven't thought about her and wondered where she was. I have regretted my decision every single hour of my life.'

'Well,' her mother said, tightly. 'What else could we have done? We did what was best. You were in a terrible state.'

'I was a *child*. I needed your support.'

'You needed us to protect you. We had to sort out the mess you'd made. Daddy and I couldn't have looked after a baby for you.' She looked at her husband for his approval and he nodded in agreement.

'Your mother's right. We have very busy careers.'

'You could have thrown money at it, like you always do. I could have left school, had home tutors, had a nanny to help me. There were a dozen different scenarios that could have worked if the will had been there.'

'I don't think so, Autumn,' her father said. 'It was the *only* solution.'

'It was the quickest and easiest for you. My wishes weren't even considered. You wanted my baby swept under the carpet and that's exactly what happened.'

Her mother's eyes narrowed. 'I don't know how you can say that. You knew nothing of life, Autumn. Otherwise you wouldn't have found yourself in that situation. You barely knew the boy. From what I recall, he was a casual labourer at the school.'

'He was a gardener.'

Her mother pursed her lips. 'Could he have looked after you? What future was there in it?'

'We'll never know, will we?'

'You jumped into bed with the first person who asked. That's no way to behave.'

'All I wanted was some affection, some love.'

'Well,' her mother folded her arms. 'You certainly got more than you bargained for then.' She snorted. '*Affection.*'

'You had no idea how lonely I was. I loathed every minute I was at that school.'

'It's the finest school that money can buy,' her father said.

'And look what good it did me and Richard.' Tears burned behind her eyes. 'You packed us both off to school as soon as you possibly could, without a backward glance. You couldn't even bear to look after your own children, let alone my baby. We were never anything other than an inconvenience to you.'

Both of her parents had blanched.

'You know that isn't true,' her mother insisted. 'We did our best.'

'It wasn't good enough,' Autumn said. 'Richard and I were everything to each other because we had no one else. You were never there for either of us. Even when we came home for the school holidays you hardly saw us. There was always something else you had to attend to.'

'You had excellent care.'

'We had a string of nannies. Some better than others. Even if you took us abroad, you'd be socialising with your friends while we were left to entertain ourselves.' Now that she'd started, she felt as if a dam had burst inside her. All the hurt of her childhood years came pouring out. Things that she'd never said to her parents before were rushing to the tip of her tongue. 'We were desperately unhappy children and both of us struggled for years. Richard never did find what he was looking for.'

'Your brother is an entirely different matter,' her father said. 'He was very troubled.'

'And you left him to sort it out all by himself. He *needed* you. I did all I could, but he needed you, too. You're his parents. Yet you were never there for him.'

'I beg to differ,' her father said. 'We bought him a place to live – a very nice one. Paid for his rehab. Time and time again.'

'But did you ever sit and talk to him? Did you ever want to know what he felt like inside? Did you spend an evening with him where you didn't lecture him about being a waste of space?' Her blood was boiling. Even talking about Richard still caused her so much pain. 'You've never even grieved for him. You don't even mention him. It's as if he never existed. I don't even know if you remember that you had a son.'

'I'm sorry you feel like that.' Her father was grim faced.

'We gave you *everything*,' her mother said, a note of sadness in her voice.

'Not the things we needed.' She fixed her eyes on her mother. 'All I ever wanted was for you to love me, and it seemed as if that was just too much to ask of you. All you ever cared about was money and status.'

Her parents sat there looking stunned. It wasn't surprising, as she'd never spoken to them like that before. She'd always been the good daughter, kowtowing to their wishes. Not anymore. As soon as she could, she'd get a job, stand on her own two feet and would cut them out of her lives. They were toxic and she wanted nothing more to do with them. She felt that a weight had lifted from her chest.

Autumn stood up and shrugged on her coat. 'I just thought you'd want to know that my daughter is back in my life and I couldn't be happier. There's been a terrible hole in my heart since the day you took her from me. I want to prove to her that she is and has always been the most precious person.'

Neither her mother nor father responded. They were top barristers, paid hundreds of pounds an hour to argue in courts, yet they didn't have anything to say to her. They simply sat ghostly white and open-mouthed.

'I thought you might want to meet Willow, your grand-daughter. I see that was pie in the sky.' She snatched up her handbag. 'Well, I'm going to do all that I can to make up for abandoning her. I'm going to try to claw back those lost years by having her in my life. She's beautiful, clever and feisty. It's you who'll be missing out, not her.'

With that she left them wide-eyed and gaping and slammed the front door behind her.

Chapter Thirty-Five

Chantal thought that the first meeting after Ted and Stacey returned from the States would be slightly awkward and she wasn't yet being proved wrong. The atmosphere was tense. Stacey could barely meet her eye and both of the girls, as if feeding off the mood, were fractious.

Ted had a squalling Lana on his lap and, though he was jigging her as if his life depended on it, she wouldn't be consoled.

'Here,' Chantal said. 'Let me have a go.' She lifted Lana from him and settled her on her hip. Vaguely, she remembered that the hospital had told her not to lift heavy weights after having the lump removed, but how could a mother with a hyper-active toddler not do that? 'Shush, shush, shush,' she soothed as she swayed from side to side.

It was only a few days since she'd come out of hospital and she was still tired and tetchy herself. If she didn't stay a little bit cross, she started to cry. But it had been a relief when Livia had said she could come home.

'Do you think she doesn't recognise me?' Ted asked sadly.

'I don't know. It may take her a while to get used to you again. She's going through a bit of a clingy phase.' It hadn't helped that Lana had been passed around her chocolate-loving aunties for babysitting duties while she was attending various hospital appointments. Since she'd been home, Lana had been more clingy than usual. Also, it had been several weeks since she'd seen Ted other than on Skype – how good was a baby's memory? Would it be easy for Lana to forget that Ted was her father when she was rarely with him in person?

'It's been harder to set up this project than I imagined,' Ted said. 'Once it's up and running I can come back to London more.'

When he'd moved to New York he'd promised that he would be back regularly, but that hadn't happened. Of course it hadn't. He was heading up a big team and the project was on a tight deadline. Chantal could imagine only too well the stresses and strains. Throughout their marriage it had always been the same. It was a huge job that he'd taken on and he was earning a mega-salary. You couldn't just take a few days off and hop on a plane at that level.

Chantal wondered how Stacey and Elsie had fared in New York. They probably saw precious little of him. While she soothed Lana, she cast a sideways glance at her husband's new love. She looked tired and she'd lost weight. They might not be as close anymore, but she still felt for Stacey.

Picking up Lana's favourite doggy, Bill, Chantal handed it to her and, as Lana clutched him to her, the tears gradually subsided. If only Jacob were here to support her but, at the time, she'd thought it was better to meet Ted and Stacey alone.

'I'll try to put her down for a nap. I think she's overtired.' She'd kept Lana awake waiting for Ted to arrive. It had been a mistake. Their plane had landed late and then they'd gone to the hotel first to check in and freshen up. Now Lana was heavy-eyed and crotchety.

'You could put the kettle on, if you don't mind.'

Taking Lana upstairs, she settled her in the cot. Chantal kissed her daughter's pink cheek, closed the curtains and checked that the baby monitor was switched on. Then she went back down to face Ted and Stacey once more. Was it going to be more difficult than she'd thought to maintain a relationship with him across the miles? Already they felt like strangers, and he'd only been gone a few months.

Ted was taking a call in the kitchen, shouting tetchily into his phone. She swerved into the living room, where Stacey was setting out cups on the coffee table.

'Sounds a bit fraught out there.' Chantal nodded towards the kitchen.

'It's a very demanding job,' Stacey said. 'I don't think either of us had realised how much.'

Chantal was sure Ted would have been under no illusions. Stacey poured the tea and handed Chantal a cup.

'Thanks, Stacey.'

She stood up and looked squarely at Chantal. 'I do miss this,' she admitted softly.

'Me too,' Chantal agreed. But how would they breach the gulf between them with a bit of social chit-chat? It would take a lot of time and that was the one thing they didn't now have.

Ted came back, as red in the face as Lana had been. Chantal smiled to herself. Like father like daughter. Neither of them dealt well with not getting their own way. They all sat down together and Stacey gave Ted some tea. An awkward silence ensued while they sat and fiddled with their cups.

'I was really sorry to hear about your illness,' Ted said, eventually.

No one ever willingly used the word cancer.

'I'm dealing with it,' Chantal said. 'The girls are being brilliant. So is Jacob.'

'I'm glad you've got good support.'

'The best.' She couldn't look at Stacey. They had readily embraced her into the fold of the Chocolate Lovers' Club and, in return, she hadn't been a good friend at all. Would that splinter of hurt ever be extracted?

'How's the treatment going?'

'I've got another appointment with the consultant later today. She's got the results back from the lab. I'll know more then.'

'If I can do anything . . . ' Ted's voice tailed away.

'We have lots of papers to sign,' Chantal said. 'Can you spare a couple of hours to see the solicitor together?'

'I'll make time,' he said determinedly.

'Good. I'll give him a call. Maybe tomorrow?'

He nodded.

Chantal folded her arms. 'This bit is difficult.' It would be easier if she and Ted were alone.

Perhaps sensing it, Stacey said, 'I have to feed Elsie. Should I go into the kitchen so you two can talk in peace?'

'That would be great,' Chantal said. 'It won't take long.'

She took Elsie and left the room, leaving Chantal and Ted together.

'She's a good woman,' he said.

'I'm pleased for you,' Chantal said honestly. 'I hope you look after her.'

'I do my best.' He sighed. 'But it's never quite enough. I'm trying to work on it.'

'Spend more time with them than you do in the office. That's always a good place to start.'

'And the one I struggle with the most.'

'No one said that raising a family was ever easy.'

'No one told me it would be this hard, either.'

They both laughed, but it had a hollow ring.

Then Chantal said, 'I'm sorry that you're missing Lana growing up.'

'It's difficult,' he agreed. 'I admit that I didn't consider *how* difficult. We won't be in New York for ever. I have a two-year contract and I can see us coming back after that. Hopefully, I can be involved more fully in her life then.'

'She's a good girl. Apart from her little tantrum just now. She's really no trouble.'

'I'm jealous of Jacob,' Ted admitted. 'He's just stepped into my shoes. He's having the life I should be living.'

'It didn't work for us, Ted. We did try. And Jacob's doing a great job,' Chantal said softly. 'Be grateful that we have someone who adores our little girl as much as we do.'

'I know. In theory it's easy, but I still can't help but feel sidelined.' He held up his hands. 'Still, that's my problem. I'll deal with it. So what did you want to talk about?'

'I know that I wasn't in a rush, but this cancer has made me feel differently. I'd like to finalise the divorce as soon as possible. If anything happens to me, then we should have everything cut and dried. It's for the best.'

Ted looked shocked. 'But you're going to be OK?'

'I sincerely hope so, Ted, but you never know. A few weeks ago I thought this was nothing more than a pulled muscle. We should press on and get all our paperwork sorted. You should be free to marry Stacey and vice versa.'

'Is this what it's about? Are you and Jacob planning to get married?'

'He has asked me, but I don't want to do anything until my treatment is finished and I've got the all-clear. Something like this does make you reassess your thinking.'

'I want to help,' Ted said. 'What can I do?'

'Let's get this divorce done and dusted.'

Her husband looked sad. 'If that's what you really want?'

'It is.'

'We could just let things ride until you're better.'

Ted has always shied away from emotional confrontations and though this was only the paperwork part of separating, it was tough and Chantal was feeling the strain too. 'I think we're past that point.'

'It seems so hard, so final.'

'It's for the best though.'

'I still love you,' Ted said. 'In my own inadequate way. I probably always will.'

'I love you too and I hope we'll always be friends. We should make that work towards giving our daughter a happy and stable future.'

They stood up and hugged each other tightly.

'This is shit,' Ted said. 'All of it.'

'I know,' she soothed. 'I know.'

This was life. You made the mistakes, you took the knocks, you carried on, you got stronger. Giving up, rolling over, dying – that wasn't an option.

Chapter Thirty-Six

Nadia was having a fantastic time in the Lake District and wondered why in all her years she hadn't discovered this beautiful area sooner. Lewis was in his element. The furthest he went at home was to the local run-down park where he had to watch out for broken glass, used condoms and discarded needles. Here there were miles and miles of unspoilt countryside to run wild in. They'd both discovered they had a penchant for fell walking.

James was up and out early to tend to the farm, but he was back by the time they were all having breakfast. Lewis had been eager to help and had enjoyed being involved with the animals. As promised, James had allotted a tiny lamb to Lewis. It was only a few weeks old and was currently being bottle fed. There was no doubt that it was a sweet little thing and Lewis fell in love instantly.

The sheep were Herdwicks, or Herdies as they were usually known; James told her they were a strong breed, well-suited for living high on the fells in all weathers. For something so tough they were surprisingly cute. They had stocky white legs, brown curly coats and smiley faces. Lewis called his little Herdie

Wellyboot and he cuddled the lamb's wriggling body to his chest and gazed at it adoringly. Despite setting out the terms and conditions as only a parent could, Nadia knew it would be hard for Lewis to leave it behind when they had to go home again.

After the chores were finished, James had shown them round another part of the local area every day. Some of the sights she'd seen had been stunning. They'd walked round Buttermere and had stopped for delicious ice-cream in a farmyard at the end. Lewis had been in heaven, sharing his cone with the enthusiastic collie dog who was clearly a resident.

The next day they'd climbed up Haystacks, taking it slowly for the children – and her. Lunch had been an alfresco picnic they'd carried in rucksacks. They'd eaten it sitting beside a tarn that was as smooth as a looking glass. The view at the top down the valley to Derwentwater was stunning. She'd never done anything like that before and it felt like a great achievement. For the first time, she knew what it was like to have fresh air in her lungs and there was a colour to Lewis's cheeks that was sadly missing in London.

They'd made the short, sharp climb up Catbells, James tempering his pace to match hers, as Nadia discovered muscles she never knew that she had. If he'd kicked out with his long, determined stride, she'd never have been able to keep up. To compensate for all the exercise, they'd also eaten the best cake ever at a trendy café by the river Brathay at Skelwith Bridge. Then they'd gone to explore the waterfall, a short distance away, that thundered over the rocks. James was solicitous and eager, his joy in their surroundings never waning.

'My parents never walked for enjoyment,' he said. 'That was something tourists did. To them, this was always our working landscape. Nothing more. But I love getting out on the fells when I can. I've not travelled much, as I've never had the urge to go far from here. For me, there's no place like it. I try to find time every week to sit, nice and quiet, with my sheepdogs for half an hour and just take it all in.' He grinned at her. 'Sometimes, I even manage it.'

His enthusiasm was infectious. She liked that he was very keen to show them his home in a good light. By some miracle the weather had been kind, with bright sunny days and the isolated showers reserved for the evening when they were tucked up and cosy at home.

Today they'd visited Castlerigg, a circle of standing stones like a mini Stonehenge. It was a beautiful and atmospheric area surrounded by hills. The sun had cast a golden glow on the mountains and purple brooding clouds stooped low over them. You could keep your sandy beaches and palm trees; this rugged landscape had spoken to her soul. Nadia watched on, smiling, as James patiently named each of the surrounding hills for Lewis.

They'd walked up to another beautiful and hidden tarn. Sitting on smooth rocks, they'd eaten the sandwiches and fruit cake from their backpacks that she'd prepared for them this morning. It was becoming a welcome habit. After lunch they'd all pulled off their socks and boots and had, very bravely, paddled at the edge of the tarn. James had held onto her tightly and she'd tried not to shriek too much as the breathtakingly cold water hit her skin.

Afterwards they'd walked through the fields of sheep and over stiles. She and James had taken their time while the children had run ahead of them and tired themselves out – they would be ready to go to bed early, leaving James and Nadia to have a long and leisurely evening by themselves.

There was only one problem: the week was flying by too quickly. Any fears she'd had about them not getting on together were completely unfounded. Even the children had slotted into a comfortable routine, with Seth and Lily welcoming Lewis like a brother. It would be good for him to have siblings, she thought. Being an only child must be miserable. It had always been the plan for her and her husband to have another baby. It had just never happened. It wasn't too late for her, though. There was still time to give Lewis a brother or sister. She looked shyly at James, hoping he couldn't read her thoughts.

James turned to her. 'Happy?'

'Blissfully,' she said. 'This place is heaven.'

'Think you could live here?'

The question pulled her up short. 'I don't know.'

'What else can I do to sell it to you?'

'Nothing,' she said. 'It's all wonderful.'

'It can be harsh and unforgiving, too,' he said. 'Wait until you've had six solid weeks of sheeting rain and all the coats and boots in the house are permanently damp and we're having to catch drips in buckets in the loft where the roof's leaking. You might view it differently.'

'Should us townies only come in the summer months then?' she teased.

'I could give you a great life,' he said, frankly. 'But I can't leave here. Ever. This is my home, not just somewhere I live. This is me right down to my bones. The farm is my life, my heritage. My family have farmed here in more or less the same way for generations. I learned all this from my grandfather.' He swept a hand around to encompass the hills. 'I went off to university in Sheffield to study Business Management because my dad insisted I use my brain, but I loathed every moment I was in the city. Any spare time and I'd run straight up here. When I got my degree, I wanted nothing more than to be back on the farm.' He gave her a rueful glance. 'Now, I don't think I'd know how to function anywhere else. You know that I couldn't uproot that.'

'Yes,' she said. 'Of course.' This was his land, all that he'd known. And why would he want to leave? His life was hard work, but it was pretty idyllic. She thought of herself sitting in a call centre all day, being mugged outside her own home. Who would choose that over this?

'I don't want you to go home.' James threw his arm round her shoulders and pulled her close as they walked. 'It's been great having you here. We've all got along so well.'

'It's been a fabulous week.'

'Why don't you make it more permanent?' He tried to make the question sound casual, but there was an underlying tension in his voice.

Everything in her heart wanted to scream 'yes' at the top of her voice, but she had to be sensible about this. It didn't matter what she wanted; it had to be what was best for Lewis. She watched him running across the hills chasing Seth and Lily, all of them shouting joyfully. Was this what he'd want?

'Say something,' James said.

'It's a tough decision,' she said. 'I have family back at home. I have commitments. Your wife was from a farming family and could help you. I'd be useless. My family have jewellery shops. I didn't even know there were different types of sheep until this week.'

James laughed at that. 'I'll soon have you in wellies with hay in your hair.'

'I'm sure!' She knew that she couldn't come to live on a working farm and be a bystander. It would mean rolling up her sleeves and getting stuck in. Was she cut out for that? If she saw a worm in her garden at home, she ran a mile.

'I realise that it's a lot to ask, but I don't want this to be a part-time relationship, Nadia. I know we've only known each other for a short time, but it feels so right. I'm not a man to rush into things . . . ' He ran out of words.

She knew exactly what he meant, though.

'You get on so well with the children and they need a mother figure in their lives. You're brilliant with Lewis and I want that for them, too. I do my best, but I worry about Lily. She needs a mum. Perhaps not so much now, but in a few years.' He grinned. 'I find it hard enough to answer her questions now. What's it going to be like when she hits her teens?'

Nadia laughed.

'More importantly, they love you.' He stopped still in the field and kissed her warmly. 'As do I.'

'Oh, James.' Her heart was in turmoil. This could be so good for them, but she was stepping into the unknown. It would mean giving up her job, her home, her family and, most difficult of all, her friends. She wanted change in her life, but could she cope with something quite so radical?

She felt as if she was falling in love with James, but she'd been burned so badly before. Could she really turn her back on everything she knew and throw in her lot with this man and his family?

'You could do what you liked to the house,' James added. 'It's a bit battered round the edges. Like me.'

'It's wonderful,' Nadia said. 'Like you.'

'I make enough money to support us all. You wouldn't need to work if you didn't want to. I know that it worries you that you're not around enough for Lewis. He could start school here in September at the same one as Seth and Lily. So he wouldn't be on his own.'

'It sounds as if you've been giving this a lot of thought.'

'It's kept me awake at night,' he admitted.

'Mummy, Mummy!' Lewis shouted. 'Come on! There are more sheeps!'

'We'd better catch up.' She called back to her son. 'We're coming!'

James caught her hand before she could move and put it to his lips. 'Tell me you'll think about it.'

'Like you, I expect it's going to keep me awake tonight!'

'Good,' James said. 'I can think of an excellent way to occupy ourselves while we mull it over.'

Chapter Thirty-Seven

My parents are going! Yay! Whoopee!

I'm sure I shouldn't be quite so deliriously happy about this, but it's all I can do to stop myself throwing off all my clothes and running round the living room. Instead, I smile sweetly and say, 'Oh, really. That's a shame.'

They're holding hands and looking coy. 'Daddy's going to come home,' Mum says.

I don't point out that my dad doesn't even know where she lives now, let alone call it home, but I don't want to spoil their fun. Or say anything that might make them change their minds and stay. If I'm honest about it, I can't wait to hustle Dad off my sofa and wave goodbye to him with his bag in his hand. I love him, but well . . . you know how it is. I want to be the one having noisy sex in my flat, not my parents.

'We're thinking of getting married again,' Mum says. 'Aren't we, darling?'

My dad nods.

'That's great.' I'll give it six months.

But then I think that in their own strange way, their love is enduring and I'm pleased for them for that. Perhaps the key would be for them to buy houses next door to each other rather than try to live together in one.

'We'll have a little breakfast and then we'll leave you alone.'

'I'll put some toast in.' Not that I'm trying to rush them or anything, but I dash into the kitchen.

I can't wait to tell Crush. We will have hot water. We will be able to watch what we want on the telly. We will be able to get down and dirty on the rug. Hurrah!

'That's great news,' Crush says when I whisper it to him down the phone. 'I knew they would.'

He is so wise.

'I'm going to ravish you when I get home tonight.'

'Oh, excellent,' I say, going a bit jelly-like. 'I'll look forward to it.'

I think when my parents leave, I'm going to change the locks. It's a plan.

I am happy, happy, happy when I get to Chocolate Heaven an hour later. I'm singing to myself as I open up. I hang up my coat and then dance round the tables, tidying the chairs and picking up bits and bobs that have been left behind. I don't even get cross that it was Ms France's job to clear up last night and she has obviously made a half-hearted effort at it.

I'm still singing when Marcus opens the door. 'You sound cheerful.'

That stops me in full flight. 'My dad is finally vacating my sofa. I couldn't be any happier. He's driven me bonkers.'

'I always got on well with him.'

'You didn't,' I remind Marcus. 'He thought you were a slimy toad and would barely give you the time of day after you'd dumped me a dozen times.'

'Ah, yes.'

I raise my eyebrows. They don't call me Elephant Memory for nothing. Actually, they don't call me that at all.

'They're getting back together,' I tell him. 'I don't think Taylor and Burton had as many ups and downs as my mum and dad.'

'Sometimes people just don't realise when they're meant to be together.' He gives me a longing look.

'Don't start that, Marcus. It was all going very well.'

He moves closer to me and uses his sincere voice. 'I'll never give up, Lucy. It should be me and you getting married. That man . . . '

'Aiden.'

'He isn't your type.'

'He very much *is*.'

'I'm trying to stop you from making the biggest mistake of your life.'

'Oh, really.' I nod my head back towards the upstairs flat from where Ms France has yet to appear. 'What about your current squeeze? Would she like to hear you talking like this?'

'Marie-France understands me.'

'I doubt it.'

'We were a great team once, Lucy,' he presses on. 'We could be again.'

'Let's content ourselves with being a great *business* team,' I suggest. 'Sales are up, profits are up, Chocolate Heaven is bustling again. Thank me for that, Marcus, and let's leave everything else in the past.'

He sighs at me.

'I'm a most excellent manager. Stop trying to mess with my heart and let me get on with my job.'

Now he grins at me and I hope that signals him knowing when he's beaten. 'Oh, Lucy, Lucy, Lucy.'

'Oh, Marcus, Marcus, Marcus,' I mimic. 'Now, if that's all,

I've got stuff to do.' I point to the ostentatious Ferrari parked on the pavement. 'If I don't keep your profits up you'll never be able to afford to put petrol in that hideous thing.'

He has the good grace to laugh. 'Where's Marie-France?'

'Probably still in bed. Punctuality isn't her forte.' I'm not exactly sure what is. I wish Marcus would let me give her the bullet and get in someone decent. Autumn isn't working at the moment and she might be glad of a few hours.

Marcus glances at his watch. 'I'd better get going too. I'll call back later.'

I watch him jump in his car and roar off. We used to be good once, but it seems like a lifetime ago. I don't like to think of Marcus being unhappy, though. Sometimes I look at him and, despite having everything you could want in terms of material things, I can't help but feel that he's lonely. And that sort of stops my singing for the day.

It's gone six o'clock when I'm getting ready to leave Chocolate Heaven. I don't want to linger tonight because I am a woman who is going home to a flat without pesky parents in residence who has been promised a jolly good ravishing. I can't wait.

Marie-France is imitating sweeping up by trailing a brush lethargically across the floor.

'Can you make sure that you take everything off the tables tonight, please?' I say in a slightly crotchety manner. 'I don't want to turn up in the morning and have to do it all before I start.'

She raises her gaze to mine and looks down her nose at me in her own very French way. There's not much in the way of an *entente cordiale* between us. I give up.

'I'll see you in the morning. Have a good evening.'

'*Bonsoir*,' she says in a way that sounds more like 'fuck off'.

Grabbing my coat, I swing out of the door. About half an hour to ravishing is my calculating. Can't wait.

Dropping into the local supermarket, I pick up some meals that go ping. Can't waste our precious first evening alone by cooking. I earmark some fishcakes and a bag of greens for dinner – healthy stuff, right? I add some baked churros with chocolate sauce and I'm thinking I could introduce these at Chocolate Heaven. Yum. I wonder if Alexandra would be able to do them for us? Then in a facepalm moment, I remember that the cake order I've scribbled out is still on my desk and I've forgotten to email it to her. If she doesn't get it tonight then that will throw us both out. Bum.

I glance at my watch. I'm going to have to nip back to Chocolate Heaven and do it. If Marie-France was a different person, then I could ring and ask her to complete this simple task. As it is, I don't trust her as far as I can throw her. It won't take a minute. My ravishing will have to wait a little bit longer but, surely, that will add a little piquancy to it.

Hurrying, hurrying, loaded carrier bags in hand, I retrace my steps. Soon, I'm right back where I started, outside Chocolate Heaven. Marcus's car is parked at the kerb and I have a momentary heart-sink. I don't want to get embroiled in another conversation with him about the suitability of my fiancé as opposed to him. I'm going to run in, do what I have to do and make a sharp exit.

Shaking my head, I notice that the tables haven't been cleared and there's no sign of Ms France. I tut to myself and head for the back room. Throwing open the door, I see that Marie-France is bent over the desk with her dress hitched up to her waist and Marcus is . . . er . . . well . . . Marcus is doing what Marcus does best.

I stand and stare, transfixed, feeling ever so slightly sick. Marcus isn't mine, but it still hits me like a punch in the guts. This feels like déjà vu. I have been in this situation too many times before with him. My heart was broken by his infidelity and its scars are still there.

Half-frozen, I force myself to tiptoe out backwards and feel behind me for the door handle. Which, of course, squeaks as I blindly make a grab for it. At that moment, Marcus's head whips round towards me. 'Lucy.'

'Oh, Marcus.' All those things he was saying this morning and now this. I want it not to affect me, to be able to laugh it off. I want to be immune to everything that Marcus does. But I'm not. Even now it bloody hurts.

Marie-France jolts upright, aghast. I shield my eyes. I have no desire to see this much of her.

'I can explain,' he says.

'Sorry.' I hold up a hand. 'Very sorry.' Then, rather like shutting the stable door after the horse has bolted, I do tiptoe out. Fast.

'Wait,' he shouts after me. But I'm out of there as quickly as my legs can carry me.

Slamming the door behind me so that it rattles on its hinges, I rush outside. The cold air slaps my burning cheeks. As I hurry along the pavement, my stomach is churning. I shouldn't let Marcus mess with my emotions. He does it every time: I think I can handle him, but I can't.

I set my jaw and stamp towards the Tube. I know that I'm doing absolutely the right thing in marrying Crush. Of that I've no doubt. But I do wonder whether I can, realistically, continue to work at Chocolate Heaven.

Chapter Thirty-Eight

When they got back from their great day out walking on the fells, Nadia was tired but elated. She wondered if she could sneak off for a long, hot bath before dinner. Unaccustomed to walking so far or up anything so steep, she was sure she'd ache tomorrow.

Her heart sank, however, when she saw Penny in the kitchen, busy at the stove. It was also quite alarming that she was dressed up to the nines. The woman had been here every night of the week and, no doubt, was a great cook. Dinner every night had been wholesome home cooking – if a little bland for Nadia's taste. At first, she'd seemed quite a plain woman, mid-forties, no make-up, jeans and a sweatshirt, her brown hair pulled back in a scrunchy. Not a look that would turn heads. Penny had, however, got steadily more glamorous each day. Which was worrying. This evening, her grooming had reached new heights. Her hair had been done and was falling around her shoulders in waves that spoke of hours spent in jumbo rollers. She'd clearly taken care in applying her make-up and looked much more attractive than she previously had. Her outfit was a very Bodenesque dress in a mocha colour that flattered her curvy frame. Nadia frowned. Rather over the top for slaving over a stove.

'Wow,' James said. 'Look at you all spruced up. Got a hot date?'

Clearly, Penny had hit the level where he actually noticed and she flushed furiously.

'No, no. Of course not.' That didn't stop her from batting her eyelashes at him, then casting a sly glance in Nadia's direction.

'Don't let us hold you up if you're going out,' James pressed on. 'We can manage here.'

'No, no. Just a night in for me.' Penny fluffed her hair. 'I'm a real home bird.'

Nadia sighed inwardly. So that was the game. Not only had Penny proved herself an invaluable help to the family, she was now trying to win James's affections and obviously saw Nadia as a rival.

'Dinner's nearly ready,' she said with more eyelash-batting on the side. 'I've made your favourite.'

James rubbed his hands. 'Great. No one makes steak and kidney pie like you.'

Salad was not in this lady's repertoire. Nadia would probably go back a stone heavier after all this stodge on top of her usual chocolate and cake consumption.

To James's credit he hadn't allowed her near the cooker all week. Which was just as well because she'd never used an Aga before and it looked like a thing of terror. Her mind went over their situation again. Could she really consider living here? Would she be able to slot into the role of a farmer's partner or even wife? It was all so alien to her.

But then did she want to stand back and leave James to the charms of this woman? Penny was looking increasingly likely to put up a fight for him. What would happen when she was far away and back in London? Could Penny turn James's head with her cottage pies and apple crumbles? It was clear that she wasn't going to let a usurper in if she could help it. In fairness to James, he did seem completely oblivious to her overtures. But how long would that last if Penny decided to up her game and come in dressed for the catwalk every day? If Nadia dallied too long in making a decision about whether they had a future together, would Penny swoop in and snatch James from under her nose? He might be unaware of her intentions now, but with Nadia out of the picture she might ramp up her efforts and, at the end of the day, James was a red-blooded man and that looked like an extremely good pie.

Nadia pulled off her boots and, after quickly sprucing herself up, sent the children to wash their hands. Then she put on an apron that was hanging on the back of the door. 'I can take over now, Penny,' she said. 'That looks lovely. I don't want to hold you up.'

'No rush,' she said tightly. 'I'm not going anywhere.'

James was opening a bottle of wine. Please don't ask her to stay and have a drink, Nadia thought.

Nadia manoeuvred herself in front of the cooker and took control of the oven glove. There were new potatoes in one pan, carrots and beans in another. She smiled sweetly at Penny. 'This looks lovely. Thank you so much, but I really can manage.'

Thankfully, James only poured two glasses of wine – a promising sign – and Penny seemed to take the hint from that. She bristled slightly, but moved away from the cooker and removed her apron. Nadia suppressed a victory fist pump and gave herself a silent cheer instead. Winner of the Battle of the Aprons: Nadia Stone! The Chocolate Lovers' girls would be proud of her for standing her ground.

'I'll see you tomorrow,' Penny said, addressing James. 'Anything in particular you fancy for dinner?'

'Oh, I don't mind,' James said. 'Whatever you cook is always gratefully received.'

She turned and forced a smile at Nadia. 'It's your last day, isn't it?' Parting shot.

'Yes,' Nadia said. 'But I'll be back as soon as I can.' Then she realised that she meant it. She had to go back to work on Monday, but in her heart she knew that she didn't want to leave at all.

Penny pursed her lips and left. It didn't seem to be the end of the war as far as she was concerned.

When she'd gone, James passed the glass of red to her. It was a good bottle, rich and fruity. She sipped it gratefully. 'Mmm. Lovely.'

'You look quite good in a pinny,' he joked.

'Would you dispense with Penny's services if I came to stay?'

'That's not why I want you here,' he said. 'Surely you know that. She's been with me since . . . well, you know. I'm sure she'd be more than happy to stay on, if that's what you want.'

'Hmm. Would she? I'm not so sure,' Nadia said. 'She likes you.'

'And I like her.'

She raised an eyebrow. 'Oh, do you?'

'Not in that way!' James laughed and came to catch her round the waist. 'Do I detect a touch of green eyes?'

'Just assessing the situation,' Nadia countered. 'I like to know who my competition is.'

'She's not that at all,' James said. 'I can assure you.'

'I'm not sure Penny sees it that way. If it was left to her, I think she'd like to have a more permanent position here.'

'Well, it's not going to happen.' James was emphatic. 'If you turn me down, I shall simply pine for you for ever.'

'Would you?'

'Yes.' He kissed her warmly. 'I'd be inconsolable.'

'That's good to hear.'

'I might let Penny give it her best shot at cheering me up, though.'

Nadia thumped his arm. 'Bastard.'

'She does make exceedingly good pie.'

They laughed together and he held her close.

'I might not have made this lovely dinner but, if you want a big slice of said pie, you'll need to keep on my good side.'

He gave her another squeeze and said, 'I love you. Nothing will change that.' Then he winked at her. 'You dish up and I'll call the children.'

Nadia's heart skipped a beat. He'd said that he loved her. She watched him saunter from the kitchen – his long, easy stride, the way he had to duck to avoid the beams – and she was filled with a surge of happiness. She loved him, too. He was a good catch, no question. They might be joking with each other, but Nadia knew full well that if James was alone here, then Penny would do her very best to get her claws into him. She would be mad to let that happen.

For the children's sake, she'd had a separate room at the house. But when the children were fast asleep, she sneaked into James's room and lay in his arms in his vast bed amid a sea of covers. It was the first week that Lewis had been content to sleep all night without her – which was a relief, but also left her feeling a little sad. Her son was growing up quickly. He was sharing a bedroom with Seth and she knew that they were probably both up playing with Lego and goodness knows what else when they should be asleep, but she didn't begrudge him the fun and companionship. She hadn't seen him so happy in a long time.

'I do like it here,' she said, resting her head on James's shoulder.

'Here in particular or Cumbria in general?' he teased as he stroked her hair.

'Both.'

'Then don't go back,' he said. 'Stay.'

'It isn't that simple.'

'It is if you want it to be.'

'There's a lot to think about, James.'

'Just think about us. That, surely, should make it easier.' He sat up, leaning on his elbow and traced a meandering finger down between her breasts. 'I worry about you. I don't want anything happening to you while I'm not there to protect you.'

She knew what he was referring to. The mugging was always there somewhere at the back of her mind. It was only when she was out walking on the hills that she could say she'd completely forgotten about it.

'The worst that can happen here is that you stand in sheep poo.'

'If that's the worst that can happen, then it doesn't sound like a bad life.'

He moved above her, kissing her with increasing passion. 'I'll miss you.'

She melted to his touch. It had been so long since she'd been loved like this and it was intoxicating.

It was raining now outside, the downpour pelting against the windows. She'd left the curtains open so that she could see the black silhouette of the mountains. In here it was cosy, safe. If only she didn't have to leave ever again . . . but they were both fully aware that their time together was running out.

'If you won't stay, then come back soon.'

'I promise. Lewis's half-term holiday is only six weeks away.'

James sighed and feathered kisses on her neck. 'That's a lifetime away. Just think of how many of Penny's pies I'll have to eat before then.'

She grabbed his bottom and dug her fingernails in. 'You fiend.'

He laughed and flipped over, pulling her on top of him. His hands roved her hips, the curve of her buttocks, and she'd never wanted him more. He looked so handsome, lit only by the moon shining through the raindrops on the window.

'I love you,' he said, softly. 'Marry me.'

Her breath caught in her throat. Had she heard him right?

Then his mobile phone on the bedside table rang.

'Don't answer,' she said.

'Hold that thought,' he told her before he picked up the phone and said, 'Hello?'

When he hung up, he was frowning. 'One of the lambs has fallen between the bars of a cattle grid further down the road. My neighbour was on his way home from the pub and saw it in his headlights. They've had a go, but they can't get it out. I'd better head down there.'

'You're going out in this?' The rain was pelting the glass even harder. 'Now?'

James was already out of bed and slipping on his jeans. 'This would be the joy of being a farmer's wife.' He took her hand and kissed her fingers to his lips. 'I did, however, mean what I said.' He pulled on his shirt and headed for the door. 'I'll be back as soon as I can. Hopefully, it won't take long.'

As he left, Nadia flopped onto the bed and stared at the ceiling. He'd asked her to marry him. There was a big squiggle of happiness inside her, but it was tinged with terror. Now what should she do?

Chapter Thirty-Nine

The day after Nadia comes home from her travels, we are all sitting in a wedding-dress shop in Sloane Square. It's a very posh one, even though I don't have a very posh budget to warrant it. But this place has a great reputation and I thought it would be worth a lickle-ickle, teeny-tiny peek.

Maybe it was a big mistake.

The dress I have on is absolutely beautiful. It's a lace number in a gorgeous champagne colour, slightly retro style. I wouldn't have looked at it at all, but Chantal picked it out for me and I have to say that she has fantastic taste. It has a scooped neck, three-quarter-length lace sleeves, a nipped-in waist and a full skirt. It says demure, but sexy. If you know what I mean.

When my Executive Bridal Consultant – their term, not mine – has zipped me up, I step out of the changing room with a 'Ta-dah!'

The girls, who are sitting on a curved sofa sipping a glass of fizz while waiting patiently, gasp.

'Oh, Lucy,' Chantal says, dabbing tears from her eyes as if she's the mother of the bride. 'That is *perfect.*'

I'm sure she's tearful because her emotions are running so high at the moment. I smooth down the skirt. 'Thanks. It does feel amazing.'

The Executive Bridal Consultant wanders off to the accessories area to get me a hat and shoes to try on.

When she's gone, I lower my voice and whisper, 'It's perfect except for one thing. It has three noughts on the price tag rather than the two I can actually afford.'

'A small consideration.' Chantal dismisses my concerns with a wave of her hand.

'You *have* to get that,' Autumn agrees. 'You look stunning.'

'It also blows half of my wedding budget.'

'You'll never get anything else as nice as that,' Nadia says.

'I'll *have* to try other dresses. This is monster expensive.' I give the skirt a little swish. Oh, so nice. 'Maybe we could pop along to Debenhams instead? Don't they do wedding frocks?' Which are likely to be hundreds rather than thousands. See how sensible I'm being?

'This isn't any old *frock*, Lucy. It's your bridal gown,' Chantal says.

'I know, but . . . ' Then I catch sight of myself in the mirror again and, they're right, it does look incredible. I am the hottest bride there ever will be.

'It's elegant, sophisticated,' she continues. 'I'd wear that in a heartbeat. It's going to be the best day of your life. You deserve to feel fabulous.'

I do feel fabulous, but Crush will kill me if I blow all our cash on this. We are on a Budget with a capital 'B'.

'This is the second time I'll have splashed out on a wedding dress,' I remind them. 'And I got a measly few quid on eBay for the last one when I didn't even actually use it.'

'It *was* covered in chocolate, Lucy.'

Oh yeah. I'd forgotten that. I had a slightly emotional coming together with the chocolate fountain at the reception after my non-wedding to Marcus, now you come to mention it.

'That won't happen this time,' Autumn says.

'I know.' I turn this way and that and look longingly at myself. 'But it's a lot of money.'

The Executive Bridal Consultant returns. 'I have a little pillbox hat that I think would go perfectly.'

And, of course, it does. The crown is embellished with glass beads, crystals and tiny seed pearls. I am in love. It's exactly the same colour as the dress and a wisp of net covers my eyes in a coquettish manner. Beautiful. More gasps from my girls.

'And some silk shoes.'

Oh, these are beyond divine! They're tiny and are fit for a princess. She places them at my feet and, of course, they fit as wonderfully as the glass slipper did when Cinders slid her tootsies into it.

I check out the mirror again. I'm a vision of bridal loveliness.

This could end my wedding-outfit shopping now. I could walk from one end of the High Street to the other, make my fingers raw with surfing online, but I'd never find anything to better this.

'I'd say that your search was over,' Nadia agrees. 'That was easy.'

'Not quite.' I torture myself by posing this way and that. I pout and preen. 'I can't buy this one. As fantabulous as it is. It's waaaaay too much money.'

'Are you sure?' Autumn says.

'Sadly, yes. We'd have to have a packet of crisps each instead of the wedding breakfast and, tempting though it is, I can't do that.' Jacob would kill me just after Crush did; his plans are well underway too. 'The caterers have been booked, the champagne selected.' It's so pretty and it breaks my heart to put it back on the silk-covered hanger and step away. 'Perhaps I could get a second-hand dress on eBay.'

Chantal drains her champagne flute. 'Excellent plan – eBay it is.'

My spirits plummet. 'You think so?'

'You've said so yourself, Lucy. This is *wildly* extravagant.'

I know that. In my head I know that. I give one last twirl and smile sadly. This is all so perfect but I know I'm right to walk away from it.

'Now go and get changed,' Chantal says, briskly. 'We all need coffee and chocolate.'

I head back to the changing room, heavy of heart. The Executive Bridal Consultant whips the dress off me – rather quickly, if you ask me. And the adorable hat. And the Cinderella shoes. She disappears. As does her commission.

When I come out, back in my jeans and shirt, feeling like a leaden lump, they're all standing there grinning like loons. 'What?'

'I've ordered the dress for you,' Chantal says.

Now it's my turn to gasp. 'You can't. I haven't got any way of paying for it.'

'Let me worry about that.' She links her arm in mine. 'It's my wedding present to you.'

'No, no, no. It's too much.'

'It's better than a Hoover or a dishwasher.'

'And ten times the price!' I protest. 'You could buy me a Hoover, a dishwasher *and* a small family car.'

'We've bought the hat, too,' Nadia says, brushing a tear from her eye. 'Between me and Autumn. All you have to do is pay for the shoes.'

'Oh, girls.' I have a little tear too and give them all a hug. 'How can I ever thank you?'

'You can buy the coffee,' Chantal says. 'And I'll have a great big piece of cake.'

'What did I ever do to deserve friends like you? You're *too* kind.'

'I can't wait to see you in it on your wedding day,' Chantal says. 'So that gives me an extra incentive to still be here.'

'You *will* be here,' I say fiercely. 'And you'll be fine.'

Then we have another group hug and this one is tighter than ever.

'Come on,' I say. 'We're not going to be sad today. Big cake is definitely required.'

I only hope that they've ordered my dress in a . . . ahem . . . generous size.

Chapter Forty

Accordingly, we find the nearest café and order the biggest slices of chocolate cake they have.

'I'd better get back to Chocolate Heaven soon – I've left it in the tender loving care of Ms France and I'd like a business left when I return. She and I have avoided each other like the plague since the unfortunate shagging-over-the-desk incident.'

Their heads all swivel in my direction and, in unison, they say, 'The what?'

Ah. Hadn't told them about that.

'I had to pop back to Chocolate Heaven late the other night and saw Marcus having it off with Ms France over the desk in the back room.' I shudder at the thought. How am I ever going to use that computer again without having a flashback? 'I saw more of Marcus's bum than I wanted to. It was probably worse than listening to my parents have sex on my sofa and that, quite frankly, has scarred me for life.'

They all laugh.

'It wasn't funny, it was *totally* traumatic.' I seek solace in my chocolate cake. 'I'm seriously considering my future at Chocolate Heaven. If she stays, then I go.'

'You need the money,' Chantal reminds me.

'Oh, yeah.' So much for the grand gesture. 'Maybe after the wedding I'll look for another job.'

'You won't, Lucy,' Nadia says. 'You're destined to be at Chocolate Heaven whatever happens.'

It certainly looks that way.

'How can I get rid of Ms France then? We need one of my cunning plans.'

They all groan.

'That's the *last* thing we need,' Chantal says. 'You get into enough trouble as it is.'

So. No new career. No cunning plan. No getting rid of pesky French assistant. Gah. I must hold on to the thought that I have my lovely, lovely wedding coming up. 'What else has been going on then?' I ask. 'That's all my news.'

'Willow is coming to stay for the weekend,' Autumn says. 'Well, overnight. I can't wait.'

'That's great. I'm so pleased it's working out for you.'

'We're speaking or texting every day,' she adds. 'I'm so happy. The only fly in the ointment is that I've had a big bust up with my parents. I went to tell them about Willow and they were their usual uninterested selves.' She blushes and fiddles with her hair. 'I was very cruel. I said things that I shouldn't have said.'

'You've been bottling it all up for a long time.'

'That doesn't excuse it, though,' Autumn says. 'I've phoned my mother to apologise but she hasn't returned my calls.'

'You have us,' Nadia says. 'And we can't wait to meet Willow.'

'I saw Ted and Stacey,' Chantal says when we turn to her for an update. 'It was a bit awkward at first, but Ted is trying his best. Stacey stayed out of the way and we didn't have much to say to each other, but it was OK. Ted has agreed to finalise the divorce quickly. While he's here, we're going to sign the papers this week. All being well. Then I'll be a free woman.'

We all toast that with our coffee.

'And you're feeling OK?' I ask, anxiously.

'Yeah. Good but not great.' She rubs at her shoulder. 'My chest is still aching where the lump was removed and my arm is still weak, but I'm on the mend. I've got an appointment with Livia later this week and I'm hoping she'll give me the all-clear.'

'Amen to that,' I say.

'I'm keeping my fingers crossed.' Chantal holds up crossed fingers on both hands.

'You know you only have to ask if you want any help,' I say.

'I do.' Chantal smiles at us all. 'You lot do more than enough for me. We'll all go out and down enough cocktails to sink a ship when this is over. My treat.'

Last but not least, we turn to Nadia. She's only just come back from her holiday and we haven't even had time for a proper download yet. 'Right, Madam. We want to hear all about your week in the wilds of Cumbria. How was it?'

She looks very coy. 'It was fantastic.'

'In what sense of the word?' I want to know. 'Rampant sex every night? More cake than you could shake a stick at?'

'Quite a lot of passion.' Even more bashful. 'Some excellent cake. Though there isn't a decent chocolate shop as far as I can tell.'

We shake our heads in sorrow at that terrible news.

'Though you can buy everything your heart desires – as long as it's made of fleece.'

'He'll make a country bumpkin out of you yet.'

Nadia laughs. 'He had a good go! Even in a week. We did a lot of walking on the fells which, weirdly, I really enjoyed. I learned to love my walking boots. And I now know more about sheep than I ever thought I would.'

'And that's it?'

'Not quite.' Nadia shrugs shyly. 'James asked me to marry him.'

'Nooooo,' I cry. 'Why didn't you say? We could have tried wedding dresses on together.'

She holds up a hand. 'I haven't said yes, yet.'

'*Yet*.' I jump on the word.

'It's a big step.' She pulls an anxious face. 'He's great and I love him, but I hardly know him.'

'You don't have to marry him tomorrow,' I remind her. 'Take it slowly.'

'He wants me to move up to Cumbria. There's no way that he can leave his farm and, I have to admit, the lifestyle really appeals to me. I didn't think I was cut out to be a country girl, but I loved being out on the hills. The scenery is stunning. It beats dirty old north London any day. And Lewis adored it. He gets on really well with Seth and Lily. He cried when we had to come home. Me too.'

'So the downside is?'

'I'd have to leave all I know behind. My family, you girls. The thought really scares me. I'd be up there all on my own, starting out again. I wouldn't have a job or any friends. I'd be reliant on James for everything.'

'There's always a catch,' Chantal says.

'It's a *fantastic* opportunity.' Autumn is vehement. 'You could have a new life, a great one, with someone you love.'

'I'm a firm believer in grabbing happiness while it's on offer,' I say. 'But we don't want you to go either.'

'And that's the problem,' Nadia says. 'I feel absolutely torn.'

I blow out a breath. 'Tough call.'

Nadia spreads her hands. 'So what do I do?'

And, even though we consider it thoroughly while we have another slice of cake and more coffee, none of us seem to be able to give her the definitive answer to that one.

Chapter Forty-One

Chantal could hear the sound of her own heart beating in her ears. She was still alive and that was something. The shock hadn't killed her.

On the other side of the desk, Livia wasn't her usual smiling, positive self. 'I'm sorry,' she said grimly. 'I would have liked to have given you better news.'

Jacob's hand slid over hers.

'Having a faulty cancer gene is literally the luck of the draw.' Livia went on to explain more about it, but her voice quickly turned into white noise.

Chantal was struggling to take it all in. She couldn't think straight at all. It was as if there was a disconnect from reality and this was all really happening to someone else. It was like a body blow. After she'd had the lump removed, it had all seemed so positive, so simple. She'd thought that it was all behind her and that the cancer would be gone. Another thing to tick off as one of life's experiences. Now it seemed as if that wasn't the case at all.

'Your mother hasn't had cancer?' The question pulled her back to the present.

'No.' She shook her head. It was one of the first things they'd asked at the very start. 'She's still hale and hearty.'

'Your grandmother?'

'I don't know.' She'd died young, before Chantal was born, so no one had ever told her. Could it be that this had been lurking in her family history all along? Perhaps she'd have to put in a call to her mother so that she could check it out. But they hadn't spoken for a long time and, at the moment, her brain wouldn't process that.

'I'm concerned that there's some cancerous tissue in the breast that I couldn't remove. It can be so minute that it's like grains of sand, but it's there and has to come out.'

Her face was wet and she realised that she was crying. Jacob's face was white as he took a tissue from the box conveniently placed on Livia's desk and handed it to her. Bad news, it seemed, wasn't unusual here.

'But she looks so well,' Jacob said.

Livia allowed herself a smile. 'And that's good news. Chantal is strong. Together we can overcome this.'

'She's right,' Jacob said.

Chantal nodded as it seemed the thing to do.

Then Livia was briskly professional again. 'There are several options and we can go through them all as many times as you need to. It's a big decision to make.'

'What are my options?' Her voice wavered.

'We can try chemotherapy first. I'd like to hit it hard. That might be enough to kill it off. It depends how you respond to it. If that doesn't work, then you can opt to have a mastectomy.'

It was the word every woman feared. Surely the breasts were the core of your femininity. Without one, would she feel less of a woman?

'Or you can have a mastectomy first and then we can be less aggressive with the chemotherapy.'

Neither of these options seemed to offer a wonderful choice or a miracle cure. Her mouth was dry, her mind reeling.

'I know it's a lot to process,' Livia said. 'If you opt for a mastectomy, then we can do reconstructive surgery. Sometimes we do it immediately. In other cases, a little way down the line.'

Chemotherapy or mastectomy? What a choice.

Chantal found her voice. 'What would you do in my situation?'

'I'd have the mastectomy straight away. No messing about.'

'Will that give me the best chance of survival?'

'Yes,' Livia said, bluntly.

'Then let's do it.'

'OK.' She made a note on her pad.

'Then that's it? Done?' Jacob asked.

'Not quite.' Livia was tight-lipped. 'The faulty gene doesn't go away, I'm afraid. In the future, you might also consider electing to have the other breast treated. We can monitor you closely, but there's always going to be a risk there.' She slipped off her glasses and fixed Chantal with a steady look. 'You might even want to have a hysterectomy.'

A hysterectomy? Chantal hadn't seen that coming, either. She'd left it late in life to have Lana but, somehow, she'd still imagined that she might have a child with Jacob. Wouldn't he want that? It was something they hadn't yet discussed, but it looked as if they'd be talking about it sooner rather than later.

'It's a big step,' Livia said. 'I know that. We don't have to make the decision right away. Let's get this sorted first. But they'll both minimise your risk of developing cancer again.'

Wow, Chantal thought. This was the illness that just kept on giving. 'If I have this gene, then presumably Lana could have it, too?'

'Yes, it's a possibility. She'll need to be monitored later on in life.'

Oh, her poor child. How could she have handed this ticking time bomb down to her?

'At least they'll be aware of it,' Jacob said. 'That's not a bad thing.'

'I'm also going to request a CT scan, Chantal. I want to be absolutely sure that it hasn't spread anywhere else.'

Chantal was numb, right down to her core. It felt as if there was a seething, black mass inside her trying to destroy her body. But it wouldn't. She would fight this thing. And she would triumph. For her daughter's sake.

'I want to start as soon as possible,' Chantal said. 'I want to live to be an old lady. I want to be here to see my grandchildren.'

'Good.' Livia looked relieved. 'Let's get this party started.' Now she was scribbling furiously on her pad. She glanced up and said, 'If it's OK with you, we'll schedule your operation as soon as possible.'

Chantal steeled herself. 'Absolutely,' she said and her voice sounded strong.

There was going to be a positive outcome to this. She was absolutely determined. Watch out cancer, she thought, I'm coming to get you.

Chapter Forty-Two

Autumn had been so excited to see her daughter again. This time she was staying overnight at her flat and Autumn had made up the spare room. No one had stayed in here, not properly, since Richard left and it made her sad to think that her brother would never get to meet Willow. She was sure they would have really got on well together. One day, when the time was right, she'd tell Willow all about the uncle she'd never know but would have loved.

It consoled her to know that there were still people keen to meet her daughter and this weekend was the time to introduce her to Miles and Flo. Willow couldn't help but adore them, surely? And vice versa. Miles and Flo were almost as excited as she was.

In a short while, Autumn was going to meet Willow's train and then they'd head down to meet Miles and Flo at the South Bank to take in some of the entertainment there. This time of year, there was the annual Wonderground, which had a great carnival atmosphere. She thought Willow would love it. And, to be honest, she was still at the stage where she felt she needed to offer Willow a carrot to come down to London to meet up with her.

Wonderground was a colourful event that ran through until September and it was a little bit edgy, a tiny bit dark, which – along with the usual hordes of tourists – attracted some wacky, bohemian characters and downright freaks. There were always a few rides – a carousel that would keep Flo amused and a couple of more white-knuckle things for Willow. There was a variety of music and a food court with offerings from all round the world, which would be fun to sample for lunch.

She wanted to show her daughter so much of her world. Willow had been given a lovely, stable upbringing by Mary and her husband, but it was clear that the girl was itching to spread her wings. She was far too young to lure away to London on a permanent basis and Autumn wouldn't dream of doing that, but perhaps she could give her a few tasters over the next few years. If Willow enjoyed Wonderground, then maybe they could take in one of the shows next time she visited.

Autumn waited impatiently at the station. The train was twenty minutes late and it was clear from the minute Willow arrived that all was not well. Her daughter's face was dark and scowling.

'Hey,' Autumn said. 'Good to see you. Have you had a horrible journey?'

Willow shrugged. 'It was OK.'

She gave her a hug, but the girl remained rigid.

'Everything all right?' Autumn studied her pinched little face. It was the epitome of teenage angst.

'Yeah. I'm fine.'

It was obvious that she was far from fine.

'We're due to meet Miles and Flo,' Autumn said. 'I thought you'd like that and they're dying to see you, but I can easily call them and say we've popped for a coffee. Would you rather sit and do that so we can have some time by ourselves to chat?'

'I haven't got anything to say to you.'

Ah. So it had all gone swimmingly last time and now she was being tested. Well, that was fine too.

'I'll call them and let them know we'll be another half an hour. We're heading off to the South Bank; there's lots to do down there. I think you'll like it.'

Willow didn't look convinced.

'In the meantime, there's a nice café just around the corner that we can go to.'

'Let's just go to the South Bank or wherever.'

'OK. We can do whatever you like today.'

Willow fell into step beside her and Autumn linked her arm. She thought it was promising that Willow didn't automatically pull away.

She was glad that she hadn't arranged for Willow to meet her parents this weekend. If Willow was in a difficult mood, it only reinforced the need for her to take this very slowly.

Autumn texted Miles before they got on the Tube. She couldn't risk warning him of Willow's mood in case she saw, but it was a shame that he wouldn't get a good first impression of her. It would, however, give him a foretaste of how Flo was likely to behave in another ten years. She smiled at that.

The South Bank was bustling as always, the atmosphere buzzing. It was one of Autumn's favourite places in London. A trip down here never failed to lift her spirits. She hoped it would do the same for Willow. And quickly.

There was a steady breeze off the Thames but the day was warm and bright, the temperature climbing surely but steadily. At the entrance to the Wonderground there was a carousel and a number of sideshows featuring curiosities, eccentricities and death-defying acts. A couple of jugglers worked the crowd with an act that was making everyone laugh. The obligatory living statues – Charlie Chaplin, Marilyn Monroe, William Shakespeare,

236

Yoda – stood stock-still along the wall by the river and the food stalls were doing a roaring trade. Willow looked down her nose at them all and Autumn pitied poor Mary trying to keep her child entertained in the countryside.

Autumn found Miles and Flo waiting for them by the carousel. Flo was waving madly and bouncing around happily.

He hugged Autumn in greeting and said, 'Hey.'

'This is Miles,' she said to Willow. 'And Flo.'

Willow couldn't have exuded more reluctance if she'd tried.

'I'm five!' Flo said.

'In your dreams, little lady,' Miles said. 'Tell Willow how old you really are.'

'I'm three going on thirty-three,' Flo obliged.

The scowl stayed in place, the hands firmly wedged in her pockets. Behind Willow's back, Autumn raised her eyebrows apologetically at Miles. This looked as if it would be a long, difficult day. Still, she was spending time with her daughter and she was happy to give her all the attention that she needed. It was just going to be hard work for Miles and Flo and she'd cut them loose if this continued.

Poor Flo took in Willow's Goth make-up and black clothes and seemed to regret her initial excitement and, instead, clung to Miles's legs.

'Hi, Willow,' Miles said, amiably. 'It's lovely to meet you. We've heard so much about you. Haven't we, Flo?'

Poor Florence looked as if she was about to burst into tears and Autumn was cross that Willow had scared the little girl and didn't seem to care.

'I thought we'd go for a coffee,' Autumn said, biting down her irritation and trying to sound upbeat. 'Chill out for a bit.'

'Can I take Flo on the carousel first and then we'll join you in a little while?' Miles had obviously appreciated that they needed a little space together.

'Sure. There's a bar behind us that's pretty cool,' Autumn said. 'We'll be there when you're ready. No rush.'

Miles nodded. 'Carousel again, Princess?' he asked Flo.

'Yes. Carriage,' she said. 'Not horsey this time.'

The carousel stopped and Autumn laughed as she watched Miles squeeze himself into the princess carriage and settle Flo on the seat next to him. It looked as if it was killing Willow not to smile too.

'She's a lovely little girl,' Autumn said.

'Yeah? I was too at that age. But you wouldn't know,' Willow retorted.

'Sorry,' Autumn apologised. 'That was thoughtless of me. Mary did show me photographs of you as a child. She said you were adorable.'

Willow grunted. 'Bet she doesn't say that now.'

'Have you two had a row?'

She shrugged. 'No more than usual.'

'It's perfectly normal to think that your parents are idiots when you're a teenager. But there'll come a time when you realise she's only on your case because she loves you.'

'But she's not really my mum, is she? And neither are you, so don't lecture me either.'

Whatever she said today, it was going to be wrong. 'I understand that your world is changing,' Autumn offered. 'I want to try to make it better for you. Not worse.'

As the carousel started and Flo waved at them madly, they moved off towards the bar. It was a fun area in front of the elaborately decorated Spiegeltent, where the nightly shows were held. The seats were made of old cars from fairground waltzers and, at this time of day, it was pleasantly busy whereas, when the shows started later in the evening, the place would be heaving. Autumn ordered them both a cappuccino and a brownie while Willow found somewhere for them to sit.

When she came back with their coffees, she sat next to Willow in the car.

'This is nice, isn't it?' she said, gesturing at their surroundings and resolutely ignoring the stony face of her daughter. 'We could get tickets for something later on in the year, if there's anything that takes your fancy. I'll grab a programme while we're here. There's a lot to choose from – comedy, music, freak shows. All kinds of things.'

Willow spun towards her. 'I don't want to come and play happy families with you. This is rubbish. You don't know who I am.'

'I would like to,' Autumn said calmly. 'I want to spend time together getting to know each other.'

'What if I don't want to know you?'

'I'd be devastated,' she answered honestly. 'It would be like losing you all over again.'

'You didn't seem to mind last time you walked away.'

Autumn leaned forward and gently cupped her daughter's face in her hands. She looked into her eyes. 'You can be as horrible as you like, Willow,' she said softly. 'I'm not going anywhere. Now that I've found you, I promise you with all of my heart that I'll always be here for you.'

Willow's lip was trembling.

'Mary's been your mum for fourteen years, I get that, and she's done a fantastic job. Look at you: you're beautiful, bold and feisty.'

The girl's eyes filled with tears and she tried to blink them back.

'But you are my blood, Willow. I've loved you since the day you were born and I will love you to my dying day. It's my biggest delight that I've been able to see you again. I hardly dared to believe that day would come. You can't even begin to imagine how much I feel for you. You are in my heart, my soul and always will be. Whatever happens, that will never change.'

Silent tears rolled down Willow's face.

'I know that I have to earn the right to be in your life and I want to do that. You can push me away as much as you like, but I'll always be here for you. If you're in a good mood or an evil one, I still love you. I love you more than life itself.'

She took her daughter in her arms and, despite some initial resistance, eventually Willow let herself be held while she sobbed. When the tears subsided, she pulled a tissue from her pocket and dabbed at her daughter's face.

'You've completely ruined your mascara,' Autumn said. There were tracks of black down her cheeks. 'You'll frighten poor Florence even more now.'

Willow gave a watery laugh and wiped her face.

She saw Miles and Flo picking their way through the increasing crowd. 'Here are the others. There's lots to do here. If you're up for it, we can even risk the Skyride.' Autumn waved them over to where they were sitting. 'Shall we start again and have a lovely day together?'

Her daughter nodded and Autumn kissed her cheek tenderly. 'This is going to take a lot of working out,' she said. 'And I'm going to make mistakes and piss you off.'

Willow smiled at that.

'But I'll do my very best not to.' She took Willow's hand in hers and squeezed it. 'You can trust me,' Autumn said. 'Today and always. I promise you that. I'll do everything I can to prove it.'

'OK.'

'Now,' Autumn said. 'Shall we polish off this cake and go and have some fun?'

Willow risked a smile. 'I'd like that.'

Chapter Forty-Three

Nadia stared out of the window of the call centre. Outside the sun was shining, women were starting to bring their summer dresses out of the wardrobe and there were a few businessmen in shirt sleeves. She, on the other hand, was in an air-conditioned office kept at a cool eighteen degrees so that none of the staff ever felt that delicious afternoon sleepy warmth. She pulled her cardigan around her shoulders and suppressed a shiver.

She took her next call. 'Customer services. Nadia speaking. How can I help?'

The woman started to tell her what seemed like the hundredth tale of woe she'd heard today.

As Nadia jotted down the details, she thought of her time in Cumbria – walking on the fells, the magnificent waterfalls, the ice-cold tarns, the lovely tea rooms and, best of all, ending the day in James's arms. She wondered what it was like there now and resisted the urge to Google the weather in Keswick, just to check. James would be out in the meadows or on the hills making sure that his sheep were all right. Maybe there'd be more lambs to look after. The children would be back in school. Penny would be collecting them each evening.

Hmm. Last bit, not so good.

'Do you think that's acceptable?' the woman said into her daydream.

'I can understand why you'd feel like that,' Nadia said to placate her. Sometimes she felt that whatever she said it didn't matter. The customers – who were, generally, treated shabbily by her company – just wanted to shout at someone, anyone.

She and James had fallen back into the pattern of speaking to each other every evening since she'd returned home, but there was a special poignancy to their calls now as they both knew how much they were missing. He didn't mention his proposal again or press her to give him an answer, but it was there dangling between them and she thought of little else. Oh, how she missed him.

On auto-pilot, she managed to resolve the issue for the woman and braced herself for the next call. Her own mobile tinged the arrival of a text and, though she wasn't allowed to take personal calls at work, she took a quick look at the message.

It was from Anita. *Come to dinner tonight. Mum and Dad will be here. It would be good for you to be together again. A xx*

Her instinct was that meeting up with them like this was too rushed, too soon. She needed time to prepare herself, as she hadn't seen her parents in years. On the other hand, there was no time like the present. She wasn't doing anything else tonight – as usual – and, as it was school tomorrow for Lewis, they had the perfect excuse to leave early. Should she just bite the bullet and do it?

There was another call coming in that she needed to attend to and, before she could think better of it, she texted back to Anita. *OK.*

It was done. Now she only had a few hours to stress about her long-awaited reconciliation with her parents.

At six thirty she stood at the end of the drive at Anita's house, filled with trepidation. It was all she could do not to turn straight round and rush back to the safety of her house. She knelt down and tried to smarten up her son. His coat was askew, one side of the collar of his polo shirt in, the other out. His hair wouldn't stay tidy. It sprung up at all angles as if it had a life of its own. Sometimes he looked so much like his father. She ran a hand over his hair trying, once again, to smooth it down.

'No more, Mummy,' he complained, pushing her hand away.

'I'm just trying to make sure that you look nice to meet Grandma and Grandpa,' she said.

He frowned at her. 'Who are they?'

'This is my mummy and daddy.'

'Oh.'

It felt awful that he didn't really understand the concept of grandparents. The joy of having a fractured family. Toby's parents had never enjoyed particularly robust good health, but they'd both gone rapidly downhill since their son had died. At first they'd tried to see a lot of Lewis and popped round regularly. However, if they were hoping to find comfort in their grandson, then they'd been terribly wrong. It seemed only to highlight that their own son was gone. His father was always grey with the pain of grief. At the end of each visit, Toby's mother would end up in tears, which was dreadful for all of them. Now they'd sold up and moved back to Waterford, back to their roots and where their remaining relatives lived. She hadn't really seen it coming, but Nadia thought there was relief all round that they didn't have to go through the torture anymore.

Now they emailed her occasionally and had sent a Christmas card with a generous cheque in for Lewis, which was lovely. But that was hardly the same as having them around the corner.

Soon, Lewis had begun to forget them so that when they called to talk to him, he had only a vague idea of who they were.

Her heart went out to her son. The relationship with grandparents could be so special, it was a shame he'd only briefly enjoyed that. Maybe she should make the effort to take him out to see Toby's folks in Ireland.

It only threw into relief how important it was for this meeting to go well. For Lewis's sake as much as hers.

'Try to behave, sweetheart.' Of course, he would. Lewis was a good boy, but it suddenly seemed crucial that they should like him. Part of her also wanted them to appreciate what they'd been missing for so many years.

With a deep and steadying breath, they headed up the drive to Anita's house. There was a car that she didn't know parked there and she assumed that her parents had already arrived. Nadia felt sick. Her palms were damp with fear and she was trembling inside.

Her hand reached out for the bell but, before she pressed it, she pulled herself up short. Why was she so nervous? She wasn't a fearful little schoolgirl now, frightened of her father's wrath. She was a grown woman who had successfully overcome tragedy in her life. She was a single parent doing a great job of bringing up her boy. There was no way that she should let the thought of this meeting reduce her to a gibbering wreck. She should remember the good times with her family. Her parents had been good people. They'd been strict, but kind. It was only when she'd gone against their wishes and had married Toby – a rather ordinary English boy, instead of some moneyed distant cousin she'd never met – that their relationship had gone wrong. After that, they had all become entrenched in their opposing views. Well, now they had a chance to put that right. Perhaps they'd mellowed over the years and had simply been waiting for the chance to be reconciled. Well, this was it.

She pressed the bell and within seconds Anita had rushed to the door. Her sister was giddy with excitement, clearly relishing her role as the family peacemaker. Nadia suppressed a sigh. If this all went well, then Anita would be crowing about it for years. But then, if it did go well, she'd have every right to.

Ushering in Lewis before her, Nadia stepped inside. She normally tried to avoid coming to Anita's house as her relationship with her brother-in-law, Tarak, was never going to be easy.

As if reading her mind, Anita said, 'Tarak's working late this evening. Something at one of the shops has delayed him. He said he'd make it back if he could.'

Tarak and Nadia shared a mutual mistrust so, if she knew her brother-in-law, he'd stay away until he thought the coast was clear.

There was a wonderful smell of dinner cooking coming from the kitchen and it made Nadia realise that she hadn't eaten since her sister's phone call this morning.

'I brought onion bhajis that I quickly made when I got home,' Nadia said. 'Not much of a contribution.' She wished she'd thought to go into Chocolate Heaven to collect some cakes or a lovely selection of chocolates from Lucy. That would have been a better peace offering than onion bhajis, and she cursed her stupidity.

'They'll be so surprised to see you.'

'What?' Nadia hissed. 'They do know I'm coming?'

'Hmm. Not exactly,' Anita admitted, wincing. 'I thought it would be best this way.'

'For who?'

'I didn't want them to worry,' her sister said. 'You would only have got all stressed about it if you'd known they weren't aware you were coming.'

Rightly, too.

'I did tell them we were having a guest,' Anita added. 'Who else would it be?'

'Oh, Anita. You said you'd talked to them about me.'

'It will be fine.'

'I could kill you for this.'

'Come on, let's get it over with. Soon it will be just like old times and you'll be thanking me.'

Nadia sighed, resignedly. What else was she to do? She could hardly cut and run now.

Holding Nadia's hand and grinning, Anita pulled her into the living room. In turn she led Lewis who, perhaps sensing that all wasn't well, dragged reluctantly behind her.

'Mum, Dad!' Anita sounded over-bright and false. 'Look who's here to see you.'

Her parents glanced up, smiling and then blanched with shock. The smiles froze on their faces and they both remained seated. No jumping up to take their long-lost daughter into their arms, Nadia noted.

'Hello,' Nadia said calmly, although her stomach was churning. 'It's good to see you both. You look well.'

The expression on her mother's face made her look as if she'd chewed a wasp. Her father seemed to have shrunk so much in the years since she'd seen him that he was no longer the imposing character he had been.

Lewis clung to Nadia's leg. 'This is your grandma and grandpa that I told you about.'

'He seems a fine boy,' her daddy said.

'Why so shy?' That was her mother. 'Is he a clingy child?'

'He's been through a lot,' Nadia said tightly. 'He's always nervous with strangers.'

Their faces told her that they hadn't missed the barb in her words. Anita fluttered about anxiously. 'Tea, Nadia? Mum? Dad? More tea?'

This obviously wasn't going as her sister had planned. And what had Nadia expected? Did she really think that they'd welcome her back with open arms? She'd hoped so, but looking at her parents she wondered whether too much time had passed for them ever to be able to get back to where they had once been. They'd been estranged for far too many years to be easy in each other's company.

She could understand their reticence with her, but what about Lewis? He was innocent in all of this, yet this was their first meeting with their grandchild and they'd hardly rushed to embrace him.

'Come and sit with us.' Her father seemed to be softening the most. He patted the seat next to him. 'It's been a long time and you must have a lot to tell us.'

If she was honest, Nadia couldn't think of a single thing she wanted to share with them. She perched nervously on the edge of the chair, Lewis still attached to her like a limpet. Her mother was scrutinising him with her unwavering, cool gaze and she wanted to protect her son from that.

'Go and find your cousins,' she said to her son. 'I'll shout for you when dinner is ready.'

Glad of the chance to escape, Lewis rushed off.

'We've just been to the Lake District,' she said pleasantly, as if talking to someone she'd just met on the bus or at the hair-dresser. 'It's very lovely up there. We hadn't been on holiday in a long time.' She didn't tell them of the reason for her visit, her gorgeous farmer with whom she was falling in love, or how she was holding a marriage proposal in her heart. They'd have to earn those confidences and, right now, it didn't look as if they were even interested in trying.

'He looks like his father,' her mother said, curtly.

'Yes. A lot. Sometimes I turn round and it's just like seeing Toby.'

'Let's hope he doesn't turn out like him,' she added.

And that really set the tone for the rest of the evening.

Anita served dinner and it looked delicious. Her sister was a wonderful cook. The biriyani smelled divine, the rice light and fluffy, the lamb tender and succulent. Anita's chapatis were second to none, but Nadia could hardly touch a thing due to the acid swirling in her stomach. Conversation was worse than stilted and every comment felt deliberately hurtful and personal. The boys were eating in the kitchen together, so at least Lewis wasn't subjected to it. She could hear the chatter and laughter from them and was glad that he was having a nice time.

'It's a shame Tarak is so busy,' her mother said. 'You know how much I love to see my son-in-law. He's been a *wonderful* husband.'

They praised Tarak to the roof and Nadia wanted to tell them what her brother-in-law was really like. He was a deceitful man who liked to cheat on his wife – even with her own sister given half the chance. Nadia smiled sourly to herself as she remembered how Tarak's relentless pursuit of her had turned out. She still had the photographs, locked away at home, that proved just how far he was from an ideal husband: Tarak in a very compromising position in a hotel room – one of Lucy's hare-brained plans. She wondered what her parents would think if they got a glimpse of those candid shots or knew that in the past he'd been guilty of propositioning Nadia? Why, when they'd seen every fault in Toby amplified, were they seemingly blind to Tarak's failings?

'Your boys are so clever, Anita.' Her mother again. 'Always top of the class. I'm sure Daman will be a doctor or a lawyer.'

Even Anita looked discomfited and she never missed an opportunity to talk about her beloved sons.

'They're great kids,' Nadia agreed, refusing to be lured into competitive boasting.

'I'm sure it's down to you being at home for them.' Her mother dabbed at her mouth with a napkin. 'That's where a mother should be.'

Nadia bit down a retort. The subtext was there all the time. Anita was wonderful. Nadia wasn't good enough. She hadn't realised that her mother could be so vindictive. By the end of the first course, she'd certainly seen her in a different light. When Anita brought in their favourite family dessert of creamy milk and rice studded with cashews and raisins, Nadia felt so nauseous that she couldn't eat a mouthful. Only her father looked slightly abashed, but he didn't speak up in her defence and Nadia's heart felt sad at the loss of him. Once, he could have been smiling and rubbing his considerable stomach at the thought of his favourite treat; now he ate the pudding in grim silence with the rest of them.

It was the longest dinner of her life. So different from the chattering affairs with all the family gathered round their parents' dining-room table that they used to enjoy so many years ago. How heartbreaking that she seemed destined never to have that with them again.

By the end of the meal, she was longing to leave. If she'd had more courage, she'd have stood up and left earlier. This hadn't been a family reunion, it had been a character assassination. She'd never thought the evening was going to be easy, but she didn't think they'd still be so set against her. Clearly, her mother felt that the honour of the family had somehow been besmirched and could never again be scrubbed clean.

'We'd better be going,' Nadia said, standing. 'Lewis has to be up early for school tomorrow.' She turned to Anita. 'Thank you for a lovely dinner. It's been a pleasant evening.'

They all knew it was far from that.

The truth of the matter was, as they'd aged, her parents had become small-minded and judgemental. They were so entrenched in their opinions that they didn't even consider those of others. Did she need them in her life if all they wanted to do was undermine her efforts and belittle her? If they had embraced her again and welcomed her back into the family fold, then she would have found it hard to break free. As it stood, it was clear that she was here on tolerance. Apart from one token effort from her father, neither of them had said a single kind thing to her all evening. There'd been no offer of condolences – no matter how belated. No praise for their grandson or how she'd managed by herself. It was as though, if they didn't mention it, then they could forgive their own shortcomings. She couldn't imagine a time when she'd ever be able to behave that way towards Lewis, no matter what he did.

She called her son in from the kitchen and they prepared to leave. Anita brought their coats and Nadia helped Lewis to button his up, feeling pride in how well he'd behaved.

'Say goodbye to your grandparents, sweetheart,' she said.

'Bye-bye, Grandma.' He gave a shy little wave. Still as much a stranger to them now that they were going as he had been when they arrived. 'Bye-bye, Grandpa.'

Even though her face was set as stone, she thought she saw her mother choke down a sob. Nadia sighed inside. How easy it would be for either of them to scoop Lewis into their arms, hug him and make it all right. Even now, it wasn't too late. But neither of them made a move.

Taking her son by the hand, she walked to the door.

Anita followed her, and at the door she mouthed, 'I'm sorry. So sorry.'

'That's OK,' Nadia said. 'You tried.'

'Speak tomorrow, sis?'

'Yeah. I'll call you when I'm home from work.'

'I love you,' Anita said. She ruffled Lewis's hair. 'Both of you.'

Walking down the drive, hand in hand with her child, Nadia held her head high. That was an ordeal that she never wanted to repeat. She thought she could feel her parents watching her through the window, but she didn't look back.

The sad thing was that it would now make it easier for her to leave the area. She wouldn't have wanted it this way, but it had given her some kind of closure on their relationship. Her parents wouldn't be the ties that bound her here; it would be her friends. The Chocolate Lovers' Club ladies who'd stuck with her through thick and thin. They were the ones who'd always been there for her. They would be the ones it would be difficult to leave.

Then she realised, with a smile to herself, that she *was* thinking of leaving.

Chapter Forty-Four

We all stand in front of the rows of toilet bags on the shelves. Chantal looks at us anxiously. 'It's hard to know which to choose.'

I pick one up. 'Pink cupcakes. No contest.'

Chantal gnaws at her lip. 'Is that the image I'm trying to convey?'

'The image you're trying to convey is Clean Person in Hospital for a Couple of Nights. This works.'

'I don't think you're taking this seriously, Lucy.'

Laughing, I hug Chantal to me. 'Of course, I am.' I've already realised that this isn't about us having a shopping outing to get Chantal ready for her hospital stay, it's about bolstering her confidence, providing a distraction so that she doesn't really have to focus on the operation that's looming large. A few more days and she'll be having a mastectomy, which still seems such a radical form of surgery. I keep my reassuring smile in place and gesture at the shelf. 'My razor-sharp and stylish brain has already eschewed the others as unsuitable. Tartan – says old biddy, might smell of wee. Black with silver piping – too chav. Powder-blue paisley – too boring. No one wants blue paisley.

The designer should be shot. Pink cupcakes say youthful with a frivolous side.'

'She's right,' Nadia agrees.

'As always,' I remind them.

Chantal knows that resistance is futile and shrugs her acceptance. 'Pink cupcakes.' She puts the toilet bag into her shopping basket.

'Have you got all your toiletries? Shampoo, deodorant, toothpaste?'

'I think so.'

'Now what?' I ask.

'Pyjamas,' Chantal says. 'Which floor are they on?'

'Up,' I say. So we all troop off towards the escalator. We stand in a line, holding the rail. The store is busy and I want to put a big cordon round Chantal to protect her so that no one knocks into her, even though she's no more fragile than the rest of us.

Autumn, behind me, taps my back and mouths, 'Is she doing OK?'

I nod in confirmation and whisper, 'She'll be fine.'

A moment later we're faced with racks and racks of nightwear and lingerie.

'Nothing with cartoons,' Chantal warns. 'No one over the age of ten should go to bed with Minnie Mouse on their chest.'

'You'll have a hospital gown on for most of the time,' I remind her.

'Not if I can help it,' she says darkly.

We fan out and flick through all the unsuitable pyjamas and nightdresses until Chantal holds a pyjama set high. 'This,' she declares. 'A perfect blend of sophistication and functionality.'

They're non-crease cotton in the palest of pinks: roomy, cut boyfriend style. They are, indeed, perfect.

'They'll be comfy,' Autumn says.

'And they match your toilet bag.' My input.

'You'll be the most colour-coordinated patient they've ever had,' Nadia says.

'No point in letting standards drop just because they're going to cut bits of you off,' Chantal jokes. But I hear the catch in her voice.

The pyjamas go into the shopping basket.

'Anything else?'

She lets out a wobbly breath and says, 'The nurse said that I should get a couple of post-surgery bras too.'

'Do they have them in here?'

'Yes. I Googled it last night.' We drift off in search of the lingerie department and, tucked away in a corner, find the post-surgery bras. To be fair, they might not be that easy to locate, but there's quite a range.

'They're even worse in real life than they were online. Some of them look like something my grandma would wear,' Chantal says, disdainfully.

It's true that a number of the bras seem as if they've come straight from a 1950s underwear catalogue. They're enormous great things with wide straps and cups like buckets. Chantal could use one as a hammock.

'But there are good ones too,' I point out. 'This is pretty and super-soft.' I turn to show a little lacy white bra to Chantal and see that her eyes have filled with tears. 'Don't cry. Don't cry,' I soothe. 'We don't have to do bras.'

'I'm scared,' Chantal says. 'I'm going to have to wear a bra with a prosthetic because one of my own boobs will be gone for good.' She folds her arms across her chest.

'It will be temporary,' I offer. 'Livia said once they're sure it's all gone, you'll have your reconstruction.'

'It could be months yet. Longer. I thought I was coping well,' Chantal says with a tearful sigh. 'But, occasionally, it hits me all over again. It all seems so real now.'

'You'll be glad when it's all over. Not long to wait.'

'It's the waiting that's the worst thing,' she agrees. 'It's so stressful.'

'Let's get these things.' I take the shopping basket from her. 'That's enough for today. Don't try to do too much at once. Small steps, small steps. Coffee and cake is calling.'

'We'll be with you every inch of the way,' Nadia says.

'You know we'd move into the ward with you if we could,' I add.

Autumn looks close to tears. 'Don't ever think you're alone with this.'

Chantal fills up again too. 'I couldn't manage without you all.'

Then words run out. I drop the shopping basket to the floor and we all have a group hug in the middle of the shop. If I'm honest, we're all scared for her too.

Chapter Forty-Five

The next few days pass in a blur and Chantal goes in for her mastectomy. It's a scant two days after the operation and she's already out of the hospital and recuperating at home. That has to be a good sign, right?

We all put little personal notes in her overnight case for her, but we barely had time to visit her in hospital. The pink pyjamas and the cupcake toilet bag, so carefully chosen, hardly got a look in. But we all let out the relieved breath that we didn't realise we were holding. She's through another hurdle.

After work, we all meet up at the Tube station and head off to visit Chantal at home. I'm anxious as we stand at her front door and there's a collective nervousness as we wait for Jacob to let us in. It's all very well coming out of hospital quickly but it's a different kettle of fish once you get home and have to cope with everything yourself.

We are, in the time-honoured fashion of patient visitors, bearing flowers and chocolate. I picked a lovely box of Chantal's favourites from Chocolate Heaven – nothing better to help get you on your feet. Nadia is clutching them to her while I ring the bell.

'Hey,' Jacob says as he lets us in. He looks tired, drawn and has a very lively Lana wriggling on his hip.

I give him a hug. 'How's the patient doing?'

'OK,' he says. 'Not very patient. I might have to staple her to the sofa to keep her there. She keeps wanting to get up and help. Go on through. I'll put the kettle on.'

'Let me take Lana,' I say. 'Come to Auntie Lucy, you delicious thing.'

Jacob hands her over and I give her a big squeeze. 'How's my best girl?' She answers me in her own scribble talk.

We head to Chantal's living room and peep our heads round the door. She's lying on the sofa in her fancy new pyjamas watching an old episode of *Antiques Roadshow*.

'Hey,' I say. 'Can you cope with some visitors?'

'Get in here,' she says. 'Hand over those chocolates.'

'How did you know we had chocolates?' I ask.

'You'd better have them.'

I laugh. We are too predictable. I show her the chocolates and then put them on the coffee table.

'Flowers, too,' Autumn says, holding out the bunch we bought.

'You're spoiling me.'

We all go to hug her, gingerly.

'I'm fine,' she says. 'I'm not going to break.'

She's pale and looks a little frail but, considering what she's been through, remarkably well.

'How are you doing?' I ask.

'Well. I'm sleeping a lot and my arm hurts like a bitch. I'm not allowed to lift Lana yet or anything else for that matter. She doesn't understand why I can't play with her, bless her.' She smiles sadly at her daughter. 'Other than that, I'm all right. Sort of.'

She pushes herself to sitting with a wince. There's a notice-able flat space in her pyjama top where her breast used to be and it breaks my heart to see it. Chantal is holding her arm awkwardly, nursing it to her.

I sit down with Lana on my lap.

'Considering what you've been through, you still look amazing,' Nadia says.

'Thanks. It's fair to say that I'm not exactly firing on all cylinders, but I'm better than I expected to be. Clearly, Hamilton ladies are made of tough stuff.'

'If anyone can breeze through this, it's you,' I tell her.

'I hope you're right, Lucy. There's a long way to go yet until I'm out of the woods. The worst thing is that I'm bored out of my head already,' she admits. 'I'd forgotten how dire daytime television is. I'll go mad if I have to spend the next few weeks watching *Jeremy Kyle* and *Homes under the Hammer*.'

'We need to get you loaded up with box sets to keep you amused,' Nadia says. 'I've got plenty from my sad, single nights alone. I'll bring some round.'

'Good. Jacob won't let me move.'

'Of course I won't.' He comes in with a tray of tea for us. 'Doctor's orders.'

'Livia has been great,' Chantal tells us. 'She says the operation has been a success and seems a lot happier now that I've had the mastectomy. I've just got chemo to look forward to.'

'You have to keep that fighting spirit up.' I bounce Lana up and down to keep her entertained. 'We'll help you.'

'I am feeling like a warrior woman,' Chantal says. 'This isn't going to beat me.'

Jacob serves our tea and says, 'I'm going to grab a shower while you've got Lana. Is that all right?'

'Good plan,' Chantal says and Jacob beats a hasty retreat. 'He's been fantastic,' she adds when he's gone. 'I couldn't feel more cared for.'

'Here's to Jacob,' Nadia proposes and we all toast him with

our tea. Then I break open the chocolates and hand them round. Chantal nibbles one appreciatively.

'Glad to see you haven't lost your appetite,' Nadia says.

'As if,' Chantal replies. 'Never underestimate the restorative powers of chocolate.'

'Isn't chocolate full of antioxidants or something?' I choose a particularly fine salted caramel. Yum. I give Lana a tiny taste too and she smacks her lips together. 'I thought that was supposed to prevent cancer?'

'Obviously we aren't eating nearly enough,' Autumn concludes.

I rectify that by having another one. Good job I brought a big box.

'I've been told to take it easy. Nothing too strenuous. Livia wants me to start the chemo treatment as soon as possible and they're hoping to fit me in some time in the next few weeks. So I need to be fit and healthy for then,' Chantal says. 'I'm going to have to do something to distract myself, though. If I just lie here doing nothing, I'll go out of my mind.'

Then a light bulb pings in my head. 'I have a cunning plan!'

Everyone groans.

'It's my best idea yet,' I say. 'You leave it with me. I just need to make a couple of calls.'

'Your plans always worry me, Lucy,' Chantal says.

'They're wonderful! And I don't want you to fret about a single thing,' I tell her. 'Leave it all to me.'

'Leave *what* all to you?' she wants to know.

I bat away the question. My mind is in overdrive. 'This plan is going to be just fabulous.' I'm so excited I could squeeeeeee.

Chapter Forty-Six

Another few days later, we are all standing outside Chantal's house once more. It's a warm, sunny day – just right for our escapade.

Autumn nibbles her fingernails as she turns to me and says anxiously, 'Are you sure this is a good plan, Lucy?'

'Of course,' I say. 'What could possibly go wrong?'

'I feel like a fool.' Nadia throws in her two-pence-worth.

'Don't stress,' I insist. 'It will all be absolutely fine.' I look down at my attire. I hope.

When Jacob opens the front door he looks at us in amazement – or maybe it's disbelief.

'Wow,' he says. 'You've surpassed yourself, Lucy.' He laughs out loud. 'Oh, my. I can't wait to see Chantal's face.'

'Do you think she'll like it?'

'I've absolutely no idea. I know she'll think you're mad.'

'Is she doing OK today?'

'She's good,' he tells us – which is a relief to hear. 'Don't tire her out, though.'

'We won't. Is she ready for us?' I ask.

'I'm not sure *anyone's* ready for you,' he teases.

'Yes, very funny. Ha, ha.' Then, 'You gave her the team T-shirt?'

'I did. Just a few minutes ago. She looked very bemused but, as we speak, she's upstairs putting it on.'

'You didn't tell her what was happening?'

'No. Only that you were coming along today. My lips were sealed.'

'Do you think she'll kill us?' Now I'm a bit worried.

Another laugh. 'She might do. Let's see. I'll go and get her.'

We have a few minutes of fluffing our outfits and then our friend comes to the door. Chantal's eyes widen when she sees us. 'You are kidding me?'

'Your chariot awaits, Madam,' I say.

She takes in the wheelchair that I've pimped and bursts out laughing.

Tied to the chair are two bunches of pink helium balloons. There's a glittery pink cushion to make it more comfortable. The arms are covered with pink and white ribbons and fake flower posies. I've bought sparkly tiaras for me, Nadia and Autumn. For Chantal there's an especially glamorous jewelled crown from eBay. We're all wearing pink T-shirts bearing the legend *BREAST CANCER MESSED WITH THE WRONG CHICK* and there's a cartoon chicken doing kung fu beneath it. On the back, I've had it printed with TEAM CHANTAL. We're all wearing white jeans and sparkly shoes.

'I'm glad I'm appropriately dressed,' she says, taking in our outfits and her mode of transport. 'That's one hell of a chair.'

'I've borrowed it from the Red Cross for the day and we're going on an outing. Yay!'

Her eyes are agog. 'Where the hell are you taking me in *that*?'

'Ah! It's a surprise.'

She shakes her head in disbelief, but I'm relieved to see that her smile is still in place. 'This I can't wait for.'

261

I give her the crown – which fits her perfectly, I must say – and we're ready for the off. Chantal's moving better now and she's got a full face of slap on. She looks so great that, if you didn't know, you'd think that nothing was wrong. I hand round the tiaras and we all put them on. I also have a banner for her which says PATIENT ON BOARD.

Chantal turns to Jacob. 'Do you know where I'm going?'

'Not a clue. But if Lucy's organised it, you're bound to have fun. I wish I was a fly on the wall.'

'I'm not going to remind you that Lucy's outings usually end very badly,' Chantal says.

'I didn't know that Ms Flipping France would call the police,' I mutter darkly.

At that moment our taxi arrives, which is an excellent distraction from my shortcomings as an events organiser. 'Oh, here we go. Can you manage to walk that far?'

'I'm not *actually* an invalid,' Chantal says. 'I can walk.'

'You'll be glad of the chair,' I tell her. 'Just trust me.'

'I'd be a fool not to,' she says with a certain amount of sarcasm.

'I admit that my previous plans may have involved a modicum of danger or risk or even a certain amount of unnecessary foolishness . . . ' I know my faults. 'But this will be just happiness all the way.'

'It doesn't involve drugs, having my photograph taken while wearing minimal clothing, driving a getaway vehicle?'

'None of the above,' I assure her.

'I won't end up in a canal or in a cell?'

'Probably not.'

She grins at us. 'Let's do it then. I can't wait.'

'Right. Let's load up.' Nadia wheels the chair to the taxi and loads it in.

Chantal kisses Lana and Jacob goodbye.

'Have a great afternoon,' Jacob says. 'Come home safely.'

I escort a very perplexed Chantal to the taxi and we all head off to Mayfair.

Lovely Jen from Chocolate Ecstasy Tours is waiting for us outside a chocolate shop. She's wearing her tiara and Team Chantal T-shirt as instructed and has dropped everything to put on this special event for our friend.

'A chocolate tour?' Chantal grins at me as she climbs into her pimped-up wheelchair. 'What a treat. This has to be your best ever cunning plan, Lucy.'

'Thanks. I think so, too.' I beam widely. 'I told you not to worry.'

So we set off on our tour, me pushing Chantal's wheelchair. People smile and wave as we pass them and they step aside on the crowded pavements to make way for us.

Jen takes us on a tour of the chocolate shops around Mayfair and Soho, stopping at each one to sample their wares. We try some champagne truffles with a hint of strawberry, crisp hazelnut and ginger crunches, velvety soft pralines and decadent molten caramels. All divine. This outing might be a bit of fun to cheer up our friend, but I'm also picking up some great tips for Chocolate Heaven along the way.

We laugh and joke as we go and Jen tells us some of the history of the area when she can get a word in edgeways. Halfway round we stop for a coffee break so that Chantal can catch her breath.

'You're not getting too tired?' I ask.

'No.' She touches my arm. 'Thanks, Lucy. This is great fun and just the tonic I needed. I was going mad cooped up in the house. I haven't laughed so much in ages.'

'Just let me know when you've had enough. We can take you straight back home. I don't want you to overdo it and feel poorly.'

'Strangely, this is helping me to forget my pain. Only a cock-tail or two would help more.'

'Are you allowed alcohol?'

'The doctor didn't say that I *couldn't* have any.' She looks all wide-eyed and innocent. 'One or two wouldn't hurt, surely?'

I look to the girls. 'Next stop cocktails! What do you say?'

'We're in,' Autumn and Nadia agree.

'There are two more chocolate shops on my route and there's a nice hotel just around the corner from the last one,' Jen says. 'I'm happy to stop there afterwards if you are.'

'It's a plan.'

So we set off again and this time Autumn takes over pushing Chantal's wheelchair. We visit the last two shops, tasting rasp-berry liqueur truffles, bite-sized morsels of pecan brownies and a dark chocolate Florentine.

When we've finished Jen asks, 'Have you had enough choc-olate?'

'You can never have enough chocolate,' I remind her. 'But I'm sure we've had enough for now. It's been great. What better way to round it off than with some cocktails?'

So we head straight to the hotel, parking Chantal's wheelchair in the foyer, and are shown to a table in the airy lounge. Less than ten minutes later we have our first cocktail in front of us.

I hold my glass aloft. 'To the patient!'

'To the patient!' they echo.

'Ah, this has been fabulous,' Chantal says. 'We must do it again when I can *walk* round.'

We make Jen an honorary member of the Chocolate Lovers' Club in respect of her astounding chocolate knowledge and capacity for endless consumption of our favourite foodstuff, then we have another cocktail to celebrate.

We're getting even more giggly.

'This feels like it's turning into a proper hen party. We certainly look like the hen party from hell,' Chantal says, pulling out her T-shirt for inspection. 'It won't be long before yours, Lucy.'

'I can't wait,' I say. 'I haven't decided what to do yet.'

'You'd better get a move on,' Nadia says. 'It's not long.'

'Everything's in place now,' I tell them. 'I think. Jacob's sorted the catering.'

'I did have a little hand in that,' Chantal confesses. 'I think you'll love it.'

'It's going to be wonderful. I had a phone call this morning to say that my dress has arrived at the shop. The groom is still in love with me.' Never a given with my history. 'All I need now is perfect weather.'

Chantal clutches my hand. 'You're doing the right thing,' she says. 'I couldn't be happier for you. As soon as I'm well again, I'm going to whisk Jacob down the aisle. We talked about it again last night. He's as keen as I am.' She sighs. 'All this has made me realise that life is a very precarious blessing. I'm going to waste no more time. I wish I could do it now, this minute, before I start chemo. That's going to set me back six months, at least. Plus I'm likely to lose all my hair.' She grimaces at that. 'Then I might have to have radiotherapy as well. By the time I've recovered, a year could have gone by.' Her voice catches in her throat. 'There's always the possibility that I might not recover at all.'

'No there isn't,' I say. 'Of course you'll get through this. Look at that T-shirt. Believe.' I point to the kung-fu chicken emblazoned on her chest. 'You are going to kick cancer's arse.'

'I know. Sometimes, I worry that I won't be here to see Lana grow up. That Jacob and I won't make it to our seventies together.'

'You will.'

'It is playing on my mind. I can't help it. The divorce is nearly finalised. It's only a matter of days before it's done.' She rubs her arm. 'I know it's irrational, but it feels as if being married to Jacob would make the future feel all the more believable.'

I stop with my cocktail halfway to my mouth. 'Have my wedding,' I say.

Chantal laughs.

'No, I mean it.' Maybe it's the drink talking, but it suddenly seems exactly the right thing to do. 'There's a wedding organised and ready to roll. Your need is greater than mine.'

'Lucy, you are so lovely, but I can't do that. It's your big day. And you've waited long enough.'

'I'm serious. Deadly so.' I hold up a hand. 'Bad choice of words. There's going to be *no one* dying in this club. *No one.*' I can see Chantal wavering. 'You picked out the dress and have paid for it. You've just said that you helped Jacob to source the catering. You'll *love* the venue. It could almost be your day already.'

Chantal bites her lip and I can sense her growing excitement at the idea. She needs this. I know.

Tears spring to my eyes. 'I couldn't bear for anything to go wrong and you not be married to Jacob.'

'I want it with all of my heart.'

'Then nothing's stopping you.'

'We could just slope off to the register office and have a quiet dinner somewhere. That would be the thing to do.'

'No,' I say. 'You're not sloping off anywhere. You're going to have a lovely wedding and there's one already arranged. It's the obvious solution.'

Chantal's eyes are bright with tears, too. 'Do you really mean it, Lucy?'

'Of course. Nothing would give me greater pleasure.'

'Could we actually do it?'

'I'll phone the register office and check straight away, but if they're already booked for the venue and date, then it can't be that hard. Can it? I'm sure it would simply be a matter of you going to them and filling in your paperwork.'

'When would *you* get married?'

'Don't even think about that. We can arrange it all again as soon as possible. It's not a problem.' I take a deep gulp and cross my fingers behind my back. 'Truly.'

'You're *absolutely* sure?' Chantal still looks dazed.

'Yes. It's my gift to you.'

'I guess that's sorted then.' Chantal giggles into her hands. 'I'm getting married.'

I hug my friend tightly. 'I have to be your *chief* bridesmaid, though.'

'It's a deal.'

'Tell the others,' I say excitedly.

'Shall I?' Chantal taps on her cocktail glass with the stirrer. 'Ladies of the Chocolate Lovers' Club, I have an announcement to make.'

Autumn, Nadia and Jen turn to look at her.

'I'm going to be married!' She looks at me, eyes shining brightly. 'Lucy has very kindly said that I can step into her shoes and take over her wedding so that Jacob and I can tie the knot as soon as possible.'

'Seriously?' Nadia says.

I nod.

Autumn adds a 'Woo hoo!'

'We should drink to this,' I say. 'Ladies, charge your glasses. To Chantal and Jacob.'

We lift our glasses.

Then Chantal frowns. 'What about Crush? You're certain that he won't mind?'

'No, no, no,' I say. 'Not at all.' And then I wonder how on earth I'm going to tell him that I've just given our wedding away.

Chapter Forty-Seven

I go home the worse for drink. Chantal, very sensibly in her condition, limited herself to just two cocktails. I did not.

I'm in the taxi on the way home before the realisation that I've just given away my wedding really hits me. Yikes. What *will* Crush say? I am supposed to be the new non-stupid version of me and look what I've gone and done. But, in all honesty, how could I deny my friend this chance?

By all accounts, her operation was a resounding success, but we all know what a terrible thing cancer is. It has a habit of biting people on the bum. How could I go ahead and get married knowing that Chantal could be waiting on an uncertain future? If anything went wrong, that would always be on my mind. If that's what she wants, she should marry Jacob and she should marry him now.

I only hope that Crush agrees with me.

He's on the sofa watching some car-chase programme when I stumble into the living room.

'Hello, party animal,' he says wryly.

'Too many cocktails.' Slightly more slurry than I'd like. 'Excellent day out.'

'At least you didn't fall in the canal.'

'No.' Good point, well made.

'I take it Chantal isn't in the same state as you?'

'No. Mush more shenshible.'

'Did she enjoy your surprise?'

I nod too much. 'Lovely time.'

He comes to give me a cuddle and then recoils as my alcohol breath hits him. 'Would you like me to make you some strong black coffee, Gorgeous?'

I cling to him tightly. 'Yesh pleash.'

'Relax the death grip, Lucy. Relax. Relax.' Gingerly, he unwinds himself from my arms. 'Some toast with that?'

As he heads towards the kitchen I blurt out, 'I've done something terrible.'

That stops Crush in his tracks. I was going to leave this until tomorrow when I'd had a chance to think about what I was going to say and when, essentially, I'd be a bit less drunk than I am now.

He raises his eyebrows. 'Does it involve Marcus?'

'No. Not this time.'

He looks quite relieved by that. 'Does it involve you getting naked with strange men?'

'No. Absolutely not.'

'Is candid photography of any kind involved?'

'No. No. No.' I shake my head vigorously. Then feel decidedly dizzy.

'Have you swallowed expensive jewellery?'

'No.'

Crush sighs. 'But I do need to sit down for this?'

'Yes. Maybe.'

My beloved sits on the sofa, head in hands, braced for the worst. 'Go on then. Hit me with it.'

I take a deep breath. In for a penny, in for a pound. I've done it now. No going back. I can hardly ring Chantal tomorrow and tell her it was a big mistake, can I? No.

'We can't get married,' I say sadly. 'Not never. Just not now.'

'Why?' Crush says. 'I thought we were getting on really well.' He looks at me, eyes sorrowful. 'This is to do with Marcus, right?'

I shake my head and it makes me a little bit dizzier. Must stop shaking head. 'It's not me. It's you.'

Crush frowns.

'Other way round,' I correct. A conversation like this should *not* be attempted in a haze of alcohol. 'It's not you. It's me.'

'What's made you change your mind?'

'I haven't,' I reassure him. 'There might just have been a tiny-weeny change of plan.' I steel myself. 'I might have told Chantal that she can have our wedding.'

His head snaps up at that. 'You did what?'

'I gave our wedding away,' I confirm and then look at him anxiously. 'She really, really wants to marry Jacob as soon as possible and I was worried that her cancer might get worse or come back or whatever and she might never make it. She'll have to have chemo and all her hair might fall out. And you don't want to be a bride when you're bald. Although it's perfectly acceptable for the groom to be bald.'

'Is that it?'

I stand there trying to look suitably penitent. 'Yes.'

'It would have been nice if you'd called me to check first,' he says.

'I know.' I hang my head in shame. What was I thinking? 'I'm an idiot. It came out of my mouth before it went through my brain.'

'Why doesn't that surprise me?' Crush laughs. 'But it's fine, Lucy. Of course it's fine.' He stands up and breathes out a sigh of relief. 'That's what I love about you most. You're so selfless.

You put everyone's needs before your own. I know Chantal's situation and it's awful. If we can help then we should. If that means you want Chantal to have our wedding, then she must.'

I jump into his arms and hug him to bits. 'But we can get married really, really soon?'

'We'll set another date just as soon as you like.' He kisses me deeply.

'We could skip the coffee and toast and go straight to bed,' I suggest, fluttering my eyelashes at him in what I hope is a beguiling manner. 'I'm very squiffy and someone who was less of a gentleman might take advantage of that.'

He spins me so that we're heading towards the bedroom. 'I'm no gentleman,' he growls.

I stroke his hair. 'But you are,' I say earnestly. 'You're the kindest, most gentlemanly person I know. And that's why I love you so very much.'

Hours and hours later, when we have loved and loved again, and I'm feeling all dreamy and slightly more sober, Crush gets up and makes us coffee and toast. And we sit in bed cuddled up together eating it and making plans for our next wedding day.

Chapter Forty-Eight

Chantal couldn't believe how the last few weeks had flown. They'd gone by in a blur and that was probably a good thing. Organising the wedding had taken her mind off the hospital visits and the discomfort from her scar. The girls had been fantastic, nothing too much trouble for them and they'd laughed a lot as they pulled the last-minute bits and bobs together.

Now, the night before her wedding, she seemed to be in a little bubble of peace. Everything was organised and there was nothing much else that she could do other than relax and enjoy it. There was just one last hurdle. She was going to take off her dressing gown and look at herself properly for the first time.

Chantal stood in front of the mirror and took a deep breath. The moment of truth. She'd managed, so far, to avoid looking at herself fully. She'd caught glimpses of her scar – when she'd had the dressings removed and the drains taken out had been a terrible moment. While the nurse had tended to her, she'd kept her eyes tightly shut, refusing to look.

She had great tits. No doubt about it. They were full, curvy, with flawless milky white skin. They still looked good in a tight jumper and they didn't sag when she took her bra off at night.

But they hadn't always been her pride and joy. At school she'd been teased mercilessly about them and they were a source of great misery. When all the other girls were flat-chested or were sprouting bee-stings, Chantal had blossomed early. She'd been one of the first girls in her class to wear a bra, which always amused her fellow classmates when they'd had to get changed for sports lessons. Then they laughed at her during the PE lessons when she ran or tried the vault or anything that involved her boobs swinging around. Afterwards, while she showered, they considered it fun to hide her bra and leave her sobbing in the changing rooms. Then she'd be late for the next lesson and would receive a detention for that, too. How she'd hated her breasts then. She would have gladly cut them off.

A few years later they'd become powerful weapons. She only had to flash a hint of her ample cleavage and men were putty in her hands. They'd also got her into a lot of trouble. A stranger in a bar had asked her if he could spend all night kissing them and see if he could try not to kiss the same place twice. She'd let him. One of her bosses had been unable to refuse her anything if she undid an extra button on her blouse before meetings and, shamelessly, she'd revelled in it. Ted had said it was one of the first things he noticed about her. Though she hoped it was her sparkling personality that had, subsequently, won his love.

Then she'd left the bad boys behind and had moved onto a different stage in her life. Bearing a child had changed her perception of her breasts as they'd become a food source for her baby. They'd swollen, grown full and ripe; the nipples had been cracked and sore to the point of making her weep, yet she'd never been more proud of them. They were nourishing her child. What greater purpose could they have?

Yet now, sadly, they'd become a risk to her health, her life.

A liability. What had once been nothing more than decorative ornaments were now threatening to kill her. Some innocuous tissue that had gone rogue throughout the generations of her family threatened her very existence. The luck of the draw. A bad hand for her.

Well, it was on its way out now. With some good fortune, a following wind and some well-aimed chemo, it could be eradicated.

Chantal looked straight ahead at herself, slowly unbelted her dressing gown and let it fall open. She slid it down her arms and let it drop to the floor. She gave a sharp intake of breath as she saw the damage wrought by the surgeon's knife. It was a neat and tidy scar, no doubt, but it still slashed raw and angry across her chest. The pink bud of her nipple was gone. Her other breast seemed mockingly healthy, but it was also a potential war zone. That might have to go as well. And, somehow, it seemed better that both of them went.

Reconstructive surgery was on the cards, but only further down the line when she'd completed her chemo and radiotherapy, if she needed that too. It was still in the lap of the gods. She'd been told that she could have adhesive prosthetic nipples afterwards, but that sounded too awful for words. She'd try to wear her scars loud and proud. In time. Maybe one of those fancy tattoos sweeping from shoulder to shoulder would be the way to go.

She wanted to touch the area, but couldn't get her fingers to obey her brain. Perhaps it was too soon. If the reconstructive surgery didn't take place until after she'd had her chemo it seemed as if she was going to look like this for quite a while, so she'd better get used to it.

The girls were coming round this evening to have a quiet drink together and she'd open a bottle of champagne or two for them all. There'd been no hen party as such, as she'd need all her energy for the ceremony and celebration afterwards. Since her operation, she'd had to rest a lot more and didn't want to wear herself out before her big day. Plus she wanted to be quiet and reflective rather than kick up her heels. There'd be time for that when this was all over.

Her wedding dress hung on the front of the wardrobe ready for tomorrow. It was really beautiful and she couldn't believe how well that had turned out. She was glad that Lucy had been persuaded to choose this one; it was so gorgeous. The fact that she'd actually ordered and paid for it had helped convince her to wear it, but she'd buy Lucy a new dress as soon as she was ready. However, if she was honest, she'd have been happy to get married in an old sack if that's what it had taken. All this was the icing on the cake. The important thing was that she was marrying Jacob and she couldn't be happier. Of all the things she was going to lose in this fight against cancer, she didn't want one of them to be Jacob. She needed him firmly by her side throughout this.

Perhaps, if the circumstances had been different, they wouldn't have rushed so much. But it felt just right. Lucy had been so incredibly kind – a true friend. The dress, with a little nip and tuck here and there, now fitted beautifully. The dear little hat and the matching shoes had been handed over to her too and they looked just as good as they had on Lucy. For Lana, she'd found the most adorable dress and matching headband. She'd have a basket of flowers, which Lana would probably destroy in minutes. Chantal laughed at the thought. In more practical terms, she had a soft bra with a gel-filled breast form that fitted into a little pocket and she only hoped that her lop-sidedness wouldn't show too much, and that it wouldn't chafe against her scar if she wore it all day. Hopefully, she'd be having too much fun to even notice. Chantal picked up her dressing gown and slipped it back on again.

She smiled contentedly at herself. This was the right thing to do. She was confident enough in Jacob's love to know that they would see this through together. Tomorrow – two boobs, one boob or no boobs – she'd be the happiest woman alive. With the emphasis very much on *alive*.

Chapter Forty-Nine

It's a glorious day, just as I knew it would be. The sun is shining, the birds are tweeting, the clouds look like fluffy marshmallows – all that kind of stuff. It's a wonderful day to be getting married. And I know this is terrible, but there's a tiny part of me that still wishes it was my wedding rather than Chantal's.

The bride looks stunning – of course. The knockout dress that the girls picked out for me looks absolutely perfect on her. The lace bodice, the colour of champagne, fits like a glove. The lace skirt has exactly the right amount of swishyness; the matching pillbox hat and veil sit at the ideal jaunty angle. She looks as beautiful as a bride deserves to be.

'You look fantastic,' I say to her, slightly choked.

'You can't notice any difference?' She glances anxiously at her breasts.

'Not a thing.'

'You'd tell me if you could.'

'Of course, but I don't think that's what anyone will be looking at today. You look radiant, glowing. There's never been a hotter bride.'

'Thank you, Lucy.' There are tears in her eyes. 'Thank you

so much. You don't know what this means to me, to both of us.'

'Don't cry,' I say. 'Not yet. You'll start us all off and then we'll have to redo our make-up. We'll all have a good sob later.' I push a recalcitrant tear back above my lashes.

'I don't want anyone to mention the C-word today,' Chantal warns.

'Chocolate?'

We all laugh at that.

'The *other* C-word! Cancer may have temporarily hijacked my life, but I'm not letting it dominate my wedding day. Today, I'm a cancer-free zone.'

'Well said.' Autumn kisses Chantal and hands her the bouquet of white roses she's chosen.

Nadia, Autumn and I went off to the high street a few days ago and bought lovely floaty numbers in coordinating shades of tea rose and mink. We also have small posies of white roses.

This morning we all assembled at Chantal's house for a wholesome breakfast of choc chip muffins. We did each other's hair, make-up and started on the bucks fizz early. The taxi has just dropped us off at the gates of Golders Hill Park and it's a few minutes' walk to the Belvedere pavilion – in my mind, the most beautiful place to get married.

'Are you ready?' I ask. 'Jacob will be waiting.'

Chantal nods.

I hold her tightly and kiss her.

'I can't believe I'm so nervous,' she laughs and holds a hand against her chest. 'My heart's racing.'

'Racing is a good thing. I think. Anything more and I'll call the paramedics.'

'I'm fine, Lucy,' she says. 'Just anxious to do this.'

'You've nothing to be worried about,' Nadia says. 'You're marrying the loveliest man.'

'I know, and it's even more important to me now.'

'I've brought just the thing for nerves, but I don't want you touching them.' Out of my handbag, I bring a packet of Minstrels. 'Ta-dah! These are the least melty chocolates I could think of. Open wide.'

Chantal does as she's told and I pop a few into her mouth. Then I dish them out to Autumn and Nadia, saving a few for myself.

'Are we all feeling good?'

They nod at me, mouths full.

'Let's do it then.' I pop in my own chocolate and we set off through the park. On our way we get smiles and good wishes from the dog walkers and joggers which, as well as the chocolate hit, helps to settle Chantal's nerves.

We climb the steps up to the pavilion through a maze of ivy-covered walkways. The clematis and roses are out in full bloom, a superb tangle of flowers. The scent of the roses is heady and sweet. Oh, this is just magnificent. Everything that I hoped it would be.

I look at Chantal and she squeezes my hand.

'It's lovely, Lucy. I couldn't have chosen anywhere more charming myself.'

'Good.' There's a slight ache in my heart that this isn't my big day, but I'm so happy to see Chantal being married. She's recovered well from her mastectomy and is due to start her chemotherapy soon. This is the ideal window in which to get hitched.

She and Jacob are spending tonight at The Ritz, then they're heading off to Cornwall on honeymoon. They've booked into a boutique hotel for a week while Ted and Stacey look after Lana. They're also holding the baby today, so to speak, and it's nice to see that they've come back from the States for Chantal's wedding. I think that bodes well for the future. I'm sure if she and Jacob manage to have a restful break then it will help to strengthen her health for what lies ahead.

Then we turn the corner and in front of us I see the wedding party waiting. It's an intimate gathering, but our closest friends are here and I don't think Chantal would have wanted more.

There are rows of gold chairs dressed with ivory sashes and, at the head of them, Jacob and Crush – the best man, in so many ways – and the celebrant wait patiently. They both look so handsome in light grey suits and crisp white shirts. Ted and Stacey are there with Elsie and Lana. Clive and Tristan have come back from France for the weekend. There's Miles and Flo with Willow, whom we'll be meeting for the first time today. James and his children have left the farm for a couple of days to be here, which is lovely for Nadia. Lewis looks very much at home with them.

We pause between towering stone pillars at the entrance to the pavilion. My friend has bestowed on me the honour of giving her away and I take my place at her side. Autumn and Nadia fall into place behind us.

I link my arm through hers. 'This is it,' I say.

Jacob turns and grins at his bride.

Now there's a beaming smile on Chantal's face too as she nods at me. Together we walk towards her groom.

Chapter Fifty

When the service is over, we throw white rose petals over the happy couple.

'Congratulations, Mrs Lawson,' I say and give her a kiss.

'That sounds strange,' she laughs. 'I'm going to have to get used to not being a Hamilton anymore.'

We move back through the park to a formal garden by the pond where a table is set up with glasses of champagne and jugs of Pimm's. There's a guitarist perched on a chair plucking out mellow tunes and we mingle with the bride and groom and the other guests while we down a few glasses. It's good to see Clive and Tristan, the former owners of Chocolate Heaven, have come back from France for the wedding. They're both looking so well and are on fine form.

I hug Clive. 'I miss you guys.'

'We miss you, too.' He nods towards the bride. 'How's Chantal doing?'

'Good,' I say. 'Being ridiculously strong.'

'I still can't believe it.'

'None of us can.'

'Make sure that you keep us posted.'

'I will.' Then Clive whispers to me while Crush is chatting away to Tristan. 'How's it working out at Chocolate Heaven with Marcus?'

'It's OK,' I tell him. 'We have our ups and downs, but I'm glad to be there. I still love it.' In fact, I haven't seen Marcus for weeks. That familiar red Ferrari has stayed firmly away. He has adopted a surprisingly hands-off approach, given his usual style. It seems quite weird not sparring with him on a daily basis. I hate to say this, but I might even be missing it a little bit. Also, if Marie-France is still seeing him, then she never talks about him and he hasn't been to Chocolate Heaven to see her. Since I saw her bent over the back-room table, we have very little to say to each other and communicate with a series of short sentences relating only to work.

Still, I don't want to be thinking about Marcus now; I turn my attention back to Clive. 'What about you two? Not fed up with rural France yet? No hungering for the bright lights of London?'

'No. We love it there. The bistro will be ready at the end of summer. Hopefully. Building work seems to move in slow motion in the Haute-Vienne, but when it's finished it will be fabulous. It's going to be very kitsch and quirky.'

I'm sure their village won't know what's hit them.

He hugs himself, excitedly. 'Everyone will have to come for the grand launch.'

'If you make it half as good as Chocolate Heaven, it will be wonderful. Try to keep us away.'

I move on to chat to Ted and Stacey and it's good to see that they look happy, too. I have a cuddle with Elsie, who drools on my dress.

'Lunch is ready, everyone!' Jacob shouts. 'Enjoy!'

Set out on the meticulously manicured grass, there are woollen picnic rugs covered with red hearts and each one has had a large wicker hamper delivered to it. Chantal and Jacob continue to work their way round the guests and the children are already running on the grass, all decorum forgotten.

Crush and I take another glass of champagne each and sit on one of the rugs. He puts his arm round me. 'How are you feeling?'

'Happy for Chantal and Jacob,' I say. 'But a bit sad as well.'

'This would have been a wonderful wedding day.'

'I know.' I try not to succumb to the melancholy that threatens to settle on me. 'Let's organise ours again very soon.'

He kisses me. 'I have no problem with that.' Crush peeps into the picnic hamper. 'All looks delicious.'

Distracting me with food. Excellent plan.

Crush scans the little menu that's been popped in the top of the hamper. 'Jacob has excelled himself.'

'He's a good man,' I say. 'He'll look after Chantal.'

Nadia comes to join us with James, both of them stretching out on the rug. My friend looks very loved up.

'It's good to see you again, James,' I say. 'It's great that you were able to make it.'

'I rarely leave the farm,' he says. 'Even more rarely that I get an occasion where I have to dress up.' He plucks at his smart jacket. 'I think it's time I took this off. My tie's about to strangle me.'

'I think we can dispense with formalities now.'

So both he and Crush take off their jackets and ties and roll up their shirt sleeves.

'That's better,' he says with a heartfelt sigh.

'Have you been to London before?'

'Not for years,' he admits. 'I'm not one for cities. I prefer the hills.'

'I can't say that I blame you. Looks like you've turned Nadia into a country girl, too.'

He beams at her adoringly. 'I hope so.'

'Shall we make a start on this hamper?' Crush says. 'It all looks cracking and it's been a long time since breakfast.'

Inside there's a gourmet picnic. There's pork and pistachio terrine with spicy chutney, Rosemary and sea salt bread, smoked salmon roulade, lemon and thyme skewers, mini Melton Mowbray pork pies, pea and parmesan tartlets and marinated olives.

'Mmm,' Nadia says. 'Delicious. This is a feast fit for kings.'

To follow there's a selection of cheeses and, most importantly, a whole host of chocolate petit fours, chocolate orange brownies and white chocolate-dipped strawberries.

We spread out the picnic and tuck in.

After a few minutes, Autumn, Miles, Flo and Willow come and settle themselves on the next rug. Willow cuddles Flo on her lap as the little one chatters away.

'This is wonderful,' Autumn says. 'What a day.'

'Fabulous,' I agree. 'The picnic's lovely.'

'You should have made it a double wedding, Lucy,' she teases.

'No, our day will come. This is definitely Chantal's time to shine.'

'And didn't she just? It was a charming service. You next, though.'

I lean against Crush. 'I have *everything* crossed!' Sometimes I do wonder whether I'll ever manage to have a wedding where I actually end up married.

'Can I introduce you to my daughter?' Autumn says.

The girl regards us shyly. She's wearing what Autumn has said is her trademark heavy black eye make-up, but she has on a pretty red and black dress and shiny red Doc Martens which look very trendy.

'It's so nice to meet you at last,' I tell her. 'We've heard so much about you.'

284

'Autumn talks a lot about you, too,' Willow answers shyly.

'That's because we are fabulous. You'll have to come into Chocolate Heaven with your mum – you'll love it.'

She flushes; maybe it's because I referred to Autumn as her mum. 'And I'll make sure that you get VIP treatment,' I add.

'Thanks.'

When we've eaten the picnic, the wedding cake appears. It's a three-tier chocolate sponge oozing cream and decorated with raspberries, blueberries and fresh flowers all prepared by Alexandra. Chantal and Jacob cut the cake while we all take cheesy photographs. Then, thankfully, they don't stint on the portions.

Too soon, it's time to pack up and leave, though I'd like to stay here in the park for ever. A taxi has arrived to take Chantal and Jacob to The Ritz and they say their goodbyes.

'It's been fantastic,' Chantal says to me. 'Have you enjoyed it?'

'It's been idyllic.'

She gives me a rueful smile. 'You should be the one going on your honeymoon now.'

'Don't even think about it. This was your day and it's been divine. You've got some wonderful memories. Now go away and have a fabulous rest and come back fighting fit.'

I hold her tightly and then we both do cry.

'Now,' I say, sniffing back the tears. 'One more task. You have to throw that beautiful bouquet to some lucky lady.'

'I hope you catch it.'

'I shall fight to the death for it,' I assure her.

So we all gather to wave them goodbye, and Chantal turns her back to us and tosses her bouquet over her head. I make a dive for it, but Nadia beats me to it and catches it neatly in both hands. She winks at me and laughs. James catches her round the waist and twirls her.

Meh. That had *my* name on it.

Bouquet or not, I am determined to have a wedding ring on my finger soon!

Chapter Fifty-One

Nadia opened the front door and with a welcome sigh said, 'Here we are. Home, sweet home.'

It had been a lovely but tiring day and now she was glad to be back at the house. Yet, in her heart, this felt less like home now. She was still feeling anxious about going out after dark and every single noise seemed to make her jump. It didn't feel safe here anymore.

James and the children had arrived late last night and had done little more than dump their bags and go straight to bed. She and James had stayed up too late, chatting and sharing a glass or two of wine. It had been nice to lie in James's arms again.

This was to be a flying visit, just for the wedding, as the children had to be back in school on Monday and their train left to return to Penrith at lunchtime tomorrow. But she was grateful that they'd made the journey at all. It was wonderful to have had them with her at Chantal's wedding and not to be at yet another social occasion alone. At one point during the day, she'd stopped, arm-in-arm with James, and had taken time to look round at their children playing together; at that moment she felt that she could really make a go of them being a family.

Now, they all flopped down on the sofas in the living room, grateful for the rest after the long day. If they felt this tiny, terraced house was a world away from their rambling farmhouse back in the Lakes, then they didn't mention it. Another time, it would be nice to show the children the sights of London. Perhaps take them to Buckingham Palace and the London Eye.

'Thank you for coming,' she said to James. 'It meant a lot.'

'It was lovely to see everyone again and meet new friends,' he said. 'I'm only sorry that we've got to dash back, but there's school, and I've got so much on at the farm.' He shrugged apologetically. 'You know what it's like.'

She did. Her visit had shown her that James was very firmly tied to his land and the rhythm of the season and the farm.

Still clutching Chantal's wedding bouquet, Nadia went through to the kitchen, only relinquishing it to put the kettle on. She smiled as she looked at the pretty white roses, wilting slightly now after their afternoon in the sunshine, and wondered whether it was a sign. If you believed the tradition, she'd be the next one of the girls to be married. She laughed at the thought.

'What's making you chuckle?' James said as he came into the kitchen after her.

'Oh, I was just smiling about catching Chantal's bouquet. Lucy was so determined to have it. I should have let her catch it, but I was feeling mischievous.'

'Hmm. I like the sound of that.' He came behind her, slipping his arms round her waist and nuzzling her neck. 'You could be the next bride,' he murmured against her skin, making her shiver with delight. 'My proposal still stands. Have you given it some thought?'

She turned and let herself relax into his embrace. 'Yes, I have.'

He gazed earnestly into her eyes. 'And?'

'It's a *huge* decision, James. It would be really hard to leave here,' she said. 'Not so much this house.' She gestured at the kitchen that needed sprucing up. Everywhere you turned, something was broken or bashed. 'That wouldn't keep me here. To be honest, my family wouldn't keep me here either. I thought it would be a wrench to leave them, but I don't think there's any chance of reconciliation with my parents. Not really. We managed to be civil with each other for an evening – just about – but I don't think they're going to be rushing round here for babysitting duties for their grandson any time soon.'

'That's sad.'

'It is. Yet, in some ways, it makes my decision easier. Anita will miss me and I'll miss her. But we'll survive.'

'She could come to us on holiday any time she likes.'

'I know that.'

'If you want to we can move back into the big cottage, then we'll have plenty of room for everyone to come. We could rent out the farmhouse instead. It would need a bit of tidying up here and there to make it suitable for a holiday let, but it's definitely doable.'

'Oh, James,' she said. 'You seem to have thought of everything. It all sounds so very feasible when I talk to you.'

'So what's holding you back?'

'It's the girls of the Chocolate Lovers' Club. That might sound silly, but they've been like a family to me for years. They're the ones who've seen me through the ups and downs. They were here for me when Toby died. They've looked after Lewis and love him as much as I do. They've propped me up when I didn't have the will to go on by myself. I don't know what I would have done without them, if I'm honest. If I come up to live with you, it's such a long way from my support network.' She gave him an anguished look. 'I'm not sure how I'll manage without them.'

'You'll have me,' James said. 'I know it's not the same, but I'll try to be a good substitute.'

She put a hand on his chest. 'You're wonderful,' she said. 'That's not in question.'

'Wouldn't they want you to be happy? In a perfect world, I'd live just down the road and we could see each other all the time, but that's not how life works. I know it's a big compromise for you, but wouldn't we have a better future together than apart?'

'I'm frightened that I'll be lonely. I don't want to rely on you for everything. That would be exhausting for you.'

'There are lots of clubs and activities, if you wanted to get involved with that kind of thing. The natives are quite friendly.'

'Some more friendly than others,' she noted.

He waggled his eyebrows mischievously.

'Or you could get a job if you wanted to. It would be nice for you to stay at home while the children are young, but it's entirely up to you. We've muddled along all this time with some help from Penny. I'm sure we can continue with that.'

Ah, Penny. Yet another thing to consider. If she didn't snap James up, she was pretty sure that Penny was waiting in the wings for her chance. What if she decided to stay here and, one day, had a call from James to say he was tired of waiting and had chosen to throw in his lot with Penny? The thought of letting him go made her feel sick.

Her mind felt in turmoil. When James was here, she knew in her heart that she never wanted to be without him. As he said, wouldn't the girls want to see her happy in a settled relationship? Didn't she deserve that after all she'd been through? Would it be foolish to give up this chance of love? But there was so much to weigh up.

'It's not just leaving the girls behind; I also have to do what's right for Lewis.'

'He gets on brilliantly with Seth and Lily,' James countered. 'I'd love us to be a family.'

Tears pricked her eyes. James would make a great father to Lewis and her son had taken to him instantly. What should she do? Take this once-in-a-lifetime chance to find happiness with her farmer in Cumbria or struggle on alone?

'Wouldn't you like to swap this for my ramshackle house and the mountains?'

A sob caught in Nadia's throat when she said, 'Yes.'

James rocked back. 'So you'll come?'

'Yes.' She laughed and wiped the tears from her cheeks. 'Yes, I will.'

Chapter Fifty-Two

From the kitchen door, Autumn watched her daughter laughing. It was a rare sight, but Willow's face lit up when she let herself go a bit and it made her look even more beautiful. Autumn smiled with pride. She was a good kid and, thankfully, their relationship was still developing nicely.

Willow was on the sofa with Flo engaging in a tickle fest. The little girl was squealing and giggling while Willow pretended to be the tickle monster. After initially being terrified of Willow and her 'witchy' make-up, Flo now adored her new big sister. It was lovely to see their closeness.

Willow pounced again, growling, and Flo shrieked again. She didn't mind them being noisy for a while. It was good for them to blow off some steam; they'd both behaved beautifully at Chantal's wedding yesterday and she was so glad to have finally introduced her daughter to the girls. They'd loved her, of course. For the first time, Willow was staying for the entire week and Autumn couldn't wait to spend time with her. Tomorrow she'd take her into Chocolate Heaven and introduce her to the many delights there. Later today, maybe they'd go up to Hyde Park and Flo could run off some more of her endless energy.

Miles finished tidying up after the carnage of breakfast and came to lean against her. 'Happy?'

'Yes. It's all working out better than I could have hoped.' She smiled at him. 'When I take her home, I'm going to stay there overnight to spend some time with Mary, too. I don't want her to think that I'm monopolising Willow.'

'I'm sure that having done the last fourteen years, Mary might be glad of the break.'

'You're probably right, but I don't want to step on her toes.' She turned and gave him a hug. 'Thank you for being understanding.'

'She's your daughter; why wouldn't I be? You've accepted Flo into your life without question. It's only right that I do the same.'

'I know it's not always easy.' Willow's moods were, at best, mercurial – but she was becoming less difficult to manage as they spent more time together. As Willow relaxed into their relationship her desire to punish Autumn by being awkward seemed to be diminishing. Sometimes, one of her tantrums caught Autumn on the hop, but she was learning to read when the darkness was coming and was able to nip it in the bud. Mostly.

'She's got to learn to trust you. That's going to take time. Plus she's a teenager.' Miles shuddered. 'All those hormones crashing around.'

Autumn laughed. 'We'll have another one going through it before you know.' She nodded towards the screeching Flo. 'Enjoy her while she's still a delightful little bundle.'

'Do you think we might add to our growing clan any time soon?' Miles cuddled her close.

'Feeling broody?'

'Yeah,' he said. 'I think I am. I like kids and I'm getting seriously outnumbered by women. I need some boys on my side. I'm fed up with having my nails painted and rollers put in my hair. I want someone to kick a football with.'

'And you want a train set.'

'What red-blooded male doesn't?'

The doorbell rang.

'Are we expecting anyone?' Miles said.

'I don't think so.' After the long day at Chantal's wedding, they were all having a lazy morning. She was still in her pyjamas and hadn't even made an attempt to brush the mass of tangles that was her hair. Wondering who it might be, she went across to the intercom and said, 'Hello?'

There was a hesitant cough and then a familiar voice said, 'It's us.'

Her *parents*? Autumn didn't think they'd ever visited her in this flat before and now they were turning up unannounced.

'We don't mean to disturb you.' Her father this time and he sounded very apprehensive. 'But we'd rather like to see you. Is this a good time?'

No. It was the *worst* possible time. She quickly scanned the flat and put her hands to her head. The place was a total mess and they'd never met Miles or Florence. Willow was here, too, and she never thought they'd want to see her after their last meeting. Yet here she was and they'd have to like it or lump it. She could hardly turn them away, but was taking no trouble from them today. Even though she didn't necessarily want a fight with them in her PJs.

'Yes, yes. Of course. I'll buzz you in. You'll have to take us as you find us, though.' She pressed to undo the door lock and turned to Miles. 'It's my parents.'

'Wow. I wish I'd washed my hair,' he joked.

'I wish I'd *combed* mine,' she said. Then she looked round at the debris of toys on the floor and realised that her hair was the least of her worries. 'I wish I'd got an hour to tidy up.' Maybe two.

'Too late for both now, I guess.' Miles grimaced.

'They'll be here any second.' Autumn's heart was in her mouth. 'Girls, girls. My mother and father are coming to see us. Can you quickly put some of the toys away?'

Willow stopped tickling the shrieking Flo and they both looked at her blankly as if to say 'Have you seen the number of toys on this floor?'

It was true. It would take hours to clear this lot away. Her one-toy-at-a-time rule had lasted about five minutes.

Willow stared at her, wide-eyed. 'My grandparents?'

'Yes.'

'Now?'

She went and held her daughter's hands. 'I would have loved to have had more time to prepare for this, but shall we just do it? No time like the present.'

Her face creased with concern. 'What if they don't like me?'

She wanted to say that, of course, they would. But, the truth was that you could never tell with her parents. They could equally turn on their heels the moment they clapped eyes on Willow.

'I can't promise anything, but I can't turn them away from my door either. We'll face them together. You do understand?'

Willow nodded.

She took in the two girls, who now sat expectantly. Flo was pink-faced, the remains of her breakfast were still down the front of her dress and her hair looked like a wild bush. Willow was in full Goth make-up, sporting a ripped Alien Sex Fiend T-shirt and equally ripped black jeans. Oh, goodness. Her parents were in for something of a shock and she'd so wanted them to love the girls. Well, they'd simply have to take them all as they found them.

'Do they even know about me?' Miles asked.

'Not really.'

'Oh, good. I always imagined I'd meet my future in-laws at a civilised dinner in an upmarket restaurant rather than in my oldest joggers and a skanky T.'

'Me too.' Then, despite her panic, she smiled. 'Future in-laws? Is that a proposal?'

Miles grinned at her. 'It might be.'

At that moment her parents knocked at the door of the flat. Damn. Their timing couldn't have been worse.

She held a finger up to Miles. 'We'll continue this conversation as soon as we can. I won't forget.' Then, with a deep breath, she opened the door.

Her mother and father stood there looking as awkward and as out of place as she'd ever seen them.

'Hi,' Autumn said, pinning on a smile. 'An unexpected pleasure.'

Her parents both looked sheepish. Her father was clutching a bouquet, which he held out to her.

'Thank you.' Autumn took it and, looking down at the beautiful and extravagant arrangement of flowers said, 'What's this in aid of?'

'A peace offering,' her mother said, licking her lips uneasily. 'We felt things went badly when we last spoke.'

Something of an understatement. Autumn flushed as she remembered it. 'Yes. They did.'

'We wanted to make amends,' her father said. 'If you'll let us.'

Well, that certainly was a surprise.

'You'd better come in,' Autumn said. 'This is as good a time as any. You can meet your granddaughter.'

Chapter Fifty-Three

Her parents picked their way through the maze of toys in the hallway. Luckily, neither of them was barefoot so standing on Flo's piles of discarded Lego wouldn't cripple them.

'I'm sorry about the state of the place,' Autumn said. 'We're having a lazy day. My friend Chantal was married yesterday and we're recovering.'

'We should have phoned ahead,' her mother said. 'This is very rude of us.'

'It's lovely to see you,' Autumn said, softly. 'Really lovely.' It wasn't the time to discuss the fact that it shouldn't be necessary to make an appointment to see your daughter – or your parents. That could wait for another time.

It was the first time in years that she'd seen her parents in their versions of casual clothes. Normally, they were both in black business suits for their lunchtime meetings in between appointments. Today her mother wore a pretty blouse, an A-line skirt and a string of pearls. Her father had on a blue shirt and what could only be called slacks. They were old before their time and still starchy, but it did make them seem more like normal people.

'Come on in. Just mind where you stand.'

'We've been thinking about things,' her father said as he followed her into the living room.

Autumn held up a hand. 'Before you say another word, I'd like you to meet some people.'

Her parents looked up from the toy minefield. 'Oh, we didn't realise you had visitors.'

'They're not quite visitors,' Autumn said. 'This is my boyfriend, Miles.'

'Hey.' Miles waved. 'Pleased to meet you.'

'This is my father. Terrance. And my mother, Anna.'

'Delighted,' her mother said.

'This is Florence.'

'I'm fiiiiiiiive!' Florence shouted.

'You're three,' Miles corrected, as usual.

'I'm threeeeeeee!' Florence shouted. Then she launched herself into a boisterous dance routine. The little girl was obviously still totally hyperactive after her tickling session.

'Lovely,' her mother said, fanning herself. 'Very lovely.' She looked quite terrified.

'And this,' Autumn blew out a breath, 'is your granddaughter.'

Her mother's mouth dropped open.

'Come and say hi, Willow.'

Her daughter stepped forward and Autumn put an arm protectively around her shoulders. If they were horrible to her child or said one single thing out of line, they'd be given their marching orders and that would be the end of her contact with them. She hadn't come this far in building her relationship with Willow to have them ruin it with a few cruel words.

To her surprise, she looked up to see her mother crying. 'Oh, my,' she said. 'My granddaughter.'

Willow clung tightly to Autumn. 'Hi,' she said, reluctantly.

298

'I know this is a difficult situation,' Autumn's mother said, wiping her eyes, 'and neither of us were prepared for it, but I'm so very pleased to meet you.'

Willow risked a small smile.

'We all have a lot of talking to do,' Anna said, 'but I would like to start to build bridges. If you'll let us.'

'I'd like that.' Autumn turned to Willow. 'How does that sound to you?'

The girl shrugged awkwardly. 'OK.'

'Perhaps we could seal the deal with a little hug?' Autumn suggested.

Tentatively, Anna held out her arms. It made Autumn smile to herself. Her mother wasn't a natural hugger but at least she was prepared to try.

Equally tentatively, Willow sidled into her embrace. Autumn's mother kissed the child's hair and, self-consciously, her father stepped forward and hugged them both.

It was a hesitant start, but it was something that Autumn had never dared to hope she would see. She turned to Miles; tears were in his eyes, too. 'Go on,' he said to her.

So she also embraced her mother, father and Willow. And they cried together.

When they finally broke away from each other, Miles gave them all a piece of kitchen roll to wipe their eyes.

'It's been too long,' Autumn's mother said. 'So much wasted time.' Then she cried again and Autumn squeezed her tightly.

'I feel a bit silly now.' Her father gave a watery laugh.

'We did a terrible thing,' her mother said. 'A truly terrible thing. That's what I came to say. What *we* came to say.' She grasped her husband's hand.

'It's working out all right,' Autumn said. 'Thank goodness. I've found Willow again – or she found me. That's all that matters.' She realised this was the first step towards building a proper relationship with her parents and she was more than keen to do that – for Willow's sake as well as her own. It was important for Willow to feel as if she was part of a big, real family. She didn't want the strife that had been between them to continue for a minute longer than it had to. 'Let's put the past behind us. We should go forward from here. I can forgive you and I hope that Willow will, too.'

Willow nodded tearfully. 'I'm cool.'

'You are a very beautiful young woman.' Her mum glanced anxiously at the Alien Sex Fiend T-shirt and the ripped jeans. 'Just like your mother.' She turned to Autumn. 'I know we've let you down, but we'd like to try to be more of a family. If you'll let us.'

'Well.' Autumn looked around her. 'You've just inherited a few more members. If you can cope with that, then we'll give it a go.'

More tears from her mother. 'I'd like that.'

'There's only one thing that families do in this kind of situation.' Miles grinned. 'I'll put the kettle on.'

Flo sat on Terrance's knee. 'This is a finger puppet,' Flo explained earnestly. She showed the little knitted toy to Autumn's father. 'Edward Bunny.'

'He's very nice.' Terrance looked as if he was holding an unexploded bomb.

Autumn smiled to herself. They might want to build a family, but it was clear they had a long way to go. If anyone could break barriers down, then it was dear Flo.

'Put it on. Put it on,' she said bossily.

Her father slipped the pink rabbit onto his forefinger.

'Now do a voice,' Flo instructed. 'Like this.' She demonstrated her best squeaky voice.

Autumn's father imitated.

'No,' Flo said with an impatient shake of her head. 'Daddy does it better than that. Do this.' She jammed another fluffy character on one of Terrance's other fingers. 'It's Mr Carrot.'

Autumn thought the orange scrap of fluff looked as if it had been through the washing machine one too many times. Her father was trying hard not to look appalled. Just wait until Flo got out the rollers and the nail varnish. No one was safe.

Thankfully, her mother was getting off more lightly. Willow was perched next to her on the armchair flicking through some photos on her phone with her.

'Shall I rescue your besieged dad?' Miles whispered. 'The poor man looks mortified.'

'No,' Autumn said. 'It will do him good. Baptism of fire. I expect the last time he held a child that age, it was me.' A wave of sadness engulfed her. She never actually remembered being cuddled by her father at all. Still, even if she hadn't had the relationship with them that she'd wanted in the past, perhaps there was hope that she could in the future. For Willow's sake, she should give it all she'd got.

'I've got some nice chocolate-chip cookies in the kitchen,' Autumn said. 'Who would like one?'

'Yay!' Florence shouted at the top of her voice, making her father jump. For a little girl, she did have one hell of a bellow on her.

'Does anyone want more tea?' Autumn asked.

Her mother and father nodded gratefully. They both risked a wary smile.

Autumn grinned back. This was all she'd ever wanted. A family to love. She thought of her brother and how much he would have enjoyed this. He would have loved Willow. And Flo. What fun they could have had together. It was a crying shame that he hadn't lived long enough to have a family of his own.

She hoped he could see them now gathered together, the hope of reconciliation in their hearts.

Brushing away a tear, she collected the cups from the coffee table and said, 'I'll go and put the kettle on again.'

Chapter Fifty-Four

I'm in Chocolate Heaven very, very early. I have my feet up and, before the day begins in earnest, I'm enjoying a coffee and a cherry and chocolate granola bar for breakfast – a new and very welcome addition to the menu from Alexandra. I can see these selling like hot cakes, if only I can stop myself from eating them all.

It was a busy weekend for Chantal's wedding, but I'm still floating on a little cloud of loved-upness. It will be me next, if it's the last thing I do. I can hardly replicate the last one and have exactly the same wedding as Chantal, can I? So a whole new raft of planning will have to begin. Hurrah! The thought of it is making me happy.

There's also something else bringing a little lightness to my heart. I'm currently reading a brochure for a renowned school which specialises in courses on how to become a chocolatier. I know! I sent for it last week in a moment of madness and it was waiting for me this morning on the doormat when I arrived at Chocolate Heaven. As I can't hear Ms France moving about in the upstairs flat yet, I've stolen a few minutes to myself to have a quick look at it.

So now I'm flicking through its delicious pages with my mouth drooling. The course is modular and it goes without saying that each one costs an arm and a leg, but I'm sure it would be worth it. Wouldn't it? I'd be investing in my future – mine and Crush's. I could be a proper, professional chocolate expert rather than an enthusiastic amateur. Hurrah! One day I might have my very own version of Chocolate Heaven with LUCY LOMBARD, CHOCOLATIER above the door. I'm liking the sound of that.

It might scupper the wedding plans a bit if I splashed out on this right now, though. Hmm. I'd have to give it very careful consideration, but I'd so love to be able to do it. And I could take my time and work through the modules slowly as finances allow. That sounds like a plan.

There is, however, one space left on a course at the end of the summer. Wouldn't it be great – now that I have a dream – if I could embark on it sooner rather than later? Let's face it, I'm not getting any younger and there are babies to fit in, too. I can't hang about for ever.

I take a slug of my coffee to help sharpen my brain while it wrangles with my dilemma.

I'm sitting here, grinning to myself like a Cheshire cat, imagining myself in pristine chef's whites designing my own chocolates and drifting about my own establishment with an air of gravitas, when I hear the familiar throaty roar of Marcus's love machine pulling up outside. I haven't seen him for weeks and my traitorous heart lifts slightly instead of sinking as it should. Damn you.

He breezes in like he owns the place. Which, of course, he does.

'Hey, Lucy,' he says. 'Early bird.'

'Hello, Marcus.' I slide the brochure down the side of my chair. The last thing I want is a conversation with Marcus about this. At the moment, this is my private dream. 'Trying to get ahead of the day.'

He flops in the chair opposite me. 'Shouldn't this have been your wedding weekend?'

'Yes.' Thanks for rubbing it in, Marcus.

'So you're still a sad single?'

'I'm still engaged to be married,' I correct. 'It's just a matter of timing. I'm already making plans again.' Not quite true, but nearly so. 'Chantal deserved this wedding more than me.'

'I know. I'm teasing.' He gives me a longing look. 'You've always been a softie, Lucy.'

'Yes.' My glance is more pointed. 'You should know.'

'Did it go all right for her?'

'It was perfect,' I tell him. As will my wedding be when I eventually get it. 'The groom stayed for the ceremony and everything.'

He smiles sadly at me. '*Touché.*'

'To what do I owe the pleasure? Just passing?'

He checks his fancy watch. 'Sort of.'

'Shall I get you a coffee? Some breakfast?' I nod towards the remnants of my breakfast bar. 'These are very good. New line.'

'A double espresso please, Lucy. Nothing to eat.'

'You really should try some of your own wares one of these days, Marcus.'

'I like to watch my figure.'

Finishing off my brekky, I lick my fingers. 'I like to watch mine,' I quip. 'Getting bigger.'

'I quite like to watch yours, too,' he says as I head towards the counter.

'Shut up, Marcus.'

I make him a coffee and, when it's ready, put it on the table in front of him. Marcus regards me while he takes a sip, then he folds his arms. 'I've given up, you know.'

'On what?'

'On you.' He sighs at me and those baby-blue eyes shine with sincerity. 'No matter how much I love you, I have to accept that I've lost you.'

A lump comes to my throat and I sit down again.

'That doesn't change how I feel, but I've got to move on or I'll go mad.' He pulls a sad and resigned face at me and it breaks my heart. 'You love another man. I fucked up and I can't undo that. You don't know how much that hurts.'

I think I liked it better when Marcus was pursuing me hotly and I was continually rebuffing him. This is too distressing. I don't want to be the reason for Marcus's unhappiness.

'I have everything I want,' Marcus says. 'Money, charm, good looks.' His eyes twinkle with mischief.

This is more like the old Marcus.

'Everything I want but you. And I'd give it all up in a heart-beat to have you back.'

'Don't, Marcus.'

He holds up his hands. 'I came to tell you that I've just accepted a contract in Dubai. I'm going to be working for an investment company out there. It's only a two-year contract but, if I like it, I don't plan on coming back. I'll be out of your hair once and for all.'

I feel sick to my stomach. 'Oh, Marcus.'

'I thought you'd be glad to see the back of me.'

'Never,' I say. 'I can't be with you, Marcus, but that doesn't mean that I don't have feelings for you.'

He laughs without humour. 'Don't give me a glimmer of hope, Lucy, or I won't go at all.'

'I love you as a friend, Marcus. That's all.' His face falls. 'You should go,' I tell him. 'It sounds like a great opportunity. But only if that's what you really want.'

'I don't know what I want,' he admits. 'Surely this is worth

306

trying?' He looks up at me. 'Marie-France has agreed to come with me.'

More shocks. 'She has?' I'm so stunned that I'm not sure what else to say. Eventually, I manage, 'I didn't think you two were that serious.'

'I'm not sure if we are. We're too alike. Perhaps that's what keeps me on my toes.' He rubs a hand over his face and suddenly looks weary. 'I want to settle down. I want a family.'

I smile at that. The last person on earth I can imagine being a dad is Marcus. He's too selfish, too self-absorbed.

'I do,' he insists when he sees the scepticism on my face. 'I just don't seem to be able to stay with women who want that too. What's wrong with me, Lucy?'

'I don't know, Marcus. You never seem to be content with what you have. You may say that you love me, but I was never really enough for you.'

'You don't know how wrong you are,' he says. 'I just didn't appreciate you at the time. I was young, foolish. I took you for granted.'

'That's as may be. It's all water under the bridge. I'm happy with Aiden now. And I *will* marry him as soon as possible.'

Marcus scowls at my determination.

'I hope you and Marie-France can make a go of it.'

He shrugs at that. 'She's a feisty one. I don't get an easy ride with her.'

'Perhaps that was my problem. I was always too much of a pushover for you.' We stare at each other, unspeaking. 'So, I've got to find a new assistant soon?'

'Um . . . ' Marcus says. 'She actually moved out of the flat this weekend. She's at my place now.'

That's obviously why I hadn't heard her this morning. 'She's not coming back?'

He shakes his head. 'Already I can't get near the bathroom.

Her stuff's everywhere. My cupboards are no longer my own. How am I going to manage?'

'You'll work something out.'

'Tell me I'm doing the right thing,' Marcus pleads.

'I can't do that. You have to make your own decisions. If it feels right, then go for it.'

'Nothing feels right without you.' His eyes fill with tears and he comes to kneel at my feet. He folds his arms across my knees and rests his head on them.

This is the Marcus I loved. The stripped-back one without the gloss and bullshit. We were at our best when we were like this together. I stroke his hair as I feel him sob. The tears run down my cheeks, too.

After a few minutes he rights himself and I hand him a napkin for him to wipe his face. I brush away my own tears with my fingers.

'What a twat,' he says, blowing his nose. 'What a fucked-up twat.'

'You're not,' I insist. 'Of course you're not. You're a fabulous man who could achieve anything that he wants to. You just have to focus, Marcus. Find out what it really is that you want from life and go for it.'

'And what if I can't have what I really want?'

I have no answer to that.

Marcus stands up. 'I should go.' He blows his nose again. 'Please don't tell whatshisname about this.'

'*Aiden*,' I supply. As usual. 'Of course I won't.'

'I'll leave the running of Chocolate Heaven up to you, Lucy. Do what you want with it.'

'I do have plans.' I don't know why, but I pull the brochure out from behind the cushion and risk showing it to him. 'I'm thinking of training to be a proper chocolatier.'

'That would be great.'

'I know.'

'So what's stopping you?'

'Mainly money,' I admit. 'Some confidence issues, too. I wouldn't want to do this and fail.'

'I can give you the money. Lend it to you. Whatever.'

'I'd rather do it myself,' I tell him.

'Don't let being stubborn stand in the way of your dreams.'

'I'll manage. Somehow. I think we both have to cut the umbilical cord between us.'

'You're right. Of course.'

I fiddle with the brochure. 'In the meantime, as you're running away with my assistant, how would you feel if I took on Autumn to work here? I'm sure she'd jump at the chance.'

He holds out his hands. 'It's up to you. My name's on the lease, but that's where my interest ends. After all, I did this for you.' He gives me a wry look. 'Even that wasn't enough.'

'I do appreciate it, Marcus. And it hasn't been too bad working together, has it?'

'It's been great,' he says. 'But I can't see you every day, Lucy, and not be with you. I'm just torturing myself. You're making a good go of it. I don't have to worry about that, at least.'

'Would you let Autumn buy into the business?' She has some money that her parents gave her and I know she's looking for a job.

'Is that what you want?'

'I'd like to put it to her. I'm not sure how it would work, but perhaps somehow we could both take it over. In time.'

'Then I'd have no ties to you at all,' Marcus notes.

I smile sadly at him. 'Perhaps that would be a good thing.'

'Come up with a plan and let me know,' he says. 'I'm open to offers.'

'Thank you, Marcus.'

'That's it then.' He looks at me bleakly.

The words I want to say will hardly come out. 'When are you thinking of going?'

'I'm not sure. We've yet to finalise the start date. But it will be soon. No point in hanging around. I won't come back to Chocolate Heaven again. This is goodbye, Lucy.'

I can't believe it ends like this. My life has been intrinsically linked with Marcus for so long that he almost feels more like a brother to me than an ex-lover. Even while hating him, underneath it all I've never really stopped loving him. However, the truth of the matter is that just because you love someone it doesn't mean that they're right for you. Don't I know it.

Marcus might think that we were destined to be together for ever, come what may, but we would never have lasted. What we wanted was too different. I wanted Marcus and, well, I don't think Marcus ever knew quite what he wanted. I don't think he's changed. I think the only reason that he still believes that he wants me is because he can't have me.

And, when it all boils down to it, I adore Crush. He's the perfect man for me. He's shown me what love really means. We get along so much better than Marcus and I ever did. We laugh, we love, we try never to hurt each other. He is steadfast and loyal. Two particular things that Marcus could never manage. We want the same things from life. That's how you make a lasting relationship. I would never ever dream of leaving him to go back to Marcus. Of that I'm absolutely sure.

Now, perhaps, Marcus finally realises it too.

He opens his arms. 'One last hug for old times' sake?'

Despite what my head says, there are still too many occasions when I can't deny this man. My heart is a much more impressionable thing. I step into his arms and he holds me tightly, rocking me against his chest. I can feel the solid beating of his heart. He presses his face against my hair and brushes my cheek. The aroma of his aftershave takes me back to the days when we first fell in love and used to spend all day in bed together. I couldn't get enough of his body, his scent, his love.

I once adored this man so much, so very much.

Then Marcus breaks away from me. 'Goodbye, Lucy,' he says.

And I stand while he walks out of Chocolate Heaven and out of my life for ever.

Chapter Fifty-Five

After a blissful night at The Ritz, Chantal and Jacob had travelled down to the wilds of north Cornwall. Jacob had organised a beautiful boutique hotel in Watergate Bay for them and it was all that a honeymoon should be. The hotel was chic, quiet and right on the edge of the sweeping sandy beach. Jacob had booked the best suite in the house and it was gorgeous. Their room had a spacious balcony and a spectacular view of the sea. The walls were covered in sanded driftwood and there was a big brass bed covered with sand-coloured throws and cushions made of pale-blue ticking. In the main room, blue leather chairs were set in one of the bay windows; the other held a roll-top bath.

For the last few days they'd explored the area at a leisurely pace, having a few gentle walks, indulging in some shopping in touristy art galleries and taking in a restorative cream tea or two on the way. She tired easily and didn't want to overdo things.

Back at Watergate Bay, they'd meandered barefoot along the beach feeling the sand in their toes, as happy families started to pack up their colourful towels and beach games for the day.

When Lana was a little bit older, they'd bring her back here. She'd love it. Chantal felt a twinge of longing for her baby. It was the first time she'd left her for any length of time and, though she was loving being with Jacob, it was so hard being away from her.

She watched a little girl of about six or seven skipping along the sand with her parents. Before too long, that would be Lana and it felt good to know that she had a fighting chance of being around to see that.

Jacob saw her watching the child. 'Missing Lana?'

'Like mad,' she said. 'But it's nice for us to have some time to ourselves. She's in good hands.'

Ted had booked a week's holiday to stay in England while they were away and she was grateful that he'd offered. It had felt a little strange to have her ex-husband at her wedding, but the awkward feeling had soon gone.

They were both living at Chantal's house so that it wouldn't be too disruptive for Lana. It had been lovely to see how thrilled Ted was to be having her for more than a few hours and it would give Lana and Elsie plenty of time to play together. 'I'll ring Ted soon and talk to her.'

Arms entwined and heads together, they sat on the sand, watched the paddle-boarders bob on the gentle waves and let the sounds of the sea soothe them. Chantal didn't think she'd ever felt more settled and restful.

After a while they went back to the solace of their room and Jacob ran her a bath. She was now luxuriating in it with a glass of champagne in her hand. The French doors were open and Jacob sat on the balcony in one of the steamer chairs. All they could see was the vast expanse of the ocean and the slowly sinking sun. It looked as if it was going to be another spectacular sunset. What bliss.

She rearranged the bubbles over her chest and, beneath the

water, tentatively dared to touch the scar where her breast had been. Her battle scar. It still didn't quite feel like her own body, but she was beginning to learn to live with it. As soon as they were back from honeymoon then she'd start nearly six months of chemotherapy. It sounded weird, but she couldn't wait for it to begin. All she wanted was to be sure that they'd got every scrap of this cancer out of her body.

They'd consider too whether she'd need to have the other breast removed. After that, she'd have reconstructive surgery to return her curves to her. She'd never look quite as she once had, she supposed, but it was a small price to pay for being able to stay around to see Lana grow up.

She was still awkward in front of Jacob and hadn't yet let him see her completely naked. He would be marvellous about it, she knew that, but she had to be ready herself. Instead, she treated herself to some pretty post-surgery underwear – thank heavens for the companies who made it. When she'd finally steeled herself to buy it, she'd chosen something pink and very lacy to make herself feel more feminine, and wore that to bed instead. It didn't seem to have dimmed Jacob's ardour, though he did hold her as if she was porcelain.

She stood out of the bath and wrapped herself in one of the luxury dressing gowns provided by the hotel. The weather was gloriously hot, but a cool breeze from the sea tingled against her skin. Chantal paused for a moment. When this all got too much, she wanted to remember the small things, to hold on to some golden memories. This honeymoon was one of them. She went out on the balcony to join Jacob.

'Top up?' he asked.

She nodded and, reaching for the champagne, he poured some more into her glass.

He moved up and she curled along the length of him on the

steamer chair. The sky was turning orange, pink, purple. The sun a burning ball on the horizon.

'This is heaven. Thank you for organising it.' There was no way that she could have faced getting onto a plane and jetting off to one of the places more usually considered a honeymoon destination – the Maldives, Seychelles, Mexico. This was just what she needed.

'You're looking much better,' he said.

Normally, Chantal shied away from exposing herself to the sun, slathering her face and body in sunblock and wearing an enormous sun hat so that her skin wouldn't age or wrinkle. This week, she hadn't been nearly so rigorous and, for once, had enjoyed feeling the rays warm her limbs. It felt as if it had soothed her down to her bones, comforting her. As a result, her face had a golden glow and freckles that she didn't even know she had were dusted across the bridge of her nose.

They were due to go down to dinner soon and her tummy rumbled in anticipation. Each night they'd dined by candlelight on locally caught seafood, beautifully prepared. A bit of sunshine and sea air had certainly brought her appetite back and she was feeling ready to face the rigours ahead.

Jacob stroked her hair, tenderly.

'Will you still love me when it all falls out?'

'I don't remember promising "in hairiness or in baldness",' he teased.

'Apparently, it's the pubic hair that goes first.'

'Sexy,' Jacob said.

Jacob nuzzled against her as the sun said goodbye for the night.

'Cancer may have its claws into us at the moment, but I don't want it to shape our future.' She ran her fingers over Jacob's chest. 'I want you to be my husband. Not my carer.'

He tilted her chin and kissed her intensely.

'Whatever happens,' he murmured, 'I'll love you for ever.'

'Hmm.' She kissed him back.

'I promise you with all my heart, Mrs Chantal Lawson, that we are going to have a very long and very happy life together.'

She settled into Jacob's arms. 'I like the sound of that.'

Chapter Fifty-Six

'This is the sixth venue we've looked at,' Crush notes. 'Or maybe seventh.' I can hear the weariness in his voice.

It's actually the eighth.

'Shall we get married here then?' He shrugs at me, hopefully. 'It's nice. No? Yes?'

'Yes.' I look round the room at the Mayfair Library and can find nothing wrong with it. Nothing at all. It's perfectly acceptable. I'm sure lots of brides get married here and love it. But I'm not sure that my heart's in it. It isn't the lovely temple in Golders Hill Park. We won't be able to have a picnic on the grass.

The registrar is enthusiastically pointing out the plus points of the building, but I'm struggling to concentrate.

'You don't seem all that keen,' Crush says.

'It's lovely.'

He frowns at me and says to the registrar, 'Can you give us a minute, please?'

'Certainly.' Hastily, she backs out of the room, leaving us alone.

When she's gone, somewhat reluctantly, Crush says, 'We can look at other venues, if you want to.'

Though, as he already pointed out, we have been around more than half a dozen already and I have discounted them all for various reasons: too big, too small, too expensive, too chav, not chav enough.

'This is fine.'

'If you want to we can arrange everything at Golders' Hill Park again.'

'No.' I shake my head. 'That was Chantal's wedding and it was perfect.'

'Couldn't we use one of the other areas there? They all looked great. Maybe Jacob could organise something different to eat?'

'Like what?'

'I've no idea,' Crush admits. 'Making decisions about food is above my pay grade.'

'No. We can't go there again. Everyone will compare it. We have to do something different that makes it ours.'

'If you say so,' Crush concedes. Though his voice actually says 'I will never, not in a million years, understand women.'

'It has to be special.' I feel my chin begin to wobble. 'It's just that . . . '

'What?'

I burst into tears.

Crush takes me in his arms. 'You don't regret handing our wedding over to Chantal?'

'A bit of me does,' I admit. 'It was all so lovely and it should have been me. But how could I begrudge her?'

'It was a really nice thing to do. I'm sure it gave her a real lift and will help her get through the next few months. They're going to be pretty awful for her.'

'I know,' I sniffle. 'I know all that. And they're having a lovely time on their honeymoon. It's just that it was a really special place and nothing will ever be able to match it. Well, not on the budget we've got.' All of the hotels are just so ridiculously expensive. I'm sure the minute you say the word 'wedding' it adds twenty-five per cent to the cost. I want to have a lovely day, but I don't want to be ripped off either.

'Let's postpone it and save up some more,' he says. 'I want you to have the day of your dreams.'

'I'm trying to be sensible,' I say. 'I just want to marry you.' Then I cry a little bit more.

'Your coffee and chocolate levels are dangerously low.' He holds my shoulders and smiles at me. 'We need to fix that.'

'I am feeling a little bit weary.'

'Let's book this,' Crush suggests. 'Then we've got something in the diary. If we happen across somewhere better then all we have to do is cancel.'

'Good idea.' I don't want to be negative while he's being proactive. It's his day as much as mine.

So I dry my eyes and we go through to the office. We book a date that seems like a long way down the line and fill in all the paperwork we need. In my head, I try to convince myself that I like it here.

A short while later, deed done, and we have a wedding date. Together, we breeze out of the building and Crush is grinning. 'Happy?' he asks.

'Very much so.' I pin on a smile.

But, to be honest, since he said the word chocolate, he lost me completely.

Chapter Fifty-Seven

Now that it's properly summer, I've dressed Chocolate Heaven with swathes of pastel-coloured bunting and it looks fabulous. We've got a summer-fruit range of chocolates and Alexandra's cocktail-inspired cupcakes on offer – piña colada, strawberry margarita, lime mojito, classic gin and tonic, and Pimm's ones which have a strawberry, orange and cucumber garnish with a sprig of mint on top. It would be nice if, next year, we could perhaps have a small selection of ice-creams. They would go well.

Finally, when all the customers have gone, I turn the sign on the door to 'closed' and breathe a sigh of relief. Today has been completely manic and, I have to confess, I'm even missing Ms France. I should go and wash my mouth out with soap for even saying that.

We're having a meeting of the Chocolate Lovers' Club; even that has to be after hours as I've been too busy to grab a few minutes to myself these last few days. Chantal is back from her honeymoon and, although Nadia has popped in, I haven't had a chance to sit and chat to her. Autumn has been busy with her daughter and, though she brought Willow in, I didn't think it was the right time to talk about my proposal – so I can't wait to have a chat with her when she comes.

Behind the counter, I select us some of the yummy cocktail cupcakes – though there's not that many of them left. I tried the gin and tonic one, which was utterly fantastic. It felt as if it had health-giving properties. I'll swear my stress reduced just inhaling it. I think I'd like to make some of the flavours a regular feature on the menu for the whole of the summer. I'll see what the girls think.

I phone Crush. 'I'm going to be late home,' I say.

'Telling me something I don't know.' His tone is indulgent.

'Not work this time. The girls are all coming by soon for a catch up. I'll be about an hour. I can bring some food in.'

'I'll make something for us. There are noodles in the cupboard and vegetables that aren't too floppy in the fridge.'

'Those are the words to make a woman's heart glad.'

He laughs. 'Don't eat too much cake or you'll spoil your appetite. I'll see you later, Gorgeous. I thought we had some wedding planning to do?'

'I'm too tired,' I confess. 'Maybe at the weekend?'

'Sounds good to me.' Then he adds, 'Is Autumn coming in tonight? Are you going to talk to her about coming in to help run Chocolate Heaven?'

'Yes. I hope she'll agree. It can't happen soon enough. Then we can think about the wedding.' I've yet to tell him that I still have qualms about the place we've booked.

'See you later,' he says. 'Love you.'

'I love you, too.' I hang up just as Nadia knocks on the front door. I let her in.

'A lock-in at a chocolate shop,' she says. 'What kind of joy is this?'

'I thought you'd have Lewis with you.'

'I've just dropped him off at Anita's so that he can play with

321

his cousins. They're very good with him. She's making dinner for us later, so I can't stay too long.'

'How are things with your sister?'

'With Anita, they're fine. She's disappointed that my parents weren't so keen to welcome the prodigal daughter home, but at least we both tried. I feel quite ambivalent about it, if I'm honest. Besides, I have a lot more to worry about.'

'Tell all,' I say.

'Soon. When the others are here.' She hands over a couple of bottles of wine. 'Let's put it this way. Tea isn't going to hit the spot. I thought we needed something a bit stronger.'

'Sounds like a plan.' While she sits on the sofa, I get some wine glasses from the back room.

I'm just pouring the first glass when Chantal and Autumn arrive within seconds of each other. 'Did you smell the scent of Pinot Grigio?'

'No,' Chantal says. 'It was, as always, the lure of chocolate. And good company, of course,' she adds with a laugh.

But she takes the wine with a welcome sigh, nevertheless.

We all kiss each other and they sit with Nadia.

'Look at you,' I say to Chantal. 'Ms Beach Body.' She looks tanned, healthy – deceptively so – and relaxed. You'd think she hadn't a care in the world.

'We've had a fantastic week,' Chantal says. 'I highly recommend honeymoons.'

'Nice to see you all loved up.'

'It's been very therapeutic to take some time out and think about anything other than you-know-what for a week.'

I wrinkle my nose. 'I thought honeymoons were all about you-know-what?'

'The *other* you-know-what!' Chantal chides.

'Oh, *that*.'

'Well, you look great,' Autumn says. 'And you're feeling good?'

'Yes,' she says. 'Ready for the next stage. I've been into the chemo ward today for a first glimpse. It's like an airport lounge with IV drips. Not quite as scary as I'd imagined.'

'We'll make sure we have a rota so that we can all take turns in coming with you.'

'That would be great. The whole session will take about three hours, so it would be good to have some company.'

'Sitting around gossiping, we can do very well.'

'There were some very young and fit-looking people in there, too. Just goes to show that cancer can strike anyone.' She takes the glass of wine that I hand to her. 'I might have to knock this off soon. It depends on the drugs they give me and how I react.' She sighs longingly at her glass. 'At least there's no adverse reaction between chocolate and chemotherapy; then I really would be stuffed.'

'Ah,' I say. 'Speaking of which.' I bring the assortment of cocktail cupcakes from behind the counter. 'I need your opinion on these babies. They've gone really well today and it would be nice to know which ones you think should be regulars.'

They fall on them the minute I put the plate down. I'm not sure that this will be a discerning audience for my wares.

I pour myself a glass of wine and join them in the cupcake research. The strawberry margarita is particularly good. However, I too am at the point in the day when I'm not very discerning. It's cake. What can I say? 'I also have news. I think it's good.' They look at me expectantly. 'Marcus is heading off to work in Dubai. Ms France is going with him.'

'No,' Nadia says, aghast. 'I didn't see that one coming.'

'Me neither,' I admit.

'It'll certainly be more difficult for him to meddle in your life from Dubai,' Chantal says. 'I'm pleased to hear it.'

I cringe before I say, 'Is it wrong of me to say that I'm going to miss him?'

'Lucy!' they all shout.

'I know. What can I do?' I nibble my cupcake for comfort and, when that's not enough, take a swig of wine. 'It'll be funny without him.'

'A blessed relief is what it will be,' Chantal tells me.

'Crush said pretty much the same,' I admit. 'There was one good thing, though . . . ' I turn to Autumn. 'He said he'd be open to you putting in an offer to buy into the company. That's if you want to.'

'Really?' She looks surprised.

'Would you be up for it?'

'I still have the money from my parents sitting in my bank account. I can't think of anything better to do with it. Are you sure?'

'I have lots of plans,' I say. 'It would be lovely if we could do it together.' I show her my chocolate-course brochure. 'I'm thinking of training to be a chocolatier. A proper one.'

'That sounds great, Lucy.' Autumn looks quite animated. 'Perhaps we could both do it.' She flicks through the pages, scanning quickly. 'What do we have to do?'

'We'll need to put a proposal to Marcus about buying the business and we can take our time with that, but I'm desperate for help here now that Ms France has gone,' I tell her. 'If you want to come and work here as an assistant, in the meantime, it would be fantastic. The sooner you can start the better.'

She looks at Nadia. 'Is that going to be possible? I'd love to do it, but I don't want to let you down with childcare.'

Nadia touches her arm. 'Autumn, you help me out on an entirely voluntary basis. You owe me nothing. You have to grab this chance. It would be terrific if you and Lucy could run this place together.'

Autumn grins. 'I'm so excited.'

'What would you do with Lewis?' I ask.

'Ah,' Nadia says. 'You're not the only ones making major changes. I have some news of my own.' She sets down her cake and puts on her serious face. 'I've decided to sell up and go to the Lake District to be with James.'

We all sit there, stunned.

'I've had the estate agent around to value the house and that's going on the market this week. He said he didn't think it would take long to sell.'

I'm the first one to speak, but all I can say is 'Wow!'

Nadia looks at us anxiously. 'You do all think I'm doing the right thing?'

'Absolutely,' Chantal says. 'He's a great bloke and that's where your heart is now. But, heaven only knows, we're going to miss you.'

'Don't.' Nadia holds up a hand. 'You'll start me off crying again. I've done nothing but blub since I decided. What am I going to do without you?'

'We're all just going to have to spend our holidays in the Lakes from now on,' I tell her.

'I'm pleased that I've made the decision,' she says. 'But I'm scared to death as well. There's so much to think about.' She holds out a hand to Chantal. 'I want to be here for you, but I'm looking to move up there as soon as possible, so that I can get Lewis settled before he starts school full time in September.'

'I'll still be here,' Chantal says. 'There are phones. We can Skype. You have to take this chance of happiness. I'm having six rounds of chemo and then radiotherapy afterwards. This could go on for ages. Don't even think about putting anything on hold for me.'

'You can come to stay with me for some rest and recuperation,' Nadia says, sniffing back a tear.

'I'll hold you to that.' Then they hug each other tightly.

'Now you're starting us all off.' I wipe away a tear. 'How can we let you go to the untamed wilds of the north without a celebration? There's only one thing for it. We have to have one hell of a party before you go.'

Chapter Fifty-Eight

Pushing my noodle surprise around my plate, I stare into the middle distance and try to calm my whirring mind.

'You seem a bit quiet, Gorgeous,' Crush says. 'Are the noodles not to Madam's liking?'

'It's not that. They're lovely. No one else could create something so tasty from such meagre ingredients.'

He gives me a sideways glance. 'I'll take that as a compliment.'

I eat my noodles with feigned gusto.

'Sure you didn't eat too much chocolate or cake?'

'No. Well. Maybe. Yes.'

He laughs.

'In my defence, we have some excellent summer chocolates and cocktail cupcakes just in. I've put a couple in the fridge for you to sample later.'

'This is why I love you. How many other women come with free chocolate and cake?' He smiles at me. 'Everything else OK?'

'I don't know.' I try a light-hearted shrug, but my heart is too weighed down to give it the levity I strive for. 'There's so much going on at the moment, I feel as if I can't keep up with it all.'

'You said you had a nice time with your girls. You haven't had a proper catch up in ages.'

'We did. We always have a great time together.' I put down my fork. 'But there are so many changes in our lives, I can't help but worry. Most of them are good. Yet it's still a lot to get my head round.'

'Tell all,' he says.

'Well . . . ' I fiddle with my food some more. 'Nadia is going to live with her new man in the Lake District.'

'That's going to be tough on you all. I know how much you love Nadia.'

'We're distraught. But pleased, too.' Those two emotions are quite difficult to hold in one head.

'It has to be a good move for her, doesn't it? It's a fantastic part of the world and I confess that I'm quite envious.'

'Part of me is, too. It's so fabulous up there and it would be lovely to escape London, but I'm tied to Chocolate Heaven now.'

'Are you?' Crush asks. 'In my view, you could walk away at any time. You don't owe Marcus anything and now he's scuttling off to Dubai you don't have to bend to his every whim.'

I'd like to argue the point that I don't bend to Marcus's whims, but I probably do. 'Autumn's agreed to come and work at Chocolate Heaven, which is fantastic. She's going to start straight away, but part time so she can carry on helping Nadia with childcare until she goes to Cumbria.'

'Seems fair enough,' Crush says.

'When I last spoke to Marcus, he said he'd consider Autumn buying into the business. She still has a large sum of money from her parents and they're getting on much better now, so she's keen to use it. I chatted about it to her today and she was really enthusiastic.' That would prise another couple of fingers of Marcus's grip from me. 'I might be able to get a slice of it too, further down the line.'

'If that's what you want. But surely it would be mega-bucks? It's in a great location, no doubt, but it might always be out of our league.'

'What if I do the course to become a chocolatier?'

'I'm all for that,' he says. 'I'll support you in any way I can. It also gives us more options. In the future, we might be able to set up our own place and it would be a lot easier to do that out of London. Don't you fancy your own little shop or café somewhere ridiculously picturesque?'

I do. In fact, I can just imagine it. 'Is it really something you'd consider?'

'I can't see myself being at Targa for the rest of my career; I'd be burned out by the time I'm forty-five. Besides, there are redundancies on the horizon.'

'You didn't say.'

'It's nothing new, Gorgeous. There are *always* redundancies on the horizon. It's just that, this time, the spotlight is turning on my department.'

'Are you worried?'

'It depends,' he says. 'If they give me a big enough payout, it could be a blessing in disguise. When we have a family, we might want to have a different lifestyle. Would we really want to bring up children in the middle of London? If we have a lump sum, we could do something radical.'

'Wow. That's even more to think about. It's all so unsettling.'

'It will sort itself out. Fretting about it won't help. And you won't lose touch with the girls whatever happens. Things change. We're growing up, settling down, coming into a new phase of our lives. Nothing stays the same.'

'But *we* will, won't we?' I reach out and grab his hand.

'No. We'll change, too. We'll have good times, bad times. Ups and downs. We'll stay together through it all, though. That's what matters.'

I abandon my noodles and go to sit on his lap, winding my arms round his neck. 'You are very wise.'

'We can even spend the rest of the evening looking at endless wedding stuff on Pinterest if that will take your mind off things.'

'Even the wedding is stressing me out,' I admit. 'I was all raring to go, but inspiration has deserted me. Chantal's was so lovely and I don't want to spoil her day by replicating it. Now I don't know what to do.'

'We don't have to rush it,' Crush says.

'I really, really want to get married.' I lay my head on his shoulder. 'But something doesn't feel right.'

'Let's wait.'

'I'm scared that if we postpone it, I'll do something stupid and it will never happen.'

Crush laughs. 'The odds on you doing something stupid are very high, but I'll still be here. I'm going nowhere, Ms Lucy Lombard.'

'And I so want Chantal to be there.' My voice catches on a sob. 'What if she doesn't make it through this? Cancer is such an awful thing.' We've talked about it in a jolly, bolstering manner and I know that we're all trying to stay upbeat for her. But what if the chemo doesn't work? What if she's one of the more bleak statistics?

'You need to be there for her,' Crush says. 'We don't have to rush it all at once. We can get married any old time. Support Chantal while she goes through her chemo, then sort out your chocolatier's course when you can give it your full attention. After that, when we know what my job situation is, we can think about buying into Chocolate Heaven or doing our own thing. Then, when we've got lots of time to plan something fabulous and it all feels right, we should do it.'

A feeling of relief floods over me. That's what I love most about Crush. He makes everything sound so easy. 'You're quite the most logical and adorable person there is.'

'A result of far too many team-building courses at Targa.' He smiles smugly. 'I knew they'd come in useful one day.'

'I'll phone and cancel the register office.'

'Let me sort it out,' Crush says. 'You've got enough on your plate.'

'You are so very wonderful. As a reward for your utter wonderfulness, I think we should now focus on some team-building of our own.' I turn so that I straddle him and, when I kiss him, my cares go out of the window. At least for a short time.

Chapter Fifty-Nine

It was the first time in many years that Nadia had been to her parents' house. She'd tried to convince herself that a telephone call would suffice, perhaps a letter, or even a message sent through Anita but, in the end, she'd decided to do the right thing and say goodbye to her parents in person.

Now that she was standing outside the door, she wished that she had written a letter instead. The house seemed somehow to look smaller, scruffier than when she was last here. They lived in a quiet street of semi-detached houses, but it was all looking a bit more run-down now, including her parents' house. The wheelie bin was in the garden and the grass was overgrown. There were a few bricks missing from the top of the boundary wall and the windows looked grubby, as if they hadn't been washed in a long time. Her father wasn't getting any younger and clearly the jobs he used to take such a pride in weren't now being done. Her heart squeezed with sadness.

If it was up to her, she'd be round here regularly making sure these things were done. It would take a couple of hours every week to get it back up to scratch. She felt cross with her sister. Obviously, Anita didn't notice and, even if she had, she wondered if her no-good brother-in-law would care enough to give them a helping hand. As a family, you had responsibilities. But then she wondered whether she had taken her own family responsibilities seriously enough. Should she have tried harder, especially in the early days, to build the bridges between them?

It was too late to think about that now. This was tough. She might not see her parents for a long time or, if anything happened to them, ever again. She could just turn away and avoid the conflict. It sounded very tempting, but she'd come this far and so she steeled herself to knock.

A few moments later, her mother opened the door. She hadn't dared to turn up unannounced, so she'd left a message on their answerphone to say that she would drop by.

'Come in.' Her mother stood to one side. No embrace. No smile.

She followed her through to the living room. 'Nadia's here.'

Nadia had to blink twice. It was as if she was transported straight back to her childhood. Time had stood still there. The house still smelled exactly the same as she remembered – an ever-present layering of the spices her mother used for cooking. They had the same carpet, the same curtains, the same awful paintings on the wall. The only thing that had changed was that her father had bought an enormous, new television which took up most of one wall. He liked watching WWF wrestling – to the exclusion of anything else – and clearly wanted it large in his living room. Her father had retired now and Nadia was glad of that. He'd sold all the jewellery shops a couple of years ago when the threat of armed raids became too much.

'Hello, Dad.'

'Nadia.' At least her father stood up to greet her and turned off the television – an honour reserved only for the most welcome guests – but she still felt like a stranger in a home that she'd once loved so much. 'Sit, sit,' he said.

Nadia perched on the edge of the sofa. Was her mother the only person on the planet who still had crocheted arm covers to protect their upholstery?

Her father waved in the direction of the kitchen and said to her mother, 'Why not make us all some tea?'

'Not for me,' Nadia said. 'I won't be staying long.' She was sure his face fell a little. Perhaps he'd thought that this was to be another attempt at reconciliation, that she'd somehow forgotten they'd all but closed the door on their relationship last time they met. 'I just came to tell you some news.'

Her mother, instead of scuttling towards the kitchen, sat back down in her armchair, too. Nadia remembered a time when her mother would have presented tea – in the best cups – and a selection of biscuits before their guest's bottom had touched the sofa cushions. But not today.

There was no need for small talk and no way of dressing this up, so she decided just to head straight in. The sooner this was over with, the better. 'I'm leaving London,' she said. 'Very soon.' When neither of them replied, she carried on. 'I've met a lovely man and I'm moving to the Lake District to be with him.'

'That's a big step,' her father said. 'Are you sure it's the right thing to do?'

'I believe so.'

Her mother tutted. 'Another man. Anita told us. She says that you hardly know him.'

She turned to her mother. 'Didn't you once want to marry me to a man who I hadn't met at all? Isn't that why you cut me out of your lives? Because I preferred one of my own choosing?'

'Look how well that turned out.'

She ignored the jibe and continued, 'James is lovely and kind. More importantly, he wants to welcome me and Lewis into his family and I'm tired of doing everything alone. I'm going to take this chance.'

'He'll send you back when he's had enough of you.' Her mother again.

'He's asked me to marry him,' she said. 'And I've said yes. It would be nice if you could be happy for me.'

'You will do what you want to do. You always have.'

Nadia pushed down the surge of temper that threatened and said calmly, 'I haven't come to argue about whether or not you agree with the choices I make in my life. Some have been good, some bad. The same goes for everyone. Including you.' There was little else that she could say. It would have been lovely if she could have brought James here to introduce him to them. Then they might see why she'd fallen in love with him, why she was turning her life upside down for him. 'I should be going now. I still have a lot of packing to do before the removal men arrive.' She stood up. 'Anyway, all I really came to do was to say goodbye.'

Her father looked shocked. 'I think we should have that cup of tea after all.'

Nadia held up a hand. 'Not for me, thanks.' She headed for the door. 'I'm not going to be back very often. But we've gone a long time without seeing each other, so I'm sure it won't be difficult. And you have Anita.'

They hadn't once sent Lewis a birthday card and she wondered whether they would start to do it now, when he was at the other end of the country. It was clear that her mother considered Nadia a daughter in name only. That made her incredibly sad.

Her father stood and hugged her tightly. His eyes were brimming with tears.

335

'My door will always be open to you,' Nadia said. 'It always has been. I'd welcome you with open arms in my new home.'

'Thank you, daughter,' her father said. 'I hope you will be happy. Please call us and let us know how you are.'

'I will.'

But her mother kissed her cheeks coolly and offered no words of comfort or good wishes.

So be it.

She looked at them both – now older and more frail – and wondered how much she'd really keep in touch with them once she'd moved. It was up to her to try, and she'd do that for Lewis's sake. When she was back outside on the pavement and the door closed behind her, she took a shuddering breath. It was done.

In some ways they'd made it easier for her to leave. If they'd have broken down and begged her to stay, would she still have had the resolve to go?

Chapter Sixty

Chantal looked at the amount of hair on the floor at her feet. It was more than she'd imagined. 'Wow,' she said.

Scissors poised and an anxious look on her face, the stylist said, 'Do you like it?'

'I love it,' she said, putting a hand to her bare neck. 'I think I should have had it done like this years ago.' At the advice of the nurse on the chemo ward, she'd had her thick locks cut and was now sporting a very short and sharp pixie cut. There wasn't much left of it at all.

'I did try to persuade you,' he said.

'I was always very fond of my hair as it was.' Now it hardly seemed to matter. As long as they got all of the cancer, she could cope without her hair. That didn't mean, though, that it wasn't worth trying to save. 'Apparently, I have more chance of keeping my hair if I cut it short and try using a cold cap before treatment.'

'Sounds horrendous.'

It did. You were hooked up to a refrigeration unit which chilled your scalp down to minus five degrees for an hour before treatment and an hour afterwards, which extended the time you spent on the chemo ward. 'I'll let you know soon enough,' she said. It wasn't guaranteed that she'd get on with the cold cap and her hair might thin or fall out anyway. But she was prepared to give it a shot. She'd been warned that it would only help with the hair on her head: her eyelashes, eyebrows and body hair would probably still disappear.

'Well, as a bonus, you now look ten years younger.'

Laughing, she said, 'I can work with that.'

'I'm just relieved that you like it!' Her stylist grinned.

In a couple of months she could be rocking a headscarf over a smooth dome. If that happened, she wondered how long it would be before it reappeared – they'd said three to six months, which didn't seem too bad. It would save her a fortune in hairdressing, if nothing else.

'Time for another coffee?'

She shook her head. 'No, thanks. I'll text Jacob and see where he's got to.'

But before she could, Jacob swung through the door of the salon and came to where she was just taking off the gown and brushing herself down. 'That,' he said, 'looks absolutely fantastic.'

She gave him a twirl.

'Sexy,' he said with an approving glance.

'I'll settle my bill and then we'd better get a move on.' The next appointment wasn't quite so appealing. She was about to have her first chemotherapy session. It seemed like a daunting prospect. The nurse had taken time to explain it all thoroughly to her but still, in her head, she didn't really know what to expect.

She'd already had a PICC line fitted in her arm through which the chemo drugs would be administered. It was covered with a bandage and was annoyingly itchy.

They wouldn't let her pay anything for the haircut; everyone in the salon wished her good luck and her stylist gave her a card and a teddy from them all. It was all she could do not to cry. When you were ill, you certainly found out who cared for you.

Back in the car, Jacob chatted away as they pushed through the traffic. It was clear that he was trying to distract her but, in truth, she wasn't really listening. The windscreen washers were clacking away, swishing away the rain from a heavy summer downpour. Autumn was looking after Lana this morning, taking her and Flo to some indoor play centre which sounded like hell on earth. She wished her daughter was here so that she could give her a squeeze and smell the milky scent of her skin.

Lucy called, which brought her back to the present. She had already spoken to Nadia, who was busy packing for her move. Gosh, how she was going to miss her friend when she was so far away in the Lake District, but she couldn't begrudge her this fresh start. She was so lucky to have found love again.

'Just phoning to wish you luck,' Lucy said. 'Call me as soon as you're out. I want to know how it went. Tell Jacob I can take the next session if you want me to.'

'Thanks, sweetheart,' Chantal said. 'If I'm feeling up to it, I might pop in later.'

'There's a big piece of cake with your name on it when you do. Love you.'

'Love you, too.' She hung up and Jacob grabbed her hand.

'Nearly there,' he said. 'Are you feeling OK?'

She nodded, pushing down the nausea. 'Not too bad. I just want to get it started now.'

In the ward, after completing the obligatory paperwork, she was shown to an area by the window with two armchairs. She took one and Jacob took the other. They were both tense now and conversation had dried up, but he held her hand and that was all she needed.

Two other ladies sat with companions in adjacent chairs. 'Hello, love,' one of them said. 'First time?'

Chantal nodded.

'It's not so bad. You get used to it quickly. Third one for me.'

Then the nurse brought the cold cap and strapped it on.

'I don't even want to see myself in this.'

'It looks like some kind of mad scooter helmet,' Jacob told her with a grimace. 'It's not a look you'd want to be seen out in public with.' Thankfully, the ward was quite private.

However, calling it a cold cap was an understatement. It was freezing and within half an hour her scalp was burning uncomfortably. She could feel it bringing on a headache. This was stage one and she'd hoped that she could waltz through it easily. Seemed as if it wasn't to be.

She bore it for as long as she could, but soon she just wanted to rip it off. Jacob called the nurse. 'I can't cope with this,' she told her.

'No problem. Not everyone can. Let's take it off you.'

She turned to Jacob, tears in her eyes. 'Looks as if my great new hairdo is going to go.'

'You'll manage,' he said. 'It's a small setback. Nothing more.'

She was going to look every inch the cancer patient now. It felt as if she'd fallen at the first hurdle.

'Don't cry,' he said. 'We'll get through this. I hate to see you upset. It's only hair. It *will* come back.'

'I know. I'm not crying about that. Not really. I'm just thinking that I'm very glad we got married when we did.'

He nodded. 'Me too. It was a great day, wasn't it?'

'The best.'

'Let's look at the photos on my phone while you have your treatment.'

'Sounds like a good idea.'

So they were flicking through images of their friends laughing, sharing their wedding day, when the nurse came back with the chemotherapy drugs that were going to be put in intravenously through her PICC line. Chantal eyed the drip anxiously.

'Promise me you'll get me to Nadia's leaving party.' Lucy was organising a big send-off for their friend and she wanted to be there with every fibre of her being. She couldn't let Nadia go without saying a proper goodbye. 'Even if you have to push me there in that pimped-up wheelchair again. I don't want to miss it for the world.'

Jacob kissed her tenderly. 'I'll get you there by hook or by crook. Promise.'

She looked up at the nurse. 'Let's get this show on the road.'

'One chemo cocktail coming your way,' the nurse said as she hooked her up.

Both she and Jacob watched as the toxic fluid seeped into her body. Chantal allowed herself a small and slightly grim smile. She was on her way now. Bye-bye cancer.

Chapter Sixty-One

The noise in Supersonic Spaceland was ear-splitting and Autumn wished she'd worn ear defenders or noise-cancelling earphones. It was a vast warehouse that had been transformed into a blindingly bright planet with aliens and astronauts painted all over the walls. There were climbing frames, ball pits and all manner of toys to keep discerning toddlers amused. A little bit of outer space re-imagined in the industrial wastelands of north London.

'This is a special kind of torture invented for parents,' Miles said over the din. 'But I thought we'd check it out for Flo's birthday party. I've learned to my cost that having twenty little girls at home and a jaded magician is a recipe for disaster. You don't know how much trauma the balloon animals caused.'

There was no doubt that Flo was in her element. She was currently wearing a sparkly space helmet and terrorising a small, blond-haired boy with a big, pink space gun. 'Hide in the grass,' she shouted at the top of her voice. 'Or the monster will get you.'

The boy looked terrified.

'Flo,' Miles called over to her. 'Play nicely.'

His daughter gave him 'the look'. Not a hope.

'Do it!' she yelled at the cowering child.

A moment later the boy's mother came and scooped him out of harm's way, casting a withering glare in their direction. Flo rolled her eyes in disdain, adjusted the helmet that was failing to control her hair and marched off in search of fresh prey.

'Sometimes, I wonder if she's really my child,' Miles said.

'She looks *far* too much like you for that ever to be in question,' Autumn noted.

'Ah, yes,' he agreed. 'She must have her mother's temperament.'

Through it all, Lana dozed peacefully curled up on Miles's lap, oblivious to the intergalactic mayhem around her. He looked down at the child tenderly and nestled her to him. 'It seems as if it was only yesterday when Flo was just like this.'

'Time flies.'

'Tell me about it.'

'I feel sad that I missed all of this with Willow,' she said. 'Even the noise and the expense.'

Miles glanced down at Lana again. She had her thumb in her rosebud mouth and her black lashes brushed her little apple cheeks. 'Let's have a baby,' Miles said. 'One like this.'

'They don't stay like that for long.'

'No. They turn into grumbly teenagers who wear Goth clothes and run up terrible phone bills. But we still love them.'

Autumn laughed. 'I could cope with two Flos. Just about. I'm not sure I could manage two of Willow.'

'She's a great girl,' Miles said. 'It's lovely to see you both together. You must be so proud of her.'

She felt herself flush. 'I am. And I'm just so relieved to have her back in my life. I'm even pleased that she feels comfortable enough to have her meltdowns with me.'

'Yes,' Miles said. 'Strangely, that's never bothered Flo either.'

Flo was currently fighting over an oversized, orange, eight-legged thing with yellow spots that was supposed to be some kind of alien. One little girl tugged one way at the soft toy, one the other. The alien thingy looked in danger of losing a leg. Maybe two.

'Flo!' Miles called again. 'Play nicely!'

She completely ignored him.

Autumn laughed.

'I don't know what you're laughing at, Ms Fielding. Next time we're here there'll be twenty of the little darlings to control. All of them hyped up on E-numbers from the dubiously coloured pizza and complimentary Haribo.'

Suddenly, Autumn was overwhelmed with love for him. He was such a kind and caring man and a great dad. Her life was so much better for having him in it.

Miles shook his head, despairingly. 'It's no good. I'm going to have to stage an interstellar intervention before Flo destroys the universe as we know it. Take this little one from me.' He went to hand over Lana.

'I've got something that I want to say first,' Autumn said.

He raised an eyebrow. 'The stuffing is going to come out of that alien any minute. Then what will happen to the cosmos?'

'It can wait. This can't.' She put her hand on his arm. 'I know it's not the most romantic of places, but Mr Miles Stratford, would you marry me?'

Miles paused and turned to look at her. Their eyes met and she could see the love in her eyes reflected in his. 'Yes,' he said. 'Of course I will.'

She pecked him on the cheek. 'Good. That's settled.'

'I was going to do it,' he said. 'Honestly. I had plans and all that. Posh restaurant, candles. Probably a ring. But I'm glad you beat me to it.'

'Let's do it soon,' she said. 'No fuss.'

'Sounds perfect.' He glanced over at the restaurant decorated to look like a spaceship. 'This is a very momentous occasion. Shall we have hot dogs and ice-cream at the starship *Enterprise* to celebrate?'

Autumn giggled. This was why she loved him. 'Yes. Why not? Let's push the boat out.'

'Here, you hold this one.' His gaze had already gone to Flo, who was now clambering up the climbing frame, a look of grim determination on her face. 'I'm just going to stop my child from boldly going where she shouldn't be.'

'Don't let me stop you from saving the universe.' Autumn took Lana from him, and she blinked awake. Soon she'd be wanting her lunch. 'Hello, little one,' Autumn cooed. 'Did you have a good sleep?'

Miles turned back to her. 'Did I mention that you are the most fabulous woman in the world and I'm the luckiest man?'

'You didn't,' she said.

'Well, I am,' he said. 'I love you to the moon and back.'

'I love you more,' Autumn said.

He winked at her and blew a kiss, then turned and shouted, 'Flo, get down from there!'

And, while Autumn looked on, smiling happily, he bolted after his child.

Chapter Sixty-Two

Nadia watched the man hammering the 'Sold' sign into her scruffy bit of front garden. So that was it. The house was gone. It had been priced to sell, the agent said and, on the first day it was up for sale, three couples had come to view it. One had paid the asking price and that was it.

She was surprised that, in its current state, the house had sold so quickly but that was the benefit of the overheated property market here. It would, obviously, take some time before the sale was completed, but she felt as if it was one less thing to worry about. Nadia glanced around the faded property seriously in need of a makeover and some TLC. Most of her possessions were now packed in boxes, which made it look even worse. It was bare, unloved. This had once been a happy family home – perhaps the right couple could make it so again. But she'd had her time here and now it was right to move on. Even if it didn't work out with James – and she had every hope that it would – she wouldn't be coming back to this house.

Despite being able to rationalise all that, it was still hard to move away. This had been her home for so long and she would be leaving her final ties to Toby behind. She was boxing up all the books that stood on the shelves by the fireplace, along with the last of the family pictures. There was one of her and Toby on their wedding day and she stroked the image of his face. He'd been so handsome when he was young and she'd been smitten. They'd set out with so much hope, so much promise, so much love – enough for her to disobey her family's wishes and have them cut her off. How naive that seemed, with the benefit of hindsight. There were days, even now, when she still missed him.

Stroking Toby's face on the picture again, she put him in the box and considered what she'd do with the photos at her new home. James had photographs of his wife and children on show all over the house and she wondered whether he'd be happy for her to put some pictures of Toby and Lewis there, too. She wanted her son to remember his dad, as Seth and Lily should remember their mum. Perhaps they could just choose a few special ones to display and put the rest in a safe place in the attic for when Lewis was older and wanted to know more. It was something she and James would need to talk about. She didn't want all these little points of etiquette to cause friction between them. Nadia sighed to herself. The joys of trying to make a modern, blended family. She was sure there'd be a few teething problems along the way, but if they worked together everything could be resolved. Couldn't it? Panic gripped her. She'd be up there alone without her girls to turn to. That was the hardest thing to bear.

Lewis came downstairs dragging his current favourite teddy bear. 'Stuart said he doesn't want to go in a box.'

'That's fine, darling.' Nadia took Stuart from him and gave the bear a hug. 'He can sit with you in the car.'

He looked placated by that. James had come down yesterday and was currently sorting out the shed for her. Then he was going to drive them both back to the Lakes the day after her

347

leaving party at Chocolate Heaven. She was conscious of the amount of time he was taking away from the farm, but was grateful to have him here to do the heavier lifting. It was quite handy to have someone around who was used to hefting hay bales.

She was also glad that he'd be with them on their way to their new life. If she and Lewis had to get on a train by themselves, that would seem too awful. Now it felt as if they were coming together properly as a family right from the start.

Her son looked downcast and she ruffled his hair as she pulled him into her arms.

'Aren't you looking forward to moving?'

'I don't know,' Lewis said. 'How long are we moving for?'

'For always.' She gave him a hug. This was the only home that Lewis had known, and she wasn't sure that he fully understood that they weren't coming back.

'Is Flo coming with us?'

'No, darling. She's staying here with Auntie Autumn and Uncle Miles.'

'Oh.' He didn't look as if he liked the sound of that. 'But I'll still be able to play with her on the swings?'

'You'll have Lily and Seth instead,' Nadia said. 'Won't that be nice?'

He considered it thoughtfully.

'Flo can come and see us for holidays,' she promised. 'You can show her the lambs and the mountains.'

'And we can throw stones in the lake?' Lewis had been very taken with the idea of skimming stones, but hadn't quite mastered it. Instead, he usually found the biggest one he could lift and tipped it into the water with a plop.

'Yes. We'll have a lovely time,' she said. 'You liked it at James's house and now it will be our house, too. You'll have a new bedroom and a new school to go to. That will be exciting.'

He didn't look convinced.

'And your pet lamb is still waiting for you.'

His eyes lit up. 'Wellyboot?'

'You haven't forgotten her?'

'No,' Lewis said. 'If we live there every day, she'll be properly mine?'

'She will.' That certainly made him look a lot happier which was a relief as she wanted it all to go as smoothly as possible. Nadia squeezed him again.

Anita came downstairs, sniffing back tears as she had done all morning. Her sister wasn't handling her departure well. Despite her distress, she'd insisted on being here to help and was currently packing up Nadia's wardrobe for her. Nadia had taken out the clothes she thought that she'd need immediately and had put them into two suitcases, but the rest were going into sturdy boxes. She wondered if James would have second thoughts when he saw exactly how much stuff they were bringing with them. She had no idea how it had all fitted into her few rooms. Perhaps moving into the bigger house in the Lakes would be a necessity rather than an option.

'How's it going?' Nadia asked.

'Nearly done.' Anita burst into tears and pulled a tissue from her sleeve to dab furiously at her eyes.

'Oh, come here,' Nadia said.

'I'm going to play.' Lewis wriggled free and bolted for the door.

'Finish your packing!' she shouted after him, to no avail. But at least it meant that her arms were free to embrace her sister.

This was the hardest part. She could just about hang on to her own emotions, but dealing with other people's reactions was too much.

'I can't believe you're leaving when I've only just got you back.'

'It's not far at all. Really. You can be up there in a few hours.'

'I've never driven that far,' she sobbed. 'My little car doesn't know its way out of London. I'd be terrified.'

'You can take the train. It's so easy. You don't even have to change.'

'I don't understand why you're going!'

'Because I've been lucky enough to find one of the few hot, single men left and I love him very much. Thankfully, he loves me. He just happens to live in one of the most beautiful places in our country.'

'Doesn't it rain all the time?'

'Quite a lot. That's why there are lots of lakes.' She rested her forehead against her sister's. 'Come as soon as you can. Then you'll see why I love it. The scenery's stunning and the house has plenty of rooms. There are lots of great cafés, too.' She chucked her sister's chin as if she were a child. 'No excuse.'

Anita wiped away her tears. 'I'll miss you.'

'And I'll miss you, too. You're still coming to the leaving party, though?'

'Yes. I'll bring the boys, but Tarak can't come. He has some important business to see to.'

It was no great loss. That was one person she would be glad to see the back of.

'Mum and Dad are very upset that you're leaving.'

'They're not,' she said, softly. 'Well, maybe Dad is.'

'You could have made more effort,' Anita admonished. 'It's not all their fault.'

Nadia sagged. 'I know. I'll try to call them once a week when I'm settled. I'll see how that goes.'

'Promise me?'

'Yes.' Nadia reached out for the box of tissues she'd kept to hand and passed one to her sister.

'I need to get home soon,' Anita said, blowing her nose.

'Then go. Let me finish off the packing. You've already been a great help. I don't know how I'd have managed without you. I'll see you tomorrow.'

Anita gave one last sniff and put her tissue away. 'Has my make-up run?'

Nadia smiled. 'No, my sister, you still look lovely.'

She got a teary grin in return. 'Call me if you need me to make anything or do anything. You know where I am.'

She showed her sister to the door and, with much hugging, waved her goodbye. Then she made a welcome cup of tea and took one out to James. The shed door was open and all her gardening equipment, such as it was, was spread out on the ragged patch of lawn. If she'd thought about it earlier, all this stuff could have gone on eBay. She was hardly going to need her little lawn-mower and strimmer with the vast acres around James's house.

When she called him, James emerged from the shed. He was sweating, his damp hair stuck to his head, his face smeared with dirt.

'I think you have the entire spider population of north London living in this shed.' He wiped a cobweb from his face. 'I'm sure working on a farm is a lot easier than this.'

She laughed, put his tea down on the picnic bench and then went to lean against his chest. He wrapped his arms round her.

'Everything OK?'

'This is hard.' Her throat all but closed and it was a struggle to get the words out. 'I've just had Anita in tears and I'm not sure that Lewis really realises what's going on.'

'It must be difficult.'

'I know I'm doing the right thing,' she said, wiping away the tears that rolled down her cheeks. 'But it's definitely tough.'

He kissed her hair. 'Thank you for doing this for me. We'll have a fantastic life together and I'll do everything I can to make sure that you don't regret it.'

351

'I'm dreading the leaving party,' she admitted tearfully. 'I can't bear the thought of saying goodbye to the Chocolate Lovers' Club.'

Then her phone rang and she pulled it from her pocket. 'Talk of the devil. It's Lucy.'

But it wasn't Lucy who spoke.

'Hi,' he said. 'It's Aiden. I'm ringing about your leaving party. Sorry to do this at short notice, but I've got a really big favour to ask.'

And, when she heard what Crush had to say, Nadia cried again.

Chapter Sixty-Three

I've put a notice on the door and have closed Chocolate Heaven for the day, even though it goes against the grain. I want this party to be perfect for Nadia so that she has some fantastic memories to take away with her and I wasn't going to be able to throw that together in the blink of an eye. When Autumn is working here full time it will certainly make life a lot easier.

This morning, I left Crush fast asleep in bed and came in here early. I've spent the last few hours decorating the café. Now it looks ready for a celebration. I've pinned paper pom-poms in pastel colours all over the place. On each table is a floral-scented candle in pretty glass holders. They smell good enough to eat. I bought some flowers from the florist down the high street and made small bunches which I've put in jam jars decorated with ribbon. There's a mix of pink roses, lilac sweet peas, gypsophila and some sprigs of herbs. Gorgeous. Eat your heart out, Jane Packer. I glance at my watch. Plenty of time yet. No need to start panicking. But I have a little panic, nevertheless.

As I knew I'd have a lot on my hands, I ordered the buffet from a local deli and they've done me proud. They delivered all the food a few minutes ago and now I've arranged the various dishes on the tables I've put out along one wall. There are mini canapés topped with brie, smoked bacon and grapes, Wensleydale with carrot chutney, smoked salmon with cream cheese, and New York pastrami with a gherkin and horseradish garnish. We've got mini cheese and onion muffins which I'm going to warm in the oven upstairs when everyone arrives. I put the platter of roasted tomato, spinach and feta quiche at one end next to a selection of delicately sliced antipasti meats. There's a platter of seafood waiting in the fridge, plus a selection of olives and a basket of rustic bread to go out when we're ready. I stand back and admire my handiwork. I think that should keep us going for a while.

I've ordered a cake from Alexandra which will form my centrepiece and she's going to bring that with her to the party. It's a three-tier sponge cake filled with raspberries and drizzled with white chocolate. It's one of her signature pieces and is fabulous. Very popular for weddings now. I'm adding some of the summer cupcakes and lots of lovely chocolates for after our coffee.

Needless to say, this has all cost a fortune, but Autumn and Chantal have very generously chipped in to cover the cost. Nadia has no idea that we're putting on such a fabulous spread. She thinks we're having a bit of cheap chardonnay and cake. I can't wait to see her face. She'll be thrilled. I do love a surprise!

I've made a great playlist – nothing that will make us cry. Well, not much. And my lovely Crush gave me some money to buy myself a new dress. I was just going to wear something that I had lurking in my wardrobe, but when I was raking through my clothes and muttering darkly, he insisted on treating me. So last night I dashed out after work, caught the last hour of late-night shopping and bought myself a fab little number. It's light chiffon material in the palest pink, with a low v-neck and some figure-hugging drapes across the bodice. At the waist there's a delicate diamante embellishment, then the skirt falls to the floor with a waterfall skirt. I'm going to look like a little angel in it. And, best of all, it was reduced.

It's hanging on the back of the door in the next room and when I've done all the tasks that could involve me spilling food or drink down myself, I'll get changed. Can't wait.

Next, I put out all the fizz. To keep costs down – a bit – we've gone for Prosecco instead of champagne and nothing wrong with that. It's very tempting to sample a glass, but I must keep a clear head until everyone else comes. The guest list is much the same as Chantal's wedding, except Nadia's sister and her boys are coming along, too. I didn't hear back from her parents but would assume they're not coming and her brother-in-law is 'busy'. Thank goodness.

By the time I've fiddled and twiddled, time is marching on and I grab my fab new frock and nip to the upstairs flat to have a shower. It seems weird being up here, but it's a nice place – two bedrooms, biggish living room, nicely fitted kitchen. Crush and I could do worse than move in here. We'd certainly have more space than we do now. Perhaps I'll talk to Marcus about it. I haven't spoken to him since he came into the shop and told me he was heading off to Dubai and, if I'm honest, it feels a bit weird. It's not that I miss him. Not at all.

Actually, I do. A bit. Not much. But, you know, it's been OK working for him and it will be odd not seeing him on a daily basis. However, as Crush says, times change, people move on. It's time for Marcus to be part of my past and not my future. Sad, though.

I quickly shower and rub myself down with the towel that, thankfully, I remembered to bring with me. Next, I refresh my make-up and regret that I haven't had time to have my nails done. Never mind. No one's going to be looking at those. Then

I slip on my dress and have a quick appraisal in the full-length mirror in the bedroom. Looking smokin' hot, Lombard! And ever so slightly demure. Which, I think you'll agree, is a killer combo.

As I make my way downstairs, my phone rings. I hitch my skirt and make a dash for it.

'Hey,' I say to Crush. 'I was just upstairs in the flat getting ready for the party.'

'I'm sorry I missed you this morning,' he says. 'I was going to come and help you, but I've not long woken up.'

'That's OK. You've had a busy week and you need your beauty sleep.'

'Are you all ready for the party?'

'Just about. I've put almost everything out. I want one last pass.'

'Can you come and meet me for half an hour? There's something I want to show you.'

'Noooo,' I say. 'Not now. I'm all spruced up. Everyone will be here soon.'

I can hear Crush suck in his breath. 'It's really important.'

'Nothing can be that important.'

'Trust me. It is.'

'What is it?'

'Hmm,' he muses. 'Can't really say, but it will be to your advantage.'

'We could go any time in the week, once the party's over.'

'I've sort of made an appointment for us,' he admits. 'I thought you wouldn't mind. I can't really cancel now.'

'Oh, Aiden.'

'Half an hour,' he pleads.

'I can't get on the Tube, I'm all poshed up. I haven't really got time to get changed again.'

'Stay as you are. It'll be fine. Jump in a taxi.'

'Are you changed and ready for Nadia's party? Then we can come straight back here.'

'I will be,' he promises.

I give in. It's so rare that he actually asks me to do anything for him that I can't really argue; it must be something essential.

'OK. Where are you?'

He gives me the address and I jot it down. 'I'll be there in ten minutes, if I can hail a cab easily.'

'I love you,' he says. 'See you soon.'

I hang up. Now I'm really stressing. And it was all going so well. I have a quick whizz round the room. Is there anything I've forgotten to do? I don't think so.

Oh, I wonder why this couldn't wait? Then I smile to myself. I know exactly what Crush has done. I'm onto his game. I bet you a pound he's found premises where we could have our own café. Grinning to myself, I dash out into the street and wave frantically at the first cab I see.

Chapter Sixty-Four

The taxi pulls up at my destination. I see Crush waiting for me on the pavement on the other side of the road. He looks so handsome in his smart grey suit that my stomach flips. He's really pushed the boat out for Nadia's party. I thought he might just rock up in his jeans and a decent shirt. But no. He's really gone to town. His hair is freshly washed and I watch him as he runs a hand anxiously through it and paces up and down.

Fumbling with my change, I settle the taxi fare. 'Thanks, love,' the driver says. 'Enjoy the wedding.'

I look blankly at him and then he drives away and leaves me standing there.

It's only then that I realise Crush is outside the register office we'd previously booked for our ceremony and my mouth goes dry. When I glance up, Crush is grinning broadly across at me and I hitch up my skirt and weave my way through the traffic to reach him.

'Hi,' he says, bashful.

I take in the beautiful Georgian building that's so familiar. 'Is this what I think it is?'

'If you think that you're going to be marrying me in . . . ' Crush checks his watch, ' . . . ten minutes, then yes.'

I feel as if all of my breath has been knocked out of me and put a hand to my chest. 'You're kidding me?'

'No.'

Throwing my arms round his neck, I whisper, 'Thank you. Thank you.'

'You're not cross?'

'No. Why would I be? This is the most wonderful thing that's ever happened to me.'

Crush blows out a wavering breath. 'You don't know how relieved I am to hear that.'

'So the party at Chocolate Heaven, that's going to be our wedding reception?'

He smiles. 'Yeah.'

'Nadia knows?'

'She does and I don't think she minds one bit that we've hijacked it. Cunning, eh?'

Almost as cunning as one of my own very cunning plans. And they really can be quite cunning.

'Well,' I laugh. 'I'm glad I made it look so pretty. It certainly looks fit for a wedding.'

He takes in my dress. 'You look every inch the beautiful bride.'

'Thank you. It couldn't be more perfect.'

'I *nearly* cracked and told you as I know you'd want to look your best. But that's really stunning.' He looks thoughtful. 'However, maybe something is missing.' He punches a number into his phone and says, 'OK.'

A second later, Chantal, Nadia and Autumn plus entourage pour out of the coffee shop a few doors down. They dash up the road and swamp me with a group embrace. Of course they're all here! How could I be married *without* the Chocolate Lovers' Club being present? They all hug me tightly.

'I'm going to have words with you lot,' I tease. 'Fancy not telling me! I thought you were my friends.'

Autumn and Nadia are wearing their bridesmaid dresses from Chantal's wedding and she has one to match.

As well as Jacob, Miles and James, Clive and Tristan are here. 'You came all the way from France?' I shriek as I see them.

'It was a close call,' Clive says, 'but we made it.'

'How could we stay away?' Tristan adds.

I squeeze the life out of them both. Then, standing at the back, I see my mum and dad. Mum's crying. That makes my eyes prickle with tears as well.

'Don't cry,' I tell my mum as she takes me in her arms while Dad stands and looks awkward. 'You'll start me off.'

'I'm so pleased for you,' she says. 'You've got a lovely man there, darling. A keeper.'

'That's the plan.' I pull away, shaky and look round my friends. 'So you knew? All of you knew?'

Much nodding and giggling.

'It was very short notice,' Chantal says. 'But we thought it was for the best. I hope we were right. I'm so glad Aiden took it in hand.'

'Me too,' I say tearfully.

From behind her back she produces a bouquet and presents it to me. The bouquet matches the flowers I've just put out in Chocolate Heaven.

I gape at Chantal. 'How did you know?'

'I spoke to the florist yesterday. She told me what flowers you'd bought and I asked her to make up something to match. Do you like it?'

'I love it.' By some miracle, the colour of the roses matches my dress and the smell of the sweet peas is heavenly. 'It's gorgeous.'

'We'd better get inside,' Crush says. 'They know I'm here, but I was on tenterhooks that you'd actually come.'

I put a hand on his arm. 'Why didn't you say anything?'

'You've got so much on at the moment that the wedding was becoming just another stress. I thought I'd take that away from you. All that matters is that we're married. The rest is just fripperies. I want you to be my wife, Lucy Lombard, and I want it now.'

I reach up and kiss him. 'So do I.'

'When we've got time, we can go on a wonderful honeymoon and maybe even renew our vows on a white sandy beach or with Elvis in Vegas, if that's what you want.'

Putting a finger to his lips, I say, 'Nothing could be better than this.'

We hold each other tightly.

'But I've no idea how you managed it without me finding out.'

'I didn't actually cancel our booking, I just rang them and postponed it. All the paperwork was still in place. Luckily, they had a space come free at the last minute and I was able to coincide it with the party you'd got planned for Nadia.'

'You're so clever,' I tell him and, suddenly, it all hits me. I get a flush of excitement and do a little dance on the pavement. 'I'm getting married!' I shout out, startling a few innocent people passing by. They smile indulgently at my outburst.

The girls do a happy dance with me.

'Let's go,' Chantal says, looking at her watch. 'We don't want to miss your slot.' She ushers us all inside.

Our guests go ahead of us, but Crush and I hang back on the pavement. He tilts my chin and looks into my eyes. 'Are you absolutely sure that you want this?'

The love I see in his face almost has me undone. 'I've never wanted anything more in all of my life.'

He takes my hand and, grinning like loons, we head into our wedding.

Chapter Sixty-Five

The Mayfair Library is a truly beautiful place for a wedding. I don't know why I didn't realise how stunning it was when Crush and I first viewed it. The sun streams through the stained-glass windows, lighting up the small but chic space. The walls are the most delicate shade of blue and there's an imposing, ornate oak fireplace. There are shelves of vintage, leather-bound books on either side of it. It's the best place ever for a wedding.

But, do you know what? We could be getting married in a swamp and I'd be happy. It's not how great the venue is or how much you've spent on the cake, it's the love in your hearts – and we have that in abundance.

My heart's pounding like a drum as Dad and I stand in the doorway at the back of the room.

Our guests are waiting in their seats and I can already hear my mother sobbing again. More importantly, the groom is here. And that's not always been a given at this stage in my previous wedding experience. Jacob is by Crush's side as his best man.

'Ready, Lucy?' Dad asks.

I nod.

'You look gorgeous,' he says.

'Thanks, Dad.'

'There's still time to back out,' he whispers. 'No one will think any the worse of you.'

'Get a grip, Dad,' I mutter. 'This man is the love of my life. I can't wait to be his wife.' It's all I can do not to run down the aisle and jump into Crush's arms.

'As long as you're sure.'

And I am. Completely sure. Mr Aiden 'Crush' Holby is all that a husband should be. We'll have a long and happy life, half a dozen kids – well, maybe two – and we'll still hold hands when we're ninety.

The music starts. We don't have a song that's 'ours' as such, but I smile when I hear the tune. 'I Knew I Loved You' by Savage Garden. It's ideal.

Yet, when Dad and I set off, in step, I realise that I'm shaking. I feel as if I've waited all of my life for this. I always thought I'd marry Marcus, but I know now that I've found my soulmate, my partner in life, the man I want to grow old with. A tear rolls down my cheek and I hurry my dad up as I just can't wait to get on with the ceremony.

Then Aiden and I are standing alone together in front of the registrar and my heart is so very happy that I think it might burst. I have never before felt such elation. Not even after *masses* of chocolate!

Chantal stands and reads a beautiful passage that Crush has chosen from the novel *Captain Corelli's Mandolin*, about two lives growing together and becoming entwined like the roots of a tree.

I hardly hear the words of the ceremony. All I can see is Aiden. Everything else is a blur.

While I'm feeling all dream-like and high, he says, 'Stop gazing at me, Gorgeous. It's your turn.'

'What?'

Everyone laughs.

Then I take a deep breath and with a voice that's loud and clear say, 'I, Lucy Lombard, take you, Aiden Holby, to be my husband, to have and to hold from this day forward, for better, for worse, for richer, for poorer, in sickness and in health, to love and to cherish, from this day forward until death us do part.'

Now everyone's crying; Aiden says his vows and I can tell from the love in his eyes that he means every word.

The registrar smiles benignly at us. 'I now pronounce you husband and wife.' She turns to Aiden. 'You may kiss your bride.'

And Crush takes me in his arms and kisses me deeply. Our guests cheer and burst into applause.

I'm married. And it was as simple as that.

I turn and look at our friends and family and feel the love in the room. These people will support us for the rest of our days.

'Are you ready, Mrs Holby?' Crush says.

'I am,' I answer my husband.

He threads my arm through his and the music plays again. This time it's The Cure and 'Friday I'm in Love'.

And, with joy in my heart and the man of my dreams on my arm, I step forward to start married life.

Chapter Sixty-Six

We all burst out of the register office and onto the pavement, giggling and laughing. Then I'm pulled up short. Across the street, Marcus is standing there alone. He has a red heart-shaped balloon in his hand with the words *I'll always love you* written on it.

Crush puts his arm round my waist. 'I phoned him,' he says. 'Told him that we were getting married.'

'Why?'

'I thought you might want him here.'

My throat closes with emotion.

'Go and talk to him,' Crush says. 'If he wants to come back to the reception, then I'm cool with that.'

I kiss my husband for being so kind and go across to Marcus.

'Hey,' he says softly, as I approach. 'Congratulations.'

'Oh, Marcus.' I tenderly brush his lips with a kiss.

'I couldn't quite hack coming for the ceremony.' He raises an eyebrow.

'You never did like weddings,' I tease gently.

'No.' He studies his feet and we each know what the other is thinking. No matter what happens, the fact that he ran out on our wedding day will always lie between us. That's the moment I knew deep down in my heart that I could never be with him. 'I'm going to Dubai next week. I wanted to wish you well and to say goodbye.'

'We'll still speak,' I tell him. 'There'll be things to discuss about the business.'

He pulls an envelope out of his pocket and gives it to me. 'What's this?'

He gives me a wry smile. 'A ridiculously extravagant wedding gift.'

I laugh, sadly. 'Only you, Marcus.'

'I've signed over Chocolate Heaven to you,' he says. 'Completely. It's yours now.'

'Don't be silly, Marcus. You can't do that.'

'Am silly. Have done it.'

The envelope is burning in my fingers. 'You're not serious.'

'I owe you, Lucy. This is for all the times I let you down, that I hurt you. I want this to make amends, to draw a line under us.'

I'm so choked that I can hardly speak. 'What can I say?'

Our eyes brighten with unshed tears as we look fondly at each other's faces. I want to reach up and stroke his cheek, but I daren't. I would fall to pieces completely.

'Say that you loved me once,' he asks. 'And that a part of you will always love me.'

'Of course.' Tears spill over my lashes.

'He's a lucky man,' Marcus says with a nod towards Crush. A single tear trails slowly down his cheek. 'I hope he loves you as I should have.'

'I want you to be happy, Marcus. I want you to find someone to love.'

'There's already someone that I love very much,' he says bleakly. 'I just never knew quite how much until it was too late.'

'Let's stay friends,' I say. 'Come to Chocolate Heaven. We're having a lovely party. Come and drink some fizz with us.'

He shakes his head. 'I've got things that I should be doing and I've said all I need to say.'

I glance back at Crush, who's waiting patiently for me.

Marcus takes my hands and pulls me towards him. He kisses my cheek, lightly, lingeringly. I can feel the pain and loneliness in his heart radiating through me and I ache for his sadness.

'You should go to your husband,' he says and I've never heard him sound so desolate. He hands me the balloon. *I will always love you.* 'Goodbye, Lucy.'

And, as he walks away from me, he doesn't look back.

Chapter Sixty-Seven

We have many, many photographs taken on mobile phones in Mount Street Gardens next to the register office and then head back to Chocolate Heaven.

The café looks fantastic and it's the perfect place to celebrate our love. I don't know why I didn't think of it before. No months of planning. No squabbling over seating plans. No stressing over table favours.

The girls get the rest of the food out of the fridge to put on the buffet and someone warms the cheese muffins in the oven. Alexandra brings along the fabulous cake and places it centre stage on the table. Jacob pours us all fizz, we switch on the music and soon everyone is laughing and having fun.

Crush comes and snakes his arm around my waist. 'Happy, Mrs Holby?'

I'll never get tired of hearing that.

'Yes,' I say. 'Very.'

'Was everything OK with Marcus?'

'I felt sad for him,' I admit. 'Beneath all that bluster—'

'And bullshit,' Crush adds.

'And bullshit,' I agree. 'He's quite a lonely man.'

'It's of his own making, Gorgeous.'

'I know that, but I can't be too harsh on him. He gave me this.' I hand over the envelope that I'm still clutching.

Crush gives me a quizzical look.

'A wedding present.'

He opens it and scans the paper. Then he looks up at me, agog.

'I'm the owner,' I say, still reeling. 'He's signed this over to me lock, stock and barrel.'

'I can't believe it.'

'Me neither.'

'There has to be a catch. This *is* Marcus.'

'I don't think so. He seemed very sincere. He's leaving for Dubai soon.' I look up at Crush. 'He's gone from our lives.'

Aiden pulls me to him. 'I know what you've felt for him and this must be hard. And I can't give you fancy presents like this.' He gestures at the café. 'But I can promise that I'll always be there for you. I'll never make you feel second best.'

I rest my head on his shoulder. 'I'd live in a tent with you,' I tell him, honestly. 'Wherever you are, that's where I want to be.'

'We're lucky,' he says. 'Many people search for a lifetime for love like ours and never find it.'

'How true.'

I look round at my family and friends. I'm glad that we all seem to be settled now. Chantal and Jacob are in the corner cuddling Lana. She's started her chemo – only one treatment so far, but she's holding up well. Ted, Stacey and Elsie have come along to the reception as well, and they all seem to have an easier relationship now.

Autumn looks so happy with Miles – and not only have they brought along Flo and Willow, but also her parents are here. It's the first time that I've seen them. I hope this means that

369

they're building bridges. They look a little awkward – and very posh – but they are, at least, smiling.

Clive and Tristan seem to have got their mojo back since they moved to France and we'll go over to see them as soon as we can. We could even honeymoon there.

My parents are still looking loved up and it's been *weeks* since they got back together. Though they're still bickering as if they've never been apart. Perhaps this time they'll make it last. I really hope so, for their sake. As I watch them, I vow that Crush and I will do better than them.

I don't want a love like theirs which seems to rely on mutual irritation and drama. I want Crush and I to be the best of friends and, when the passion has faded – as inevitably it will – that we will still adore each other. That our love will deepen into care and respect. That our two lives will grow into one. That being apart will be inconceivable.

Nadia and James are with Anita and her boys and it reminds me that this isn't just my wedding, but also her farewell party. That brings a lump to my throat. My emotions are all over the place today. It's going to be so hard to say goodbye. Our lovely little Chocolate Lovers' Club will, for the first time since we met, be one founder member down.

We eat, drink and are very merry. Then Crush and I cut the cake. Someone turns the music up and we have our first dance to Dionne Warwick singing 'What the World Needs Now'. Love, sweet love. Dionne's right: it's the only thing that there's just too little of.

'This has been the most perfect wedding ever,' I murmur to my husband as he holds me close and we sway together. 'I couldn't have planned it better myself.'

'I'm glad you approve.'

'I think I'll let you plan all our important anniversaries from now on.'

'Sounds good to me.' He gives me a wink.

After the first dance, we push all the tables right back and have a good old boogie. My mum and dad are smooching to whatever song is playing. Autumn's daughter starts off shuffling uncomfortably at the edge of the floor, but a few songs in she's throwing shapes like the rest of us. Even Autumn's parents are joining in and I've never seen Autumn look so happy.

Then I realise there's something that I have to do. I grab my bouquet. 'Ladies and gentlemen,' I shout. Slightly drunkenly. 'I have a very important traditional task to perform. The tossing of the bouquet.'

Someone makes a rude comment.

'But I'm going to give it my own personal twist.' I raise a hand. 'Autumn Fielding be upstanding!'

Autumn shuffles to the front of the group, embarrassed.

'There is only one person here who deserves this bouquet. And it's you. So here you go. Catch!'

I launch my bouquet into the air and Autumn reaches up to grab it.

'You're next,' I slur, happily.

'Actually, Lucy,' she looks round and smiles coyly, 'I've already proposed to Miles and he said yes.'

'Hurrah! *Another* wedding!' Blimey! Weddings are like buses. First there are none and then they all come along at once!

Then, all too soon, it's time to wind the party up. We've all but drunk the fizz – a pile of empty bottles gives testimony to that. And we've eaten all the cake.

'I haven't booked us anywhere,' Crush says. He looks slightly more dishevelled than he did earlier. 'I just thought we'd go back home.'

'Sounds like bliss. All I want to do is have a cup of tea and take off my shoes.' I grin at him. 'And snuggle all night with my husband.'

'I think I can arrange that.'

Nadia comes over and hugs me. 'It's been a wonderful day, Lucy. I'm so going to miss you all.'

I hold her tightly. 'We'll come and visit you as soon as we can.' Perhaps, as well as France, we can have another honeymoon in the Lake District. Maybe we can have a whole year of honeymoons.

She lets out a shuddering breath. 'This is hard.'

'Take good care of her, James, otherwise you'll have the Chocolate Lovers' Club to answer to.'

'You have my word,' he promises.

'This is it, then.' Chantal and Autumn gather round too and we have a group hug.

'It's not goodbye,' I say. 'I'm not going to entertain that word. It's hello. Hello to new beginnings.'

Our lives are changing. A chance meeting, a change of circumstances, a diagnosis of cancer – all of these things can swing us off from what we think is our ordered life plan. Two of us are newly married and there are two more weddings on the cards. Maybe there'll even be some more Chocolate Lovers' babies to come. Who knows?

I find one last bottle of Prosecco and pour us all out a glass. 'To the Chocolate Lovers' Club,' I propose. 'To love, life and chocolate.'

We all raise our glasses and drink.

Whatever happens, this won't be the end of the Chocolate Lovers' Club. We might be heading off in different directions but there are strong ties that bind us. We are true friends, and true friendships endure for a lifetime.

Acknowledgements

To all the ladies who shared their breast cancer stories with me, thank you so much. I really appreciate it. You are all fabulous survivors. The thing I found most shocking was that everyone's story was so individual – everyone has their own particular experience and treatment. No wonder this is such an awful disease to crack. I wish you all many, many years of health and happiness.

Also to Jennifer Earle of Chocolate Ecstasy Tours who has helped me so much with chocolate research over the years that she truly deserves to be an honorary member of the Chocolate Lovers' Club. If you haven't tried one of her tours, they're fab. Put it on your bucket list.

And to Yvette Hughes who inspired me with our tour of Hampstead Heath and the gorgeous Golders Hill Park. You are a lovely friend.

www.chocolateecstasytours.com